SILVER

SILVER

My Own Tale

As Written by Me

WITH

A Goodly Amount

OF

MURDER

EDWARD CHUPACK

THOMAS DUNNE BOOKS

St. Martin's Griffin · New York

M

This is a work of fiction. All of the characters, organizations, and events portrayed in this novel are either products of the author's imagination or are used fictitiously.

THOMAS DUNNE BOOKS
An imprint of St. Martin's Press.

SILVER. Copyright © 2008 by Edward Chupack. All rights reserved. Printed in the United States of America. For information, address St. Martin's Press, 175 Fifth Avenue, New York, N.Y. 10010.

www.thomasdunnebooks.com
www.stmartins.com

Map by David Cain

The Library of Congress has catalogued the hardcover edition as follows:

Chupack, Edward.
    Silver : my own tale as written by me with a goodly amount of murder / Edward Chupack.—1st ed.
        p. cm.
    ISBN-13: 978-0-312-37365-8
    ISBN-10: 0-312-37365-1
    1. Pirates—Fiction. I. Title.
    PS3603.H857 S55 2008
    813'.6—dc22

                                            2007040973

    ISBN-13: 978-0-312-53936-8 (pbk.)
    ISBN-10: 0-312-53936-3 (pbk.)

First St. Martin's Griffin Edition: January 2009

10 9 8 7 6 5 4 3 2 1

For Maria. Only Maria.
Ever Maria.

Acknowledgments

Many, many thanks to Jennifer Gates and Mary Beth Chappell of Zachary Shuster Harmsworth for their essential advice and dedication. Special thanks to the intrepid John Parsley of Thomas Dunne Books for making sure that I did not get lost along the way.

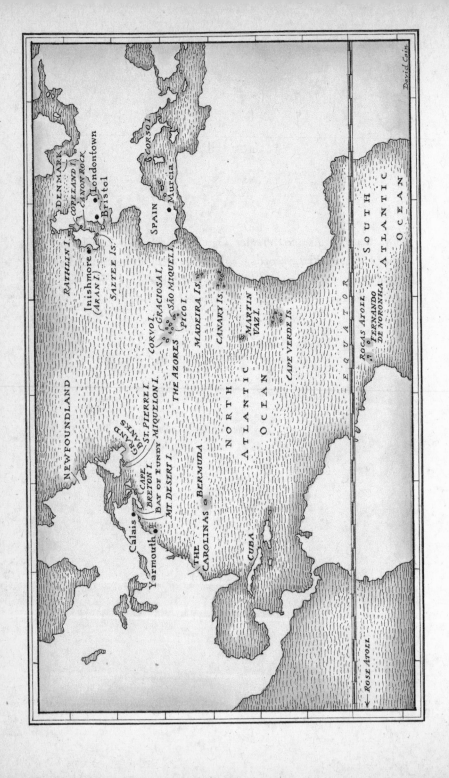

DENMARK

RATHLIN I.
COPELAND I.
CANON ROCK
Inishmore Londontown
(ARAN I.) Bristol
SALTEE IS.

CORSO
Murcia
SPAIN

NEWFOUNDLAND

GRACIOSA L.
GREAT BANKS
CORVO I.
CAPE ST. PIERRE I.
BRETON I. MIQUELON L.
MT. DESERT I.
Calais
Yarmouth
THE CAROLINAS BERMUDA
CUBA

BAY OF FUNDY
THE AZORES
SÃO MIGUEL L.
PICO I.
MADEIRA IS.
CANARY IS.
MARTIN VAZ L.
CAPE VERDE IS.

NORTH
ATLANTIC
OCEAN

EQUATOR

ROSE ATOLL

ROCAS ATOLL
Fernando
de Noronha

SOUTH
ATLANTIC
OCEAN

David Cain

SILVER

CHAPTER I.

I AM SILVER

 am Silver, and there is no other pirate like me on these waters. No other. Not you and not Kwik, not Smith and not Gunn, not Bones nor Black John. Not damned Pew. Not Bloody Bill. Not Solomon. And not Jim Hawkins, that son of a slattern.

You mustered Smollet and my hearties to blazes. That was considerate of you, as they would have died from the fever by now if you had not murdered them first.

I know what you will tell your Georgey, that middling monarch that now pays your blood wages. You will tell him that you captured me in paradise. You will not tell him that Smollet fell into a faint and was well on his way to the pintles when he, snagged in the ratlines, spied your ship sailing toward us. Smollet was turvy and saw your First Rate skimming the sky, upturned, its hull breaching the heavens whilst its topsail fathomed below. We grounded on a reef. Georgey likes his romances. Tell him that Smollet glimpsed a phantom ship. That will please the wretch.

This ain't paradise. This is the South Seas. Paradise is a gale that rocks the planks and tears the timbers and blows rime in your eyes. Paradise is a ruthless place. The rain hammers you into bits and casts you for your life. The lanyard runs through your hands and cleaves them. You laveer through the wind and gybe the sails until your arms cramp. You hang on to the gunwale so as not to end in the soundings. There ain't a bit of paradise down there in them soundings, but only Old Nick and his halters with their whips and brands and sloth-eyed children.

Tell me of a better life than climbing the cordage or riding the forefoot. Any snotty or tar worth his earring would go weatherly to oblivion rather than remain on land.

I have consulted my charts and you may be interested to know that the Linda Maria was stranded on the Rose Atoll when you appeared to us from out of the vapour and the rain. You will want to cite the name of the reef in your logbook when you provide your account to King George. I give all the glory to the reef and not to you, my sir. The month, by the by, is January and the year is 1715. It has no meaning to me, but it surely does to you. You have been searching for me for so long now, but not as long as we searched for Treasure Island.

Aye, the Bible. I should write about the Bible first. What would this tale be without that Bible that young Edward brought aboard my ship? It marked our course, and we followed that book from our youth to our dog years, trying to solve the secrets inside it.

I knew that Edward's Bible held a secret as soon as I opened it and seen the word "Blood" spilled on the first page, just 'neath the headpiece. It takes a singular creature to write the word "Blood" in a Bible, and mind you to write it in crimson. The rest of the ciphers were written in ink as black as the scribe's soul, a fine fellow by my reckoning all in all.

I weighed that book in my hand, taking it from Edward before he claimed it back, and though it could fit in the palm of my hand, it was heavy with deception and double-dealing. It had a back and front of leather and a sturdy binding, the better to keep its secrets. It was an old book, some worn, some tired from all its trickery, mayhap hundreds of years old, that Bible.

I ain't given to sentiment, but if I had never resolved them ciphers, I still would have held that book to my heart for the sake of the deceit in it. "Blood," the master brigand wrote in it. "Blood" he inscribed as his legacy. "Blood" he planted like a weed in the Garden of Eden. "Blood" he scratched out as neatly as his own epitaph.

And just above that crimson word was the headpiece that I have traced from memory, as I could never forget it or any of the other markings in that masterpiece of malevolence.

And then, under the headpiece and "Blood," the scribe scrawled the numerals "1303," which first I took to be the year of the man's birth or death, or mayhap even the year that he planned his evil.

Subsequently, the author wrote a sentence so simple, so evident that it could not have been more cunning. He wrote, "I have hidden 41 meters from the foundation 6 wooden boxes overlaid in ivory, and all empty, and one remarkable treasure covered in nothing but sackcloth not more than 2 meters deep nor more than 87 meters wide." What a prize—eighty-seven meters wide! Of course, the trickster's declaration sent us north and south and east and west, to leper lands and cannibal lands, through torrents of hail and volleys of storms, and everywhere we went death followed us. It follows us now, lurking just abaft the taffail. And waits.

I will set forth only one other cipher now, a fitting cipher as this is the beginning of my own tale, a cipher that was written in Latin and read, "*Audacibus annue coeptis,*" heartening the reader to look with favour upon a bold beginning. The deceiver wrote the cipher twice, once on the last page of his Bible and the second time on a tree blackened by lightning on Treasure Island. A craftsman, so he was.

I AM SICK with the fever and almost blind. My hide is blistered. My bones ache. I coughed so hard that I almost blustered my head off. Do not be vexed on account of my health though, my sweet. I will not faint nor fail. I will not keel over until I kill you. Stand me plumb so that I may take a drink of rum on account of my impending betterment.

I hate Englishmen.

I hate Englishmen, though I hate the Portuguese more. I despise the Spaniards most of all.

I claim no country but the North Sea, for I am Silver, Long John Silver. I set forth here my true adventures, the good, the evil, the blessed, and the cursed of my life at sea, I Silver.

The bottom of the sea is the right place for me, but you would bring your dear captain to Newgate Square to swing by the twine.

I would rather be hanged by the French. At least they would give me a last meal that would be better than biscuits. It is true that I was born an Englishman, but I would expire a Frenchman.

I am not your prisoner.

I have dashed captains from the Tortugas to Pimlico Sound. I have eaten the bread and fruit of every land and downed it all with Spanish wine. Good wine is the only attribute of Spain, by the by, as it has no other attribute except fast horses, and I assign all the credit for that to the horses.

You will not hold me here. I do not keep company with pink-livered Englishmen.

Old Nick flung hard seas and storms against me, but I never gave in to Nick or his crew. Who are you compared to Nick and his gibbets and demons? Nick tried to sentence me under his swells, but I always cut his lines. I aim to trip up Nick by his hooves. My plan is simple. The day that I go under I will challenge him to a duel. I will cheat. Nick will gallop at me, and I will, all atremble, lope at him. Just when Nick is about to grip me, I will tip my cane. Nick will tumble and his halters will all bow down before me. I will condemn Nick, I will, to a seven master. I will make him shine its deck from bulkhead to bow every day. Or, I might set him up in Londontown as a chimney sweep and fix him in the top of a flue out of pure mischief, so that Nick could glimpse but never get close to the flames. Or, I might put him in Parliament. Nick could do some damage there. But that would be a form of benevolence, and so it ain't much likely.

The Linda Maria is my ship. The men that sail on her call her mother, for she is no less to them. Who are you to hold her wheel? Have you scrubbed her pine like I done, day after day, on Black John's orders? You have not, sir. Have you mended her like I done, tied and twisted her bits of hemp twelve times by twelve times until her ropes were sturdy enough for a younker to swing by them? Have you scraped her free of all barnacles of honesty and integrity that she may have picked up in port? No, sir. I have seen to her best interests. Have you steered her clear of the rocks and floes that would do her harm? Have you brought her into harbour by night, by moonlight, so that she might show herself to her highest advantage? No, you have not. I have minded her from the day that I first come aboard her when I was a lad, to the day that I become her captain, and even now whilst you tramp her deck. Her timbers creak and moan. She knows that you are not worthy of her.

This is my history, and if I write it laggardly, it is only for the enjoyment that it brings me to recount it. My plume is from a ship, one of your King's ships, that I caught off Arcadia. I skirted Newfoundland and found her beached in foul weather. I made her brief acquaintance and killed most of her crew. I detained some of the crew in the hold and sold them to the Caribs for nuts and sugar and such. The Caribs ate the Englishmen. The Caribs have peculiar tastes and apparently enjoy their stew stringy with Englishmen. This plume is made from a peacock feather. My parchment is from that same ship, and if it is worthy of Georgey and his decrees, it is good enough for me. I do not know the origin of the ink. I have no doubt that it is exceptional. The ink runs some, like English blood, but the blame must be placed on the scribe.

I have charts of all the seas that I sailed and of all the lands that I afflicted. I am pleased to tell you that I stole every one of these charts. I took this cross-staff that I am holding from one of your fellow compatriots this past season, and may he rot where I left him, which is just off Barbary in the event that you are looking for him. You will find him in the tuck of his ship, on account of his rank, and his mates well below there. I am unable to navigate with the cross-staff in my cabin, but that is all the same with me, as I shall use it soon enough when I escape. I shall not need it to navigate your horizons. They are marly and bleak, my hearty. Marly and bleak.

This is a tale of time and distance.

Some captains gauge time by observing the run of the tide, whilst others watch the wash in the waves. They tally the speed of the ship against the markings on their charts. I prefer to throw seaweed, or preferably a man, or preferably a Spaniard, in the water, as the science is the same. The hard cases, like Black John, threw a knotted line into the water and determined the ship's speed and so the distance traveled in that manner. That is too much work for my hearties and me. We use a sundial or an hourglass to reckon time. If we forget to turn the hourglass or look at the sundial then, as far as we are concerned, time has stopped. No one is particularly concerned about it. We are never late to a murder.

Now, distance. Some captains measure distance by the Pole Star and the sun. Some send their tars into the nest to ken from point to point. Some captains sail along coasts and mark the landfalls. I mark distance with my right hand. My forefinger, held high to the heavens, marks two degrees. My wrist, so held, marks eight degrees. My murdering hand marks eighteen degrees. I hold it up to the blue and the black and sail. My hand has never failed me except in a fog, or now, in this fever. I say that distance is of no importance either. It runs through your fingers like the buntline but does not attach itself to anything. You cannot tie it to the square sail or pull it up the yard.

Aye, and this is a tale of that Bible and of gold too. And of treasure. Aye, and of treachery too.

I began writing my history this very day, my hearty, for this is the day that you locked me in my cabin. I hold my plume in my starboard hand and my dagger in my lee hand. I will damn you with these words, I will. I will damn you.

You did not speak a word to me after you killed my men. Not a word, and after all these years too.

You shut me in my cabin, but I have reckoned every day that I have been here. Aye, and I will pin my dagger to your heart for each day that I am here. I marked the exact time that your tar turned the key in this lock.

You should fear me.

I will come for you. I will.

And now there is a rap on my door.

What man is it? Is it you then? No, it ain't. It ain't any man at all. It is that lout of a cabin boy that you sent to torment me.

---

*A*re you very ill, sir?" the lout asked.

"It is an insult that your captain does not address me directly," I answered. "Tell him that I said so, boy. Tell him that. And tell him, and mind you this, that he is a doomed man. Mind you to tell him that too."

"I would not tell him that."

"That is an order."

"You are not the captain. Not anymore. The captain is standing on deck," so the lout told me.

"Impertinence," I replied. "Unlock my door. I will give you ale."

"The captain said that I should never unlock this door."

"I have a woman here," I told him.

"You do not."

"I do."

"You do not."

"You are a true torment to the world, boy."

"The captain said not to speak with you. You are sinister, he said."

"I am as harmless as a fawn, I am."

I did not tell the lout that I would murder him if he turned the key in my lock, as that might have deterred him from opening the door. Then again, he was a lout of a lad.

Mind you, I have not had the displeasure of viewing the lout's features, as he must have been hanging on to the mast-step when you attacked, but I know his face as well as the corn on my left foot. His eyes are clear and colorless, as there ain't a spoon of intellect behind them. His brow is as straight as a deadrise. His nose is flat and his neck thick enough for a rope.

His hair is black and oily and sits snug on his head, and is his only aspect of consequence. That is nature for you, sir. What it does not bestow on the inside it grants on the outside. This lad must have hair by the tonnage as there ain't a dollop of sense inside him.

His gait is wobbly, and I can hear him trudging to and fro well enough, and so the cleat must have stubs for toes. His fingers are fat, and they bespeak the boy's girth. His body would be a barrel, and so he wears a belt that barely cinches his leggings and blouse. He is mostly middlemost. He is short. There ain't much that a smithy could do with him except flatten him, and, if a smithy took a hammer to him, that smithy might do a lasting service to the populace. Not that I have any interest in service to the populace.

The captain said that I could speak to you on one matter only," the cleat told me. "Your edibles. And that is so that you do not starve. And that is so that they can hang you."

"He means to poison me," I enlightened the lad.

"He would never poison you," the lad replied. "He would not collect the reward on your head. The King himself promised him. Aye, sir, they will hang you. In Newgate. The captain said that there is a patch reserved for you in the courtyard. A fortnight, the captain said. Then they will hang you. In Newgate. In the courtyard. At sunset."

"An insult. They hang such as me at noontime. You may ask any pieman."

"I would see a hanging."

"You are determined to see a hanging, and so I will furnish you with a hanging," I told the lout. "I will hang your captain. The yardarm is choice. Then I will hang you. Aye, you will see a hanging then, boy. I will hoist you with the marline," I told him.

"You are sinister," he piped.

"You are a cleat, boy," I told him. "You might as well be made of lumber." I told the lad his composition for his own good, as I always done right by my lads. "Come in here, boy, and I will show you my musket," I told him. "I warn't much older than you when I executed its owner." When I overtake the ship, now that I think on it, I may drop the lad into the sea so that he can be of benefit to the cuttlefish. He must have some purpose in this world. "I wish to parley with your captain," I told him. I pounded the deck of my cabin with my boot to lay emphasis on my resolve. "Your captain is afraid to speak

with me. This is my ship. Do as I tell you, cleat. I am the captain of this ship. Ain't I John Silver? Ain't I?"

"I will ask the captain," he replied.

I would have this lad follow close behind me, like a tailor sewing up the hinter of my trousers, whilst I told him my history. Aye, but my butcheries would be lost on him.

"Dunce. This is my own ship," I told him.

"We will be paid dear for you."

"How much? It is a matter of pride with me, boy. There is dear and there is dear," I told him. "I will double it. Open this door, boy, and I will double it." The cleat told me that I could not be trusted. "There ain't any man that can be trusted. Alive or deceased. Do you think that your captain can be trusted, boy?"

"My name is Jim, sir."

"Just so your name ain't Jim Hawkins," I told him.

"No, sir. It ain't," the lad replied as flat as cobblestone.

"Are you of any kin to young Hawkins?"

"Jim Mullet I am. That is my name, sir. I am Mullet."

"Then you started this life with more than me. I warn't born with a name, at least not one that I can recollect. Not even a Mullet. Open this door, Mullet."

"I have my orders, sir. I would see you hang at noontime if it pleases you to hang then."

"Tell your captain that I ain't dead yet. Tell him that this is my ship. Tell him that I am the captain. Tell him that he is as doomed as a mug of ale at White's in Pall Mall. I will swallow him in one guzzle. Tell him that."

———⊱◆⊰———

I heard the lad's dull footsteps as he left. He plodded away and that was the end of our exchange, except for a cough that he no doubt muffled by holding his kerchief to his mouth. Mullet warn't only a cleat but a gentleman as well. A shame. I would have taught him better.

A lad should not plod through this world. He should tramp through it with heavy boots. Black boots. Shined boots. He should drink rum, and not wine that has been watered. He should drink until he coughs up his liver proper, mayhap somewhere in the Indies, whilst telling the simple folks there tales of Long John Silver. And most particularly, he should tell a tale of treasure, as there is such pleasure in the telling of it, like nipping from a glass of brandy in the eventide, a long eventide made of odds and chances with a red dawn in the reckoning. And, he should be sure not to leave out the blood.

CHAPTER II.

BLACK JOHN

lack John would ride a haycart from the infernal world to have at my treasure. He would clamber aboard with his cackhand and take a term of seven hundred more years just to touch my treasure. I would stake my wig on it.

Black John was the name of the sea rat that was my captain, and so his men called him until I put him in his grave.

Now seafaring men and seaside ladies don't call Black John's name no more, they don't. There ain't any that hail him since I cast him down. I cast him down below the billows. I cast him down into the depths, and he is still there I say, though there is every possibility that he has taken up a residence in Hell or thereabouts. Mayhap the man has taken a berth haunting a house on Great Street, for Black John was always a restive man. My captain was born to reside in the dusky environs. Worthy of a fair stretch of doom he was. Aye, and if Black John is in Hell or thereabouts, I will meet him there soon enough, I will, for I was born for the dusky environs too.

But it ain't my time yet, my hearty, and so I hereby write of my early term and how I come to iniquity and indecency and such other attributes that we hold in good repute.

Black John was fond of taking his meals at the Three Goats when he was in Bristol, and it was there that I met the sea rat. I was cook, thief, and dishonourable servant to Dick Peel, the proprietor of the Three Goats. Dick Peel was a landlubber through and through, but he was a dishonest landlubber, and so he and I took to each other right off.

When innkeeper Peel was of a mind to serve eggs for supper, I stole eggs for him. When Peel wanted to please his patrons with fowl, I pilfered fowl. When poultry warn't suitable, I swiped mutton. I recall running down High Street with a leg of lamb under my arm. But I warn't born for petty theft.

Peel was a fine innkeeper. He would serve a man a portion of meat, and before that man could finish partaking it, Peel would remove it and put the oddments in a stew. A lady might order ale, and if she did not imbibe it quickly enough, Peel would clear it away and top off the next glass with the dregs. Peel was strictly profitable. He taught me how to squeeze a penny until it come up a farthing, he did.

Blind Tom, who raised me until I was twelve, moored me at Peel's when he could no longer take care of me. So it was, that at twelve years of age, I brought the sea rat a black coat. I took that coat from an old seaman. That tar was the first man I ever killed, and that coat, as I recollect, had silver buttons that shone in the bright Bristol moonlight.

I spied my victim stumbling about an alley, no more than a squint away from the Three Goats, filled with naught but rum and bilgewater. I crept behind the old swab, proper cur that I was, and gave the coat a tug. The man paid no mind to me.

I said, "Give me that coat." I warn't able to summon more wit than that, as this was my first murder.

"I ain't neither," the man answered. Then he said, "I know you. You belong to Blind Tom. No coins for you nor he, boy. Leave me be."

"Tom is dead," I answered.

"That is best. That is best for you. That is best for him. And that is best for Bristol."

"Give me that coat, I said."

"That blind man was a bother and a blight on Bristol. Your Tom was an affliction, what with all his wailing. And you are too, boy."

"I will drag it off your carcass." Mark you how quick I come to wit.

"Kill me for a coat, will you? Get a trade, my sinister pup, and leave me and my coat be. I will call the constable."

"I have a trade," I answered. "This is it now."

I grabbed the coat again, but the old tar anchored his scarf around my neck and only let go when I stuck my elbow into his belly. Then the tar ran at me. He missed me by a fathom, he did, but he ran at me again, and this time he tumbled.

He fell hard and launched a scream, so I picked up a stick and stabbed him with it until he parted with the coat and Bristol and the rest of this scurvy world. There is no coming to terms with some tars.

I had no more regret about killing that drunk than I had for stealing eggs for Dick Peel. Young Silver, and fondly I recall the lad, knew that he was headed directly for Hell and not anyplace where he would be playing the harpsichord or spinet.

Had I a mother, she might have rewarded me with a piece of string for my industriousness, although most mothers take exception to murder. I walked the docks with that coat over my shoulders, and it kept the chill off my bones. What mother could do more? Industry is its own reward, I say. Aye, and there was something more to my simple act. I was proud of it. I had not barked nor begged for my prize. I had taken it. It had come as easy to me as stealing them eggs for Peel. I strode down that street, so I did.

Black John was at the Three Goats with his men when I returned. I was always a direct sort, and so I said to him straight off, "I have a fine coat for you, Black John."

"What is your name, boy?" he asked me.

"He has no name," Peel told the sea rat. That was true. Tom never thought to provide me with one. "Boy" Tom called me, and not by any other name.

"How do you hail him then?" Black John asked Peel, scratching at the only part of his face that warn't covered by his beard.

"I call him this or that. When I call him he comes," Peel answered. "Blind Tom, who brought me the boy, never told me his name. The boy will answer to whatever name you call him, Captain. He has no preference." Then he added, "The boy has a temper, Captain."

"There are ways to cure temper in a boy. It is a matter of a stiff strap and a strong arm. That is all it takes to cure temper in a boy," so my impending benefactor said.

"He would not take well to a strap, Black John. He would not."

"You do not give the boy a say in the matter, Peel. The strap does the speaking for both parties in such a matter. Headstrong then?"

"Headstrong," Peel answered. "But enterprising."

"So the boy pilfers for you." Black John tugged at his beard so forcefully that I thought that his jaw might give way and drop to the floor of Peel's inn. Aye, but that jaw was set in Black John's face too firm and would not meet the terms of the tug. He had as much chance of pulling off his beard, no matter how hard he wrenched it, as he did of pulling the black out of it. He was in perpetual war with that beard, he was.

"Some," Peel replied. "But only on account of his appetite, which is considerable, Captain. He eats as much as the royal navy."

"The boy must have a name," Black John declared. "I am not saying that he deserves one, but it is a matter of protocol. Imagine, if you will, innkeeper Peel, if I had to order my men about without nomenclature. The ship might career. A world without names carries a risk. It might fall over on its heels."

"He come to me without a name, so that is how I took him," Peel said, matter-of-factly. "I had not thought about the unfavourable effect on the world."

"That is why I am a captain," Black John said, with a swift stroke of his beard. "It ain't for naught that I command the Linda Maria. And that is, and everyone that I have ever inquired agrees, a right name for such a lovely lady." Peel nodded so quickly that his teeth chattered. "Blind Tom done right to bring this boy here," the sea rat told Peel.

"He knew that he was near Old Nick's blockhouse when he brought me the boy. Blind Tom knew, Captain, that I am such as takes pity on a boy. He done right by the boy, as you say, Black John," Peel agreed. A wisp of smoke escaped from the fireplace and curled about the room. Peel looked longingly at that bit of smoke. He warn't a brave man. He would, if he could, have joined it on its travel about the room and through the window.

"What is your name then, boy?" Black John asked me. "You must have one. Give me your name. It would not do for the tides to stop turning. You would not wish that on the world, would you, boy? Your name then."

"The captain asked you your name, boy," Peel said, before I could reply. His voice trembled as he sought to assist Black John, afraid that Black John might turn Peel's own world over on its heels if I did not answer Black John forthwith.

"I go by whatever name suits you," I said. "I could be John or Edward or William if it suits you, sir. I could be Harold or Francis for that matter. I could be honest or dishonest, sir. Cat or cur. Whatever suits you. But mostly, sir, I am hungry. For bread and meat. If it suits you, sir. And, afterwards, a brew to wash that bread and meat down."

"Meat you say. And a brew you say. To wash it down you say," Black John replied. "Doesn't Peel here fix you abundantly?" The tug on the beard again.

"He eats well enough," Peel answered quickly. "The boy has a considerable appetite, Captain."

"This is a fine coat. As fine as they come," I told Black John. I sat down at his table. Aye, and I slapped my palms on it for I was ready for hearty fare such as Black John ate. Peel was parsimonious with the edibles he gave me. He treated himself no better. He considered a clam a banquet. He regarded an oyster a feast. So long as Peel put his victuals in tallow and sprinkled them with salt he was content. He could not understand why a person might want more.

"Do not sit there," Peel admonished me. "He knows no better, Captain." Another gasp of smoke drifted out and away from the inn.

I paid no mind to Peel. "This coat," I said. "There ain't naught better than a Bristol coat for a sailor."

"He ain't a sailor," Peel said. "He is a captain." Peel refilled all of the men's tumblers with ale. The only other time that I had witnessed generosity in Peel was when a particular lady visited his inn, and that lady was his Judith. She had buried three husbands and possessed three inheritances and was therefore exceedingly attractive to Peel. He served her a whole guinea fowl as I recall. She was tracking other quarry at the time and did not set her sights on Peel until much later. I always wondered if Judith did him and the others in or if they just packed up out of pure dread. She was a ghastly woman when I first saw her, and with poor habits too. She licked her upper lip after every bite of food. I imagine that she looked at her husbands the same way that she looked at her edibles. I do not know how many bodies lay between Peel and Judith before she nabbed him. I only saw her again many years later, and after Peel had passed, and she was deaf and daft, and those were her best qualities.

"A captain's coat this is," I continued. "Only a captain's coat would sport buttons like these."

"And how did you come by this coat?" Black John asked me, fingering the buttons. "Boy," he added.

"I murdered a man for it," I said proudly. I threw my shoulders back some as I recall. My shoulders were broad even then. I was particularly skillful at freeing eggs from Peel's cupboard. It was a matter of removing the back of the cupboard. Peel would count the eggs the next day over and over and crawl around the floor searching for the missing eggs, which provided me no end of amusement. He might lose a wedge of sheep's cheese now and then. He kept those edibles wrapped in paper and locked in a cabinet, but I broke the lock so it turned at will. Peel believed that he locked the cabinet when he put his key in it, but had he bothered to turn the key in the lock more than once, he would have discovered the ruse. It warn't like Peel to turn a lock more than once as it would have been a waste of his fortitude, such as it was. Aye, eggs and sheep's cheese broaden a boy's shoulders, and if the boy happens to steal those victuals, they broaden them shoulders even more.

"Murdered you said?" Black John asked me. Pew, the hairless crab, watched Black John tow his beard nearly down to the floor. He reached for his own face and pulled, but Pew was perpetually hairless and only managed to nick his chin. If Black John took a stick and poked himself in the eye with it, I have no doubt that Pew would have done the same.

"To bring it to you," I told Black John. "A fine coat it is too. As fine as there is," so I told him. "Captain," I added, as casually as he had appended "Boy" to his address to me.

"Murdered you said?" Peel asked. His hand trembled, and I was concerned that he might spill ale on Black John or one of his men. I did not wish to lose my benefactor, and so I filled the men's tumblers on Peel's behalf.

"So I said," I answered.

"I saw this coat, Captain," Peel said. "It was in a sea chest. In my back room, Captain. A patron of mine that shipped off unexpectedly, Captain."

"And left his sea chest, Peel?" Black John asked.

"Perhaps not, Captain," Peel responded. "I am trying to recollect."

"No swain would leave his sea chest behind him," the captain said.

"Naught a one," Pew said.

"I shall wear this coat," Black John said, and he draped the coat over his shoulders, just as I done when I murdered the tar. It fit him like a second skin. "Well done," he said, "for a boy without a name."

Pew threw a phantom coat over his shoulders.

"Thank the captain," Peel told me. "That's a good lad," he said, as if I was such a creature. "It is an honour that the captain would consider wearing it. A tremendous honour. I am not sure that I have ever been witness to such an honour." He halted for a moment, then offered, "In this inn at any juncture in my recollection." I did not know what Peel had attempted to say and whether his words were meant for Black John or me. I do not expect that Peel knew. He was ever anxious to please, as doing so led to profit. But Black John was too enamoured of his coat to pay mind to Peel. The sea rat told me that he would do me the honour of wearing the coat that I gave him on the night that he sailed. He told me that I could come to the port to see him off, and as a final act of kindness, he tore the heel off his bread and gave it to me.

Peel could not bear the silence as I looked upon Black John's munificence in the form of the heel of bread. "You broke bread with Black John. And, at Black John's own table," Peel said. "The bread, I have been told, is among the best in Bristol." Peel's declamation was correct. I had stolen the loaf from an excellent bakery. Peel's shoulders flagged out of relief, and he was so pleased to have come out of the conversation without impairment, that he instantly commenced to count the number of tumblers on the tables. Nothing brought him more pleasure than tallying a bill. But I had more to say to the sea rat, and he had more to say to me.

"You may take your leave now, boy," Black John told me. "Treat this lad right all in all, Mister Peel," he said.

"That I will, all in all, Captain," Peel answered with the slimmest of bows.

"And mind you to give the boy a name," Black John said.

Black John's crumbs did not satisfy me, and so I said to the sea rat, "You have a ship. The Linda Maria," I told him. "I have an eye for the ladies." I winked at the sea rat. I warn't given to winking, but I assumed that a man of the world like Black John might appreciate a wink in the admiration of his lady. "The Linda Maria," I said again, drawing my thumb across my nose. I had seen a milliner make that gesture once after cheating a buyer of some piece goods, and it lent the reprobate an air of sophistication. Black John warn't impressed.

"He knows the name of my ship but not his own name," the sea rat told his men, who joined him in a laugh at my expense. Pew laughed the loudest.

"I also know that you must carry a piece of silver or two, or more, for him that does you a service," I said. "I speak on behalf of the lad that brought you this coat. A poor lad. That has just a piece of bread. And no name."

"But a mouth," the sea rat said. The tug on the beard again.

"The boy means no harm," Peel told the captain. "Nor slur. Of any kind," Peel said as he backed away from Black John's table. Then Peel announced, looking about, that he smelled smoke. There warn't no smoke in the room no more. Even the smoke had deserted poor Peel.

"It is no more than brimstone," Pew said. Allow me to revive your recollection of Pew as it has been so many years since you sailed with him. He was a repulsive creature, he was. Hairless, as I said. A long nose that was more beak than nose. A lip that was curled into cruelty itself. Limbs that were longer than natural. His arms gave him good reach, and he could snatch and stab with advantage. When he slept on the deck and twisted himself up he resembled nothing more or less than a crab.

"A right smell too," an even more repulsive swain known as Kwik concurred. You never met Kwik and so I will recount his features presently. They were so vile that I will wait before describing the menace of a man. It puts me off just thinking about him.

"So you want silver," Black John said to me, drawing his thumb across his nose. He abstained from the wink. "I knew a milliner once who made such a gesture whenever he cheated a customer. Kwik here was such a customer once upon a time."

"Last time in port," Kwik said. "I was wanting a patch for my jacket. I cut his throat. After I cut off his thumb."

"The boy wants silver," Black John said, stroking his beard. "Silver," he repeated, considering my request.

"A considerable appetite, Captain," Peel said. "So I said, Captain, sir." Peel's eyes darted about the room. He was always reckoning. Peel might, if the occasion arose, inform Black John that the sea rat had twelve buttons on his corset before the captain could snuff him.

"Aye, so you said, innkeeper," Black John replied. "A simple strap will not do for such a boy, innkeeper."

"Aye, Captain. Not for this boy. Not a simple strap," Peel said with some hesitation. He stopped counting the tumblers. His hands drifted into the pockets of his apron.

"I would be as enterprising at sea as on land," I told Black John. "I would sail on the Linda Maria, sir." I thumped my chest. It was a considerable chest for a lad of my term. If eggs and sheep's cheese fortify a boy's shoulders, then porridge fills out a boy's chest. There was no way to nap porridge, and so I ate whatever portion of porridge the patrons failed to finish before Peel could put it in another pot. I doubted that Black John or any of his crew had met a milliner that thumped his chest. "I am able," I offered. "Ready and willing. For anything the sea might throw my way. Storm or gale or even, if it is of a mind for it, fair weather. I ain't partial."

Pew forgot himself and thumped his own chest, hastily looking around to see if anyone had noticed his treason, before wiping his hands on the table.

"I am partial," Black John said. "He is tall for twelve years," the captain told Peel. Peel's head bobbed. "Let me see your hand, boy. Show me your hand. Put it here, boy."

Black John held out his hand, and no sooner had I tendered my own mitt, than Black John grabbed it. He mashed my hand in his and slammed it on the table to the delight of his men. "Scream for mother," he said. "Scream now, boy," the sea rat said. "Scream for mother."

"Ain't got one," I answered.

Black John released me, and whilst I tallied my digits, he said, "I know that you done me a service today. I done you a service too, boy. I let you live. I could have killed you for speaking with me so, and by rights."

"Jurisprudence," Pew sang. "Simple jurisprudence."

Then Black John imparted his law on my behalf. The magistrate of the Three Goats kicked me so hard that he felled me. But I stood up right away, I did, and said to Black John, "I aim to go to sea. I aim to sail with you."

"Perhaps he needs more jurisprudence," Pew said. "So says Pew."

"I would be pleased to show it to him," Kwik offered.

Before Black John could reply, I said, "I want to sail with you, sir. Only you. You are the greatest of all the captains that sail from this here Bristol." I was ready to throw in all the captains that sailed from Londontown if necessary.

Black John and his beard pondered my words, and after they finished pondering them, said, "True, but I have no need for a cabin boy." I heard the waves lapping on the shore. I smelled the brine. I heard, even though I had not yet made her proper acquaintance, the timbers of the Linda Maria creaking a welcome. "No need," Black John repeated. "None. Whatsoever."

"And never will for such as you," Kwik said. Most captains have such as a Mister Kwik on their ships, men that slip the captain a word here and there about another tar. I had my share of such men on board the Linda Maria too. They serve a purpose on board a ship, much like a compass, so that the captain knows where he is headed and if any storms are looming on the horizon.

I was readying my reply, but some of the crew, those who were keen to see me reach thirteen years, advised me to hold my tongue. But I was never such as would hold his tongue, and so I said, "I want silver then. I want silver for the coat that I brought you."

"I give it back to you." Black John took off the coat and carved that fine coat in twain with his dagger. "Here you are, my lad," he said. "This coat does not suit me anymore. It is torn."

The hearties roared with laughter. They nearly split their sides and near as neatly as Black John split my coat. They pounded on innkeeper Peel's tables so hard that they dashed them. Good ale spilled across innkeeper Peel's floor. Aye, and more good ale, and there ain't no bad ale mind you, ran out of those hearties' mouths, for they laughed so hard. Pew tore at the air and laughed until he fell to the floor.

I gave the coat back to Black John and asked him half a coin for half a coat.

The laughing stopped. James Kwik, that blight on humanity, told the captain, "I will show the boy silver, Captain. If it pleases you. Hard silver."

"Sharp silver too," the plague known as Pew said. Pew lacked common faculties and so was amusing in that regard. He was ready with a dagger at all times. He jigged like a beetle bug. He slipped, like Kwik, the occasional word to the captain. In his day, Pew had formidable sight and could spy a ship leagues away before any other man spied it. It may be, and I have thought on it from time to time, that we, the captain and I, kept Pew because whenever we saw that hairless crab of a man, we looked at ourselves in the glass and were pleased that we warn't him.

There was another reason why I did not murder the crab right off though, and that was that I had struck a bargain with him. He had seen Edward's Bible. He was the one, as you know, that found it. Whenever I looked on Edward's Bible I recalled how Pew appeared the day that he discovered it. The cover of that Bible turned blacker with each passing year and took on a sheen from the salt air like a polished pair of boots. But not so, Pew. He become ever more hideous, an eye and an ear leaving him, yet Pew and the Bible did have a commonality. They both smelled some musty.

But, more on Kwik. Kwik never took to me, and I never took to Kwik. We were natural foes from the first. You may be inclined to like Kwik on account of his ill will toward me, but do not become too fond of him, for I kill him forthwith.

Kwik was a man who sweated all the time. He was a greasy soul, who stood leeward to the devil. His hair, which was black, swagged down over his brow. His eyes were small, like a rat's eyes. He had two scars. One scar split his brow. The Dutch engraved that scar on him. Bloody Bill gave

Kwik the other scar. Aye, I will speak more on Bloody Bill later too, as I can't tie all of my seafaring life onto this bollard just now. Bill tried to cleave Kwik into longitudes when Kwik come between Bill and his beloved sea. No man separated Bill from his sea. It was Kwik's mistake to step in front of Bill whilst Bill was looking into the deep. That scar ran athwartships, along Kwik's chest, and then abaft to the middle of his back.

Black John paid no heed to Kwik and said to me with all the graciousness of a hangman, "I will give you your silver. Give me your hand again, boy. Put your hand on my table, and I will give you your silver."

And so, as there was no choice in the matter, I put my hand on his table.

Kwik slithered behind me. I do not abide a man that creeps behind another man unless I am the one that is doing the creeping.

Peel, who was concerned on account of his dismembered tables and spilled ale, importuned Black John, "I would you spare the boy. The boy does steal good mutton, Captain. The best mutton it is, sir. And sir, he does not know any better than to speak to you so."

Peel's words on behalf of the mutton and me were true enough.

Peel went on, "If you mean to punish the boy, Captain, you will not take him with you. You will leave him here. On land, sir. That would be stout punishment for the boy, Captain. He spouts each and every day about going to sea."

Black John covered my hand again. "Here is your silver, boy," he said. I was fully prepared to meet my doom, I was, but Black John dropped two pieces of silver into my hand. Kwik, disappointed, sat down. "Aye, here is your silver, boy," the sea rat said. Then, Black John struck the table with his fist. He struck the table so hard that the coins sprang out of my hand and back to Black John. Peel's inn thundered with the sound of the hearties' laughter.

"There is no pirate like Black John," I said to the sea rat. "There is no pirate like Black John who can steal back his own coins."

The hearties' jaws shut straightaway, and there was no more laughing then. Black John was so taken aback that he did not stir. Now it may be that Black John was too surprised to run me through. Or, it may be that he recalled the words of my advocate, Peel, and decided to take pity on me. Or, it may be that he was particularly fond of the mutton that I stole for Peel, but Black John did not kill me. He merely said to me, "You are a confounded creature, boy."

"I will work hard on your ship," I told Black John. The brine of the sea filled my lungs, and every mast on the Linda Maria called to me.

"Work hard he said," Pew repeated. "The boy will work hard. For the captain, so Pew heard."

"I do not need a boy," Black John said. "But I will give you a name, confounded creature. I name you John, for John is my name, and I let you live this day. I warn't a party to your birth, so far as I know, but I let you live this day. And so, as your sponsor, I give you my own name."

"You can still snuff him, and even if you gave him your own name," Kwik said.

"A fine name John is," Pew said. "Not a better name on a gravestone, Pew says."

"Misery, innkeeper Peel. It is misery to be the captain of these rovers," the sea rat said. "I have not yet concluded naming the lad, and Kwik would render him a carcass. Aye, and Pew would pick his pocket after that. Misery, innkeeper Peel."

Peel nodded with understanding. "Would more mutton help, Captain?" Peel asked.

"Not even the best mutton," Black John replied. The sea rat raised his arms for his next declaration. "I call you Long John, for you are tall for your years. I give you the name of Silver too, for silver may very well be your doom. Aye, and so now you are Long John Silver."

Then, Black John gave me the silver coins. Pew reached in his pocket, thought better of it, and pulled out his hand with naught in it.

"The boy thanks you, Captain," Peel said. "Don't you, boy?" Peel said.

"You may bring me black boots when I next find myself in this latitude, Long John Silver. I have no need for a torn black coat. As I said."

Peel put his fingers to his lips.

"I shall bring you boots," I answered. "Long John Silver shall."

That, my hearty, was my life before I roamed the pirate seas and took to treasure, when I was no more than what the sea rat called a confounded creature. I was a random piece of work, I was. My father, most probably, was a sailor. And my mother, most probably, was a whore. That was my likely origin according to Tom. No one ever claimed me, not ever. I do not recall a mother or father. You may tell me that all men have mothers and fathers, but I had neither so far as I can recall. My hearties have relations. Them that I murder have mothers and fathers and cousins and kin.

It is only I, John Silver, captain and confounded creature, that come into this world without milk or mother.

Before Tom took me I slept in the lanes. I ate what my patrons cast away, the food that warn't fit for their table. I ate what the dogs left behind. Those dogs are my only kin, so I say. No other kin ever claimed me, and so I claim no other kin than those curs. And Tom.

I likely come into this world on a day without sun, for there was never any sun in Bristol. Not where I slept, not where I ate, and not where I roved. The preachers tell you that Hell is hot just to throw you off the mark, but Hell is a cold place, and it lies just north of Bristol. And I do not know if it was a man or a devil that dropped me here. I do not have horns, so I expect that it was a man that dropped me here, but if it was a devil, that is all square with me too.

Bristol is as good of a place as any other to starve to death, but Tom saved me. He taught me to count. Coins ain't worth a cod if you can't count them, and I was always thankful to Tom for teaching me. There was no better service that Tom ever done for me, then bringing me to Peel.

Aye, Tom. He taught me to solicit funds too. I could bark like a dog. I could howl like a banshee. I could purr as well for a supplementary farthing. I could dance. I could sing. There was almost nothing that I would not do to acquire yellow metal.

I made my trade in other ways before I met Tom. Bristol was a careless place. It was careless with its boys and careless with its coins. I was a good thief, being so in need of sustenance, and it gave me pleasure to pinch from them that would see me starve.

Blind Tom found me one eventide, though it would be more correct to say that his cane found me. Tom tamped me on the head with his cane.

I resided in a particular lane, and it was there, behind a loose brick, that I hid my coins. Mark how I was always given to secreting my riches, even as a lad. Tom varied his choice of bursaries. And so it come to be, that on this eventide, Tom deposited his earnings behind a brick in my lane. Tom was well acquainted with lads such as me. Therefore, Tom struck me.

Tom, his cane, and I consequently come to an understanding. Tom needed a pair of eyes and I needed edification, and so Tom and I banded together as neat as braces. He took me under his wing, which warn't a wing at all but a great black cape, and Tom brought me up until he gave me to Peel.

And Peel gave me the only trade that I ever knew before I went to sea, unless thievery and murder are trades too, but most gents do not hold them enterprises to be such. I had no trade before Tom brought me to Peel. Peel taught me to mull, parch, boil, roast, bake, and steam. That is a trade for a hungry lad. There is no better place for a boy to get hale than in a tavern.

The fire in the tavern, even when it blazed, never warmed me though. My bones were too cold. I spent too many days shivering in the lanes for that fire to warm me. Aye, and the constable that tried to beat me when he saw me in the streets never struck me in Peel's tavern. Instead, he inflicted good cheer on me by pinching my cheeks. I always hated the constable.

Tom gave me to Peel, the blazing fire, and the pinching constable, as Tom was very sickly by then. He did not beg anymore. He hardly ate or drank. Greedy lad that I was, I ate the edibles that Tom left behind. I took his coins too. Them coins seemed like the treasure of treasures to me then. It is all relative, and for all I know I may be the richest man on land or sea now. But then, and as I had nothing, even them few coins was true wealth to me. If you think that it was wrong for me to take his victuals and currency, then you never starved.

Peel approached me with a pencil, a book, and a proposition one forenoon. He presented me with his book of accounts and informed me that he had decided to teach me to write, and that he was going to throw reading into the bargain as well. Peel warn't free-handed by nature or inclination, and so when I protested, as I was perfectly content to just thieve for him, he informed me that there warn't no choice in the matter. He, having taken Black John's words to heart, held a strap at his side. I am not sure what he intended to do with the strap as, even at that age, he was no match for me, but he folded it over and snapped it until it offered a weak crack. He practiced his menacing several more times until the strap complied and tendered a crack of commendable volume. I took the strap out of concern that Peel would harm himself by it and have to close the inn, the consequence being that I would be back in the street again.

I placed the strap on the table between us. Peel narrowed his eyes. He was capable of calling the constable. I had no standing with the constable but only with his pinching fingers, and so I thanked Peel for his goodwill and told him that if he was willing to summon his goodwill again that I would be willing to endure it.

Peel informed me that it would be a benefit to us both if I learned letters. I could, he said, assist him with his books of account and gain an aptitude. I could not conjure up any need for me to acquire an aptitude, but Peel pressed on. He told me that any seaman worth his salt had to know letters. He spoke about comprehending charts and writing logbooks, and squeaked on about the consequences of misreading compasses and incorrectly recording lays and berths. He had heard it all, he told me, in his tavern. He warbled on that he owed it to Blind Tom to help me. He owed Tom no debts, and it was likewise with Tom, as Tom and his pail had moved well north of Bristol and into another realm, but I decided that I would abide by Peel's wishes. I saw the potential for positive yield by entering facts and figures into Peel's book. I presumed that I might, from time to time, make an error in my favour. Peel presumed so as well. He paid me less wages from thenceforth.

Peel laid his thin book on the table, next to the strap, and I noticed that the book's cover was held together by bits of string that Peel had tied together. What a difference between this book that Peel prized above all others and Edward's book that truly held a treasure! The binding of Peel's book had broken many times and was stitched together. I would expect no less from Peel. He was thoroughly pecuniary. I had, prior to working at Peel's tavern, seen Bristol surgeons at their labours. They and their rapparees picked people up out of the streets and carried them away, and I never saw any of the people that they carried away come back. I also saw the surgeons' stabs at sewing wounds, but never noticed anyone benefit from the mending that was applied to them. That is an interesting vocation, as the Bristol surgeons are paid to malign their fellow creatures, then honoured for it, but honest scoundrels like me are hunted and hanged. The book was stitched together with an uneven hand, Peel's hand, and looked like those bodies that the surgeons hemmed or, in the worst of the cases, purloined for healing. Peel ran his fingers over the binding with a care that could have passed for affection.

The cover of the book was blackened with grease, and the edges of the book were worn and blackened too. Again, mark the difference between Peel's ledger and Edward's Bible. Edward's Bible had been blackened with care, whereas Peel's ledger was blackened by mischance. Peel's ledger had likely been brown at birth. Edward's Bible was born black. Aye, and all that touched Edward's Bible were blackened by it too.

The first page of Peel's book had notes and numbers on it that swirled about the page. Every space on the page was filled, and it was like Peel not to waste a scrap of anything that he had purchased. The second page bore the same strange markings. Peel turned the pages of the book whilst I watched him. He grinned, and I grinned back at him as I surmised that I was supposed to be impressed.

Mostly, the markings looked like the tattoos on the South Sea natives. Those tattoos mean something to those natives but not to us. It was the same with Peel. The markings in his book held great meaning for him. He was pleased whenever he looked on them. They meant nothing to me. Not yet.

"Ten years," he told me, and I winked. He looked at me peculiarly, and so I returned the gaze. "This summer," he said, as he turned a page and poked his finger on an entry. He read the entry to me and told me an event that I remembered. "Thin Jim," he said. I recalled that a man, perhaps ten years my senior, come into Peel's tavern in July and asked about the possibility of an apprenticeship. Peel told the fellow that he had no need for an apprentice because he had me, and the fellow said that his name was Thin Jim and that Peel had better remember him. Peel, accordingly, wrote the man's name in his ledger. Thin Jim told Peel that he meant to have the best tavern in Bristol one day and that it would be filled with women and song. Peel told him not to forget to fill it with patrons or he would not remain in business, and Thin Jim rejoined that the Three Goats was a dull place, and he had nothing to learn from Peel anyway. Thin Jim did run a good tavern, and likely a better tavern than Peel, as it was filled with women and song, and patrons, when I went there many years later for a brief mooring.

Peel tore out a page from his book. He tore it slowly, as he could not bear the loss of a single sheet of paper. He did dock me wages for the paper, and for the use of his pencil as well, because I read those entries in the ledger on my commencement from Peel's college of learning.

He wagged the pencil and waved the torn page in front of me as if I was an animal and had never seen a pencil or paper before, then he slowly, with a care that amounted to devotion, wrote numbers on the page. Blind Tom had taught me to reckon but not to read numbers. I could count, but I had to commit the counting to memory, and that is likely how I developed such a keen memory. Peel left me with the page, the numbers, and half a sack of barley. He told me to reckon the grains of barley, which was easy enough, but then he told me to write them down by tens and then by twenties and so on. I protested. Peel stood firm that I should do as he told me, and so, as I was hungry, I done as he said. I chewed some of the barley, and therefore immediately profited from my education.

Peel went about his boiling and parching whilst I stayed at my work, and when he returned he was amazed at what I had written. I recall that he looked at the paper and then at me and then back at the paper. He turned the paper over and looked at the other side of it, as if he could divine how I come to compose my numbers so well on my first attempt. He asked me if anyone else had entered the tavern, and I told him that I had been alone since he left me with the barley, the torn page, and the pencil.

He took away the sack of barley and brought out a sack of rice as if I could only count barley. He put his hands on his hips and told me to write the numbers whilst he watched me. I counted and composed my numbers and when I was done Peel pronounced himself astonished. He put his hand on my head to feel if I had a fever and when he concluded that I was fit, he whistled. It warn't so much a whistle as it was a wheeze, but he stopped his cookery for the night and tore another page out of his book. This time, he tore the page out quicker. He wrote the letters of the alphabet on the page and told me to copy them. I wrote them without delay. He read each of the letters and sang a little rhyme to me to help me remember them. I sang the rhyme back to him. He felt my head again.

He wrote his name on the page, then my name, the one that Black John had given me, and he sounded the names out for me. I repeated them. He wrote Blind Tom's name and pronounced it, and I done the same. He told me that if he was a swordsman and not an innkeeper, and was teaching me swordplay, he had no doubt that I would be as good as him in a fortnight. I told him that it would almost certainly take me less time than that to be as good as him. I must have perturbed Peel because he gnashed his teeth, and the only other time that I had seen him take his troubles out on his teeth was when a tar died at his table without having first paid his bill.

Peel wrote the words that I asked him to write and sounded them out for me. My first words were "sword" and "knife" and "sea" and "moon" and "rum" and "dagger" and "murder" and "milk" and "spoon" and "gold" and "Bristol" and "treasure" and "barley" and "rice" and "mutton" and "pounds" and "sterling" and "book" and "thief" and "mother" and "father" and "latitude" and "longitude" and "heading" and "red" and "hand" and, for the sake of Peel, "berth" and "compass" and "chart" and "lay" and "meat" and "fish" and "fork" and "ladle" and "pot" and "flour." Peel was pleased.

I was writing sentences, and good ones, in a week. I aim to write the truth about my history, and so I will not tell you that all of my sentences were intelligible, but I was fairly proficient right off, but not as advanced as you with all of your edification. You may recall that I sang you bawdy songs and that you sang them back to me, and so I profoundly bolstered your education. You have advanced even further since then. You can read the warrant and the amount of the reward for me in your King's own hand. I will nevertheless ask you to thank me for your tutoring when I hold my knife to your neck. That is "knife," sir. You may trill it at will.

I examined Peel's letters, and they warn't out of the ordinary for a man that kept no company except with meats and cutlery, and so I asked him for books. He brought me a bible but I already knew much of it, as Tom and I had our share of sermons whilst we stood outside the churches and waited for remuneration. Tom and I done much better standing outside the taverns and houses of ill repute, where the patrons were in better spirits than those leaving church and, as a result, gave us more coin. The Bristol preachers, now that I think on it, were like the Bristol surgeons. I never saw anyone raised up by them, and the dead never come back neither.

Aye, now Edward's Bible was a book worth its binding. I should remark on the hand of the trickster that wrote the riddles. Most folks write their words aslant, but he that wrote the riddles wrote them strictly upright as if he was particularly proud of them. I cannot blame the fellow, as I would have been pleased too to have let loose such wickedness upon the world. His hand never wavered. He was sure of his mischievousness.

The clues that the trickster offered, so simple, so plain, and so pitiless, were hidden from sight, the trickster offering no assistance other than his words. I cite one such cipher again. He wrote, "I have hidden 41 meters from the foundation 6 wooden boxes overlaid in ivory, and all empty, and one remarkable treasure covered in nothing but sackcloth not more than 2 meters deep nor more than 87 meters wide."

All them words are true as they reveal all.

All them words are false, for they reveal naught by their mere appearance.

Leave us dismember the words. Firstly, "I have hidden 41 meters from the foundation." Where was the foundation situated? What was the meaning of "foundation," and was it an edifice or something else?

The author put us on notice that he had hidden 6 wooden boxes overlaid in ivory. Now, did he mean "6" or were we to tally the "6" with the "41," or for that matter withhold the "6" from the "41"? And why were the boxes of wood? And why were they topped in ivory? Was there a meaning to these particulars?

Now, my hearty, how were we to discern the meaning of "and all empty"? Were we to take from these words that the prior clues were without meaning, that they were false clues or that they were clues at all? Should we have disregarded the prior words?

Then he wrote, "and one remarkable treasure," and that was what we fixed our gaze on all these years. That was the heart of the sentence. But what was the treasure, and why was it remarkable?

Next, and he stated plainly, that the remarkable treasure was "covered in nothing but sackcloth," but what manner of person would conceal a treasure in such fabric?

The sweet mercenary of a man.

He went on that his treasure was concealed "not more than 2 meters deep nor more than 87 meters wide," and so I again ask you what were we to make of these numbers?

The answers, and so we know now, are manifest. I have solved every one of his ciphers and this one, this essential one, as well. It took me all them years to ascertain the cruel truth. And, sir, it was worth all them years, at least for me, as I have the treasure, and you do not. Here I am below, and there you are above. But it was not always so.

PEEL BROUGHT ME books about the sea on account that I requested them books, and I read them with pleasure. I principally liked adventure books, although the primary personages in them thwarted heathens and beat them back one way or another. I rewrote them books so that they were, by my way of thinking, more truthful. I scrawled in the margins and crossed through words and so appended the tales so that they were more pleasant. The heathens thrashed the gentlemen and gentlewomen after I completed my corrections. I also drew in the books. My jots and scrawls disquieted Peel because he had borrowed the books from his aunt. I read the letters from his aunt, and I am sure that if he had read my tales to her, he would have provided her a trifle more excitement in her declining years. He never returned the books to her, and she never asked him for them, as his aunt had a poor memory, and so I continued my improvements to them.

I also read the broadsheets and took a liking to politics but not to the ministers in Rump Parliament. I put them ministers in the same company as the surgeons and preachers. I can also attest that they never done anything for Tom or me but put us out of one lane and into another. They also never raised anyone up except themselves. And strike me if these words ain't so, but I have always been plainspoken about my duplicity, whereas these ministers of the Rump hide their crimes under their periwigs. Landlubbers all.

I read recent history too, courtesy of Peel's aunt, and did take a liking to the Duke of Monmouth despite his blood. He seemed like a good enough rogue as he tried to assassinate his brother, James. Monmouth, good bastard son that he was, fought from Somerset to Sedgemoor, and it took eight hacks of the axe to sever his head and so that Monmouth was some obstinate. Eventually, his head come off, but them royals had to sew it back on for his royal portrait. I rewrote the accounts of the battles between Monmouth and James, and you may be interested to know that Monmouth bested King and country at none other than Bristol with help from Silver.

Your King, as long as I am marking the matter, has brought nothing but misery to his kingdom. Peel told me that all of the kings and queens are relations to each other. Peel also told me that the British kings and queens are as much German as English and that, he understood, there was Russian and French blood mixed in them too, and so I say that they are no better than mutts like me. All of these battles are family disputes of one sort or another. The royals never die in any of them. They send their militaries to be murdered.

I drafted some rhymes that Peel enjoyed, but he said that they warn't befitting a lad of my term. He did recite them from time to time to his patrons, and they seemed to enjoy them, but Peel gave me neither compliment nor coinage for my verse. I made no other use of my new skills. I did purloin a plume and ink bottle, the better to practice my aptitude, but Peel was less than pleased when I showed him my results. The words that I had written were fine ones, quite clever so Peel opined, but the ink run all over my breech stockings. Peel told me that he would take a sum out of my weekly wages to purchase new stockings, as he could not have me traipsing about his inn disfigured by ink. I corrected the entry in Peel's account book later.

I WAS COUNTING no more than cutlery in Peel's galley, and inscribing no more than Peel's receipts, when I saw the sea rat again. It was one year later. Black John and his men had maimed and murdered and plundered all that year, whilst I stayed anchored at Peel's, stirring stewpots. The upright life is naught but penance.

"Bring the captain his meal," Peel charged me. Peel, when he warn't quivering, was direct. He used his breaths sparingly.

"A good portion too," Pew said. "Good portions for all of us hearties, and notably Pew."

I set the salted cod and rice before Black John and his men.

Kwik said to Pew, "Look on him, Pew. Ain't his colour as bleached as bones?" Peel had told me to hold my tongue when Black John and his men returned, and so I did not reply.

"Pale, Pew says to you, Kwik. Pale like all landlubbers."

I returned to Peel's galley but kept the door open so I could hear the rovers.

"Ain't he got a name?" Black John asked Pew. "And a good name? A right name?" He twirled his forefinger all through his beard.

"Aye, so he does," Pew answered, twirling his finger. "Pew recalls that you gave the boy a name, and a right name, so Pew recalls. And a good name, so Pew recalls. Kwik, do you recall that name? Tell the captain, for it would please the captain if you told him the name, Kwik."

"Are you summoning the boy by his name, Peel?" Black John inquired, not waiting for Kwik's response.

"Silver. I call him Silver, Captain," Peel replied at once.

"Just Silver?" Black John asked, pulling harder at his beard.

"Save, when I call him John Silver," Peel replied quickly. His voice wavered, and I imagine that Peel held his breath later to make up for the breath that he had expelled in answering Black John's inquiry.

"So I named him," the sea rat said.

"So Pew recalls as well," Pew said, grabbing at his chin. "And? If Kwik were to call the boy, for more cod for instance?" Pew asked in that singsong voice of his.

"Long John Silver," Peel replied. He poured more ale into Pew's tumbler. Peel would have sighed if the cost had not been so dear.

"And so Pew recalls," Pew said.

"So do we all," Kwik said, drawing his thumb across his nose. Peel filled Kwik's tumbler. "The once and future cabin boy. We might have taken him on then but for his tongue. I might have cut out his tongue the last time we docked here. This boy, rather Long John Silver, would have gotten his wish and gone to sea directly, and we would have been spared his tongue. A pity for all concerned."

"Call him, then," Black John ordered Peel. "Call him by the name that I gave him."

And so Peel called me.

"Still obstinate then?" Black John asked.

"Ever so, Captain," Peel replied, concisely.

"And still as confounding?" Black John asked.

"As ever," Peel replied. He did not tell the sea rat of my betterment. There was no reason for him to inform Black John as there was no profit in it for Peel.

Pew called for me, and I answered the summons.

"My black boots, boy. Where are the black boots that I stipulated, Long John Silver? It is a year if it is a day since I commissioned those boots, Long John Silver."

"At the ready," I answered.

"I charted your prospects, Long John Silver," he said, squinting at me with them eyes that were too small for his face. I come to know that squint well enough in time. Pew squinted too.

"I thank you," I replied. I had decided to be careful, and so I said no more. I warn't afraid of Kwik, as I was certain that I would find one way or another to best him. He was, once I looked past his history with the milliner's thumb, which did confer him with a modicum of character, no more than a common swain with a patch on his jacket. I was careful because the Linda Maria was calling to me again, and she bade me silence.

"He ain't yet told you your prospects yet," Kwik said. "It may be that you die horribly," he sneered.

"Your prospects are fair, Long John Silver. What do you say?" the captain asked.

"Naught," I answered.

"Not naught, Long John Silver," Pew said. "Never naught to your captain, so says Pew. Never, not to your captain."

"My captain?" I asked.

"The boy grew even dimmer," Kwik said.

"I have a need for a cook, innkeeper Peel. But I sail directly."

"Pew endorses him," Pew said. "On the sake of the cod."

"And you, Kwik?" the captain asked my adversary.

"I am so inclined, Captain," Kwik answered. He added with some hesitation, "As well." I had made an enemy. My prospects were already advancing.

"Then, innkeeper Peel, your lad shall join me and my men this same night, if your lad is willing, that is, for he has not said much on the matter," Black John said.

"I am willing," I replied as quickly as I could.

"Settle your affairs then, Long John Silver. We sail on the Linda Maria this same night."

Peel, thereupon, produced four guineas from his apron pocket, which was the exact sum that Peel owed me for my labours according to his account book.

"I am obliged to you," I told Peel. The fire in Peel's hearth peeked out the grate and cast a shadow on the wall of the inn that looked for all the world like Tom's cape. "I would say more to you, and words befitting a benefactor of sorts, but I am ready to take my leave. And so I will say, and I do say, that I am merely obliged."

"That is so, boy," he answered, as tersely as he could afford.

"Get your kit then," Black John said.

"I am wearing it, sir," I said.

"And mind you to bring me my boots," Black John said.

Them boots, which I gave Black John the first night that I sailed on the Linda Maria, were excellent boots, they were. I stole them from Peel. Peel, my benefactor to the last, never missed them boots neither so far as I know.

CHAPTER III.
ON THE LINDA MARIA

lack John stood at my side that first day on the ship, and in between barks and tugs on his beard, told me about the Linda Maria. He detailed her secrets plank by plank, from the anchor chain to the top timbers, but she was much dearer than the sum of her parts. I looked at her lines and knew right off that there was more to the lady than her gunnery and locks and penny nails. Aye, Black John was right proud of her, but he described her like a carpenter paring a portrait of his wife. He might as well have told me that his lady had ten toes and ten fingers and two feet and two arms, and a head, and thrown in a torso for the sake of the accounting. I saw all of her curves and graces and charms whilst he hammered the frame into place.

He done an injustice to that lady by describing her so plainly. It would be as if I had described Edward's Bible as just hide and parchment, or that there was a number on the bottom of every page and that each chapter was numbered too. It ain't right nor proper for me to describe the book of treasure so, that most devious testament, a book that is blasphemy itself. Mind you that I ain't even set forth all the clues in that book yet, as it would be a disservice to deceitfulness. I ain't written about the first cipher wheel yet nor how it appeared on the first page of the book one night whilst the moon rose and the sun set. No, it just ain't right to write about all them deceits just yet. They must be savoured. And, I was recounting my first day on the Linda Maria and how Black John did not deserve her. Was there ever another such lady of brass and wood so loyal to her mate?

B lasted Mullet! Here he is again carrying your poisons to me, and now of all times when I was about to render a portrait of a lady. The wick is low and here comes Mullet, treading as doggedly as a gravedigger.

You must have read the passages of these very pages I write, which I slipped to Mullet under the door of my cabin by now. You want to know more. Very well then.

"Where do you hail from, Mullet? And do the people there have heads made of parsnips?" I asked your lad.

"Not so far as I know, although they grow all manner of crops. Would that not be something? A people with heads of parsnips. Would they have greens for arms and legs?"

"It is an expression, Mullet. Rather, it is an insult. Do you not understand that I have insulted you? Are you not inclined to rush in here and spike me with a dagger? Or does your captain only allow you pointed sticks?"

"I have a tray for you."

"I told you that I would not take his poisons. You may eat freely, Mullet."

"I shall then. It is from the captain's own table," so Mullet told me in between mastication. He sullied his words some whilst he spoke, speaking and chewing at the same time. He did manage to say, or I understood him to say, that he hailed from the colonies and not from the land of parsnips. His exact palatine is of no matter. If he were from a barony or a county, titled or indentured, he would still be a dunce.

He spoke his next words clearly enough.

"The captain read what you presented me." Here, Mullet stopped to swallow.

"And, boy?"

"He deemed you a liar." Mullet struggled with his next words. "A profligate liar."

"So he would. So that you would take no heed of my tale. So that you do not believe what I write about the treasure. You have read it, so I assume. Before you presented the parchment to your captain?"

"I have."

"That is almost industriousness, Mullet."

"Not at all."

"We must develop your character."

"Not at all. I am content as I am."

"Exactly so. We must make you less content. I have never been content. How could I be with the world abounding in riches and not enough of them in my pockets?"

"The treasure?" he asked with a belch.

"*Correct. I will write about the first cipher wheel shortly, my Mullet. Here was a device of inconceivable artfulness. You could read it so that it seemed nothing more than the recitation of the alphabet. The letters were placed around the wheel.*"

"*Was it a carriage wheel?*"

"*Bog. It was made of parchment and guile. The alphabet was written round its rim. You had to hold it up to moonlight to see it, and even then it revealed nothing, as it was one of the keys that unlocked—*" And here Mullet interjected.

"*One of the six wooden boxes,*" he said.

"*Mullet, do not interrupt a man who is about to tell you a secret. And now, you will have to wait. I was writing of my ship, the Linda Maria. I am writing all this for your betterment.*"

"*So you can escape the noose,*" he said, flagging, then falling against my door as the ship keeled. I was not certain if it was his head or bottom that battered the wood. I expect that they are of equal weight and worth.

"*There will be a reckoning,*" I told him.

"*So you can escape the noose,*" Mullet replied, and he was almost perceptive.

———◦◦◦———

She is a good ship, my Linda Maria, and easy to turn in a breeze or a blow. She is an English ship and as plain as a mug of tea, like all English ships, but for her bow. There are Christian saints with sad eyes carved in her bow. No Englishman could do such fine work. A Spanish prisoner who was given a tumbler of rum after he finished his work carved her bow. Then he was hung. My Linda Maria is plain otherwise. She is a small ship with a modest keel, and so it is a mystery how she can run so fast when her sails are filled with fair weather. There is no modesty to her then. She is never bashful when her sails are full and the wind is behind her. Black John, that first day at sea, told me that the Spaniard died cursing the men who hung him, and they were long and foul curses, and it was his curses that filled her sails.

My lady commenced her life in an English port under an English sky, and sailed on only an English sea, until Black John showed her the world. Black John took her one forenoon, so he said, and turned her wheel lee and abaft, and lee and abaft she has sailed ever since.

Black John told me that he had sent the Linda Maria's first captain to the bottom of the brine with a grapnel tied round the man's ankles. "Took this from him first," Black John divulged, tugging on a gold earring in the form of a heart with a dagger through it. "Wards off the sea fluxes," he told me, flicking it with his finger so that it chimed. "He didn't need it no more." Then Black John barked "South-southwest" and the Linda Maria dipped her bowsprit in a final curtsy to Bristol.

The wind blowed abaft, Black John dug his fat fingers into her rail and pronounced the points where we were headed. I skimmed my hand across his lady's rail as soon as he withdrew, and from that moment on I knew that she was to be my own ship. Just as I knew that Edward's Bible was meant for me as soon as I looked inside it and seen its odd inscriptions. I placed my palm on that Bible, and it shivered me the same as when I had placed my palm on the Linda Maria's rail. No cannibal was fonder of a shrunken head hanging from his waist than I was of that book or my ship. And what use is a head after it is shriveled down to hair and pelt and a pair of eyes? Them cannibals are impractical sorts. A ship can ferry a body to the far ends of the world. A puzzle book can occupy a person all the days of a life.

The men jumped about, and as I had not yet learned anything of the labours on board a ship, it appeared as anarchy to me. They shouted and cursed whilst they jerked the ropes and pulled the sails, climbing and racing from duty to duty, whilst I done my best to comprehend the disorder.

I watched the Bristol shore wane. The headsails swung back and forth, and Bristol come into and out of view. My lady capered. She seemed as anxious as I to be on her way, and I saw Bristol by the lee and by the wind, here and then gone, and then about and then abreast. The cottages and taverns grew dim. The greenery ebbed into a haze, and the ship pitched and swayed, then the land was gone, and the gray-blue of the water surrounded me. Twigs and branches bobbed in the water, then they were gone too. I had left Bristol behind me forever. Blind Tom was gone. Peel was gone. We headed further out to sea. The water turned darker. Luff, we turned. We trimmed the mainsail and let the current take us.

I stood at the rail for hours, for league after league as if entranced, until Pew skulked behind me and put forward that I might want to climb the rigging for a better view. The men's faces were red, and sweat sheeted down them. Their arms and legs were swollen from their efforts. Their mouths hung open, and their chests heaved as if they were still pulling and hoisting whilst they waited for me to fall to my death for their amusement.

I was keen to give them an entertainment of another sort and to prove my worth as well. I scampered up the rigging, past the cringle, as plumb as a charley noble, beyond the carlines, up to the crow's nest and close enough to the colours to hang my blouse over them. I grabbed a cordage that was dangling from the rigging with one hand, and held on to the rigging with my other hand. We were suddenly in the chop, and I gripped the cordage tighter. Pew was looking up at me, as were all the men, when Black John come on deck with a chart under his arms. He looked up, following the eyes of the men until his eyes lit on me, and ordered me to clamber down straightaway.

I disobeyed my first order.

I hung by my heels from the rigging and, still gripping the cordage, laughed. I swung arm over arm across the rigging and scrambled down it slowly, as the view was so agreeable. I saw water on all sides of me, seamen below me, and naught and no one to stop me. I saw opportunity, my hearty. I thumped Pew on his back and asked him if he would like to race me up the rigging. Pew backed away and into Kwik, who whispered into Pew's ears.

Black John asked me if I had heard him shout the order. I told him that I had not on account of the wind. He asked how I had been able to climb the rigging as I had never been on a ship before, and I told him that Pew had explained it all to me, throwing in, "He said it was your order." Black John straightaway flogged Pew with his belt, and so the men had their amusement after all.

My mates were impressed and one by one introduced themselves to me, telling me that no one had ever climbed the rigging on their first try. Billy Bones asked me if I warn't some scared whilst up the rigging, and I told him that I warn't born with that attribute.

Even Bloody Bill offered me his paw, and no man had ever seen that beast of a man offer his paw to another creature before, as Bloody Bill was all malice. He mashed my hand good before he retreated to his post by the rail, so to look at the sea. I never saw him do any work on board the ship, but put a dagger or a saber in his hand, and he was all industry. The captain talked to him slowly, carefully, as if Bill was a wild beast that only he knew how to tame. No other man spoke with Bloody Bill, as they were so afraid of him, which was as natural as could be since he had murdered so many of them swains.

Only Kwik refused to speak with me, and instead told a Mister Arrow to instruct me in the ways of the ship. Arrow warn't nearly an accomplished drunkard as Bones, but he done right well as one. Arrow taught me everything that I needed to know about the ship and the duties on board her. I learned it all before I had the chance to learn Mister Arrow's first name. He washed overboard, or so Kwik said, one evening. Mister Arrow, evidently, had taught me too well. He also gave me a sound piece of advice before he departed. He told me to stay even keel to Kwik and never to anger him on account that Kwik was jealous of me. That perplexed me, and so Arrow explained that I had found favour with the captain, and Kwik was the sort of ganger that could not abide anyone else being in the captain's favour.

The last bits that Arrow taught me were the rules of the ship. You may have forgotten them, and so it is my pleasure to remind you of them. Mind you that pirates are serious about their rules, as you may recall, for without their rules pirates would be no more than ordinary seamen. Poor ordinary seamen. Indulge your captain, my hearty, whilst I remind you of our rules.

In particular, no pirate can steal from another pirate. Death is the punishment, so you may recollect. It does not matter if it is booty or edibles that the brigand takes. Death is the punishment, my hearty, unless the thief is showed mercy. That ain't likely, though, on account that pirates ain't partial to mercy.

We all of us fight. When in doubt throw the blade.

Now if a hearty loses a finger in battle, that hearty is entitled to an extra share of booty for the loss of the finger, on account that the hearty ain't a sound hearty no more. But, if a hearty loses two fingers in battle, that hearty ain't entitled to any more shares, he ain't. The loss of one digit is hard luck, but the loss of two digits is carelessness.

By way of corollary, if a hearty loses his hand he receives five extra shares. That hearty is entitled to the supplementary shares so long as the hearty loses his hand in a single hack.

There are further shares too for the loss of an arm or a leg. A hearty that loses an appurtenance receives a score of additional coppers, though most of those who are so entitled do not claim the coppers on account that they are dead at the time of receipt.

There ain't any shares for dead men, there ain't, nor for their widows nor kin. Those are the rules on blood wages.

If a hearty kills another hearty, it ain't a crime, so long as the ship does not go off course as a consequence.

If there is no punishment, there is no crime.

The mates of the dead man may settle all matters that are in dispute. If there are no mates to right a wrong, then no wrong has been committed.

If a brother pirate slurs, offends, or insults you, you may murder him for it, unless he murders you first.

Those with sharp swords and who shoot straight are in the right. Those with dull swords and who shoot poorly are in the wrong. Good justice is simple justice, I say, and justice don't get no simpler than that.

Lastly, there are the rules on drinking with a fellow hearty. If a fellow hearty bades you to drink with him, you best do so. He would be within his rights to snuff you for not joining him in a tumbler of ale.

There are no more rules among us. We do not need more rules. We are murderers and not milliners.

Mark in particular the rules about thieving. The Bible that you took was mine from the moment that I placed my hand on its cover, just as the ship was mine from the moment I laid my hand on her rail. That Bible was meant for me. A scoundrel wrote them ciphers in that Bible for another scoundrel to solve them. You likely had to study to be a scoundrel, but I come by it most natural. So mark you not only our rules but also my enterprise, and from my first day on board the ship. It is a matter of lack of integrity, sir, and I take due pride in it.

I commenced my duties on the Linda Maria by swabbing her deck. And not with a rag or a mop, but with a lady's underslip. That underslip was linen and lace and no less, and come from a countess that Black John ransomed the season before I joined his crew. It gave me no pleasure to handle such finery so, but I wondered from time to time if my sad-eyed saints warn't grateful for their glimpse of earthly pleasure.

When I did not swab the deck, I polished the wheel. When I did not polish the wheel, I scrubbed the bulkheads. When I did not scrub the bulkheads, I oiled the windlass. When I did not oil the windlass, I mended the ropes. When I did not mend the ropes, I swabbed the deck again, my sir. I swabbed and polished and scrubbed and oiled and mended like I was born for those labours. I was as proud of my ship as some men are of their wives when walking to church on Sunday. My church was the sea, my ship was my miss, and every day that I stood on the bow was Sunday to me.

The sea has a temper, and so we took to each other right off. One day she is all tolerance and time, and the next day she drowns you. The sea is honest when she ain't a cheat. She gives you a full accounting and picks your pocket at the same time. My carved saints must have hearts of lumber, just like Bloody Bill's, to stare at the sea all day and all night. Look into their eyes. Their eyes are as broad and deep as the sea. Mayhap they demand the profane too.

My foremost duty was to cook for Black John and his men. By and by I come to murder for Black John. I never lacked spirit. Black John installed me in the galley with Brag and told me to mind everything that Brag done. "Mind it all," he told me. "Then do the adverse." Brag was no cook, though he gave a fair portrayal of one when curled over his cauldrons and kettles. And so it came to be, that Brag fixed Black John a cod stew one eventide that warn't to Black John's taste. There was more pepper than cod in the stew and, consequently, that was the last meal that Brag ever cooked for the captain.

"I have me a real cook," the captain told Brag, whilst we fiddled in the waters about Devon looking for stray merchant ships. We flew the Jack so that when we met up with an English ship, it tacked alongside us for a friendly tea, and we all waved to each other until our lines were lashed and we struck. The winds near Devon are fierce, being English winds, and are the only attribute of the country that bore me, except for its verse. English verse is choice when it blasts you like an icy wind. We were all given to singing a quality verse to pass the time, so long as it warn't reputable in any way. Brag droned a tune now and then, usually about pigs in a pot, or some other aspect of cookery, and so they were fairly obscure ditties. They assumed, in that sense, an affinity with his meals. "He is a Bristol cook, and there ain't no better cook than a Bristol cook. I paid good silver for him too," the captain told Brag whilst the winds howled. The Jack whipped this way and that as if it was now a member of our crew aiding us in our search for bounty.

It warn't until Black John spoke to Brag about paying Peel that I discovered that Peel had sold me to Black John. Peel's recompense was my gain, as I sailed with the sea rat. The only one who did not raise a profit from the transaction was Brag.

It was almost September, as I recall, and time to head for sunnier climes, when Black John announced the superiority of Bristol cooks over all other forms of mullers. The Devon wind braced all of us on board the Linda Maria, but not a one of us wore a jacket. We mostly stood on deck bare-chested, as we were hearties and unwilling to let a bluster from Devon get the better of us. We shivered from our top girders down to our deadrises, but no man spoke of the cold, as we were so accustomed to it. A dagger only hurts the first time that it goes in a body, and after that first thrust, the body pays it no mind. It is a matter of determination and, on occasion, whisky.

The men liked my cooking. The captain was particularly smitten with my fish stew. I never put any pepper in it.

Bones showed me how to fight with dagger and sword and saber. There was no one better than him with those implements. I heard him boast so much about my skill with them that I was concerned that he might meet Mister Arrow in the deep. There was no need to be concerned about Bones though, as he could always, and in any state, defend himself. The men proffered that Bones was better with a sword when drunk, but I never saw any difference in him. He cut down men dead drunk and cold sober. Bones warn't partial to pistols. He said that there was no art to firing them. I had to teach myself that pursuit by aiming between Pew's temples, to the delight of the men, who would lift or lower my arm as required.

Bones asked me on one of them first days at sea what I saw in the seafaring life. I had been poor in Bristol, and I was still poor, so that warn't it, and so I told Bones that it come down to hunger. He reminded me that I had worked in a tavern and had all the food that I wanted there. I asked Bones why he drank so much. "Thirst," he told me. "A powerful thirst." We were well away from Devon by then, but Bones's hair pointed easterly, on its permanent course to the English taverns. I told him that he could drink his fill every night on board the ship. "But I am ever thirsty," he told me. "So it is with me," I replied. "I am always hungry."

One day that year, an uncommon draft come our way and unfurled our banner. The Jack was long gone, and we were flying the skull and bones. I felt the breeze, warmer than the Atlantic blows, and that breeze filled our sails all the way to Malabar, like when we discovered the first clue in that Bible and struck our course. Greed filled our sails then, and it blowed us all around the world, and I do believe we lighted in Malabar on that occasion too.

I spied what I took to be a reef in the distance, and it warn't until we were upon it that I saw that it warn't a reef at all but another ocean, and all that had been green turned blue. Then the clime changed and the banner unfurled and I felt the warmth of the other side of the world. I remarked to Bones on the change, and he blowed into his empty bottle as if heralding our arrival in the tropics. He sniffed at his arm and seemed pleased that he still bore England on his skin. He turned back toward the green that we had left behind, and mentioned that one day I would not notice the change.

Bloody Bill howled, and Bones said that there was at least one other man on board that had noticed the change. "He has as much sense as the deadeye," Bones declared, "but he is as accurate as it as well. I always know if we will be beset by a gale if he gives forth two howls. Three howls is hail. Four howls is whales on the beam. And," he said, "five howls is doom. If he gives forth five howls, go directly below. He will grind anyone in his path."

"He is tame when the captain calls to him," I told Bones. "Like a beast on a leash. And there ain't no secret to it," I told Bones. "I seen the trick. The captain hands him a coin, strikes a flint, or flashes silver in front of him, and the sight pleases Bill. I heard the captain whisper tales to him once. They understand each other. I have tried it," I confessed. "At night," I told Bones. "I was some curious and kept a dagger in my sleeve, but I had watched the captain carefully, and so I whispered a tale to Bill and struck a flint. He looked up for a moment and was surprised to see me and not the captain and turned away. I have tried more times since, and Bill knows me now and expects a watch or a coin, and I never disappoint him. I take them from Pew. I tried a song once, but Bill grabbed my neck and so I croaked a tale to comfort him."

Bones told me that I was as sharp as a fid. I asked him why he had tacked on to Black John's crew. "Bottles and barrels," he told me. "It is bottles and barrels for me. And if fortune falls my way, it is froth on the mug and all to the good. I am partial to rum and rye. Whisky suits me too. Rum betters my disposition. If I was captain," he told me, "and I may be one day, my ship would float on ale."

Bones told me that each man on board come to account for different reasons, but when you boiled them all down you found larceny at the bottom of every pot. Black John was the most larcenous of any man on board the Linda Maria, Bones added, and therefore the fittest of all to be captain. "Kwik is fairly larcenous too," Bones said. "He would be captain when the gimblet turns his way. Likely about the captain's neck, if he can manage it."

"I am fairly larcenous too," I told Bones.

"Then," he said, patting down his hair, "you have prospects. As long as you stay out of Kwik's way."

I was anxious to prove myself among the men with something other than a ladle, and so I practiced my swordplay and waited for the opportunity to show it.

We were in quiet waters and roosting on deck like seabirds in the steamy weather, when Black John shouted, "Double rum!" He had spied a merchant ship through his glass.

The men jumped about, securing and stowing the loose articles and fetching their swords, whilst Black John stood in all his glory on the quarterdeck. We bore straight for the ship. It was a Dutch merchantman, and we were amused to see the officers dressed in their finery whilst we roamed about our ship shirtless and in torn leggings.

We were on them before they could hail us and strike terms. We winded our lady and downed her sails whilst they huddled around the lifeline, awaiting orders from their captain. By the time he ordered his men to luff up it was too late. We had already pinched his ship by sculling against it and lashing our spring lines to their masts. It was enough to bind our ships, and whilst they rode a peck in the waters, we boarded his ship and cut the lines that held their sails. The cloth fell all about them and arrested half the crew. Pew, grinning so that he bared all of his rotten teeth, scampered about the deck stabbing his sword into the sails and the men trapped underneath them. He delighted in each shriek, scurrying over the sails, stabbing here and there until he was exhausted by the effort and sat on the reefing. He saw a billow, plunged his sword into it, and heard one last cry.

We matched our steel against their steel, and cut a good number of them free from this world, but five of us stood apart from the others.

Bloody Bill, mouth gaping and vacant-eyed, lumbered toward them. He marched in a plumb line across the whole of the deck, murdering every man in his path. Our own men bounded out of his way, as no one was certain if Bill could distinguish friend from foe, or if he even desired to make the distinction.

Bones held a saber in each hand and fought two men at once, and sometimes three men at the same time, and cut every opponent down. He was drunk. I was sure of it. He had that grin and reeked of spiced rum. He readied about and saw four men advancing on him. He found the salon, downed a draft of spirits, sliced every Dutchman that dared enter there, and wiped his lips when he was done.

Kwik, though I could not abide him, fought well. I watched him carefully, ascertaining his feints and parries, minding how he stood and where he planted his hams. He warn't as skilled as Bloody Bill or Bones, but he could handle a sword.

Your captain, John Silver, found it remarkably easy to kill Dutchmen. I fought just as Bones had taught me. I even picked up the sword from one of the Dutchmen that I murdered and, like Bones, held a sword in each hand. I was good enough that the men cheered me as I cleaved through three men and toyed with the last one by backing him against the shackle. He tripped. I bade him stand. He cowered. I pitched both my swords into him. Kwik crept up to me. "Eight," he told me. "I killed eight, Silver," he said.

Aye, and the captain. He distinguished himself that day by directing the battle. He never left the Linda Maria, but perched on the boom like lace atop a bonnet and called out orders. He slapped each of us on our backs when we returned to the ship. He gave Kwik the honour of burning the merchantman. Some of the Dutchmen were still in the water. Pew played with them by throwing them sheets, then pulling them back. All of them drowned.

We watched the ship burn whilst Black John counted the coins. He gave each man a share according to his will and estimate of how well that man had fought. I received little more than tuppence. The sea rat told me that I had fought well but that I warn't yet of a term to receive more. He kept my share. The merchantman lit up the sky as it burned.

Then, we were back to quiet waters and fell about our regular duties. We sailed for the Indies, and then Corso, and found no ships of interest, and so we bobbed for the rest of the season until we returned to Malabar. We had sailed in a great arc, circumventing oceans, and finding nothing but the wind. Black John was content. The men grumbled some, but were careful not to talk around Pew, as Pew reported whatever the men said to the captain.

We took our comfort in a tavern in Malabar with an English name, the Flint, named after the parrot that flew about the tavern and rested on the ladies' shoulders. Flint was harmless enough, and almost charming when it pecked at Pew, who shooed Flint away by spitting ale at the bird.

The ale was abundant. Bones worked the spigots, a natural publican, and drank a glass for each one that he brought to the men. He would have bankrupted Peel had he worked for him. We sang, the women and Flint joining us, until we moved on to other pursuits. Flint followed Pew and his woman up the stairs, bobbing his head up and down and repeating, "Pieces of eight." Pew noticed that the woman was walking with a peg. "Only four," he told Flint. "She ain't got half of what I want." Flint replied, "Eight," and Pew conceded. The bird flew to Pew's table and doused his beak in Pew's ale, toasting his victory.

When we woke the next morning all of the ladies were gone. We dressed and left the tavern. Bones took a few swigs before the short jaunt back to the ship. The men had forgotten all about our poor season, just as the captain had schemed.

We returned to our labours once again. Black John placed me back in the galley, but I found it hard to abide my duties as I was ever anxious for adventure. There warn't much else to cook but turtles, but neither the men nor the turtles protested. If we were lucky enough to catch fish in our nets, I bathed those fish bones from Monday to Sunday. A good catch of cod, if I salted it, lasted the crew a fortnight.

Kwik was the only hearty that complained about my cooking. He come into my galley at nightfall to issue his censure. I gave good witness for both my skills as a cook and the sound character of the turtles. Kwik struck me, and that was the last time that a man struck me and lived more than two blinks. The dead warrant come down on Kwik then and there. I snuffed Kwik the following nightfall.

The summer in the Atlantic when I snuffed Kwik was another profitless one. We did not scuttle ships. We did not attack galleons. We did not sack encampments. We did not raid ramparts. No fish stayed in our nets. No boars, cows, goats, or lambs gave themselves up for the good of our gullets. Kwik's last meal, I am pleased to recount, was the same turtle broth that I had served him the previous evening.

Those who sat nearest to the captain during supper were Pew, Bones, Brag, and Kwik. I will not relate much more about Brag. There ain't much more to relate. Brag sat too close to Bloody Bill one forenoon when Bill was at his biscuits, and Bill heaved Brag overboard.

I sat down next to those rovers, and said, "It would be my honour to dine with the cursed and the damned of you."

"Then set your foul carcass beside us," Billy Bones said. "There is always room for the cursed and the damned at our table."

"We are cursed in this life," Brag said, swallowing a spoonful of broth.

"And damned in the next. So snatch what you can from this world, Pew says," said Pew.

"Gulp and swallow and swig, I say," said Bones. "Take all that you can get and take it now."

Then Bones, who never needed any inspiration to gulp or swallow or swig, drained his ale. Brag and Pew downed a good measure of ale too, and said, "Aye, true words." Bones's topping seconded them and rose up his mast.

"But it is no honour to sit next to one of you," I said, downing my broth in a single swallow. The heat of the broth steamed my insides, and I was hungry again. Kwik's bowl was full.

"And which one of us is that?" Kwik asked, tapping his spoon on the edge of his bowl, as if he was counting the ticks of the clock before he would plunge his sword into me. "We should bid you to sing for us, Silver. Before you can join us. Before you can eat. I never found a name less suitable to a person. Silver. It ain't fitting if you ask me. It ain't a fitting name, with due respect to the captain, for a beggar boy. So, which of us ain't good enough for the beggar boy from Bristol? Which of us hearties ain't up to your standards?"

"The one with the face of a rat," I answered.

Pew jumped to his feet.

"It ain't you," Bones told Pew. "Young Silver ain't staring at you."

"Speak then," Kwik told me. "Say the man's name. It would please me. Greatly. Beggar boy. It ain't our Bloody Bill, I warrant you," Kwik said. "It ain't the captain. Is it the captain, Silver?"

"It ain't Pew," Pew said. "Pew does not have himself the face of a rat." Pew looked at the back of his spoon at his reflection just to be certain. He seemed pleased by the visage that he spied on the back of that spoon, on account that he smiled, but Pew never had any discernment when it come to his countenance.

"It ain't Brag or Bones or Pew. So speak, boy. Speak the man's name," Kwik said. He stood. "Speak it," he hissed.

"You," I told him, with a hatred as fierce as true devotion.

"I will drink to the victor," Bones said, winking at me.

"And to the defeated too," Pew sang, rubbing the back of the spoon with his sleeve.

"You die, Silver," Kwik said. "You die by this sword." He drew his sword with a flourish. I could not abide the man. There is no need to flourish a sword when going about dismemberment. Mark his words and contrast them to the brandishing of his sword. "You die by this sword," he told me. He spoke five words, all stunted. Why not inform me that he would impale me on the tip of his sword and turn me round until he fed me to the sharks? Is that not a prettier manner to mark a man's demise?

"No," I replied. "You die. By this sword," I said, mocking his simple words, and drawing my own sword with a flourish worthy of an assassin. I tapped my sword twice on the deck. Style, at such times, is pertinent. It is a matter of respect for one's craft. "I would us have this dance," I told

Kwik. I bowed. He reddened, which I found exceedingly pleasing. "I have never skipped with a rodent," I told him, "and so I may not know all the steps, but I promise you that we will circle and bob as if there is no morrow. May the better man have a morrow." I bowed once more.

And what did the captain do? He leaned back in his chair to better enjoy my fatality. The sea rat, much like Peel, misjudged my abilities. Black John did speak on my behalf though, now that I think about it, for he said to Kwik, "Quickly, if you must. The lad's cod is stellar."

"Fight," Kwik said. "This will be good sport." Six more words and not the hint of a dulcimer or a lute in any of them. He certainly deserved to die, and if for no other reason than out of disrespect for our common tongue.

Kwik lunged at me. He attempted a sneer, but I found deficiency even in that effort. It warn't a sneer, such as a proper hearty might invoke when going about a piece of mischief, but an uninterested sneer, as if Kwik was mashing on a turnip. That drowsy sneer put me off, it did.

I charged Kwik and missed him, but I was able to grab his arm and fling him against the bow. The saints paid us no mind. Nothing that I ever done roused those wooden saints from their melancholy.

"Cut me. Carve me," I challenged Kwik. "Throw me bit by bit into the sea." Kwik showed a bit more interest in me, which I fathomed from the biting of his lower lip.

We went round and round each other looking for an advantage. I dropped my shoulder to test him. He thrust his sword at me and missed.

"You need be fleet. More fleet," I admonished Kwik, then I feinted by dropping my shoulder again. Kwik thrust, and I nicked his arm. I jigged around him. He appeared confused.

The men were shouting and wagering on which one of us the crabs would dine that night. Kwik sneered proper then, he did, on account that some of the men raised their wagers on me.

I feinted again, and Kwik lunged at me again and missed. I lanced him in his other arm.

"Finish him!" Pew bade me, shifting his loyalty to me.

"I will kill you, Silver," Kwik said, moving aft. "I will carve your heart." He had managed ten words, but there was still no melody to them. I was pleased that he had followed my lead and spoken of the carving of my heart. He might have had a future as a poet if he had applied himself to that trade, if I had let him live, legless, and if we had marooned him in a waterside café in Venice. He might have found a calling in the literary arts in time. Then again, I warn't particularly concerned about his future at that moment.

I recalled how Kwik fought the Dutchmen. I knew his next feint and was ready.

"My heart?" I replied. "It ain't as big as a mustard seed." Kwik turned weatherly, just as I knew that he would, as he had done when he fought the Dutchmen.

"Enough," Black John said, holding up his hand. He was keen to see that Kwik was spared, but he had not offered me the same courtesy. That was the second time that I disobeyed one of Black John's orders.

I plunged my sword into Kwik's belly. Kwik looked astonished. He clutched my sword and pulled at it over and over until his hands were bloody, but he could not draw it out. He tottered, and I waited for him to fall, but Kwik staggered about the deck. That was pure stubbornness, I say. I ran my finger along the scar on his brow, slowly. "To Hell, Kwik," I whispered. I dragged my sword out of his belly. It warn't until then that Kwik fell. "He warn't fleet at all," I told Pew.

Pew stooped over Kwik, slid his hands into Kwik's pockets, and produced a gold watch. Pew said, "I knew that he took my watch."

"That is my watch," I told Pew. "Do you not recognize the face?"

Pew gave me the watch and stepped away.

The captain nodded at Bloody Bill and went below. Therewith, Bloody Bill lumbered over to me.

The beast spoke. "Overboard," Bill snarled.

I was certain that Bill desired me to caper over the rail to my doom, but Bill kicked Kwik, repeatedly, until he had Kwik athwart the boomkin. "Overboard," Bill repeated, hoisting Kwik by his legs until they were flush with the sheer pole. I lifted Kwik by his shoulders. We swung Kwik back and forth thrice, so we did, and then we dropped Kwik into the sea.

Bill lumbered back to his post near the taffrail and sat down. He was still once again. He looked into the deep and his eyes grew wide. Bill's mouth fell open. Whether he was awake or asleep, no hearty knew.

I slept well that night. I recall reflecting that night, before I fell asleep, that Peel had sold Black John an enterprising lad. Aye, and I recall reflecting that Black John had acquired himself a right bargain.

CHAPTER IV.

THE SILENT SIR

***

A nd what of Edward?" Mullet asked me. "You write of him but never speak of him. You only speak about his Bible."

"We were the best of mates."

"You do not speak about him."

"I have referred to him. I have given him all credit for bringing me the Bible."

"But how did you acquire it? Exactly how? How did you meet Edward and where?"

"Everyone and everything in its place, Mullet."

"My belly aches." Mullet appended his statement with a groan.

"That would be the poison."

"It could not have been. It was delicious."

"All the best poison is delicious, lad. Take Edward's Bible for instance. A poisonous treatise, concocted and consumed over ages until it works its bane all the way through the body. The enterprise of it, Mullet! The stratagems! The false resolutions! Was the treasure always and ever in Britain as Edward expected, or was it secreted in another land as I inferred? An answer for each of us. We could read the answers so, neither correct nor incorrect. Poison, lad. Pure poison. And delectable."

"The ship needs repair." Mullet must have rolled over, as the planking moaned.

"Not when I was at her helm. I knew how to care for her."

"The captain says she is rotting."

"Impossible. She is only ill-tempered because your captain holds her wheel. Has he polished her rail, shined her brass, mopped her deck, and mind you only with an underslip?"

"He has scraped her barnacles."

"An affront to her."

"And mended her sails."

"*Her sails needed no mending.*"

"*They tore on our way through the Cape. Them and the spare sea-cloth.*"

"*The Cape. A circuitous route.*"

"*He said that you would say the same. My belly,*" so he bleated.

"*Then he is enjoying what he reads. Very well. Tell him exactly what I speak to you now.*"

"*I shall endeavor to remember it.*"

"*You shall not forget it, not a word of it. I am sure that he has instructed you so. Very well then. Now mind you that I will write more on this in my next installment, but you may tell him the following, some of which he knows, some of which he may know, and some of which he will swear is not true. But it is all truth, or at least as much of it as I can manage. And do not interrupt me. And do not whimper or groan or lay your head on my timbers no more. It is distracting.*"

"*But I am feeling sickly. My first voyage.*"

"*Perhaps your last as well.*"

"*More likely your last voyage.*"

"*Spirit, lad. Spirit. That is better. Lance your lobe and place an earring in it to ward off the fluxes. Did I not tell you that Black John himself wore one? Do you not see the men wearing them? Does your captain not wear one?*"

"*He removed the earrings from the men. He will not allow it. He has no earring.*"

"*Aye, I forget. He never wore one.*"

"*They are for cannibals,*" he said.

"*He would know now, wouldn't he? That time on Skeleton Island. The cannibals in their jungle and your captain in his quarters. You may tell him that I spoke of two possible solutions. The first solution come to me, and mind you do not interpose even a grunt whilst I speak, after I found the second cipher wheel.*"

"*Another wheel?*"

"*Damn you, boy! Aye, the other wheel! I spun the cipher wheel and its sister so that they aligned with each other. I can surmise your next question. From whence come the cipher wheel and from whence its sister. Quietude, lad. Listen now and read the resolution later. All will be revealed in due time. Must I say so again?*"

"*Not at all,*" Mullet mumbled.

"*I was not making an inquiry of you, Mullet. It serves me to think of you as roasted pork, sputtering now and then over the coals, and I will take any statement by you as such. Now, firstly." I waited to hear if Mullet would make a declaration, but he assumed his role as roasted pork very well and abided me. And so I continued. "The initial clue after we spun, so to speak, the wheels read 'And Last Icon,' words that had no apparent sense or meaning. There were other clues but, as I said, this was the initial clue. Your captain will recognize it, and if you attempt to resolve it, and do so successfully, you will derive a location from it. A precise location. You must reorder the letters of the clue so that they construct other words, the site of one of our voyages. I have already spoken its name to you, and so you have more than I had when I first attempted to solve the cipher.*

"Speak not a word.

"Secondly, I return to the primary riddle. 'I have hidden 41 meters from the foundation 6 wooden boxes overlaid in ivory, and all empty, and one remarkable treasure covered in nothing but sackcloth not more than 2 meters deep nor more than 87 meters wide.' Do we reorder the letters of this cipher?

"Do not reply.

"Where to begin? Perhaps at the location cited by 'And Last Icon,' then again, perhaps not. Perhaps not.

"Do not respond.

"I cannot say how many times that I counted the numbers in the declaration, as I believed that the numbers held the answer, or how many times I abandoned the numbers and read the sentence as plainly as possible. I trusted that I would have to find a foundation. I believed that underneath the foundation I would find six boxes of wood, each box overlaid in ivory, and each box containing no part of the treasure but only more clues, as the boxes were empty. And, at the same site, I would find, and how I did not know, the remarkable treasure, and it would be covered in sackcloth. I knew how far and how deep to dig."

"I have solved it," Mullet said. "The other riddle. 'And Last Icon.' "

"Impossible."

"I have reordered the letters. They can be read to have several meanings."

His words were true. Was it possible that Mullet had come across the answer that had eluded me for so many years, and so quickly?

"I found it simple. I merely reordered the letters."

"Speak then."

"My belly aches."

"That is not one of the answers."

"No, but it is a matter of fact. Are you ready, sir?" he asked. "I do not hear you, Mister Silver."

"It is Captain Silver to you. Aye, I am ready."

"Very well. 'And Last Icon' may mean, at least may mean, 'In Lot Can Sad,' although it may mean 'In Sad Not Can,' as I am undecided about which answer is correct."

"Oaf. It is senseless. It is a collection of words and not a location."

"I was not certain that you meant a location as such, but a location as in something else."

"What else? I unmistakably said a location."

"Well, 'Cain And Lost,' or, if we add letters," he went on.

"We cannot add letters. No more than we can take them away."

"But you can do so with the numbers. I recall you saying so. Or, 'Sail'd Canton.' There. A place and a means of getting there."

"No, Mullet. You cannot take away letters. 'Sail'd' is not a word. 'Sailed' is a word."

"It is close to a word."

"It is not a word."

"It is a good answer."

"'Idiot' is a word. 'Oaf' is a word. 'Pillock' is a word. 'Dunce' is a word. 'Simpleton' is a word. 'Bird-wit' is a word. 'Bully-fop' is a word. Even 'poxed ninny' is a word."

"Two words in fact, sir. As you cannot add or take away."

"And leave us not forget that 'Dolt' is a word as well. And all them words describe you. And I will add and take away as many words as I please to describe you."

"Then I will take my leave."

"Take it by jumping overboard."

"Why would I do that?"

"Because, Mullet, you are a poxed ninny. Take your leave. I will write. Tell your captain, 'And Last Icon.' There is no point or purpose in speaking of the riddle to you. At the present, and as I am in the mood, I shall write about murder." And with them words Mullet announced that his belly was much improved and that he was hungry again, and he bade me to repeat my instructions to him. I did not.

I laid a good measure of men in their graves.

I swept away all the worries of the rich with one wave of my saber. I ended all the adversities of the poor with one jab of my dagger. I murdered the master, and I murdered the slave. I murdered the lady, and I murdered the mistress. I murdered the lofty, and I murdered the low.

All were equal before my sword.

I slew Smiths and Joneses. I slew Whites and Blacks. I slew Stuarts and Jacks.

I took the lives of the fat. I took the lives of the lean.

All stood square before my sword.

Davy Dawson, I done him in. He was the captain of a frigate. Now he is a corpse crawling with sea maggots. I recall an Alan Stivy that I sent to his doom. He was a first mate, and now he is no more than a heap of bones. There was a William Tudor too, an admiral that chased me to the Indies and almost caught me. Now he is in the brine. Your fate, my hearty, will be the same.

I dispatched Spanish and English and French and Portuguese. I butchered all manner of men. There ain't much difference between a footman, a coachman, an alderman, and a charwoman, there ain't, when their blood runs. There ain't much difference between a carpenter, a wooliner, and a minister, and not and nor a planter neither, when the wind whistles through their bones.

You fear me. That is why you will not speak to me.

I murdered brave men and cowards, patriots and traitors too.

Declare yourself.

Do you recall the song that I used to sing? "A bottle of rum, a cask of ale, I sing this song before I set sail." I shall sing you that song again, my silent sir, before I murder you and take back my ship. I dare you or your brothers in blood to come for me. There is a blade for every man that stands with you. Do you hear me, Captain? I dare you to come for me. I play an open game. I have a dagger and a pistol. I need no more.

I have a looking glass. I see a man in the glass with a red-and-white beard. He does not have much hair on his head anymore, but this glass is crusty with salt, so the man likely has a tuft or two more hair than I can see. Red hair. He has a considerable nose, red too, and he is rather proud of it. That was the nose that smelled treasure. There are so many lines on his face that it looks like a sea chart, my hearty. It is a map of blood. He has wide eyes. Those are the eyes that spied treasure. Aye, and red eyes too.

You fear an old man, but you are right to fear me, for I will murder the first one of you that steps through my door. Aye, and I will murder the last one of you that steps through it too, so I will. A bottle of rum, a cask of ale, I will kill you all before I set sail.

You dare to bring Silver to justice? There is no justice but pirate justice on these waters. These are my waters. There is no justice but my justice.

The ship is listing. I feel every shift of my ship, every stirring of the boards, every creak of the wood, every turn of the wheel. The wind is blowing hard. The men are fishing the mast. You are taking me to England the boy said. To England.

My ship rides hard on the waves. She fights you, Captain. She fights you.

Doom to you.

My ship will not bear me to England. She is loyal to me to the last. The waves roll away from my ship on account of the man who dares to walk her deck. Doom, sir.

Do you hear how the timber groans? She defies you, Captain. She defies you with every crest and curl. It is doom for you.

You best tell every tar that this ship will never reach England.

This is my black sea.

And now the wind sputters. Even the wind abandons you. But doom walks the deck slowly, sir, and there is time to tell the tale of Silver, the confounded creature, of Long John Silver. How he bested you. How he learned each secret of the book of treasure, and how each solution led him to the next secret and its solution. Why is it that Silver found the first cipher wheel? It was because he understood the contrariness of the man that had written the ciphers.

Patience.

Do not be vexed. I will lay out all the ciphers near as neat as a seamstress laying out a pair of pantaloons.

There is time to satisfy your curiosity. There is time for everything in its season. Even time for murder.

There was no wind the night that I killed Kwik either. We dropped anchor for the lack of the blow. We stayed in those waters for weeks. Weeks, my sir. Weeks, that season. We rolled bones. We swabbed. We mended. Weeks and weeks, my sir. We fished. We fought. We even bathed.

The captain stayed in his cabin, where it was cool, though we still worked at our labours. I brought him his supper, and when I asked to take my leave, he replied, "Ain't there an apple here? Fetch me an apple, Silver. There ain't an apple on my plate."

"No, sir," I answered. "We finished all the apples."

"The barrel was full. I took an apple from the barrel three days ago, and it was brimming with pips."

"The men ate all the apples, sir," I told him. "Every one of them delicious pips. To a man and to a pip."

"It was brimming," the captain glowered. Aye, but it was cool in his cabin. We worked like plough horses on deck whilst our captain lazed in his cabin, the wretch. "And at the bottom?" he asked. "The very bottom of the barrel?" He reached out for a stretch and wiggled his fat fingers. Black John was a beefy man, but his fingers were thicker than the rest of him on account of him exercising his fingers whilst totting up his fortune. I watched him at night pacing back and forth in his cabin. The shutters were drawn, but I watched the wraith walk about and count his fortune. Mayhap it was Black John's shadow, and just as larcenous as its master, that I saw strolling about the cabin when the moon was full. If so, I wager that it stole the nightcap off the sea rat's head one night when he was at his slumbers. That nightcap disappeared one chilly eventide, and so I say that even Black John's shadow was a rascal. "The bottom, I asked you, Mister Silver. That barrel was full. Such as you are used to searching at the bottom of barrels."

"Aye, but rotten. They are all rotten at the bottom. Some, even at the top of the barrel, had rotted, sir. You find such pips now and again. I venture that they floated to the top by chance and were above their station. I would not bring you a rotten apple," I told Black John.

"I heard that there is such an apple, Mister Silver."

"A black pip. That has worms, I say."

"Fetch me the apple," he ordered me. Black John pulled a kerchief out of his sleeve and mopped his brow with it. He was hot, even in that cool cabin of his. I had heard that Black John was born at sea, and was the son of an honest seaman, a man that was a captain himself. Some of the men said that Black John tottered his own father and took over his ship when he come of age. He was born with larceny in his heart, the men said. Black John never spoke on his ancestry, and I never inquired about it, but I doubt that the tale was true. Black John was born in a pool of gravy, I say.

I say that he went to sea as a young lad, and, like most swains, tired of the square life and took up plunderage to enhance his earnings.

"I will look for it, sir. High and low and fore and aft," I told Black John. "I will look wherever that apple might be, sir. I will search every sack on board this ship. I will look in every vessel. I will peer through every lubber hole, sir. I will ask every man."

"What is that in your blouse, Mister Silver? It looks like an apple to me."

"So it is," I said, taking the apple out of my blouse, and turning it round in my hand, as if I was surprised to find it.

"Then you brought me an apple after all. A green and tart one. A long way from a black pip. I venture that this apple floated on the top of the barrel, and as soon as you saw it you thought of your captain."

"Aye, so I did," I replied. "I forgot that I brought you the very last apple. It is the heat that brings on the forgetfulness. It is exactly as you say, sir. This apple floated to the top of the barrel, and as soon as I saw it I thought of you. Aye, so I did. It is for you, sir. Top of the barrel."

The captain took the apple and polished it with his sleeve. "Mister Silver," he said. "I cut out the tongues of those who lie to me."

Black John had them broad eyebrows too, as you recall. And he had that beard that covered most of his face so you only saw his eyes, and the man squinted from all those days under the sun, and so you never saw all of his eyes, but just beads. And, what with the mass of hair and squinty eyes, you never knew what mischief the man might be charting at any moment.

"I have not spoken to you about Kwik yet, Silver," he said. "I sailed seven years with James Kwik. Seven years, Mister Silver," he said, whilst he peeled my apple. "I heard that Kwik struck you. About the ears. So Pew told me. If I struck you, about the ears, would you draw a blade on me, boy?" Those black beads of his grew wider.

"No and never, sir. I would be careful with that apple, sir. I have every expectation that it is faultless, but the center of some apples have the odd spore in them. If a man expects tart, he should receive it, I say. Tart enough to warrant his expectations. Mind the spore, sir. Enjoy the pip, sir, but care is required with every bite."

"But you drew a blade on Kwik," he said, ignoring my treatise on the fruit of Eden.

"Aye, sir. I ran him clean through with it."

"If Pew struck you, would you draw a blade on him, Silver?"

I answered Black John directly enough. "It ain't likely that he would, sir. But if Pew struck me, I would. Aye, sir. I would. I would run him through."

"And, Mister Silver, if Bloody Bill struck you, what then? What would be your rejoinder then?" He gave his beard a tug. I had been waiting for the tug. He was a bit tardy with it on account that he was so perturbed with me. He took a small bite of the apple, looking it over.

"I would run him through, sir," I answered. "The apple looks to be in fine form. I am glad that you recalled it, sir."

He took great bites of the apple now. "Would you run him through? Would you, Mister Silver? Would you send our Bloody Bill to his grave then too? As strong as he is. Would you, Mister Silver?" He put his kerchief back into his sleeve and crossed his arms. He had eaten the apple down to its core.

"Aye, sir. I would run him through, sir. Unless he ran me through first."

"But you say that you would not run your captain through if he struck you. Are you certain of it, Mister Silver?"

"Aye, sir. I am as certain of it as I am certain that there ain't no more apples on board this ship."

"You may take your leave now, Mister Silver. And Mister Silver?"

"Aye, sir?" I asked, and I was innocence itself when I answered the captain, as I had hidden another apple under a stretch of canvas and was anxious to eat it.

"I ain't inclined to lose any more men. At least not until we get to port."

I turned to take my leave when I heard a whistle. The captain's dagger was quivering in the cabin door. He had just missed me.

"Don't you ever lie to me, Mister Silver. Ever," the captain said, husking up the sleeves of his cutty sark. His kerchief fell out of his sleeve. He crossed his arms again. I was, evidently, no longer in his favour.

I never feared Black John. I never feared any man.

What does a Bristol dog fear? What does a Bristol dog fear of darkness when all that dog knows is darkness? What does that dog fear of thunder when all that dog ever hears is thunder? What does that dog fear of the whip when all he ever feels is the whip? What does a Bristol dog fear?

I am that dog, sir.

I am the dog that bites the other dogs. What do I fear? I am John Silver, and I am more dog than man and more dog than dog.

BUT NOW I luff from the tale of my own youth at sea to tell of my chance meeting with young Edward, as you have been patience itself. Aye, and so I will write on that certain cipher now, the declamation that we traversed the world trying to solve.

Hold on now, my sir. Patience, so I have heard, is its own reward although I much prefer my brand of remuneration.

To find a treasure is one matter, and a sweet matter it is, but to undo a man and take all that is precious to him is another matter entirely. I must savour the moment. Aye, but now that I think on it I am eating two sweets. I am not only drawing my share of the treasure but also casting you to davies, and so I am twice the beneficiary. Aye, twice. One and one. Or, in your case two less two, as I will leave you with naught but the hair on your head and then only so long as you ain't hanged by that fine head of hair. Numbers are important, my hearty. How many leagues is it until we reach England?

There. I have taken my satisfaction, and hereby divulge an element of the answer to the simple statement that appeared on the first page of the treasure book. Recall, "I have hidden 41 meters from the foundation 6 wooden boxes overlaid in ivory, and all empty, and one remarkable treasure covered in nothing but sackcloth not more than 2 meters deep nor more than 87 meters wide."

I ascertained that the numbers might correspond to the pages in Edward's Bible, and so the 41 meters might therefore correspond with page 41 of that book.

The passage on page 41 read so:

41:2 And, behold, there came up out of the river seven well
favoured kine and fatfleshed; and they fed in a meadow.
41:3 And, behold, seven other kine came up after them out of
the river, ill favoured and leanfleshed; and stood by the other
kine upon the brink of the river.
41:4 And the ill favoured and leanfleshed kine did eat up the
seven well favoured and fat kine. So Pharaoh awoke.
41:5 And he slept and dreamed the second time; and, behold,
seven ears of corn came up upon one stalk, rank and good.

41:6 And, behold, seven thin ears and blasted with the east
wind sprung up after them.

41:7 And the seven thin ears devoured the seven rank and full
ears. And Pharaoh awoke, and, behold, it was a dream.

Now what did that cipher represent? Was I to add up all the sevens and
arrive at forty-two and should that be a bearing? Was I to take away the
seven fat kine and seven thin ears and arrive at twenty-eight? Was I to
look for a "meadow" or the "brink of the river"? Was I to follow the "east
wind" and let it blow me to the fortune? Was it a false clue, as after all, it
"was all a dream" of Pharaoh and so the passage read? Did the word,
"rank," hold any meaning? And what of old Pharaoh? Was he a symbol
for your King? Leave us say, for now, that I turned that page over and
about and that some of my suppositions were accurate and others wore a
windward tide.

I looked on that cipher day after day at sea, and I see the solution
clearly now, as I have already resolved it, but there was a breach in my reasoning wide enough to sail a frigate through it. I did not spy the solution.
It warn't for a good many years, long after I had murdered Kwik, well after Edward had joined our crew and leagues later than our adventures in
Spain and other points of plunder that I finally solved the cipher. And the
other ones. All of them. Which is how I come to rightfully own the treasure whereas you do not.

It is also time that I introduce my lad to the world, my Edward, and as
I found him. He brought us his King James Bible, and I dare say that but
for young Edward we would not be jousting this same day.

Edward. Do you recall the slip of a lad? I first met him outside the
Abbey near Bartholomew Close. Black John had granted the crew leave in
Londontown, and I was strolling in the shadow of the Abbey when Edward
bumped into me, and said, "Pray, pardon me, sir. I beg your pardon."

"I beg your pardon," I said, and I straightaway cut open the pockets of
his coat with my dagger. A string of gold beads, a piece of cambric, a
swath of velvet and, lastly, my gold watch, fell out of his coat.

"My mother is ill," he sputtered. "I am on my way to the milliner."
Years later Edward told me, whilst deep in the rum, that he had never been
caught before that day.

I held his wrist. "Aye, by way of a run through Little Britain and Blue-
coat Hospital. You pay your milliners handsomely," I told him. "More

than in Bristol. In Bristol," I went on, "our cutpurses are more careful too. I will accompany you," I told him. "Your milliner is no doubt waiting for you in his foreshop for payment." The lad commenced to struggle. He tried so hard to escape that his cap and a pair of silver-fringed gloves that he had hidden under it fell away.

"To heel," I said, and Edward told me his troubles. I always had a way with the wayward lads, having been such a one myself. He told me that his mother was lying in, that he had a pair of starving sisters and three starving brothers, and that he hoped that his sad history would, upon the whole, weigh in his case should I bring him to account. He said that his mother was in the wicked trade. And, he said, that was how she come to be lying in. Further, he continued, his father was dead. Moreover, he said, if his father warn't dead, he would have sent a proper sum to him and his pair of sisters and three brothers to set them all to rights. However, he said, that his father, in truth, went to Ireland. And, he died there. Therefore, he said, if I would but give him leave, he would walk straight to the Abbey. And, he insisted, toward the infinite. He would pursue the pristine life. He gazed forlornly at the goods and said that the sight of them rested hard upon his spirit.

The lad might have convinced an honest man of his words, but he warn't speaking to an honest man. He was speaking to Long John Silver.

"We have better liars in Bristol too," I told Edward. Then I made him an offer. I spied true talent in the lad, and so I told him that I would make an honest thief of him. I turned him round and told him to look at the drapers, weavers, and mercers in their shops and how they all hung their heads. They are landlubbers, I explained to him, and all landlubbers hang their heads because they are a pitiful people. Not a one of them, I told him, had ever chanced a rope or even a paper of lace around their necks. I looked into his eyes and told him that I spied oceans in there. I told him that he was a born blaggard and had a better future than even an alderman on the skip. He only needed a ship and, by chance, I had one for him, and there was no better one that sailed the brine. I put the goods in my pocket and brought him directly to the Linda Maria.

Some repined the seafaring life the first time that they hoisted a hook, as they warn't accustomed to labour of any kind. Some put in their regrets when the first storm blowed. Some come to low water as soon as they drank the bilgewater that passed for sustenance under Black John's watch.

Edward at first bells had a hard time of the seafaring life too. I say that on account that his head was in a bucket for ten days after we put to sea. I raised his spirits when I told him of the Canaries and the Carolinas and the Indies. I raised them even more when I cursed. He enjoyed cursing. I damned the Spaniards, the French, the Scots, and the Irish. Still, I could not keep the lad's spirits high, even after I damned the Portuguese. There were days when he walked from the castle to the quarterdeck as if he was dragging the anchor behind him.

"Ain't he on even terms with the grand jury?" Bones asked me. He offered Edward a drink of rum, which was particularly generous for Bones. Edward declined and stuck his head in the bucket again.

Pew scuttled over to me, and said, "Summon an ordinary as soon as we light. It seems to Pew like the boy is in need of his last good words." I told that hairless son of a rector to bluster off. "You look like a bill was preferred against you, boy," Pew told Edward. "Pew says that the lad looks like he is in the dock in Guilder's Hall." I lifted my leg so to put my boot in Pew, but he scurried off before I could dispatch him.

Edward, in time, took his head out of the bucket. I instructed him on swords, sabers, and pistols. I taught Edward the art of plundering, cheating, ransacking, and all that a young rover should know. I taught him to roll bones, and though Edward was reluctant to hazard a single shilling, when he played he prevailed. Edward won Black John's own cape in one game to the captain's embarrassment and my amusement. Edward looked a right gentleman in that cape. So he did, my good mate.

It was on one of Edward's first days at sea that Pew went rummaging through Edward's belongings such as they were, which warn't much at all, and found the Bible. The pages of the Bible were dog-eared and yellowed, and when Pew first brought the Bible to me on account that he wanted to cause some mischief, I did not yet perceive the value of the book. Pew had already taken an interest in the scribblings inside it, and the one scribble in particular that read, "1303."

I took more interest in the other ciphers, particularly them that I have already written on and the one that read, "Blood." That was the only word that warn't written in deep black ink. It was written in crimson, and so I wrote.

I was intrigued, my hearty. Pew had him some musings about the book, and namely that it was the good for tinder on a cold night as the pages were so brittle. He offered to take it, but whilst he held it he said, "1303" again. And then he said, "Blood," and looked about as if he was trying to recall a matter.

I pledged Pew never to tell anyone of the Bible, and vowed that if Pew did not hold to his promise, I would murder him in a manner befitting his betrayal. That manner, by the by, was boiling him as it is the best way to cook crab. Pew's hands shook as he handed me the Bible, and mind you that his hands never shook.

Edward, only a trice after Pew left me, discovered the larceny and told me of it. I, true hearty to all, told Edward that Pew likely took it, and thereupon Edward commenced to search through Pew's hoard. It does please me, as I had planned it so, to relate that after I put the finger on Edward he was surrounded whilst rummaging through Pew's articles, and that Black John decreed that the lad should be appropriately punished. I presumed that Black John would order me to convey the punishment, as Black John knew that I was fond of the lad, and my presumption was plumb. I delivered twenty lashes to Edward and afterward carried him below deck.

I went hard on the lad. It would not have done for Black John to suspect that I had gone easy on Edward, as the captain would have tormented the life out of the lad just to pester me. I also reasoned that Edward might disclose the origin of the Bible and the significance of the markings in it whilst I cared for him.

Edward, some dazed from the pain, did not disappoint me. He complained that he should not have been whipped like a commoner, and when I conferred him with a sip of rum and assured him that he could confide in me, he told me his true story. He warn't born nor bred for thievery but took to it as his only recourse when the King's own guards murdered his family in its entirety. My lad was highborn and come with a pedigree, and enough of one that Georgey's guards cut the throats of Edward's mother, father, brothers, sisters, and even, and as if they knew the family's secrets too, their tawny cat and yellow-beaked canary.

That warn't all though, as Edward said that his family had been tortured before their throats were cut and he described what he saw without expression as if he was back there again, what with his father's limbs hanging from the lampion post and his mother's arms tied to the bedpost and her split in deuces. His father heard the hooves of the horses, pitched the Bible into Edward's hands, and told him to run and not look back nor never come near the manse again.

I tried to cheer the lad, and told him, "Why, Edward, you ain't no simple knave at all but a sort of baronet. You are pomp and circumstance itself." He took no comfort in my compliment, and his face darkened when I advised him that he should leave me hold the Bible as his bailiff so it would not fall into the hands of his foe.

He held the book to his chest and said that it was all that was left of his family and that he meant to keep it.

I slapped Edward on his back, and he winced some, but I told him that highborn or not, I had been right about him as he had showed sound fortitude. "I always knew it," I told the lad. "All of the royals are naught but robbers and no different than you nor me for all their origin. But they got them their robes and finery, and underneath them accoutrements they keep all their secrets, whereas we stand shirtless on deck for all to see." Edward responded, "Not all their secrets, John." I placed my hand on the lad's shoulder. He grimaced some, and I told him that he should tell no one else of his lineage so as not to get spliced like his dear mother. I also advised him to say nothing of the Bible. "You come onto the ship a simple Peach and you will leave it as one, and that is a promise from me to you. You can always trust me, Edward. Aye, if you cannot trust the man that lashed you within a league of your life, then whom can you trust? Still, we must eat us this royal cobbler. Tell me more, lad."

Edward opened the first page of the book and showed me the elaborate headpiece and the writings 'neath it. I had seen the headpiece before. It was the same one as is in every Bible, and I would know, as enough of them had been bowled at Tom and me whilst we were at our begging. There warn't nothing special about the headpiece at all, so it seemed, and look here, I traced it once more.

"There is a meaning to all this," I told Edward. "Enough of a meaning for your family to be murdered for it. Your father gave it to you for safekeeping. He died on account of it."

I rubbed the front of the book with my thumb, expecting some of the dye to come off, but the black stayed. I run my thumb through its pages and they did not crackle. If the book was from 1303, its pages were in excellent condition. The pages purred like a cat, a cat that only I should pet. Them pages were yellowed, but only a bit, and the first page was darker than the rest, as if the trickster had imparted some of his spirit onto it.

"But these must be clues," I said, and Edward readily confessed that he believed so too. His expected that his father had hidden a fortune, or so he said, and he surmised that his Bible might somehow disclose where the fortune was concealed.

"Would you help me find it, John?" he asked me innocently enough. "I might restore my family name as well."

I encouraged Edward to speak more, applying a poultice for his wounds and pouring more rum down his throat.

Edward downed the rum, and I offered him my full assistance, putting forward that we should divide the spoils equably. Edward agreed to split the fortune, as I knew he would, as there was no other choice. I would be captain one day, and so I told Edward, and on that day we would search for his fortune. Until that time, so I told him, we would abide Black John. But, our time would come, and when it come, we would be ready for it. We would determine the meaning of these words and sail straight for his fortune, so I told the lad.

"I might be your first mate," Edward added.

"I would myself recommend you to the Rump if our hearties would not kill you upon the recommendation," I told him. "But have you told me all, boy?" I inquired. "For if you are holding anything back, anything at all and no matter how small it is, it may be near impossible to solve the riddles inside your book."

My poor lad fainted at them words, and so I poured another dram of rum down his gullet to revive him. I assured Edward straight off, whilst he was hacking away, that Pew would be no trouble, as the only thing that he cared for more than his trinkets was his life.

"And 1303," I questioned Edward. "The date of the printing of the Bible? The date that it was given to your father? The date that he took it from another?"

"I expect the date that it was printed," Edward replied.

"And this word, 'Blood,' that is so striking?" I asked him. He answered that it held no significance for him. "The other writings? Anything at all? Any meaning that you can sight?"

"None," was Edward's reply.

"We will have to keep this book a secret. Guard it," I told him. "Be at the ready to defend it. For the sake of your fortune," I added. "And your family name." Edward agreed, quite readily once again, confessing that he lacked mastery of the sword and dagger. I told him that I could think of no one better than me to provide him with them skills.

And so there we have it, the commencement of a quest and a lasting friendship between two blaggards, and even though one of them blaggards was highborn and the other one a Bristol dog.

One last matter, my hearty, before the fever takes me again. The waves will roll and the wind will come back, but this ship shall not go to England ever, and you shall be a dead man, and your crew shall be dead men, and you shall all be dead men, for a Bristol dog has sharp teeth.

CHAPTER V.

A TWICE-DEAD SPANIARD

was writing, so I was, before the fever come on me. Aye, I was writing about Edward's early days at sea and the ciphers. Aye, the ciphers. Mullet read the parchment and was most inquisitive about how Pew's hands shook upon reading the year, 1303, on the first page of the Bible. He also queried me why I had not written more about the headpiece, as warn't that a clue too.

I have just now slipped the tracing of the headpiece under my door and importuned Mullet to fix his gaze on it. His breathing grew heavier on account that he ain't got any proclivity for deliberation at all.

I charged him to recite back every matter about the treasure that I had told him and that I had written, or at least as much as he could remember, and he registered his usual protest about taking orders from a man locked in a cabin. Then he blowed the air out of his nostrils as if he was about to begin an oration, but did not speak. The lad stayed moored. And so here is what I told the lad, as I expect that he may not be able to recall anything except his last meal.

I told him that there were two letters on the headpiece and bade him to find them, which he done, and then I told him that one of the letters was dark and the other was light. Mullet thumped his head against the door. I imagine that when he turned to see them letters his head keeled from the labour. I explained that the letters are on the headpiece of every one of the King James Bibles. There are many means by which to interpret the letters, and it might interest him and so I said to him that the headpiece is a code.

I told him to look closer at the tracing. You might even say that there are two forces in opposition to each other, I said, for each of them creatures is pulling on a strand that holds the bundle together. I solicited his response regarding which one of them creatures would prevail if they pulled the strand at the same instant, and he could not say as both had the same advantage. Now it may be, I told him, that the creatures are land-lubbers or hearties, or that one is a landlubber and the other a hearty, but there is no way to discern so from the drawing. And so I told him, it may be that them two are not creatures of any kind at all but two hemispheres, mayhap a longitude and latitude, and then I asked him which side would prevail. He could not answer. But one of them is as right as fair weather and the other is as wrong as foul weather. Which side would prevail then? He could not say.

Now, I told him, the two sides, the dark and the light, may represent the sun and the moon, day and night as it were. He sparked to that and said that day follows night, and then reconsidered and said that it may be that night follows day, but he warn't exactly certain. A last question, so I told him. If the two blaggards in the drawing pull on the bundle of sticks at the same time, will the bundle fall apart and will they be left with naught, or will the secret inside the bundle be revealed? And of course Mullet could not say.

Mullet did offer that if one looked beyond the letters, past the middle, that there were strange animals in the drawing. Aye, there is truth in that too, I told him. Them are their mates. Then again he said it might be that it is just a pretty picture.

Mullet left, one foot sliding behind the other as if he was as lame as me. It warn't in him to mock me, so I expect that his leg had gone dozy on him.

And Mullet, when you read this, you must understand that when I deem you a cleat or a drowsy lad or by some similar nomenclature, I mean so with sincerity.

I wonder what is to become of our world. It may be that a cleat is a cleat, but if Mullet portends the future, I prefer to remain bolted in my cabin. He hails from the colonies, and if he is the best that breed has to of-fer, they shall be of no consequence. Mullet is more kin to a carp than he is to Hawkins. Hawkins had a futurity to him. Hawkins, in the right hands, could have grown into a ganger. Mullet will ever be what he is this day. You can dress Mullet in greens and pour gravy over him, but he will still be Mullet.

*   *   *

FEVER AGAIN.

And there is Mullet outside my door when I wake. He has returned like a fish bone caught in my craw.

———◦◦◦———

L eave me be," I told Mullet when he told me that he had brought me more fare from your table.

"But the captain ordered me," he replied. I imagine that Mullet has a knob in his neck that jumps up and down like a bobbin when he speaks. I have given more thought to the lad and have determined that his purpose is to serve as ballast.

"I ain't inclined to be poisoned, boy. Your captain means to murder me." I heard Mullet swallowing and almost saw the bobbin rising and falling, whilst he contemplated his response.

"He means to feed you first," Mullet replied. I have no doubt that he stands stock-still when he speaks. His arms hang by his sides, and he only moves them from time to time like any fish that must open its gills now and again for air.

He cleared his throat twice and waited before speaking. I could have crossed the globe, I could have, whilst waiting for him to tell me what you told him. "Captain says." And here he cleared his throat once more. "You do not have much time left."

"Tell your captain that he will never find my treasure without me. I shall therefore bide my time before presenting him with another solution. You must understand that I have all the solutions and that your captain only has some of them. That is how I come to find the treasure before him and how I come to hide it and all my other riches from him. He must read my account as carefully as I read the clues in the treasure book. I will now recount the manner in which I found another part of my fortune, now buried with the treasure of treasures in a place that only I know. I will tell you about a Spaniard by the name of Don Jorge."

———◦◦◦———

I poured the whole history of the San Cristobel over Mullet, and he did not say a word. He is so drowsy a fish that not even my gravy could spice him. Now Hawkins enjoyed the tale of the San Cristobel, asking me all the particulars, which I hereby write, as it pleases me to do so and as Mullet will not give the best account of it.

And I shall allow Black John more ink, although I don't owe him any-thing, as you cannot understand how anxious I was for plunder without un-derstanding how he maddened me by his miserliness. We generally fail to foresee how one act leads to another, but Black John's refusal to attack ships made me ravenous for recompense, and his rebuttal of my plea to pursue Don Jorge's bounty made me want it all the more. That Spaniard's riches, when I found them, weighed me down so that I had to bury them. And where did I bury them? Where? What better place than alongside the treasure that you seek.

LARCENY IS OUR business. It is as good a business as any other, and more honest than most others, as we admit to the principle of our enter-prise. Black John, except when it come to filching from his own men, was a mediocre merchant. We rolled about the oceans, Black John being con-tent to assault only one or two ships a year, then retreat to port. A small crew of men always stayed behind to guard the ship, and we rolled bones to determine which men left and which men stayed, and so I cheated when-ever possible.

Black John was free with his currency in port, which always took me aback, as he was so miserly with his men. He did increase my share of the spoils as I matured, but I always believed that I deserved more and so, from time to time, I visited his cabin on one pretense or another and took an item that caught my eye. I stowed the goods in Bloody Bill's locker. Bill never knew the difference, and if the captain ever discovered the theft, he dared not accuse Bill of it.

Aye, Black John was right generous to everyone in port but his men. He spent his blunt on ladies and lodgings, and always fitted himself out with the finest of luxuries. His men slept on pallets or on the floors of the inns where Black John took up residence. Black John bought a room only for himself and his ladies. He never shared a nick of his fortune with his men in port. Ben Gunn had a malady that turned him puce, and the men entreated Black John to buy him a night's bed. Black John refused on the grounds that Ben would likely die and not be able to manage the remuner-ation. Ben spited him and lived.

Ben Gunn was an exceptional hearty, he was, and that was because he returned from the grave. Now, he warn't particularly solvent when he returned from the nether region, but at least he paid his respects. That merits mention, and so I shall write more on Ben Gunn in time. In time, sir. In my time, sir, as Ben bears on the treasure too.

The men that borrowed money from Black John were ever in his debt. He found new and various ways for them to squander their currency, such as prompting brawls between them, then setting the wagers on it, or persuading the borrowers to buy him another round of drinks. He trimmed all of his men one way or another.

The men stayed true to him. They had no choice, as the sea rat would have killed them if they tried to leave, and no other captain would let one of Black John's men join his crew. It warn't for fear of retribution that them other captains did not chew on Black John's scraps. It was their code. Once in a while a midshipman did escape, and if Black John did not capture him, he flogged another man for the sedition.

Now and again Black John lost a man in port, usually on account of a mashed head. He soon found someone else to take the man's place, as there was an abundance of idlers in port. The new men only saw the Black John that materialized in port and not the miser on board the ship. What man would not want to sail with Black John, that most beneficent man among men, that fine free-spending fellow? Who would not want to tack on to the crew of such a sporting sort?

And so I grew more restless as each year passed. We had our conquests. We pulled the Jack down and the Skull up and did not even have to hoist a sword. Our quarry always surrendered.

The sea rat took it into his head one year that we should sail to Denmark. My lady was buffeted by squall after squall, and any sensible man would have turned the ship around, but Black John had never seen Denmark. Men, who had never been ill, laid up green. We did not have proper clothes for the clime, and shivered so constantly that I thought the nails would burst from the planks. Black John remained in his cabin, cozy in two jackets, woolen slippers, and a long stocking cap. I was used to detriments on account of my early years, and so I fared better than most of the men. Bloody Bill remained at the taffrail, watching the waters turn to ice whilst a frost settled on him. We come to predict the day's weather by how long it took him to shake the rime off in the morning.

We took turns on the lookout for floes and sailed slowly through the peculiar sea, a sea that was all head like the froth on a mug of ale. But, it warn't froth. It was deadly white. The sea there is thick, and we spied broken planks and cracked masts, and I had no doubt that underneath them planks and masts were blue faces staring up at us from their graves.

Bloody Bill howled when we come to the ice and after we left it. The captain passed him a coin for each of his howls. I struck a flint for him twice at night, when we were at anchor and all but the beast and me were at their slumbers.

Black John had more luck than he deserved. Whilst we shivered and Black John consulted his charts, we encountered a battle between the French and British navies. The ships were equally matched in gunnery with forty guns apiece. They might have been looking at their own reflections in a glass, or taken the place of them adversaries in the headpiece, as they sailed board and board to each other. The French ship, the Cherbourg, and the British ship, the Offence, maneuvered about each other, each trying to pull the strand.

Neither frigate had fired a shot when we arrived, but as soon as the Offence saw our Jack, it tried to gripe and fired its cannons at the Cherbourg. The Cherbourg returned fire. We lowered our flag and retreated to a safe distance.

The ships circled each other, looking for an advantage. The ordinaries of the Offence must have been coiling the ropes, as they turned in less than eight minutes in rough seas, which warn't fast enough though as the Cherbourg was wearing ten minutes. The ships circled each other, the Offence closing the gap until it was no more than five hundred yards apace, and then it fired. The Cherbourg tacked, sustaining light damage, but immediately returned fire and struck the Offence, which rose out of the water and crashed back as if Old Nick himself had hauled it down. They were board and board again and the Offence fired, this time to the Cherbourg's disadvantage. The shots breached the Cherbourg's hull. Aye, but then the Cherbourg fired and struck the Offence. The Offence listed, pulled by Nick once again, and then righted itself.

The Cherbourg was doomed on account of the breach in its hull, and the fellows of the Offence, gentlemen all, piped aboard the fellows of the Cherbourg. Black John gave the order to strike the Offence. We raised the Skull and blasted through the Offence's masts whilst those good fellows were still at their tea. We lashed our lines, fought both British and French and killed all of them, not being particular to either of their extractions but only to their blunt.

The Cherbourg was ready to go down, and so we grabbed what we could from the Offence before we saw a Dutch ship on the horizon and headed aback. We hoisted a Dutch flag and sailed away with our fortune.

The men gave all the credit for their spoils to Black John, but I knew better. It was chance. We had altered the fortunes of them two ships by pulling harder on one of the strands that separated them from their natural fate.

Black John was content to loll about for two seasons after that catch. We only captured one ship, a French troller of some class, beneaped, that was notable only for the cambric that it carried.

Then chance turned again.

I had been with Black John for nine years, Edward having tacked on board the crew during the eighth year, when we come upon the San Cristobel. The ship was listing, and I knew that it might split in two at any tick, but I wanted plunder. I had long past given up my wooden spoons for a curved saber, and was deft with a sword, apt with a hatchet, and able with an axe. I was stronger than any man on board the ship except for Bloody Bill. I was always the keenest man on board the ship.

My hearties threw the crew of the San Cristobel overboard. We had no room on board the ship for their beasts, so we threw them into the sea too, and they drowned with their masters. There were casks of rum, tierces of meat, and barrels of wine in the brine. Our bowman was jouncing on the waves. Pew and him come to a misunderstanding over the pike. Our bowman grabbed the pike to skewer one of the barrels, and Pew done the same. Pew skewered our bowman instead. A mischance, so Pew said. We hoisted the barrels and casks and tierces onto the ship with handspikes, and the bowman onto the ship with our boat hook, but the bowman was dead. We laid the barrels amidships. We threw the bowman and his marly soul back into the sea.

Billy Bones pried open the hand of one of the Spaniards. The devil was barely alive and still clutching a box when Bones broke the latch and found a lock of hair in it. Fair hair, as I recall. Bones tossed the box back to the Spaniard and the Spaniard obliged Bones by drowning forthwith.

Aye, but the greediest of the men, your Silver, roamed the low hold of that sinking ship. I hoisted myself over the kentledge and even such as I that had seen most every sight in my jaunts never seen a sight such as I found, for there in the depths I spied a Spaniard chained to a wooden barrel. He thrashed at the rising brine, kicking to keep his head above water and paddling when the barrel rolled him over.

The Spaniard pleaded with me to free him. I was perfectly content to let him drown as he was a Spaniard, but I found his cries for help and thrashing most diverting. I almost forgot that the ship was sinking. He swore on the grave of his mother that he was rich and avowed that he would reward me if I saved him. "You may ask them all about Don Jorge," he said, as the barrel rolled him over. I told him that he did not, at least at the moment, look much of a man of means.

He declaimed once more that he was rich and offered to give all of his wealth to me if I would save him. He opened his hands and spread his arms as a demonstration of his wealth, but as soon as he done so, the barrel rolled him onto his back. He kicked and flung his hands about, and I would have been more amused by the spectacle if the ship warn't going down, and I warn't in the hold with the devil. Aye, but flies and buccaneers are attracted to a rotting carcass even if it is a Spanish carcass.

He managed to gargle, "Spare me," before the barrel rolled him over again. He spat out the water and tried to speak, but I held up my hand.

"Mother's milk," I told him. I held my sword above him. "I may very well miss," I warned him. "It would be best if you remained still," I cautioned him, as he rolled yet again. He thrashed about, rather desperate. It was a shame that the San Cristobel was sinking, as we could have larked about so all day. I ran my blade along his shoulders, as I did not want to miss him in the dark and bade him again to remain still. No doubt he preferred death by sword to death by drowning, and so he obliged me.

I held my sword with both hands, the Spaniard's eyes grew wide, and I heaved my sword with all my might and split the chains that bound him. He lashed away at the water, frantic to leave the depths of the ship until I put my dagger to his neck. "Speak of your riches," I told him.

And so, in the foul air of the hold of that sinking ship, the Spaniard told me his tale. He was rich and in love, so he said, and those were his only crimes.

My Spaniard, so he told me, knelt on his breeches the Sunday before the San Cristobel set sail and asked his love to wed. She replied that she was carrying a child. She had been assaulted, she told him, by her brother. They talked about love and vengeance, and for some time, because Spaniards enjoy nothing better than to talk about them matters.

My Spaniard visited the brother, and no doubt waved his arms and shouted, and mayhap even scared the brother, because the brother drew his pistola and pointed it at my Spaniard.

Life is a simple matter, I say, and the more evil a man is, the more simple life is. Good men are vexed. They vex themselves. They are vexed about the effect of this on that and of that on this and, when they finally finish their vexings, they vex themselves again. By the time they end their vexings, a cow could learn to dance the jig. And so, before Don Jorge could grab the pistola from the brother, whilst Don Jorge was contemplating rejoinders and pondering rebuttals, whilst he was considering replies, the brother, who warn't a good man, struck Don Jorge on the head with the pistola.

Consequently, Don Jorge's lantern blowed out, and he fell to the ground senseless. He come to in time to see the brother's servants throwing a rope over the branch of a tree. The brother put the noose around Don Jorge's neck.

"You should be dead then," I told my Spaniard, "but you look too ripe for a corpse." He warn't, in any event, a poor-looking fellow for a Spaniard or a corpse. His skin was dark but not brown, dusky, like the colour of the others of his kind. His face was more bog than beard. He had not been able to wash or trim his whiskers, and so it grew some wild on his face. His eyes narrowed, and it seemed to me that he saw his riches hard alee of him. He had all his teeth and showed them when he spoke of his wealth. He was neither weathered nor withered but for his cheeks, which were sunken, although a good mason could have put him to rights without much mortar.

"I should be twice dead," he said. "Once by hanging and once by drowning." He almost seemed proud.

The ship listed, and we clambered onto the forecastle deck. I was able to see more of my Spaniard, and now he looked like a specter, as he lost his substance in the light. He had a slender build and not nearly the bulk that I had presumed in the dark. The sun hit us plumb then, and I would swear to you that I was almost able to see directly through him.

I grabbed his arm, a spongy mass of skin and bones, to drag him forward. He must have had them riches, as spongy sorts like your King always do. The taffrail cracked as he began to speak, and my Spaniard jumped aft and almost into my arms.

"I hung from that tree for at least three hours," he said, and he showed me the rope marks on his bony neck. "I grabbed the trunk of the tree with my legs and held to that tree with my legs, Englishman. And there I stayed. An eternity, Englishman."

"You don't look to me to have the might to hold on to a twig," I told him, and I christened him a liar like the rest of his countrymen.

"Then I saw an angel," he said. "And with a horse," he said. "And a hatchet."

The angel was none other than his beloved. He told me that his love gave him the hatchet and that he hacked at the rope that bound him until he was free. It was a fine ending, and so I told him, but I reminded him that I had found him chained in the ship and drowning like a rat.

"Gold, Englishman!" he shouted. He snatched at my arm, and his fingers barely surrounded a quarter of my limb. I swatted him back and told him that I would let him live a whit more so long as he spoke of gold. There is always time to kill a Spaniard.

Don Jorge went to the brother's home that same night. The brother was sitting at his writing table, my Spaniard said. Two candles flickered in the room. The brother was hunched over the parchment on the table, and there was a goblet filled with wine on the table. That was what Don Jorge saw when he crept into the room with a dagger up his sleeve.

Perhaps the brother saw Don Jorge's reflection in the window, or perhaps he heard his footsteps. Perhaps the flames of the candles waned. Perhaps the brother felt a chill when Don Jorge entered the room, for the brother turned. The brother turned, he did, but he turned too late. Don Jorge struck the brother with the goblet.

Don Jorge was no pirate. He was a farmer. A pirate would have finished the brother then and there.

"I clasped the dagger," Don Jorge said. "And he begged me for his life. He promised me his gold. All his gold, Englishman. Doubloons, Englishman. A fortune," he said, as he spat out some of the water still in him.

The Spaniard and I climbed through the main hatch and onto the deck. The San Cristobel's bow was tipped to the heavens whilst her stern had already resigned herself to the deep. The deck was slowly snapping as it fell beneath the weight of the waters. I told him to grab the bowline.

"He took me to his bodega," the Spaniard said. "I saw bottles and casks stacked to the thatches. There were scores of casks. Hundreds of bottles. Inside one of the casks," he said. "The gold, the fortune is—" Then the Spaniard stopped his tale for we heard a crack as thunderous as the hammer of a hanging judge. The foremast crashed to the deck. The top gallant mast swung aft and lee and round about, until it dropped no more than five meters from where the Spaniard and I stood. "The ship is sinking under our feet," the Spaniard squalled.

"Aye," I answered. "The topmast will come down next, it will. Then the devil's helmsman will turn to and the devil will blow, and we will go down to the deep together." He was eager to abandon the hulk, but he had spoken of a fortune, and I was prepared to stand there until the waves washed over us. "Stand fast we will, Spaniard. I will lash us with the bowline to whatever mast that stands. We will not leave this ship, we will not, Spaniard. We will not leave this ship until I know all. The fortune, my Spaniard. Tell me all."

"In the name of heaven, we must leave or we will die."

"No, you will die, Spaniard. I will live. You will die."

My Spaniard told me, as quickly as he could, that the brother took a spar and lifted one of the casks. Then the brother split the cask with the spar, and the cask spewed forth a river of coins. The brother struck the cask again, and the river become a waterfall of charms and gold and jewels. Don Jorge sat in the middle of all those riches. He dug both of his hands in the treasure, he did, and laughed until the brother struck him with the spar. My Spaniard woke on the ship in the chains where I found him.

He begged me to take him to Spain. He told me that the treasure would be mine and mine alone, as all he wanted now was revenge.

I told him to heave up his final words whilst I advised Old Nick to stand by the braces. I told him that he was an exceptional bard but a middling actor. I did not believe a word of his tale. He, with all haste, as we stood at the prow, which was all that remained of the ship, told me how to find the treasure. He grabbed my arm again. His eyes were ablaze. He told me the way through the woods, the clearing that I would come upon, the house that I would find, then the bodega that I would sight behind the house. I only needed to ferry him to Spain. Aye, and provide him with a pistol.

He dug his bony fingers into my arms and did not let go until I pried them off one by one. And then he grabbed me again and swore that all he had told me was true. There warn't nothing between the deep and us now but a foursquare of deck.

I recalled that Tom told me that last words were generally truthful, on account that a person wants to lie straight for eternity, and so to pay heed to sworn particulars at such a time. And so I believed the Spaniard. Every word, sir.

I called out to my hearties, "Avast the halyards, men! Make still those sails! I bring you a tale from Spain, a tale of gold! Lower a boat for me, Bones, and heave to. Pull the oars for me, Mister Bones, and you shall be the first to hear the tale. Call the captain, Mister Smith. Call him, I say."

"What is this, Mister Silver?" the sea rat declared. "Are you giving orders now?"

"We sail for Spain directly, sir," I answered. "We sail, sir, for gold. We sail, sir, for riches beyond measure." The water around me churned and boiled. It would not be long before there was nothing left of the San Cristobel, the Spaniard, his tale, or me.

"We will not, Mister Silver," the captain called back, husking up his sleeves again, just like he done when he threw his dagger at me. "We are on a course for the Indies. The compass points east, and so we sail, Mister Silver. By the by, Mister Silver, you are drowning." Bones's hair confirmed the course.

"The fortune is in Spain, sir," I called to him with a crossness that took him aback. The prow was ready to go under, I was standing on my toes, speaking of treasure, and he was paying me no heed, and so I had every right to be some cross under the circumstances.

"I spoke, Mister Silver. We sail for the Indies. After the Indies, we sail for these Tortugas again. Then, we sail for Madagascar. And after Madagascar, we sail for the balmy seas. The Carolinas, Mister Silver. But wherever we may sail, wherever we may go, Mister Silver, we will never sail for Spain. Never, Mister Silver."

The beads in the captain's head grew as large as farthings. He pulled at his beard, and hard, and I thought that there might be every chance to spy the man underneath that thicket, but I only caught a glimpse of him. All of the men took a blade to their beards now and again so as to be presentable to the ladies in port, but not the captain. It must have been a matter of pride with him. Or, it might be that he had seen what was underneath his beard and did not particularly care for it. He regained his composure and looked at Pew, who was already stroking his own chin.

"Pew here ratifies the captain's order, for Pew has him no desire to die in Spain. So says Pew." I heard the last moans of the San Cristobel. A ship always moans, the same as a man, before it goes under. Don Jorge tore at my sleeve.

"Now get back on board my ship, Mister Silver," the captain ordered, as if I had a choice in the matter. "We have picked the San Cristobel clean. We are headed for the Indies, Mister Silver, and the San Cristobel is headed for the bottom of the sea."

I snaked loose from Don Jorge and swam as fleet as I could to the Linda Maria. I thought that there might be sharks in the water on account of those rotting Spaniards and their beasts. I saw Don Jorge jump into the water just as the prow sank below the waves.

Bones pulled me aboard.

Some of the appendages of the ship bobbed to the surface as if they warn't good enough for Old Nick, and so he spewed them out. The block come up and then a portion of one of the masts. I saw the foredeck. It peeked once more at the sun, and must have decided that it preferred the dimness of the sea, for it descended. The rudder rose. A good number of the transverses emerged. The longitudinal looked over the waterline, nodded, and sank. But one sight particularly struck me, and that was Don Jorge swimming as fleet as he could for the block. He had, at least for now, escaped death once more.

I pointed my finger at the Spaniard. It was a remarkable sight, and I bade the captain to look on him as he tried to climb onto the block.

"I do not see anyone," the captain replied, turning away. "Is there a man on the block, Mister Pew?" he asked.

"Not a man that Pew can see, sir," Pew sang.

By Nick, the Spaniard settled on the block. And then he found a swath of sail floating on the water and began to rig the sail. And then, of all things, he grabbed at a pair of pantaloons that he pulled off a swain that had broken to the surface. And then the Spaniard relieved the man of his blouse. "A sight this is, Captain." I tugged at his arm just as Don Jorge had tugged at my own arm only a few moments past, but the captain and his beard went below.

I did not find the Spaniard's treasure for a score more years, and I will draft the particulars in time, so to mark your treachery. But now I will give you a full account of Mary and Evangeline, for a reckoning man I am, and then I will scrawl some on Solomon, so to set down your deceit there too. I will write more about Bloody Bill and Pew and Bones, and about the captain and Ben Gunn. And young Edward. I must not forget young Edward, who had so recently come aboard the ship with his Bible. Aye, and I will write more ciphers and their solutions. A reckoning man I am, and this is a reckoning it is.

CHAPTER VI.
MARY

———

Every child should be issued a dram and a dagger at birth, those articles being necessities of life. Mullet must have been issued a biscuit and a bat. He surely did not eat his biscuit, and must have clodded himself on his head with his bat.

"Are you dead yet, boy?" I asked Mullet. He had not spoken a word since I had told him the story of the San Cristobel, whilst he ate the victuals that you sent me. "Ain't you foaming at the mouth? Ain't your belly so swollen that it might burst?"

"I ate it all. I licked the plate, sir," he said. He should have sounded delighted, but his voice trailed off as if he was contemplating a mincemeat pie laced with arsenic. Mayhap the lad had a taste for arsenic.

"Then you may tell your captain that his poison was superb," I told him. "But Mullet," I added, "it may be slow poison."

"Yes, sir," he replied. "I will tell the captain," he said, with a voice as flat as the deck, and with no more thought than if I had told him that there would be no sun on the morrow.

———

All of the ciphers are important, as each one of them points to the treasure of treasures, but each cipher by itself ain't much use without the others. The ciphers are no different than a chart. A hearty can't sail nowhere with only half a compass rose and half the degrees marked on the chart. But one of the ciphers is distinct as it is a number code, and most damnable, even though I eventually rendered it into the King's English. You never solved it, but chose to skip about as you saw fit, finding one solution, then another, never realizing that the ciphers are best solved in a particular order. The number code describes a locality. You have been there, my hearty, and know the place but cannot solve the code. You may ask why would I present the code if you know its answer, but to leave it out would render the tale incomplete. Aye, and it pleases me that you cannot solve the riddle even though you know the resolution.

Now you may believe that you have no need to solve it, as you already know the answer, but I have written that I hid my treasure. I might employ this same code between these pages to mark the point where I buried my treasure. And consequently, I bestow on you this opportunity.

One of the ciphers led me to a tombstone, as you know. These were the numbers etched on the tombstone, and in a fine hand I might say, as if the scribe had all the time in the world before he dug his grave.

$$1\text{-}1\text{-}4\text{-}4\text{-}5\text{-}7\text{-}9\text{-}12\text{-}14\text{-}14\text{-}14\text{-}15\text{-}18\text{-}18\text{-}19\text{-}19$$

I wrote and rewrote, read and reread them numbers. I split the numbers and put them back together and, just as with the kine and the corn, tallied and took away from them. I totaled them with "1303," then deducted the numbers. I put all them numbers together and withheld them all from each other and still could not solve the code. Then, one fair eve, I sat on the deck with a woman from the Carolinas, and the way to solve the cipher come to me. Well, sir.

After I escape this ship I will head straight for the Carolinas. There is a woman there that I would see before I left her again for the sea. She has raven-colored hair, breeding of sorts, a sound dowry, and no high expectations. If I ain't yet killed you, my hearty, and you are in the Carolinas, I would be obliged if you would find my Mary. And if I drift to the Carolinas, after I kill you, I will find my Mary myself.

My Mary has blue eyes as you may recall. Her skin is as white as whalebone. She is thin, she is, and when she shivered on board the ship, a sip of rum stiffened her. Straight and all square my Mary walked, except when she had her that sip of rum.

You spoke most eloquently about my Mary once upon a time, but I take it that you ain't of a mind to hear about her at the moment. As soon as I mentioned Mary to Mullet, he retired, telling me that you had ordered him to take his leave if I spoke her name. Very well, my sir. In that case, I will leaven my account with clues as to how to solve the number code. So, you see, you must read about my Mary.

You have instructed Mullet, and so he told me in between slugs of wash water, that he ain't to read what I write about Mary neither. No doubt you do not want to taint the boy with such a rich tale, but never you mind, as I will edify him all the same.

You must have surmised that each number of the list of numbers denotes a letter in the alphabet, and therefore each number has a precise significance and the letters form a series of words. The means to crack the cipher come to me, as I noted, whilst Mary bustled about in her frock. She wore them layers and layers of fine clothes, and it got me to contemplating their purpose. What use is it to a woman to wear all that fashion? None at all, sir, except to hide what is under it. And what use is it to place all them numbers in a row? None, my hearty, except to hide the import of them. So here is what I conjured the night that Mary and I sat on deck, her being the only woman that ever sent me straight to a bible.

Leave us look at the numbers once more.

1-1-4-4-5-7-9-12-14-14-14-15-18-18-19-19

I assigned a letter to each number. It was as simple a reckoning as a reckoning can be, and no different than counting barley for Peel. I ascribed an "A" to "1", a "D" to "4", an "E" to "5" and so on. The man that wrote these ciphers was no fool, bless his larcenous heart, and so if you assign a letter to each number you still ain't out of the dock. The letters form the following bit of nonsense.

A-A-D-D-E-G-I-L-N-N-N-O-R-R-S-S

You may look for a pattern in the numbers and in the letters, there being four pairs of equal numbers and letters.

Or, you may align the numbers and letters to form words. I made out the word, "Norse," right off and so believed that perhaps the treasure lay at the top of the compass, past the icy waters and floes where the Norsemen once lived. You can look on any configuration of numbers and letters and find what you want to find in it. I seen a "Dale" in there too. I found me a "Sail" and a "Den" and a "Rail," but each and every time the remaining letters formed no words that I could comprehend, until I come to believe that I had erred and that this was not a number code.

As I wrote, I have solved the cipher, and now it is your turn to do so. I give the cipher to you and recommend that you heed it. I play an open hand. But for now, leave us recall my Mary, as it was she as much as the treasure that come between us.

Mary's husband was a highwayman outside of London before he become a gentleman in the Carolinas, growing tobacco and tea. He was a gambler too, and it warn't long after Mary and her highwayman married that she found out that he was a better highwayman than a farmer and a better farmer than a gambler. He warn't inclined to settle his gambling debts, so Mary and her highwayman sailed to the Carolinas.

Mary's highwayman reformed. He laboured on a plantation and gave up thievery. He gave up his gambling too, Mary said. He worked on that plantation for four years. Then he purchased his own land. It was good land too, Mary said, and her highwayman turned a profit from it. Three years later, Mary said, she buried him. A creditor from London come to the Carolinas to settle old debts and foreclosed on them pledges with an axe to the forepeak of Mary's husband. That is what comes from honest work, I say.

Mary is tall, and almost as tall as I was in those days. Do you remember how striking she looked? I know that you remember her sister, Evangeline, for you gave her a gabardine coat, and you ain't the sort to ever forget a gift that you gave a person.

I had a thick red beard in those days, Captain. And thick red hair. Aye, and my hide was burned red by the sun. Young Silver had himself a firm jaw and good teeth. He was lean. He swaggered. I spy him still if I squint at the looking glass. There were no furrows on his brow then. There were no blotches on his face. He walked plumb then, so he done. His shoulders were broad, his back was wide, and his legs were as long and tough as marlines.

I spy young Silver in this looking glass. There he is. Look sharp now. There he is. And there is Mary by his side. There you are too. We were mates then. Aye, there you are too, Captain. But is that Silver there? Or is that figure no more than what comes from a good measure of rum? For I drank a good measure of rum tonight to draw off my fever.

All men feared me in those days. You feared me too. I say you fear me still. I strode the deck like a king. When I walked the deck the men stood aside. All except Bloody Bill and the captain. Bloody Bill never stood aside for any man. The captain never gave way neither as he was the captain. Still, even he feared me, for I spoke to the men like I was already their captain. Black John knew a usurper when he saw one, having been one himself.

Bones told me to mind Mister Smith too. I had no use for Smith, because he warn't only the pimpled son of a preacher, but the collateral of a vicar as well. Mister Smith, in turn, had no use for me because he was the first mate and wanted to be captain upon Black John's demise. I suggested to Bones that we kill them both, the captain and Mister Smith, so to cut to the quick. I could take my rightful place at the helm, and Bones could stand at my side as first mate.

Bones smoothed down his hair, but no matter how much he tried to pat it down, his hair always rose up again. The man was just filled with too much rum. His paw could not keep his hair down, and so it climbed like ivy toward the moon that hung over England. "I would be captain," Bones confessed. "And if I become captain, I would kill you. I would kill you, Silver, before you killed me."

I told Bones that, in my opinion, he warn't fit to be captain because he was always bilged with rum, whereupon Bones replied that he only drank rum when he was sober. And so, thereupon, I reminded Bones that he warn't never sober.

"That is a puzzle then," he declared, then pronounced me less fit than him to be captain, on account that my mind had been clouded of late. "You are taken with her, ain't you?" he asked. He bent forward as he spoke, and as he did so I thought that I heard the yarn in his trousers call for mercy.

"As if I would have me a heart. As if I would," I told him. "I only have eyes for one woman, and she would give me splinters."

The barque on which Mary sailed was laden with molasses, tobacco, and tea and was headed for England before we altered its course. Mary was on her way to England to plead for the life of her brother, who was in Newgate Prison for horse thieving. Is it any wonder that I took to Mary, who had a highwayman for a husband and a horse thief for a brother? What countess could surpass those attributes?

The schooner not only gave up its molasses, tobacco, and tea, it gave up its crew too. We murdered them. We let the passengers live so that we could ransom them. Bloody Bill heaved no less than seven men overboard. Bones took away the first mate's sword. That was a sight, for after Bones took the sword, he held the man up by his hair and slit his throat. I, so I recall, strangled the captain. Every man proved his mettle that day, except the captain and Pew. The captain directed the battle from a perch outside his cabin. And Pew collected the watches from the corpses.

Bones told poor Edward, as you recall, to drop the corpses overboard. And poor Edward did. I call him poor Edward because he trembled the rest of that night. Do you recall how he trembled, Captain? The ladies and the children cried, and Bloody Bill hooted himself to sleep. It was Spring Tides and Summer for Bill, it was, as he was never happier than after a murder. Bones drank more Madeira. The captain gaped at his charts. My hearties went about their duties. And Silver watched the waves wash the bodies under the sea.

The next morning, Bones and Charles Trundle took several swigs from Bones's flask and dressed in the fine clothes that they found on the barque. Whitman played a shanty. Whitman played so sprightly that Bones hoisted Trundle and carried him on his shoulders fore and aft and fore again. Then Bones tossed fair Trundle to Morgan, who tossed him to Shiling, who tossed him to Pining, who tossed him to Smith, who dropped fair Trundle on fair Trundle's head.

You knew these men as well as I, and I only mention their names because they sailed with us, but they are of no importance. Forget them all except Billy Bones. They did not have the same stuffing as you and me. Do not bother to recollect their names or faces or virtues or vices. Forget them, I say. They were all cods of one class or another, and I reminded you of their names only to give you leave to now forget them. Aye, forget them. If I knew the surnames of the cods that I consumed over the years, I might be inclined to distinguish them too. It is a matter of accuracy.

The women covered their eyes. Except for Mary. She looked straight at us.

"Would you give me the honour?" I asked her.

"I am not in the mood for dancing at the moment," she replied.

"He is a crack fiddler," I told her.

"They are murderers," one of the ladies said.

"Mary," another of the ladies counseled her, "you should not speak with him."

"There is no harm in speaking," Mary replied without hesitation.

All the ladies turned their backs to my Mary.

"Those poor men. I prayed for them," Mary said.

"Not me," I said. "I do not spew prayers. Not me. Praying never got me anything. Not a hot meal. Not a warm coat. I do not spew prayers."

Do you recall those natives that we spied in the Pacific? They danced about their cauldron and hammered at their drums whilst the steam rose all about them. They shouted and sang, and all of them were happy except for them that they were cooking in their pot. They were all praying. The men stoking the fire and throwing wood on the flames were praying. They shouted and lifted their heads to the heavens. The women who joined the men in their dance were praying. They threw themselves down on the ground, jumped up, looked in the pot and gave thanks by holding their arms to the sky. And I suppose that them that were in the pot were praying too. They were all good prayers. I have no doubt about that. But, some cooked and some got cooked, and I believe it likely that some of them that were doing the cooking got cooked at the next feast. Therefore and therewise I do not spew prayers. And, as I have written, the churchfolks in Bristol never did much on my account except toss their prayers at me one by one.

Moreover, I bid you to recall spindly-legged Ben Gunn, whose name I drafted some sheaves back, and who has an unfortunate habit of turning up at odd times. You may consider this a diversion from the tale of the treasure, but it ain't so, nor am I off course on the telling of my history. You will see that it is so by and by.

Bones was drunk and left Ben Gunn on one of the islands, but Bones was never able to recall which island. Bones and Ben rafted to shore to go hunting. Well, Ben hunted, and Bones drank. Bones returned at night with Ben's boar whilst Ben closed his eyes and slept. Bones thought that the boar was Ben. They both did have them spindly legs and so looked the same to Bones. We never found Ben or his spindly legs again. Ben toted a bible around with him. He even took it on the hunt with him so that it would bring him favour. Edward, in contrast, always kept his Bible inside his shirt or jacket or hid it under his rump at night. He secreted it all about the ship during the day, no different than Tom or me done with our reserves in Bristol. I had already written the ciphers on parchment. If I wrote them once, I wrote them by the hundreds, using them as wicks to light my candles so that no one would read them, ever in hope that the embers that drafted upwards might reveal resolutions before they snuffed. Moreover, I had memorized the ciphers, and so believed that I had no need to hold Edward's Bible in my hands. How could I forget the clues that I had read over and over?

That bible did Ben no good. The boar was delicious. I imagine that Ben pranced up and down that island with his bible until some beast ate him. I should have liked the chance to introduce him to Solomon. Aye, Solomon. I spoke his name before but ain't introduced him proper. I will, so I will, my hearty. That would be a sight. Ben would flounce around with his bible and quote scripture, and Solomon would heave his oaths at Ben. They would be as content with each other as an old cottager and his mistress.

The lady that had counseled Mary not to speak to me, heathen that I am, said to me, "For your soul. That is why you pray, sir."

"I am glad not to have one," I answered. "For if I did, I would have starved to death by now. I would be as stiff as a plank."

"Then you are damned," she said indignantly.

"I was never anything but damned," I replied. I patted her hand. She removed it instantly, as if she had been poked with a branding iron. "Do you speak for all the ladies?" I asked her, and she replied that she spoke for the ladies that were respectable.

"You may speak to me then," Mary said right off.

"No harm ever come from a brisk jig," I told Mary, offering her my hand. "The bransles cause the detriments. Those and minuets. A man can turn an ankle on skips such as those, but not on a brisk jig. No jig ever harmed anyone."

"I would be obliged if you would bring me water," Mary answered. "And if you could bring a pitcher for the others, I would be obliged as well," Mary said. I would have drowned the hag in the pitcher, and I wondered if Mary had the same notion, as she asked me for the water directly after the hag spoke.

I brought Mary her cup of water and a pitcher for the other women. Mary held the cup to her lips. A rill of water ran down her chin. She dabbed the water with her kerchief.

"Gracious indeed," the hag said. "Such low ways. You and your sister. Lack of breeding. And your husband sold brown tea and black tobacco. Everybody knows it. And for a price too. My Edgar said so." The other ladies waggled their tongues in agreement. I could have drowned her in a beaker. A pitcher was too good for her.

"My husband done the best he could. Farming did not come naturally to him, as you may know," Mary replied without hesitation, as if she had answered the affront many times before.

"We all know it. Whoever did not pay the price that your husband set for his rotten goods paid a different price," the hag said. "They paid with their lives," she said, lofting her head backwards so as she would not have to breathe the same air as my Mary.

"Lies," Evangeline said.

Mary's sister, Evangeline, did not speak much on account that Mary spoke so well for both of them. Evangeline was darker than her sister and some shorter. They both had blue eyes and silky hair. A man could have done worse than Evangeline, but her best attribute was that she was Mary's sister.

Then Mary spoke. "Brown tea and black tobacco are too good for some," she said. "From where we hail, with our low ways and lack of breeding, the hens eat meal and sawdust. If we gave those hens green tea and tobacco, they would get themselves high ways," Mary said. "High ways do not do for hens. Those hens might begin to believe that they were ladies."

"You are low," the hag replied, dropping her voice to stress just how near the bottom of the world Mary belonged.

"When they are no more than just clucking hens," Evangeline said. Aye, that Evangeline did have her some good qualities. She had her some spunk too, my hearty, though my Mary had more.

"Hens indeed," the hag answered. "I feel faint," the hag went on. "I feel faint. Fan me, Matilda," she told one of the other women. "Fan me before I faint dead away. Water."

"There is no more water," Matilda told her.

Mary whispered, "More water please." I done exactly as she bade me. Smith was treating with the ladies when I returned.

"Give me that cup," Smith told me. "Here," he offered the hag.

"Not from your hands, sir," she said. "Matilda, if you please." Matilda held the cup, and the hag swigged the water as if it was the last cup of water in the world and she the only person on it.

"The woman will drink us into dry docks," Smith said. "More water, Silver," he commanded me. I brought the hag another cup. "I will serve it to her now," Smith said. The hag looked at Smith and fainted. Smith threw the water on the hag, who woke, looked at Smith, and fainted again. "Leave her be then," Smith said. "I ain't as bad as all that," he said, running his paw over his face.

"She is rather proud," Mary told Smith.

"No one will harm you," I told Mary.

"Nor my sister," she said, taking Evangeline's hand.

"Nor her," I said.

"We are proper sorts," Smith said. "Silver here is the most proper sort among us proper sorts. Ain't that right, Mister Silver? And that is on account of his pedigree. Ain't that so, Mister Silver?"

"Just like there are hens," I told Mary, "there are roosters. And just like hens cluck, roosters strut. Ain't that so, Mister Smith?" I asked.

"Get you to your work, Mister Silver. The wheel needs more polishing. Now," he said, departing without a word of farewell to the ladies or me.

"You will protect us?" Mary asked. I answered that I would be pleased to provide her my service. The hag, who revived as soon as Smith left, inquired as to who would protect the ladies from me. "This man will defend you," Mary told her. "I believe him." Mary put her hand on my shoulder and patted it as if I was a stray dog. That took me aback. Our kind ain't used to the gentle touch on the shoulder.

The hag glared at Mary and me. "Now I am certain of my fate," she said.

I come to Mary that eventide well after the last dog watch. All of the ladies were asleep, with the exception of Mary, her sister, and the hag. Mary put her finger to her lips. She bade me to follow her and led me straight off to the lanterns. The hag, forsaking her duties as sentinel, looked up but turned away after Evangeline cut her a look. The waves were particularly choppy and no one was sleeping near that part of the deck, lest the waves wash over them and disturb their slumbers. It warn't a quiet night on account of the breaking of the waves, and that was fine with Mary and me, as we did not hear the hisses and rasps of the hearties on deck, but only the sound of the sea. Mary gasped when the sea sprayed us and I told her that the sea was merely bidding her a good evening, whereupon the sea sprayed us again, but this time Mary remained still. She refused to offer the sea any further encouragement, and the sea, recognizing an unyielding will, capitulated for the moment.

I was used to the nights at sea, but Mary warn't, and so I asked her if she was cold. She replied that she liked a little dampness in her bones. She would have made a stout hearty, she would, what with her affinity for the cold and her estimable character, if I could have cured her of her womanly garments.

Then, to my bafflement, Mary produced three farthings and a watch from under her corset. Her corset was well-rigged and so it took her a few moments to turn out the hoard that she had hidden there. I was impressed. I recognized the watch at once as belonging to Pew. She swung it back and forth, then put it back in her corset. She showed me the farthings, and I rubbed them between my fingers and gave them back to her. "Well?" she asked. "Enterprising," I told her. I could think of no greater compliment to give her. She had slipped her hand into my hearties' pockets and stolen from the best thieves on the waters. "Enterprising," I told her again. She beamed and returned the coins to the bursary beneath her dress.

She asked me if I would indeed protect her. The wind, which was clearly in concert with her, blowed the backstay of her dress off kilter, and I caught a glimpse of her white shoulder. I agreed.

Mary sat back against the rail. I crossed my arms. She crossed her arms. I moved next to her. We did not speak. This was a challenge. She uncrossed my arms and I done the same to her, and she let loose a laugh from deep inside her that was different from the laugh of any woman that I had ever heard. It was a cavernous laugh, straight out of the bottom of her bursary, but with the timbre of tiny bells at the end of it. It was like a man's laugh, except for those bells, and I wondered if she had swallowed her highwayman whole. Aye, but there was no way that she would have let anyone, dead or alive, into her bursary.

I was used to the women in port. They were all industry. They undressed themselves and me, and quickly, and accommodated me as swiftly as they could whilst they watched the pendulum.

The sea's respite ended, and the waves washed over us. I put my arm around her waist. She pushed it away. Mary warn't at all like the women in port.

Tom and I heard a good many sermons about Delilah and Jezebel. They were some of the favourite subjects of the Bristol preachers, and they condemned Delilah and Jezebel, but I always thought that if Delilah and Jezebel were truly dreadful, the preachers would not have spent so much time mulling over them. The preachers must have found some comfort in those women.

I could write fathoms about the parts of a ship, but Peel never taught me the words for a woman's accoutrements, and I never saw any reason to learn them as they were flung off so fast. There was something like a clevis pin that held Mary to her mounts. She pulled it out, the mounts dropped to her waist, and I was able to see most of her fine figure, though she was still covered in various-coloured finery.

I waited for her to unfasten the other parts of her assemblage, and imagined that it might take her some time to disengage all of the buttons and hitches that held her together, and so I pulled off my boots and stockings. I recalled the sermons once more. Adam and Eve were ashamed by their natural state, so the preachers said, however if they were ashamed, then they must not have looked as fine as Mary and me near the lantherns.

I was preparing to slack off my buckle when she held up her hand and engaged me in conversation for the longest time.

She spoke about her plantation and the need of a man to mind it, and I told her of my exploits at sea. She said that she grew corn and other crops on the plantation, but took the greatest interest in the corn. Some stalks grew high as high could be, she told me, and other stalks stayed stumps. The stalks stood side by side, were watered the same, and got the same sun. She said that she would stand in the fields and watch the corn, and she never detected any difference in their care or conditions that would account for their divergence. She told me that it seemed to her to be a matter of will. Some stalks wanted to grow straight up to the sky, and other stalks preferred the dirt. I told her that I warn't a farmer but that I expected that they were all cut down in the end. And, I told her that there was no use in coming to a philosophy about corn on that account.

It was then, as I said, that I got me the notion of petticoats and ciphers both hiding what lay beneath them.

We looked into the waters, and the fish that followed the ship fascinated her. They were jumping that night, and she could not take her eyes off them. I asked her, after a time, why she thought some fish jumped higher than other fish. She said that she presumed that it was just like the corn, a matter of will, and I told her that it was possible, as no fish in its proper mind wants to be eaten by another fish. I told her that I had regarded the matter and determined that some fish are born stronger than others, whereupon she reasoned that both strength and will determined their fate. She said that it was no use in coming to a philosophy about fish as the best of them end up in the skillet.

She spun one of the farthings that she had stolen, all the while talking about her life in the Carolinas, the cotton and the corn, the servants and the ease of it all. Her voice had a sugary air, and soon enough she had me on her porch sipping tea with her. Then she laughed, and I heard the highwayman. I grabbed the coin. She did not protest. She had expected me to take it.

She solicited once more, in the most melodious tone, my promise to keep her and her sister safe. I gave the farthing back to her, but she pressed it into my hand and held it there. I took her wrist. Mary took the coin out of my hand and traced a line on my hand with her finger. I loosened my grip on her wrist. She held my hand in front of my face, and I watched the impression that the coin had left on my palm vanish. I dropped her wrist. She closed my fingers, ran her hand over them, then opened them. The coin was there. And, my hearty, it shined.

She hitched up her dress and told me to keep the farthing. I heard the highwayman again. I forced the farthing into her palm. Her eyes grew wide and I apprehended that I must have hurt her. I opened her hand and threw the coin over the rail, and I ain't never committed such a heinous act before or since, however I meant to show her that coin or no coin and shine or no shine, there are some things in this world that are just beyond reach. I poked my finger into the hollow of her hand and told her that she held a promise. She had nothing to fear from me. She laughed, and this time I only heard the bells. We had come to a draw.

I perplexed her only once that evening, and that was when I told her that her figure was as fine as a ship's bow. I explained that I meant her the greatest compliment. She told me that I warn't fit for society, and explained that she meant her statement to be a compliment too. When we had concluded our compliments, Mary told me more about her life. She had been born poor, just like me, and had forced her way into favourable circumstances. She waved her hand and said it was all parlor tricks, but, winking, said that it did not hurt to have a good ship's bow.

We were so engaged, treating with each other and jesting with each other, and for some time, when the men began to stir. I walked Mary back to the other women. They were all asleep, and even Evangeline, except for the hag. Not long after that, the captain called for me.

Smith was in the sea rat's cabin. He put his hand on my shoulder and declared straight off that the captain had a service that he wished us to perform. They, the both of them, smiled. I could have sailed a sixteen-cannon man-of-war through those smiles. They were good and pleased with themselves, the dastards.

I, per usual, told the captain that I was ready to perform whatever service he required. Aye, but when he told me the service that he wished me to perform, I felt the rime in my spine.

The tug of the beard. The squint. "You will take two of our bonds," the sea rat told me.

"Mary and Evangeline, sir," Smith said, slipping his hand off my shoulder. He must have felt the ice rising through me.

Black John wanted a ransom, so he said, and he wanted it to be a handsome one, so he said. And, he added, that he could think of no man more suitable to be at my side when I collected that ransom, than Mister Smith.

Any other man on board, mayhap with the exception of Pew, was more suitable than Smith. Smith was good for slipping a word to the captain now and again, and that, so far as I know it, was his only accomplishment. He warn't much good at anything else. We had men that were good with saw blades and sabers. They could slice a man in thrice before the man blinked. We had men with aptitudes for the dagger. They could strike a man square between the eyes from fifty paces. Some men were profound with a garrote and others that could wring a man's neck like it was a bird's gullet. We had all manner of men that could lay a man to his eternal rest, and by whatever means that struck their fancy, and all of those men were better men than Henry Clive Smith.

I knew why Black John wanted Smith to accompany me. Smith was to kill me. Bones told me as such, and warned me to keep Smith poleward of me. I told Bones that I intended to come back alive and not as a carcass, and that must have comforted Bones, for he took a long swig in my honour and promised to take two more swigs upon my return.

A man that can feed a crew is a popular man, and I always cooked a fair meal for the crew, I did. So too, I always gave a spare morsel of meat and a sound skimmer of soup to anyone that asked for more food. The men never forgot my kindness when I gave up the carving knife. I cured them of their ailments too with my bandages and brews. Aye, and I told the men tales too. Proper sea yarns. I gave them battles and blood. I told them the tales that I had heard from the seamen who sojourned in Peel's tavern. They all took to my tales, and even you, though you may deny it. My hearties always called for a tale after their sup. Even Bloody Bill, I suppose, favoured my tales, because he leaned forward when I told them, though I expect that he had a difficult time hearing me from the taffrail.

The other men seconded Bones's warning and my own conjecture. They told me that Smith would try to kill me as soon as I put the toe of my boot in the Carolinas. Then, after he killed me, so they said, Smith would return to the ship and say that I come to my doom at the end of Carolina twine. That was the plan.

The next morning, whilst I was polishing my dagger, Smith asked to have words with me.

"Always at the ready," he said, eyeing my dagger.

"I would not want my dagger to stick on a Caroliner's ribs," I told him.

"There is no chance of that, Silver. If you stick a man with your dagger, that man is dead. Fall that man will, and before you can pull your dagger out of him. Silver, the captain means to give you the wheel when we return. I thought that I would tell you. Out of gratitude," he said.

"When I return," so I said.

"When we return. With the ransom," Smith replied. Mayhap I could have sailed a fleet rather than a man-of-war through those teeth.

"And how will the captain show you his gratitude, Smith? It ain't right that the captain should only bestow his gratitude on me. I would that you get some of that gratitude. A good measure of it. At least as much as me. You would deserve it. You should receive it. And, as you are accompanying me, I guarantee you my own gratitude as well. I pledge it, and so you may count on it."

"A saber. I saw it," he said. "It is as fine a saber as any man would ever need. That is what the captain promised me. Upon my safe return," he added.

"I look forward then to our return," I told him. I put my hand on his shoulder. "Our safe return. And the captain's gratitude." Whereupon, we attended the ladies, after I threw in, "I only wish that I had as fine of a saber to give you."

The ladies, except for Mary and Evangeline, drew closer to each other when we advanced. Smith stroked Evangeline's hair.

"He will not harm us," Mary told her sister. "I trust," Mary said, looking at me.

"They will murder us all," the hag said. "They will. As soon as they get the ransom, they will murder every one of us." She commenced to throw her head back again so not to breathe the foul air, but before she could complete her show of disapproval, Smith told her to shut her gullet. The hag gasped and nearly fainted dead away again, which would have been fine with me.

There was no fanfare when Smith and I set off for the Carolinas. We dressed for the parley with the Caroliners in our finest attire. Smith sported a green jacket and a yellow cravat. He looked like a right gent from Threadneedle Street. And Silver? He sported his best clothes too. He looked like a beggar, he did. Silver's jacket was torn. The only attribute that Silver's jacket had in common with Smith's jacket was that they were, by circumstance, both green.

"Come back," the captain told Smith. "With Mister Silver and coin," he appended. Then the captain caressed his beard, turned to me, and said, "A pair of queens is all a man needs in his hand to win at whist, and you have you such a pair, Mister Silver. A fine-looking pair." Pew rubbed his chin. "I would drink to the both of you," the captain said, "upon your safe return." He stroked his beard once more.

The men bade me to bring back silver, but Bones advanced a request for mash whisky, if I happened to spy a jug. Bones had his priorities.

Smith took the oars. When we were a good spit away from the ship, Smith told me to raise the fingle sail. "Whisky," Bones called after us. "Remember, whisky." The men hailed after us and wished us good luck and fair tides. Even Bloody Bill tramped to the bow, though he did not call after us. I noticed that Pew tipped his hat to the captain. That is how Henry Clive Smith, Evangeline, Mary, and I set off for the Carolinas, my murder, and Bones's jug of mash, if I could find it.

Smith said, "You will drop the sail at three leagues."

"At noon," I replied. "There is no chance of anyone spying it."

"I will give the order," he insisted. Then, "Mind you the wind, Silver," he cautioned me.

"The wind is shifting," so I told him. I commenced to hum, and Smith importuned me to stop, and so I done for a time until I said, "I would sing you a song, Mister Smith."

"I am in no mood for a song, Silver," he said, checking the wind by whistling into it, and telling me that the wind had not changed at all.

Smith had no feel for the sea. "But plumb this song is, and good for a cold day such as this day is. Cold, Mister Smith. Cold this day is," I told him. "This song will warm you though." I caught Mary looking at me out of her weather eye. "Look at this lady," I said, tipping my head toward Evangeline. "She is shivering down to her davit. I would give you my jacket," I told Evangeline, and so I did, and Evangeline was grateful and thanked me, even though I only gave her the jacket to suit Mary.

"Now you are cold," Mary said, and I told her that I was never cold, which was true enough, and Smith told me to mind the sail, barking, "Luff."

"Aye," I answered. "Luff it is." I asked if Mary was cold, but she was cast from the same oakum as me, and declined my offer to give her Mister Smith's jacket. Not that Mister Smith would have readily parted with it. I would have given him no choice in the matter if Mary had deemed his jacket worthy of her shoulders.

Mary put her arm around her sister, and Smith barked, "Luff" again, and I could not help but notice that Mister Smith's hands gripped the oars. I asked him if he would like me to relieve him of them and take a turn with the sail, and he declined that offer too, though he pitched a sneer at me on account that I was some persistent in talking whilst he was ferrying me to my murder.

I did not want to disquiet the ladies, though I doubted that I could disquiet Mary, and so I once more offered to sing to Mister Smith. I told him that it was a bawdy song, but he paid me no mind. I told the ladies that they could batten their ears, and Evangeline did, but Mary would hear my song and have her sister hear it too, and so pulled her sister's hands back and waited for my recital with all anticipation. She smiled, as I recall.

"Belay it. Turn hard to," Smith bade me, giving me a stare like anchor ice.

"Come to quid now I do, Mister Smith," I said.

"All your songs end with a quid. Fitting for a beggar." If Smith had told me those words on the ship, I would have cut him into deuces. A man needs to protect his reputation on board a ship. I would have told him that all my songs end in pound notes before I cut him.

"I was no more and no less such a grandee," I told him. "At one time, Mister Smith. At one time."

"A beggar, ladies. A beggar still. Sing, Silver," he told me. "Sing then. I may give you a copper," Smith said. It brings a certain calm to a man when he knows that another man hates him so. He knows where he stands with the other man, and so there is no need for artifice but only daggers. But, a man's murder is a special occasion, and so I sang a song to Smith befitting the occasion.

My song began with a ditty about a poor sailor and his wife and brood. The poor sailor was, of course, Mister Smith, and the wife and brood belonged to him as well.

Smith's ears perked up as if I had pulled a rope and hoisted his family up the mast. He had five sons and a gaggle of daughters. Aye, it was a plumb song. It perturbed Smith to no end.

Smith gripped those oars and his knuckles, so I recall, went white. It don't do for a man to gybe back once he has set his course, and so I continued my song. I tossed in, just so Smith would not present arms on my behalf, that none of the men could afford better on Black John's sea wages. That calmed him some, as I was singing the truth, and so he did not take it personally that his family was starving to death.

Mister Smith's daughters had no dowries, and such as Mister Smith, with his gaggle of daughters, would need stiff dowries to attract eligible suitors, as he warn't precisely what landlubbers considered an upstanding citizen. And I sang all this to Mister Smith, whilst his hand gripped them oars. I thought it a most seemly song. Timely too.

I trilled about how beholden we were to Black John for all that we had received from him. And, how we could not just count what he gave us in pounds and farthings. Nor even in coppers. Smith's hands loosened on the oars, and so he was either readying to shoot me or hear the rest of my refrain.

I lofted up my next verse in the most consoling tone I could muster, like a man in a church choir that Tom and I had heard many times as we plied our trade in the street outside the church. He sang with a quietude that softened the consequence of eternal damnation for everyone in that church. And so I sang for Mister Smith.

"No one but us will know the true amount of the ransom down to the farthing. We will take our share, and it will be a good share," so I sang. Smith took his eyes off the sail. He looked at me, then at the sail, then back to me. "We divide the remainder when we return, and will take another share then, we will," I sang. And then, my hearty, I set my face dead calm like those carved heads on board the ship that were all patience and virtue and lack of understanding. And so I imagined that man's face in the choir become too, after he finished his solo, whilst Tom and I quaked outside in the icy air waiting for some of that warmth to waft our way.

"Still the beggar boy," Smith said. "Reef," he said. He would not look at me. He was contemplating his preferences. He had to choose between murder and fortune. Smith warn't, on the whole, imaginative, as an imaginative man could have calculated how to carry out a murder and take the fortune too. I had already done so.

"That is my song, Mister Smith," I said, dropping my hands to my sides as if there was no other matter in the world to consider.

"Back," Smith said.

"Think about your wife and sons. Your daughters," I hummed.

"Reef."

"The captain would never know."

"Enough of this tattle."

"It is only thievery, Mister Smith. And we are masters at that," I told him.

I knew that he was in the same anchorage as me when he said, "Steal from the captain no less." I told him that I could not name me a better man. Smith inquired about the amount of our take, and I told him no more than enough. And so Smith, innocent murderer that he was, asked me how much was enough. I gave him a distinct answer. I told him that the take would be more than Black John would give him for my murder.

Mary turned her head into the wind to watch me. Some of us have more larceny in us than others, and such as you and me, and Mary too, have good holdings in that currency. She seemed mightily pleased, as she slapped her sister on her thigh.

Smith, dishonest to the core and with his own holdings in larceny, replied that he warn't going to murder me. "Hard to," he said.

I pressed on. "Aren't those your orders, Mister Smith?"

"Hard to, I said."

I asked him, and Mary may have fluttered her eyes at me when I made my inquiry, when he planned to shoot me. I was naturally curious, I told him, as it was to be my murder. I opined that he might want to blast me before we reached land. I offered that it might also be worthwhile for him to discharge his pistol into me now, so that he could dispose of my body by tipping me over the side of the yawl. There were benefits, so I explained, to killing me before we got the ransom. But, and to the contrary, there were also benefits, I told him, to killing me after we had taken the ransom. I mentioned the ladies, and Evangeline screamed some, and so Mary had to calm her, and I advised Smith, in case I had not been clear on the matter, that I had an abiding interest in the matter. Evangeline screamed again, and Mary, in the kindest manner, clouted her sister on her knee, and so Evangeline sputtered and stopped. I importuned Smith to spare the ladies. Mary took a sniff from her snuffbox.

"I follow my orders," Smith replied. Now here, I had just sung a song, and a pretty one to Smith. I had just offered him riches, and I had also counseled him on the various manners in which he might kill me, and he replied without any heed to any of it. I do not begrudge him his insipidness. That is, of course, why I am here, and Mister Smith ain't among us no more.

His main failing, and he had many failings, was that he was loyal. He might as well have been a tailor's apprentice. I told him so, and he took it as an insult, even though I was only speaking the truth. There is a puzzle, as whenever I have lied I have come to advantage, and, generally, whenever I have spoken the truth I have been disadvantaged. I make no claim to the finer points of discretion, and that may have played a part in Mister

Smith's rejoinder as well, and that is because Smith answered me by point-ing his pistol at my chest.

"But the ransom," Mary told Smith. She was better practiced than me in discretion.

Smith replied calmly, as if he was describing the way that the light played upon the breakers, turning them from white at their tops to the deepest and darkest blue at their fathoms, that his orders were to kill us all as soon as we come to shore. Thereupon, Evangeline shrieked yet again, and it is a rather ordinary statement to make when a man has a pistol pointed at you. Mary rebuked her sister still again, by tugging ever so gen-tly at her long tresses that had, by now through the wind and the rocking of the yawl on the waves, come undone.

"If I would be you," I told Smith, and I folded my arms to show that I had neither the means nor the method to take his pistol from him, "I would take the ransom. Leave my marly corpse in the Carolinas. They will surely hang me, and you will get the ransom. It weighs up fairly well for you." I assured him that Black John would do no different, and declared that I was a dead man whether he put a shot in me or whether the Caroliners put a rope around my neck. That seemed to give him some comfort. "But spare these ladies," I said. "On account that there ain't no profit in killing them. Take the ransom. Profit is profit, Mister Smith," I told him. "Kill me, but take the blunt first." I would have said the same to me if I had the oars, and he had the sail, but my words confused him all the same. Honesty is a profitless business.

"It is rather simple, Mister Smith," Mary threw in by way of assis-tance. "You bring us to shore, and safe, mind you. You take the ransom, and there will be a ransom no matter what you heard or what your captain told you. We are ladies of means, sir," Mary told Smith. "Leave this fel-low with my countrymen. We will hang him." She crossed her arms, just like she did the night before when we were together. Those were fine words, and I could not have said them better myself.

"Well spoken," I told her.

"You are too kind," she replied. She took her sister by her waist, and it was meant to be a comfort to Evangeline, but Evangeline nearly keeled over the side.

There ain't no proceeds that come from conjecture. I am a pirate, a blaggard, and not a planter or any other form of landlubber. My life is the sea, and I pledged my nub, such as it is, to the sea. I ain't the sort to tie himself into an eye splice. Still, Mary had a way about her. I like to think that she turned her horse thief over to his creditors for the inheritance of his plantation. There ain't no call for a sword or a pistol if you can wield words with the same effect, and Mary was some accomplished with words.

Nevertheless, it seemed to me that Smith was puzzled, and even after Mary and I had elucidated matters for him, and so I bade him to speak the plan back to me.

"I take the ransom," he said.

"At the first opportunity," Mary assisted him. She did not mean to offend Smith's honour, and was only trying to be helpful, and so she went on, "Pardon me, sir. My sister and I are the intended victims and, therefore, we do have a say in the matter." Then, "Go on. Proceed," she told him. "You take the ransom," she reminded Smith.

Smith was perplexed and needed more assistance. Mary might have told Evangeline to jig into Smith's lap, if Evangeline warn't quaking and readying herself for another scream. Smith was in need of inspiration. Mary and I took turns clarifying the plan, which was truly a simple one, and Smith aimed his pistol back and forth at whichever one of us was speaking at the moment. He was distracted and not minding the oars or the sail or our heading, as he tried to understand the plan, and it took us so long to work it out for him that even Evangeline, in time, sighed.

Smith finally agreed that my song was plumb, after I pledged to him for the fifth time that he would be rich, and that the captain would not kill him so long as he brought him the ransom. I chimed, just for lather, that the men would shout his name and carry him on their shoulders. He asked me if Bloody Bill might lift him on his shoulders too, and I told him that it was certainly possible if Bill got the notion to do it.

"Those Caroliners will butcher us before we say good morn to them," I told Smith, and on account that he was rather simple, I went over the plan with him one more time. "At least this way I have a chance to escape. Why Mary here might even aid me. Put away that pistol, Mister Smith," I told him. Smith done as I bade him. "Always wait for the chorus, Mister Smith," I told him.

Mary put her hand in the water, lifted a piece of driftwood from it and showed it to her sister, and then she settled back like she was at her leisure instead of on her way to ruination. She dipped her hand in the water and let the waves curl over and around it, and closed her eyes for a good while.

"Aye, now lower the sail," Smith commanded me, taking control again. "There is the coast."

"I spy it too now. So you said, and so there it is, Mister Smith," I told him. I lowered the sail. "I would relieve you of those oars now, Mister Smith. If it suits you that is," I told him.

"So you may," he answered, and I took the oars from Henry Clive Smith.

One more matter, and I know it is so on account that I asked him, but Mister Smith did not know him any number codes. Still, I had come to a conclusion about certain of them ciphers during our voyage, and I will tell it forthwith after a taste of rum.

CHAPTER VII.

RANSOM AND HENRY SMITH

ow that I have taken my dram of rum, and prior to declaring my conclusion about certain ciphers, I have traced the head-piece once again.

What fiends these two gentlemen can be when pressed to reveal what is inside their bundle of sticks. Leave us place ourselves in the portrayal. The more that I pull on my half of the strand, the more that you pull on your half. You tug and I tug and you cease and I cease, but no matter the action the treasure is always between us.

And so it was with my destiny. I went from one land to the next in search of the prize, following each knot in that strand of rope, until I believed that I might roll scuppers until eternity.

One eventide, just after Edward went about his duties, I took the Bible from where he had secured it in his cabin. He had written "Evangeline" on a scrap of parchment that fell from the book when I opened it. The ink was still damp and had blotted one of the pages of his Bible.

I put the scrap of parchment back in the Bible, and just as I put the scrap back in the Bible, a light come through his port window and cast a shadow over the first page of the Bible. A most faint drawing appeared.

It was the first cipher wheel.

The cleverness astounded me. A person could look on that page in sunlight and moonlight and see no trace of the wheel.

The wheel had been drawn with a substance that only revealed the drawing in dim light and dampness. We were off Malabar, and it may be that the first page was damp from the weather or Edward's piece of parchment, but there was the wheel. I turned the page but a whit, and the drawing disappeared once more.

Had Edward seen it?

The page smelled like vinegar. A cook knows his fare, and the wheel had been written with red cabbage water. Such writing would only appear in the damp and in a pallid light. The wheel was almost colourless but I could make out a bare hue, most resembling brown. The letters of the alphabet were inscribed round the wheel's rim.

I heard a bustle outside Edward's cabin and replaced the book. And who was outside Edward's cabin but Pew, wearing a grin. I touched the handle of my dagger, and Pew darted topside.

The cipher wheel had to be the key to a code, but which code? I did not yet know that this wheel had a sister, a wheel more substantial than one written with red cabbage water.

Now I had me my rum, and it is time to return to the Carolinas, as a lady is waiting.

So there we were, Mister Smith, Mary, Evangeline, and me, on our way to some sort of ruination, and recall that Smith was pulling them oars and I was singing that song, and Mary was trawling her hand in the water and Evangeline was sighing as she had concluded her screaming.

I smelled the Carolinas before I saw it. The stench of that country filled my nostrils. I would tell you that the country smelled like old fish, but that would be a libel on cod. They say that there are smells that can raise the dead, but this was a smell that could send a corpse back into the clay. Aye, the perished would leap back into the loam to flee this stench. When I remarked on the affliction, Mary said, "We are in the low country."

"We are in perdition," I replied. "Tom told me it would smell like this."

"No," Evangeline said. "It is just Albemarle County."

The sun had just come up, and we were in near darkness on the beach. Smith tripped. I could have killed him then, but I decided to wait. We needed to hide the yawl, so I kept my sword at my side. Mister Smith's prospects of living much longer, in any case, warn't good. A plan is a plan, after all.

I was, nevertheless, taken with the urge to strike Smith's countenance from the earth. I always endeavour, whenever possible, to be as practical as possible about a man's murder. A hasty murder is like a hasty meal. It does not satisfy the body or the spirit. I decided to be practical about

Smith's murder and let him amble this earth a bit more, and just then I saw a fisherman searching for his hat. The wind had blown the hat to where I was standing. I picked it up and presented myself to the fisherman, whereupon Smith cut the fisherman's throat.

Smith put his hand over Evangeline's mouth before she could scream. I knew that Mary warn't the sort of woman to scream at the sight of a man missing his hat or his head, so I did not clap my hand over her mouth. We hid the man and the yawl behind the liberal bramble on the beach.

Our kind looks at the sky some regularly to ascertain the weather, and there ain't any tufts or curls or strands or swells of clouds that we ain't seen. We have counted the orbs whilst stretched out on deck before our slumbers and seen them flicker and fall. We have watched the moon tamp and trim its sails as it follows the sun across the sky. Aye, the sun. We have surveyed everything that it can effect, from the brightest blaze to the bleakest shadow. We know which way the wind will blow before the gulls can flap their wings. We have seen the portent of a storm from a thousand leagues away. We know the signs. We have felt the calm of the next day before it was upon us. We are sailors. We watch the sky.

I looked up that morn and seen a sun that warn't bright and warn't dark, as if it was sullen on account that I had ascertained the answer to the riddle. It was red and rust and pale and, lastly, black. Leave it to Silver to put out the sun itself. It was an eclipse, so it was, and that darkened sun looked just like a wheel to me. The frogs leaped back and forth, not sure if they should go about their business or hide. The sand fleas walked in circles. The birds conferred and come to no conclusion. They hopped from branch to branch, fluttered their wings, but never took flight.

We caught our feet in the roots of the brambles, as we had difficulty seeing them, and stepped in pools of tar on the beach. The wind blowed tobacco leaves our way that stuck to our boots. A dogfish flopped in the rushes until Mary set it free by carrying it to the edge of the water. The tide washed it back.

The light finally fell upon the ground in streaks and shafts. The wind blowed freely then too, and carried the sounds of the town to us. We stepped past a maple and heard the clattering of a wagon. We hunched in the rushes and spied horned cattle, followed by sows, followed by a boy with a long switch urging them on by smacking their flanks. The animals stopped to chew on the tufts of grass that sprung up out of the sand, and bite their fellow creatures, before going on their way.

We entered a marsh of stunted greenery. We crossed the marsh and come to a wild thicket. We were stealthy, my hearty, and so were sighted only by a pig who was rooting in sacks of corn, oats, wheat, and fodder. It warn't interested in our kind though, as we warn't choice provender.

Then an infantry of fishermen come our way. We repaired a good distance from the dock, behind the thicket, and had a good view of the fishermen and the town from there. From time to time the fishermen threw fish bones to the stray cats that lazed near the docks. The cats ran through the town with those bones between their teeth. I saw savages too. They walked the streets clothed in beaver and leather and smoked pipes. "Those are Algonquians," Mary told me.

Algonquians are a kind of kin to your monarch. So I say, for Algonquians hold their heads very high when they walk and do no labour except to blow smoke out their pipes. They must be his kin.

I saw rice, cotton, tobacco, peanuts, and potatoes from my hiding place. Perdition was plentiful. I saw enough horses to fit an army. Pigs and cows strolled through the streets. Their breeders greeted the butchers and the butchers greeted the pigs and cows, and such is the history of hasty pudding.

There was more in that town than sand and savages and fish and cats and horses and the makings of hasty pudding. There were ships, and they guarded the town day and night from such as our breed.

We kept to the trees and brambles until we come upon the road into town. There, we saw three men digging coal. They were standing in a pit and black from the coal dust. One of the men hoisted himself out of the pit to rest in the shade of a nearby willow. Their labour was so hard that they wiped their brows at every chance. Then and there I thanked the devil for making me a scoundrel. When I go into the depths, as I surely shall, Old Nick will sentence me to honest work if he means to spite me. He will send me to a coal pit in the Carolinas, he will.

I was parched from the voyage, and Smith said that he was some thirsty too and pointed to the bottle of spirits that one of the men was drinking, and so it was an easy matter to decide to quench our thirst.

I snuffed the man with the bottle. He was leaning back on his elbows and drawing a good swig from the bottle when I crawled behind him and cut his throat. He fell back onto my chest, and I grabbed the bottle from him before he could spill one drop. Smith took the bottle from me. He drew a swig. Smith and I were on those miners before they saw or heard us. We took their purses though there were only a few coins in them. I took a pair of boots. I still have those boots, and I mean to walk into the nethers with them. Never give up good boots, my sir.

Evangeline commenced to sob.

Smith fixed his eyes on Evangeline, and said, "I know how to comfort a lady." Mary told him to keep his promise as a gentleman. Now presuming that Mister Smith had any aspect of the gentleman in him is like presuming that a root hog would look dandy in a waistcoat. Mary threw Smith a bit of flattery to keep him at bay. She knew how to handle the likes of root hogs and Smiths.

I suppose that Smith meant to bow, but he looked ridiculous in the role of a gentleman, as he took her bid and stooped.

Mary advised us to put on the miners' clothes. It was good advice, and we did as she bade us. Mary took my hand and said that she would be honoured to walk with me through the center of town, and Smith, who heretofore been trusting of Mary, become chary. He accused Mary of intending to turn us over to the residents of Albemarle County as soon as we entered town. She had hatched a plot, he said, and would scream at the first opportunity. Mary put her hands on her hips and stared him down. Evangeline followed suit. I settled in for the sport and sat on a rock.

"I could scream now," Mary told Smith. "I am known in some parts for my articulation. I can be so loud, if I am of a mind to, that a man might want to clap his hands over his ears. Sometimes, I can just be completely out of control, and I catch myself talking louder and louder." She raised her voice whilst she said them words. "I may not be able to help myself, try as I might," she said, pitching up her voice again.

Smith told Mary that, in that case, he would be obliged to murder her. Mary had expected Smith's answer. She had drawn him to it as surely as if she had that root hog on a leash. "And the men here would kill you," Mary told him. "The men in these parts have, for the mostly, straw bones," she said. "But even men with straw bones can shoot straight. At pirates," she added. "And by the by, we do not cotton to trials in these parts. The justice is rather simple. If the shot kills you, then you are deemed guilty. If the shot does not kill you, then you are deemed innocent. That is, until the second shot kills you. It has been my experience that few men are found truly and unreservedly innocent."

After some pondering, Smith pronounced Mary's plan a good one. We put on the miners' clothes and rubbed coal dust over our faces and arms.

I sneezed and when I breached I drew in the bounty of the low country. I do not know how anything can grow there. The grass should wilt the day that it comes up from the ground on account of the stench. The stench is more putrid than a dozen sullied Englishmen, sitting astride a dozen sodden horses, commanding a dozen dirty Irishmen, pulling a dozen muddy mules. And in a fair wind, I say.

Mary chose that instant to remark on the wealth in the Carolinas.

"That must be the price of prosperity. If this is the stink of the rich, I am glad that I was born into deprivation," I told her.

"You can be rich here. A man can make a fortune. If he works hard enough," she said. She raised her dress as she walked so that it would not become soiled on the ground. The saints on the Linda Maria might have opened their eyes some wider if they had seen those legs, white as they were and leading to the profoundest damnation.

"And work is the worst deprivation of all, it is," I told Mary, after reeling in another whiff of Albemarle County. "That must be what gives this country its foul smell. This is the smell of honest work, this is."

"You forget that you are a miner now," she told me.

"A pasquinade. But a blot on my reputation just the same."

"I would improve you," she said. "Give me your dagger." She held out her hand.

"I would not. A dagger would not improve my disposition," I told her.

"Wonders. I will do wonders to you with it," she said whilst we walked. She held out her hand. "I will not harm you," Mary said. "You have my word. You gave me your word. I give you my word. It is as good as yours. Isn't your own word good?" she asked. Well, it warn't good at all, but I gave her the dagger anyway, as she had put forth her hand for it, and I warn't inclined to disappoint her, and as Smith had nominated me a damned sot to give it to her. I never could resist good blasphemy.

Mary turned my dagger round in her palm and pricked her finger with the point of it. She seemed pleased. She looked over the edge of the dagger and ran it down her dress. Then she cut a tiny piece of Evangeline's dress with it so to test the blade. "First, your hair." She walked toward Smith.

"It looks like a donkey's tail," Evangeline said, holding her hand over her mouth.

"Our men, such as they are," Mary said, "do not wear their hair like that here. And certainly not miners. They keep it fairly close to the bone.

As close to the bone as possible. Without spoiling their permanent dispositions," she added, "and letting those dispositions run into the countryside."

"You ain't going to barber me," Smith told Mary.

"Not I," she replied. "My sister." Mary gave her sister the dagger and suggested that Smith not move for the sake of his disposition and the charming countryside.

You would have been proud of your Evangeline. She pulled Smith's mane and harvested his hair in a single hack. Smith felt his scalp. It was still there, and his shoulders gave way some out of relief.

"And now you," Mary said to me, placing her hand on my arm. Evangeline gave her sister the dagger. "As if you were a lamb," Mary said to me as she lifted that dagger over my head.

There ain't much more faith that a man can put in a woman than to let her take a blade to his head. She slowly withdrew her hand from my neck after she barbered me, and then wiped it on Smith's breeches. He was too struck to speak, and so that was another good deed that Mary did that day. Then she gave me the dagger. I still have it. It is the dagger that I will use to shear you, my lamb.

WE COME UPON the town presently.

Mary put her hand in mine and told Evangeline to take Smith's hand. Evangeline warn't eager to take his hand, and so Mary put her sister's hand in Smith's paw and advised her sister that Smith did not have fleas. Smith, though, might have had fleas. He scratched fairly often.

It was our good fortune that the people we encountered warn't inclined to talk to us. Mary told Smith to let her or Evangeline speak if we were hailed. She was afraid that we would give ourselves away by our manner of speech. She also told us not to stamp our feet when we walked. "Small steps," she said. "You are not tramping a deck." So we minced our steps, and Mary pronounced us nearly respectable, and, under other circumstances, I might have taken that declamation as an insult.

We come to High Street. "You have been as fine a pair of consorts as any woman from these parts could expect. Perhaps, even, an improvement. Go in there now," Mary said, pointing to the cathedral. "It should be empty. I will see the families and bring the ransom to you directly."

"Aye, and I was born this same morn," Smith said.

"And an ugly suckling you are," I told him.

"Let us keep up appearances," Mary told me. She kissed my cheek. "I will not let any man hang you," she told me. Smith parsed her words and asked if women did the hanging in Albermarle County. Mary said that she would be tempted to accept the offer, in his sake, if it was presented to her. Evangeline readily concurred. Mary assured him that we would be free to leave with the ransom. She reminded me of my duty to release the captives on the Linda Maria, and said that we would all be free as the air soon enough. Smith, thereupon, choked, on account that he breathed in too much of that free air.

Mary looked me up and over the way that I look on a ship that I am about to sack, and told me that she would be pleased if I would remain in the Carolinas. Sometimes at night on board the ship, as you know, we put a pair of candles next to each other for illumination. Much depends on the wind, but the flames from those candles either join and grow taller or extinguish each other. There is no way to tell what will happen before the tinder is struck and the wind blows, and no one knows on any given night whether the flames will grow or give way. We have even placed wagers on it. "I am a sailing man," I told her. "To my marly soul."

"And I, sir," she answered, "am a lady."

"I would know more about you," so I said to her.

"Then sir," she replied, "I would be no lady."

Smith snickered some, and I was mightily tempted to gut him, especially when he said, and in the presence of them ladies, "There ain't no mystery to her, Silver. Not a bit."

Mary and Evangeline walked away without another word, but I saw Evangeline put her arm around her sister. Mary marched straight ahead. Mary's horse thief must have lived a charmed life, so long as it lasted.

Smith and I climbed the steps of the cathedral. The inside of the cathedral was dark but for a few wicks that lit our way. The wooden boards groaned with each step that we took. There was no other sound.

We had time to ponder whilst we waited for Mary to return, and so I mentioned that young Edward told me that men are worse than demons, as no other beast would let another starve to death. No other beast would make another thieve for his bread, then hang him for it, so Edward said, and so I told Smith. Smith did not consider the philosophy. He dismissed it by saying that Edward and I were two bumps on the same twig. Smith was suspicious of anyone with whom I kept good company. I told him that Edward did not speak much, and so when he spoke Smith should not take his words lightly, as Edward likely gave his words an abundance of thought before he let them out.

Eventually, the door opened and a man entered with Mary and Evangeline. Mary introduced the man as Andrew. There is a landlubber name for you. Andrew. I wager that he was pimply too. He had a large head and a thin frame, much like a cabbage atop a stalk. There was, it seemed to me, little risk of harm from a man with such little brawn to him. I was wrong. They grow the men differently in the Carolinas. I have never trusted a man with a cabbage for a head since that day.

Andrew was breathing hard on account that the bag that he carried was so heavy.

Smith ordered Andrew to open the bag, and I asked Mary if there were steeds at the ready. "Horses and a carriage," Mary said proudly. "All at your command. Anything that you require. Anything that you might find of necessity, John Silver. Anything at all. Within reason," she added, "Long John Silver."

Gold is gold. Even the flames from the candles on board the ship sputter as the night draws to an end. There is no permanence to flame. Gold lasts forever. I looked in the bag. There was more than gold in that bag, my hearty. There was silver. There were jewels. Coins. There were precious stones of every colour. There was a dagger in the bag with red stones on its handle. I fancied that dagger as soon as I saw it. There were pewter forks and knives. There were plates. Fine ones, they were. There were pistols in the bag, and one of the pistols was so small that it fit into the palm of my hand.

"There is enough here for thirty men," I said. "We are rich, Mister Smith. Now, ain't this better than a sword and a wheel?" Mary was smiling. She was a cutpurse at heart. I would venture that some of the coins slipped out of that bag before she reached us. I would venture that as heavy as that bag was when it was presented to us, it weighed more before it found its way into our hands. "Larceny is its own reward," I told him. "Though," I went on, "it benefits from confirmation in the form of bounty such as this."

Smith, anxious to leave, ordered Mary and Evangeline into the carriage and told Andrew to hold the reins. He gave me the honour of riding in the carriage with the ladies. He sat next to Andrew and the bag. "All speed now," Smith commanded Andrew. It is a wonder that the cabbage head atop that stalk harkened to Smith's words even then, but there is no telling what thoughts might be inside a man with a cabbage for a head. "When we are out of town you will whip that horse," Smith ordered Andrew, "until he curses the father that sired him." When we were well past the town and nigh the yawl, Smith told Andrew to pull the reins. Then Smith told us to get out of the carriage.

This part of the land was so green as to make a salt sickly. There was green all around us. The leaves were as large as whale fins. The brambles and trees grew in every direction and had roots that could snare a man's foot.

Did I ever remark on Smith's mouth? His lips were thin, and most of his teeth were rotted out. He was no different than much of the men in that regard. Not many of us had our teeth. I had all of mine, dog that I am, and you had all of yours. Billy Bones had a full mouth, as the spirits that he imbibed preserved his teeth and the rest of him too. Black John had only a few teeth left. Bloody Bill had all of his teeth, but he was a beast and was sustained as nature intended him. The rest of the men, Smith included, had little left by way of teeth. I recalled his smile on board the Linda Maria when he stood next to Black John.

"Open the bag," Smith commanded me. His lips coiled into his maw when he spoke, and I saw no tongue inside that maw, not then or ever, though he must have had one. All that I ever saw inside Smith was darkness, and when he opened his mouth to speak it looked like nothing so much as a shallow grave. I realized that Smith had not looked into the bag. He had not seen the riches, as he was so anxious to leave. Now that we were safely away, he wanted to see the treasure. "No," he said. "Do not open the bag now. Bring me the bag," he told Evangeline. "We will open it together." He looked into the woods. "We will untie the lace that fastens the bounty." Evangeline, per habit, screamed. Smith did not try to comfort her. "You cut a bit too close to my scalp when you barbered me. I ain't complaining," he said, "as what is done is done." Mary took her sister's arm and pierced Smith with her gaze. I would have feared for Mister Smith if I had not intended to kill him myself. Smith told me to guard Andrew and Mary and walked toward Evangeline.

I intended to rid the world of Henry Clive Smith. My plan had been for Smith to take our share of the ransom in jewels and keep them in his pockets. I would take the rest of the ransom on board the ship. Our hearties would gather round the bag. They would shout, they would. Aye, and then Black John would come forward. He would cut the bag open. The men would shout again whilst the coins, jewels, gold, silver, and other riches spilled out. And then I would ask, "But where is Mister Smith?"

"Aye, where?" the men would ask, turning about to look for their mate. None of them would suspect me of the dodge. They were all as dumb as deadeyes.

"But hold here," I would say. "There is more ransom than this. I recall that there was more. There was a green jewel that I saw. A yellow one too. It looked like a tiger's eye. I saw it in the bag and now it ain't here. That is curious. You best ask Mister Smith," I would tell the captain. "See if Mister Smith recalls those jewels. The others too." The captain would call for Smith, and I would aver that he might have gone below to rest after our journey, and the captain would send Pew to rouse him. Pew might even offer that Smith went below rather quickly.

Then, Pew or whomever Black John sent to fetch Smith, would find Smith and the jewels. A man would drag Smith topside. Smith would protest, fiercely, that he had not cheated the captain and the crew, but he would stop his protest when the men put their daggers to his neck. Smith would say that the jewels were mine and that I had tricked him.

I would ask, "Then why would I tell the captain that the jewels were missing?"

And one of the men would say, "There is the jewel that Silver described. A tiger's eye. Just like a tiger's eye, and so Silver said."

The men would tie Smith to the mast. Smith would swear oaths. He would disparage my name and curse it above all others. No matter. Each man would stick a dagger into Henry Clive Smith, and I would stick my dagger into him too, and lastly. Then Bloody Bill would throw Smith's body into the sea.

That was my plan. Leave it to a fool such as Henry Clive Smith, and a landlubber with a cabbage for a head like Andrew, to scuttle a good plan.

Smith, on his way to Evangeline, leaned over the bag and took a coin from it. He pressed it into Evangeline's palm and asked if she liked the coin. Mary pulled her sister back until she and her sister were at my side. Smith laughed. Andrew, who stood near the carriage, piled abuses on Smith of a class that I had not heard before. They must have been strictly Carolina curses.

"There is a dagger," I told Mary quietly. "With red stones. Tell your sister to take it from the bag. She only has to cut him. He will not expect it. I will finish him and send him to oblivion. They may not expect him there at this time of day or from this clime, but I doubt that they are scrupulous in their standards for membership. She must do it quickly though."

It has been years since I said those words to Mary, but I think about them often. There are days when there is no blow in the sails. A man has time to ponder his life on those days. There ain't much else for a man to reckon on those days but his own account. My hands are not suitable for hacking wheat or corn or cotton. They are suitable for lashing ropes and hoisting sails and turning wheels. Aye, and they are more than suitable for murdering men. I would speak about another matter as well and speak about it now before the fever takes me again. I feel it coming on me.

I have thought about you and I, my hearty, and what come between us. And of all things, a last secret. We were mates. It is a pity, I say, that the wood of this ship is more loyal than your flesh, but so it seems. Turn the ship, sir.

I say that if a dog is born brown, then that dog is a brown dog. Forever. You are a brown dog, my hearty, and so am I. We cannot change into white pups now. Neither of us. Turn the ship.

I tell you this too. Men made this world. No one else. If men made this world then there is no true justice except the justice that men make. Why hang a man in such a world? This is a world of men and not of magistrates. Turn the ship. Heave to. What is this matter between us? The world would be no better without me. It chills me to think of Silver swinging by the twine. This is our world. There is no justice. Not for you, not for me and not for any man, there ain't. So I say, and curse Solomon for telling you different. One man lays aside another man in the muck. Turn the ship. Shorten the mainsail and heave to. Give the order.

The fever has me.

I will not sleep.

Turn the ship. Turn the ship.

I will never sleep.

CURSE THIS FEVER.

I drank brandy after my slumber. Brandy ain't a cure for the fever, but it does take the bite away.

I am not crossing through a word of what I wrote when the fever was on me. Not a word. Those were good ravings. I am skilled in all matters, I am, and even in ravings.

What was that I meant to write about "1303"?

It was the preeminent clue, the sextant linking all the ciphers together. Each cipher was stitched to the others and formed the strand that we pulled. But to where, sir?

Edward knew the meaning behind "1303," and he knew it from the first and did not tell me. And I know why the King murdered his family and the reason his father trusted him, only him, with the book of riddles.

I am revealing too much too soon.

This fever.

Aye, but I was writing about that day in the Carolinas. About my Mary and your Evangeline and about Smith who lies in a grave.

Mary told her sister to grab the dagger, but before Evangeline could grab it Andrew lunged at Smith.

"No!" Mary screamed, but her scream come too late. Smith had drawn his sword. Andrew, a landlubber to the last, rushed straight into the sword.

Whereupon I drew my own sword.

Smith gave me a grin as wide and as long as he could sway up from that cavern of a mouth. "You will die now, beggar boy," he said, whilst I peered into that shallow grave behind his coiled lips. Mayhap I was wrong. I might, now that I think on it, have spied several good teeth in there, like guardians standing watch over his worthless guts.

I entreated Mary to run whilst she had the chance, and she grabbed me by my sleeve. Smith sauntered toward me. "Aye, run," he told Mary. She would not leave go of me. The air hung on me, my feet sank into the earth, and I felt the roots close about me. So this was how Old Nick would claim me. I would not die on his terms. I pushed Mary away. She fell.

I turned to the tide and faced Smith. We fought but a brief time before I put my sword in Smith. Smith warn't good with a sword, and so I told you. He crawled about the ground like a maggot for a time before he finally died. He even crawled up to Evangeline. "Help me," he pleaded with her. "Twaddle," I said to him. Then he rolled over on his back. Smith died so close to Andrew that their blood ran together.

"Mary," I said.

"Madness," she replied before I could speak another word. She turned and walked away without looking at me. She left me standing over the bodies, and the bag full up with ransom. I would have liked to have spouted some words in my favour to Mary, but I did not speak. I am a rover. This is my life. I am a rover and am suited for nothing else.

I cut the horses loose from the carriage but held the reins of the speckled gray. I hoisted the bag onto the horse and mounted him. Then I whipped that horse. No one followed me to the yawl. I rowed until it was dark, then I hoisted the sail. I arrived at the ship near dusk.

I spied Bones on the deck. "Lower the ladder, Bones!" I shouted. "Lower it for a man bringing you more riches than a sod like you ever saw!" Aye, I called to him like I did not have a care in the world and could fly to the mast.

But it was the lurking Pew who dropped the ladder and scurried down it to take the bag. Pew pounded his fists on the captain's door until the captain come out in his cutty sark, and Pew shoved the bag into the captain's hands. "Riches!" Pew shouted, pulling at his hairless chin. Then my hearties commenced a clamour that could be heard for seven leagues in a thunderstorm.

The captain, befuddled, asked, "Where is Mister Smith?" My plan had turned in on itself, like Smith's own coiled lips. It was true that Smith was below, as I had planned to tell the captain, but he had gone well below the double bottom.

I had no rejoinder but to tell the captain that Smith was dead at the hands of the Caroliner who gave us the ransom. Black John was too stunned to pull at his beard, and so Pew reached for it on his behalf, and Black John kicked Pew. Then I spiffed the captain a tale. I gave Andrew some bulk, more bulk than he deserved. I let him keep his cabbage of a head but afforded him a girth that I likened to the trunk of a tree. And, I told the captain, he needed that girth just to keep that great cabbage of a head from falling onto the ground. I gave Andrew height and bid him up as high as a nail in the gallant mast.

I told Black John that Mary and Evangeline ran off and that I was chased by a mob of fishermen, miners, and pipe-smoking Algonquians, and that I barely made it to the yawl. I cautioned the captain that they would all be after us, and that I expected them to set out for us presently if they had not done so already. I could always spiff a tale. Black John would let the captives go free and make haste to depart, as he was, I knew, thoroughly a coward, even when it come to Caroliners. But, there are times when a pistol misfires, and even when I hold the stock.

Pew slipped in between us. "Pew would see the riches," he said.

The captain opened the bag and this time he nearly pulled his beard off his face. I caught a good glimpse of him then. His skin was gray and lined with scars. He looked old and weary to me. I thought of the man that had grabbed my hand in Peel's tavern. This was a different man, it was. Each man peered into the bag and gave me a nod.

"We are all of us rich," I told the men, "and the captain is the richest among us," so I said. "With more than any man," and the captain looked at me whilst I spoke, "and even more than the marly king of England."

The captain nodded at me, not out of fondness, as he had meant for Smith to murder me, but out of satisfaction that I had ensconced him just below your King. Pew nodded as well. He told the men to make haste, as there would be a party after us, and Bones searched my pocket for a bottle of mash whilst the men cheered our good fortune. Nobody gave a thought to Smith. I told the men to put the ladies and their litters into the yawl, so we could, as the captain ordered, be off and away with our bounty.

"Serve those morsels to the sharks," the sea rat ordered the men. "You heard Silver. He said that they are after us. You heard him."

"But women and children," Bones cut in. Those were the only words that he could manage. He, for once, failed to take a swig.

"Throw them in, Bill," the captain told Bloody Bill. The sea rat's eyes gleamed. Murder suited him. "Every one of them. To the last of them."

"Pew says that it would be best to be quick about it," Pew trilled. "The quicker the better. To the last of them Caroliners. Every one of them." There was no need for Pew to second the captain's command, for Bill had already begun to follow the order.

"They ain't much fit for sea," Black John told me. "And where would I get me another yawl that is so sound, Silver? It brought you back to us safely. A piece of luck this yawl is." He knew that I had done him a turn. He would take his time to murder his confounded creature.

Edward and I were the only hearties that did not draw a sword or dagger or throw any of the Caroliners into the sea.

I strolled about the deck that evening and every man thanked me except for Bloody Bill. The men toasted and hailed me. It was late when I saw young Edward leaning against the mast holding a bottle of rum.

"Are you holding up the yard?" I asked him, clouting him on his back. I tried to put him in good spirits, and told him, "I am quite close to re-solving the riddle of the kine and the corn, boy," so I lied to him.

He did not reply.

CHAPTER VIII.
TO LONDONTOWN

as Mullet been to Londontown? What would the lad do there? He would wander its streets and get lost and robbed in the bargain. That might be an accomplishment for the lad.

You must take him in hand. We all of us captains have a duty to those that stand before the mast. Now I ain't saying that Mullet has any ability of any kind, but a captain must try to bring out whatever there is that is inside a lad. At the very worst, he would get himself murdered, and that might be a benefit to the populace.

I forgot myself. He cannot be murdered yet, as he must play his part in this history. I have more ciphers to give him, and there is much more to recount. Why, we ain't even been to Spain yet.

So leave me write them ciphers once more, and add one more for the same price. I present them to you again purely as torment, as I have solved them all while you have solved but a few of them.

We got us that headpiece.

There are the numbers, "1303."
We got us the declamation.

I have hidden 41 meters from the foundation 6 wooden boxes overlaid in ivory, and all empty, and one remarkable treasure covered in nothing but sackcloth not more than 2 meters deep nor more than 87 meters wide.

Now that declamation may represent kine and corn, not to mention a Pharaoh in the bargain.

> 41:2 And, behold, there came up out of the river seven well favoured kine and fatfleshed; and they fed in a meadow.
> 41:3 And, behold, seven other kine came up after them out of the river, ill favoured and leanfleshed; and stood by the other kine upon the brink of the river.
> 41:4 And the ill favoured and leanfleshed kine did eat up the seven well favoured and fat kine. So Pharaoh awoke.
> 41:5 And he slept and dreamed the second time; and, behold, seven ears of corn came up upon one stalk, rank and good.
> 41:6 And, behold, seven thin ears and blasted with the east wind sprung up after them.
> 41:7 And the seven thin ears devoured the seven rank and full ears. And Pharaoh awoke, and, behold, it was a dream.

Then we got us the number code carved into a tombstone.

1-1-4-4-5-7-9-12-14-14-14-15-18-18-19-19

There is blood in the Bible, and that was the last cipher that I solved, so you know.

BLOOD

We got us one of the cipher wheels by the grace of the damp and the moonlight, them letters written in red vinegar that had no meaning until I found the second wheel.

And I wrote of one of the ciphers that we found when we turned the two cipher wheels.

And Last Icon.

Aye, and here's the one more, yet another riddle in the black Bible, almost blotted out by Edward's ink. Edward, so I wrote, had entered the name of "Evangeline" on a scrap of parchment. I had most difficulty reading that page as the ink all but blotted out the words concerning a queen by the name of Esther.

> And when inquisition was made of the matter, it was found out; therefore they were both hanged on a tree: and it was written in the book of the chronicles before the king.

So we got us a queen and chronicles that were set before a king and an inquisition. And it all fit trimly. A king and queen would have treasure. The Bible was a chronicle. And what should I make of the "inquisition"? It could only mean Spain. Or so I believed. And what of the phrase, "they were both hanged on a tree"? I did not know its significance, but assumed that additional clues might hang from the tree ripe and ready for my picking.

The verse seemed to be right by poundage and tonnage. Hadn't I planned to go to Spain to recover Don Jorge's riches when I become captain? And so Edward knew, and he had chosen the page and the verse. It could be that he had discovered a clue that he had not told me, or that he was attempting to mislead me. Or, it could be that this clue corresponded with another clue that I had not yet found. It might well be that Edward, smitten near Malabar, had written Evangeline's name and placed it in the book at random. I could not decide. And, mayhap Edward had planned that too.

Lastly, *Audacibus annue coeptis.* The trickster heartened us to look with favour upon a bold beginning.

And now here comes Mullet again like the plague. There is no mistaking the tread.

I have solved it," so Mullet said as he settled against my door. I felt the ship reel from the weight of him. "And Last Icon. I have solved it."

"Your captain told you," I replied.

"He did assist me. He inquired if I saw a 'land' in the words. I did not see Britain or France or any other country as hard as I looked. I asked him how a land could be so small as to fit between letters, and if so wouldn't the people in that land be tinier than mites?"

"You are a pilchard, boy."

"My captain said that an island is a type of land too, and so I stared at *the words until I grew faint. I, just before I fell, almost saw an island floating on the parchment."*

"You keeled?"

"Only for a moment, then I righted myself. The captain told me that he meant the words might spell an island. I crossed through the letters so the phrase now read, 'Island Atcon,' which perplexed me all the more."

"I imagine so. And the captain flogged you for idiocy?"

"He has never raised his hand against me."

"The consequence is apparent."

"He asked me if I seen an animal on the island. I had not seen the island let alone an animal on it, but by and by I did see it. He did not even have to mark it for me. I seen a cat. And then it all fell into place. The phrase is meant to read, 'On Cat Island.' Am I not correct?"

"I would not tell you."

"That is unfair."

"You may be right and you may be wrong. Your captain did not tell you?"

"He laughed."

"I would have laughed too."

"But am I correct?"

"I would not tell you."

"That is most unfair," Mullet said, and he hammered my door with his fist although he did not make much of a sound at all.

⇒•⊂

I fear that Mullet does not have any blood, warm or otherwise, in him. Duty, my hearty. Duty. We must blow life into the lad like we were bellows. We have a profound duty to our lads, sir. I shall raise the lump of a lad and endow him with another answer before we strike Spain, but for now we sojourn in Londontown. The lad really is a cleat, wood through and through, but he is your cleat. You can always, if he don't progress, use him for kindling.

I SLUMBERED. THE fever.

What day is it and what is our heading? The lad does not know. He does not answer me. He has gone. I shouted to him of Calais. How we cut them Frenchmen into tartlets. I must have frightened him away. Or, you called him away. To fetch better poison.

*   *   *

THE SHIP IS turning. This is the Atlantic. Already, the Atlantic. My cabin is damp. The water would be green again.

Where is Bones?

I remember now.

Do not forget that I cured you of all your ailments, and you had heaps of ailments, even the jeebees, but I cured you of that with fish oil and brandy. But all that curing counts for nothing now. Black John had it too but he would not take my cure. Bones gave him rum and tinder powder, which is a good cure for the scabies but not for the jeebees, and the captain's hair fell out. The captain and his hair come asunder, and that served him and his hair right for listening to Bones. Aye, then the captain was willing to let me fix him. I gave him a brew of garlic and lime that was hot enough to boil his insides. I told you to pour the brew down the captain's throat. You enjoyed that deed, you did. The captain keeled over, but he stood on the deck the next day a right seaman.

I cured you. But you would kill me.

I put a poultice of tobacco and salt on your leg that time that you come up with an affliction in the Indies. I always took care of you. But you would have me hanged. And there ain't no cure for the hanging affliction.

I rid you of lice. I burned them off you with a mixture of gunpowder and rum. The lice ran to Bloody Bill and lived a good life on Bill's head.

This damned fever.

I brought you to your first woman.

The fever is taking me once more.

I GOT ALL the provisions that I need here, all I can eat and drink. When I was a boy I warn't particular about what I had for supper. I ate whatever people gave me, and when they did not give me any fare I found my meals in the streets. I wanted to live, and so I ate all that I found and even cursed creatures. Most of the other lads died of starvation. Some died from a fever such as I have now. Some died of cold. Some died of boils. Some died of bites. Some died just for spite.

And I do not blame them.

Spite, sir.

Those fellows and I fought over the same scraps. Rotted fruit was choice, and we fought the hardest for those bits. Any one of us would steal a piece of bread from the hand of another. Blind Tom would give us a morsel of meat now and then. It was Tom who showed us how to gather rainwater in a kerchief. A man need never die of thirst in Bristol so long as he has a kerchief.

We could never find Tom's coppers. He told us that he swallowed them. There was one boy, Virgil, who thought that if he split Tom in two, Tom's coppers would spill out of him. Virgil ran at Tom with a butter knife. I grabbed Virgil's feet. Virgil fell and died from a cracked head a few days later.

Tom was grateful to me after I spared him Virgil and his butter knife, and so from time to time Tom would give me some of his coins. Tom enjoyed my company and my protection from the Virgils of our world. He trusted me too.

Did I slumber again?

Tom told me to doze with my eyes open, and I could have managed it if I was of a mind to watch the crows circling us in the night sky. But I warn't. Some of the lads said that Tom had a treasure in coppers. I searched for his treasure in the cracks of every building in every lane and alley, but I never found it.

THEY WILL NEVER hang me. Not when they know your secret, the last secret.

I am deprived of the night air here in my cabin, but not of the sun nor the moon nor the stars. I have written it all down, sir.

This fever wracks me.

I will not sleep again. You will not kill me in my sleep.

This is my ship. It sails on my sea. My sea, cur. There are all manners of redress and amends. There are acts of Parliament and acts of Relief, so they call them. There are privy counsels. There are courts of Chancery. There are whips. There are pistols. There are swords and sabers. There are all manners of redress and amends. Pick your death.

Aye, this is the Atlantic. No wonder the fever has returned.

Tom wrapped my head in a wet cloth. I was ill. It was the fever then too. Tom took care of his lads.

I SAY THAT the moon come first. The moon come before the stars. The moon come even before the sun, I say. And before that the world was bleak, my hearty. The world was dark. The lions slept next to the lambs because the lions could not see their supper. Men bumped about in their Sunday clothing with nowhere to go and the world was filled with confusion. Women wore long dresses and carried parasols for no good reason so far as they could see. All was bewilderment. The children went hungry. There warn't even a piece of penny candy to pluck. The world was dark, and people could not see right from wrong and, as a consequence, there was no damnation. And without damnation there was no salvation.

The moon brings the tides. Where there are tides there are ships. Where there are ships there are men. Where there are men there are land-lubbers and seamen. Where there are landlubbers and seamen there is good and evil. Where there is good and evil there is damnation and salvation. You may presume that I am not fit to treat on salvation. I am. Only the damned are fit to treat on salvation because only they understand what they have been denied. And they can reckon it to the ha'penny.

Welcome to the church of Silver.

The sun and stars are afterthoughts. Bristol has no sun on most days, and people get along fine without it. You can see the stars on a clear evening, but there ain't many clear evenings in Bristol. I never heard anyone complain. There are those who believe that the sun come first. They are entitled to their opinion, though any heathen seaman will tell you otherwise, and there ain't a good seaman who ain't a heathen of some strain. Aye, the moon come first. And then the seas and then the tides. And then men. And then women. And then the beasts. And then the constables.

I am a heathen. I come into this world as a heathen and I will leave it as such. I only swear to what I can see with my own eyes. I seen the cipher wheel in the faintest of light, but I seen it. That is more than anyone ever saw of salvation, my hearty.

You bolted the shutters of my cabin, but the moonlight still shines here.

When I hear the men scrambling about the deck I know that it is day. When I only hear the moan of the wind and the splash of the waves against the hull, I know that it is night. I am certain of another matter too. My men are loyal to me. They will take back my ship and hang you at high tide, and then I will sleep like a crooked governor on holiday.

I have written about my crimes pecuniary and otherwise, and you know of my other treacheries, but there is more to Silver than you can fathom. I will write, in the profoundest detail, how I become captain of this ship. The contrivances are exceptional. The deliberations are acute. Hold on to your stuffing.

And, be certain to tell Mullet. The murders that follow may inspire him. He may take a mallet to you. We, as I said, owe a duty to our lads.

*   *   *

I WRITE, NOW that the fever is off me, of Londontown. The same Londontown of the Old Bailey and Newgate. The Londontown where you would hang Silver and where we are now headed. Aye, I write of Londontown, the city where I dispatched Black John the sea rat. This is a history that is written in ink but should be scratched in blood. And we know all about blood, don't we now?

The sky is as dark at day as it is at night in Londontown. The chimneys spew out tar and smoke and darken the heavens. It is a city that is as dark as my own heart.

The people in Londontown go round and round like the hands of a clock, round and round, from one street corner to the next, personages and paupers, some bearing finery and some bearing rags. And here they are, and there they are, and they go in and out of shops and in and out of carriages, and all about and round and round in Londontown. And when the day is done they have gone nowhere but Londontown.

Currency stokes the chimneys and the people in Londontown. Everyone wants it. Beggars stand in the mud for it. The highborn, those solid citizens, stroll about the town for it. There are skinny dogs and fat rats in Londontown all scrounging for the same treat. Nothing satisfies an appetite like coin of the realm. The skinny dogs starve and the fat rats feast whilst Old Nick laughs, and they all roam the streets of Londontown together.

Londontown is no place for the weak or the sick or the poor. They die. The coachman does not stop for the lame. They go under the wheel. The penniless huddle together and pick each other's pockets until the wind blows them out like kindling sticks. The thirsty pray for rain or, at least, an understanding aleman. If they get neither, they go thirsty. Tender is required. Nobody is doused without it. That is Londontown.

Five hearties walked into that city one day. Those hearties were Black John, Bloody Bill, Billy Bones, young Edward, and I. Five hearties in all come to Londontown after five years at sea.

Not all of them left it.

Those five years were good years. They were years of profit and plunder in spite of Black John. He was content to lay into the slow and feeble merchant ships. If a ship had more than a brace of cannons, he would not sail within ten leagues of it. He only struck the ships without gunnery. Still, we picked the bones of enough of those ships to raise our means. The captain, of course, had the most coinage among us. The captain was so rich that he used his drafts as stuffing for his mattress. He slept on a mound of money, he did. But he slept poorly. I saw a candle flickering in his cabin on many nights when he, or his shadow, was counting his money.

There ain't much that a man can hide about himself on the Linda Maria. He could not sleep for another reason too. He was thinking about me. He was pondering treacheries. He plotted against me regularly. He detested me as much as I detested him, and did not kill me for only one reason during those five years. No man fought like me. I killed more merchantmen than any other man on the sea rat's crew. He knew it, I knew it, the men knew it, and the dead merchantmen knew it. Only Bloody Bill, as dense but as strapping as ever, stood a chance against me. The captain never matched that creature against me, as Bloody Bill was too valuable to lose. He killed more seafarers than any other man except me. That was the captain's predicament. He could not afford to lose either of us.

And there was more to the captain's predicament.

I still cooked for the men on occasion. I still told them tales. Aye, and I saved their lives from time to time. That bred loyalty.

I grew strong, and the captain grew weak. He stooped and stumbled and knew that he was losing his Linda Maria to me. And so the captain's sleepless nights ended when he said that we would go to Londontown. He had determined that the time was right to kill me. We had both been waiting.

He promised a fine time for "you and your pup," as he called young Edward, with all the blood that was left in him. He gave Bones the task of showing us the taverns and Bill the task of bringing us the ladies, though he did not specify if Bill would bring us them ladies dead or with breath still in them.

I told Edward that same gloaming that he would live longer if he trusted the dagger in his scabbard rather than Black John or any other man. And Edward answered me most peculiarly. He said that he trusted me, and as it was near evening and the men were tottering off to sleep, he tapped on the Bible and we read them ciphers again, as we done near every night. But those were different tides then. I might have, if I was so inclined to trust any man, trusted him too.

The next morning the captain called for his medicines, his goldenseal and ginger, as soon as we launched the yawl. He looked about the yawl and ordered Pew to bring them. "Rum is the best cure for whatever ails you," Bones said, as he set his backside against the wood, to the agony of the timber. Pew tossed the captain's powders into the yawl. Bill sat silent as ever, no different than the plankings, looking up at his perch on the ship as if he had lost something dear to him. Aye, but the captain had brought him on our journey for a purpose. Malevolence was Bill's stock-in-trade. The sea rat meant to settle all scores on this journey. He needed his sleep.

The captain swallowed his roots and washed them down with water from his flask. "Digestion," the captain pronounced. "There is little in this world that is more important." Bones patted down his hair and it blowed up again. "Oars," the captain ordered Edward. "Avast." We rowed until the wind caught the sail. Then the captain took the tiller. Bill kept the watch. I manned the sail, Bones drank his rum, and Edward trusted in me. And so we proceeded, my hearty, until we come to the cove where we stowed the yawl.

Bones set about to scout for a horse, and Bill lumbered behind him. Whilst they went about that business, the captain regaled Edward and me with tales of his murderous deeds. I thought it a near pity to kill the old man after I heard his stout tales. Black John could talk about murder and mayhem like some men can talk about maids and moonlight. Black John, the sea rat, had bilgewater for blood and sea air for a soul. He was a scoundrel's scoundrel. But I would be captain. And, I hated the blaggard.

When my hearties returned, Bill said, "No steeds." Near loquacious was Bill. Bones added, much to his consternation, that they had found no taverns nearby. So we walked until we come to a farm. Bill took the horses, and we rode them until we were nigh the city. Then we left our steeds and settled into an inn named the Old Marie, which was at the end of a street and across a lane and around a corner from your dear Parliament.

Old Marie, a toothless crone, showed us to a table.

The crone brought us mutton, savoury pie, ale and more ale. We ate and drank until our bellies were ready to split. I was willing to die on the spot where I sat, not for King or country, but for savoury pie.

Old Marie showed us to our rooms, but Bones grabbed a bottle of rye and arranged himself on the floor behind the bar. We all went directly to sleep, and it had been so long since I had been on land that it was a time before I settled into the straw. Nevertheless, I was the first to wake the next morn. Then Edward and the captain woke. Edward and I come down the stairs fully dressed, as we had risen early so to course through the Bible that he had stowed on his person. The captain come down the stairs in his nightgown, nightcap, and slippers. And then Bill woke. He come down the stairs as stark as desolation. The captain walked Bill up the stairs, as a man would with any beast, and bade him to dress, and as long as the captain had expended the labour of climbing the stairs, he decided to dress for the day as well. We found Bones in the same place where he laid himself to rest the night before. The empty bottles were arranged around his body like idols, whilst he snored away behind the bar.

Old Marie, who looked even more a fright than the day before, promenaded down the stairs. "There is a thirst for you," she said, staring at Bones. The captain presented her with a fist of guineas that she snatched without delay. "Wait," Old Marie said whilst she scurried up the stairs, plucking her hem up so as not to trip. "I will make myself more presentable. As is proper for so fine an esquire what got him guineas."

We were still waiting for Bill to join us, and he had just finished dressing when Marie bustled up the stairs. They met at the landing, and with visions of guineas dancing in her wig, she wished Bill a good morn. Bill done what was most natural to him and growled. That gave her a fright, and so she backed into the wall as Bill clumped past her and down the stairs. She darted into her room, stealing a glance to make sure that Bill's boots had not caved in any of the steps.

Bill lumbered about the room, sniffing the air for seawater, moving his head back and forth. No doubt the captain wanted Bill in this condition, penned like a boar, so as to be particularly dangerous. Bill opened and closed his jaws, then let go a bellow. He might have meant to yawn. I expect that Bill slept poorly in his cage.

Old Marie peered down from the landing and asked the trouble. The captain reassured her that it was just Bones raving from the rye. "Port wine quiets him, but rye provokes him, and it will be nothing but port for him from now on. If there is any port remaining, madam."

Edward stood over Bones. "There ain't much rye left," Edward put in.

"Well," the captain said. "The lad speaks." Edward looked at me. "He need not put words in your mouth," the captain told Edward, referring to me. "You are a hearty as good as any other and can consider matters for yourself. No need to look at Silver for a reply. Speak. Tell us on what you have been considering."

"A hat with a feather," Edward said, and that was all he said.

It was natural for Edward to think of such a purchase, and he had answered the captain honestly, given Edward's unfortunate breeding.

The captain looked at him strangely. Then he looked at me as if Edward was my creation. It is true that Edward and I had a lark on the ship before we landed in Londontown. I fixed some cordage to Edward, tied it with fids, and stood behind a rotted gangplank and pretended that Edward was a marionette, such as I had seen in the Bristol lanes. We presented a diversion for the men. I cautioned him not to speak but to open and close his mouth when I pulled on the cordage. He danced when I hauled the line tied to his ankles and dangled his arms until I pulled them. Edward spoke volumes that night. He told my tales. The men asked him to tell him the tales again the next night, but Edward maintained that he did not remember a one of them.

The captain must have presumed that Edward would thank him for bringing him to Londontown. Edward was certainly pleased to be there, but he warn't able to proffer the words. That was Edward. He kept mostly to himself except when he was with me. And then we mostly spoke of the ciphers.

"Dry land does not agree with any of us," the captain told him. "Once a man sleeps above the waves he gets little comfort sleeping above the clay." Then Black John told us with two clomps on the pitted pine, "I feel stout. Good and stout. I mean to have me a romp. I mean to have me a frolic. A spree, my hearties. A singular one at that."

"Just so long as we all of us stay above the clay," I told him. I saw no reason to keep my words to myself. I warn't like Edward in that way. I was the same lad that had provoked the sea rat in Peel's inn them years ago. If Peel were with me that day in Londontown, he no doubt would have tallied the bottles on the table and dashed into his galley on some pretense.

"That mouth again," the captain replied. "Insolence as usual. That is Mister Silver for you, men. He has become all insolence. I should have left him a landlubber. A paltry thief. A wastrel of a lad. Hardly even that. A beggar boy."

Black John tried desperately to provoke me. It is important to settle on the site and occasion of a battle, so as not to allow your enemy that advantage. There is always time to murder a man. The pleasure comes from the game of it. Did you ever wonder why I always won at rolling bones? It was my timing, sir. I waited and made the appropriate wager at the appropriate moment. I tallied the odds. I wagered when all was in my favour.

"Bill," I said, "if you kill me, I will not tell you any more tales."

I had concluded that the captain would order Bill to kill me, and hastily, so that he could proceed on his singular spree with a clear conscience. A man has a right, I say, to speak directly to his murderer.

Bill bellowed once more, rolling his head from side to side, looking for his sea.

"What is that then, gents?" the crone shouted down from the landing.

"He asked the best way to Parliament," I answered.

"In a carriage," she said, laughing. "Three turns and a twist and you will be facing Oliver Cromwell himself. Or at least his head, as it is still on a pike."

And warn't that providential of Old Marie given what we learned later?

"This fellow will stay behind," the captain told her. "His name is Silver. And he will pay you for the privilege of your company. He goes by the name of Silver because he has so much of it. If you would be willing to abide him, that is." Old Marie's eyes flamed like embers at the mention of coinage. Black John did not mean just to murder me, but to bankrupt me too. He slammed his fist on the table. Again, I recalled that day when he first come to the Three Goats and the skinflint would not pay me for the coat. He stood to leave, towing his beard behind him.

Bones shrugged his shoulders and followed the captain out the door. He was resigned to one murder or another, the captain or me, by the end of the day. Bill left muddled, unsure about what he had seen and heard, no different than a savage that has set at tea for the first time. Edward left without a word, but patting the pocket of his coat where his Bible lay close to his heart.

There are ladies who are in their shifts. They live in the country until they exhaust their maintenance. Then they sell their hollands and linens. They are too proud to go into service or teach themselves a trade. They search for squires and sea captains. They scan the horizon as sharply as the best starbolin. They wait, these ladies, for an honourable proposal of marriage from an honourable man. They wait until they exhaust their pride too. Then they find the likes of you and me. We bed them and pay them. They have no need to learn a trade then. The trade learns them soon enough. They never find their squires and sea captains. But they eat. They live. And there is no dishonour in that.

Old Marie was brought low well before she settled down in an inn on the stump side of Parliament. She told me, and so I tell you, what she said when she come down the stairs in a black wig and red dress. That dress hung on her bony frame like a barley sack. Old Marie's cheeks were painted red. She wore white gloves too. And here is the pity of it.

"You look like true quality," I told her whilst she fluttered her eyes. She asked me our trade with all of the modesty she could gather, and I told her that we were merchant seamen, so to speak, and some farthings short of true gentlemen. She chided me for disparaging such an honourable trade, and done her best fluttering again, telling me that she knew our trade by our gait and going on that her late husband was a seaman too.

She took off her gloves. She said that her mister was dead. "Pirates," she said. "Left me a widow at my tender years." I told her that pirates chilled me to my marrow. "I am in narrow circumstances," Old Marie told me. "Some call my tavern an ill house. I have virtue by the ale barrel, sir. But folks, they do talk." She went on, "Just because I offer lodgings." She conjured a tear that ran down her painted cheek. "Folks. They do talk," she said. "And I am a midwife. And have helped those in need. Young ladies. And in an instant," she said. "And I do not ask any questions of the young ladies." I gave her my kerchief. She looked it over. "Silk. A gentleman. I knew it. There is a dim chamber waiting for me in Newgate. And a pallet bed. Industry is all that keeps me here. All that keeps me a lady. That. And no more." She conjured another tear. "I do not mean to place my burdens on you," she sobbed.

I proposed a friendship, and promised her that it would be a generous one. I told her that I had stayed behind because I had a mistress in circumstances. Old Marie closed her mouth. I believe that she was attempting to hold her breath, but she warn't able to conjure a blush as readily as she had conjured tears. She leaned so far frontwards in her chair that I thought that she might tumble out of it. I put five farthings on her table.

"I ain't in my groats so much that I would take money for hearing a man's troubles," she said, staring at my coins. I told her that I wanted to make amends for my wicked life and placed five guineas next to the five farthings. "Five and five will not fix matters," she told me, and I told her that I did not know the proper price for amends in Londontown these days. "It is a matter of keeping your young lady in her accustomed fashion. I know a banker who is trustable. He is better than trustable. He is discreet," she said, grabbing the coins.

I held her hand and asked her to leave at once to remedy the matter. I gave her five more farthings. She waited, and I gave her five more farthings, topped it with another guinea, and told her to take her time about it. She put on her apron and went into the street.

I take satisfaction in reminding you what next transpired. It gives a fresh meaning to malice.

CHAPTER IX.

CAPTAIN SILVER

here are no ends of ways to clip a man. You can kill like a cottager and rend a man with a rake. You can kill like a constable and slay a man with a stick. You can kill like a soldier and slaughter a man with a sword. You can even kill like an Englishman and prejudice a man with a paper, so long as you can raise a pair of witnesses.

A man might murder for vengeance. He might murder for love. He might murder for greed. He might murder for honour, shame, cowardice, or country. A man might murder for pleasure. There is no end of reasons why a man might murder. I had only one reason to kill the sea rat. I would be captain.

Here now is the account of the last of Black John, and I relate it, my hearty, without any huckabuck.

Black John, Edward, Bloody Bill, and Bones returned to the inn near eventide. Young Edward sported a new hat with a blue feather. I would never have acquired a hat with a feather, blue or otherwise, as I was always practical. I preferred pistols.

Black John did not purchase any goods. It pained him too much to spend his farthings on the same goods that he could pinch. Bones brought back a woolen cap. He bought it even after Edward told him that the cap was too small for his head. Bloody Bill broke into a shop window and stole a silver plate. He could have brought the law down on all of us if he had been caught, but nobody was inclined to reprimand Bill.

I recall telling young Edward that Bill's plate shined like Old Nick's throne, and that Bill could not say if the plate was made of silver, pewter, parchment, or dust. Bill only saw the shine. Edward stood in front of the window. He turned his head this way and that and ran his finger across the feather, but could not satisfy himself. I walked closer to him, and as I drew closer, the window darkened and Edward was able to see his reflection.

The captain took Bones's cap and ordered Bones to recount their diversions to me. The captain could not fit the cap to his head either, and so tossed it back to Bones, who persevered in trying to pull it over his skull. Bones related that they had walked about the Cloister and the Strand. Bones's eyes narrowed, and his fat fingers dug into his cap. He told me that they had met some ladies and, by way of illustration, bowed. The cap slipped out from his fingers and fell to the floor. I heard a small rip from his breeches as he stooped. Is it any wonder that Bones took to drink? He was beset on all borders. His hair defied him on one end and his flanks on the other.

We all watched Bones in his struggle with that cap, but the captain, before asking the men to recount their day and so torment me, asked me the whereabouts of Old Marie.

I suppose that I could have told the sea rat the truth, that I had sent her away on a pretense, so that we could go about our murdering in peace, but seeing the odds, largely in the form of Bloody Bill pawing at his plate, I told him that Marie was at her bath. And, in any case, it always pleased me to lie when the truth would suffice. It takes wit to tell a lie, at least a good one. A lie is peach pie. The truth is porridge.

Edward tossed his curls at his reflection, and said, as if it did not matter at all now that he had seen his likeness in the window and attended to it, that he had hired a coachman to take us back to the ship. Edward knew Londontown, he did. He knew the city well on account that he had been chased through it so many times during his days as a cutpurse. He spoke in a clipped manner, as if now that he was back in Londontown, he could resume his life of privilege. It is true that the men beat most of the privilege out of him when he first joined the crew, and that I had a hand in his discipline too, on account that he had to learn our ways, but I was the one that ended the tutelage. Aye, and I gave him my stockings too, as he shivered something terrible during those first days on board, and I did not want him to expire on account of his erudition. He paid me back for the use of my stockings, good lad that he was, and with the interest that I assessed him. And Edward was a worthwhile investment, and I knew so from the start, for the interest grew and grew the more we fathomed the markings in his Bible. He gave up his life of advantage, and I acquired it, and so it all come to even tender so far as I am concerned.

Edward preened some more in the window, and tipped his hat with the blue feather to a gentlewoman that walked by the window. Good fortune suited Edward, even if it paid no mind to Bones. Bones had given up pulling his cap over his head and was now trying to look behind him to appraise the state of his breeches. He turned whilst he spoke, like a hound looking for his tail. "Then we met in Spring Garden," Bones said. "After the Cloister in Smithfield and the Strand. Then," Bones went on, "Edward bade us to go to Covent Garden. He knows the town like I know my rum. There was a sight there. We saw a widow," Bones said. "Comely. And being chased through the streets. It added to her appearance. Most comely."

Edward later confessed that he had, for a moment, considered returning to his manse until he remembered his father's warning. He was much distracted and confessed to me that he, whilst walking about, chanced upon a rotting head on a pike outside Westminster Hall. "Cromwell," Edward said, his hand momentarily touching his curls before falling again to his side. "I have not seen him for some time. He has not changed much since they took his body from the Abbey and cut off his head. He still stares at naught all day and night." Edward was pale, so he was. "It must be onwards of twenty years that his head has been on that pike," so he said. Edward might just as well have told me the date of our visit, 1685, as I knew that as well. Everyone knew the fate of the Lord Protector. Even Old Marie had just mentioned it. Charles II had decreed that Cromwell's body be dug up, his head cut off and placed on that pike, and only on account that Cromwell had murdered the father of Charles II. Cromwell had been rotting away for years. Was there a person in all of Britain that did not know such? Then why had Edward made a point of relating it to me? It warn't like he had high tea with that head.

Even so, Edward was mistaken. His Oliver Cromwell, the great man of Parliament, the man who appointed himself Lord Protector, was staring directly at the graveyard crosswise from him, and in particular at one exceptional grave, that of a queen otherwise known in life as Lady Anne Hyde. And it was luck for me that the man's head warn't parboiled, for so the good people of London done with another head, that of Sir Thomas More's nephew, William Fisher, and for treason so they said. More's head was put on a pike too, although he had the better view as his head topped a stick on London Bridge. And these murderous people consider me a scourge? Aye, but I am about to write of an another assassination. We will come back to Cromwell's rotting head soon enough.

Bill grunted. The London air must have agreed with him. Mayhap he had committed a murder when the captain's back was turned. "Edward told us that she was no widow," Bones said. "He knew her. Said she was a good thief."

Edward was still looking out the window. I looked out the window too, but could see no one there except the gentlewoman trundling along and her maidservant shuffling behind her, carrying her woman's parcels.

"A crowd was after her," Bones said. "They caught her. Near tore her apart. I never knew that landlubbers could be so spirited, but I suppose that a chase and the prospect of a hanging brings out the best in them. Edward said that he warn't never caught." Edward looked at me, briefly, and smiled before returning to the fellow looking back at him in the window.

"Hanging," Bill said, his voice rising. The captain mollified Bill by spinning a coin on the table. Black John handed the coin to Bill, and Bill tried to spin it, but the coin skittered across the room. The captain retrieved the coin and spun it again for Bill.

Edward turned away from the window and took a watch out of his pocket. He was still a nimble lad, and said that he took it from a woman in the crowd, and as he spoke, Bill fixed his gaze on the watch. Edward slowly put it back in his pocket, but it was too late. Bill grabbed for the watch and tore it along with the Bible from Edward's pocket. Black John put out his hand, Bill looked up, Black John whispered to him, and Bill handed him the Bible. The sea rat regarded it for a moment and tossed it back to Edward, never even opening it. Edward stuffed it back in his pocket.

"I have a beggar, a parson, and a drunk," the captain said. "Here is my navy, Bill," he said, spinning the coin. "And let us not forget malice. Let us not forget Mister Silver, Bill." Now Bill looked up at me. I put a coin on the table. Bill stared at my coin. He picked it up and turned it over and over in his mitt. Then Bill set his eyes on the ale inside Bones's tumbler. Bones did not hesitate and brought all of us a mug of ale, serving the first mug to Bill.

I presented a toast to long life, Bones and Edward lifted their mugs, Black John tugged his beard and folded his arms, and Bill, deadened to everything in the world but the coin that he turned over in his hand, tilted his head one way, then the other to better see his fortune. Bones left our company for the cask of rum behind the bar and commenced to sing, and even the captain joined in the song whilst Bill tried to spin the coin. Black John forgot his beard, Edward's Bible, Bones's cap, and Bill's coin, and slapped his knee as he sang. I thought it a good time to murder him.

It gives me profound pleasure to recount Black John's murder, as it was fairly extraordinary.

The captain wiped his chin and stood. He knew that it was time to murder too, and that must have been why he was so jolly. He spoke a word to Bill, and Bill stood too. When it is time to murder it is time to murder, just as when it is time to eat it is time to eat, and so I took my dagger and stuck it into Black John's belly before he could order Bill to slay me. I stuck that dagger into the sea rat again and again until he fell. I believe that he damned me. I am reasonably certain of it. It was most hard to hear him with the blood bubbling in his throat. Bill was perplexed, and so I spun the coin on the table and handed it to him. Bill looked at the captain, then at the coin.

"Silver," Black John gasped.

"Long John Silver," I corrected him.

I took the captain's coin and placed it on the bar. Bill looked at the coin in his hand and then at the coin on the bar, and dropped my coin as if he could not contemplate the possibility of two coins existing in his world. He tramped over to the bar and grabbed the coin. Bill appeared to think for a moment and turned toward the captain. Bones, who stood fast until now, grabbed Bill's hair and pulled Bill's head back. Black John mustered some oath or another. The man did not have the courtesy to die.

Bones struggled with Bill's great head. I twisted my dagger deeper into the sea rat. His head lurched and then listed back again. Bones made a firm suggestion that Edward assist him, but before Edward could present himself before the bar, Bill broke free of Bones's grip. The captain wheezed and, almost in concert with him, Bill snarled and turned round to face Bones. Bones, with what I am certain was the greatest regret, tossed his ale into Bill's face. Bill mashed his fists into his eyes to ease the sting and, then, Edward pulled his dagger.

I called to Edward to stick his dagger in the beast, but Bill's eyes cleared and he set his sights on me. I wrenched my dagger out of Black John. Bill and I stood face-to-face.

The captain clutched his belly and importuned Bill to kill me, or, at least, that is what I presume he gurgled. Bill lifted his foot and began to lope towards me, but Bones caught Bill, slinging the bar rag round his neck. Bill snatched at the rag and dropped his dagger. It was then that Edward skewered Bill.

Bill clinched his chest, and I rushed to the fore and skewered him too. Bill, beast that he was, pulled out our daggers and dropped them. None of us could strike Bill after that because he bolted about the room, running into chairs and tables, senseless with pain and fury. Edward's sword was against the doorpost. Bill grabbed it and run at us, letting loose a bellow that could clabber stone.

Edward and I threw the daggers at Bill, but they sprung off him. Bones threw his blade, and it stuck in the beast.

Bill floundered, but he warn't yet dead. I hurled him against the bar. I was a strapping man, but Bill weighed as heavy as all the seas in all the worlds, he did. It took all of my might to bowl that beast.

The captain, with all the power that he could summon, from a strength that come from sheer hate, gasped, "Kill Silver," as if Bill could hear him. The sea rat bade Bones to dash me. He even rasped to Edward. Black John promised all of his wealth to the first of them that sent me under. If Old Marie had sauntered in just then, he would have promised her the same and thrown in a betrothal as well.

I twisted my dagger deep into Bill's chest. I held my dagger in Bill and looked into his eyes until his eyes grew cold. "Dead now, Bill. Nick's orders. You will be in your sea soon enough. And that sea ain't filled with the froth of waves or the shimmer of coins or lovely little murders. It is an empty sea, Bill. Empty. Like the driest land, Bill. And all they do there all eventide is scatter bones across the land. It is landlubber work, Bill, the scattering of them bones like the planting of seeds in May. And there ain't even a gibbet there for company. There ain't no ship. There ain't no sea. Just the toil of the bones." Bill, as if trying to find his sea for the last time, closed his eyes.

Edward strode about the room swinging and brandishing his fists like they were sabers, shouting oaths at Bill, whilst Bones downed a mug. A dagger in the belly warn't a fit demise for Black John though, it warn't. My captain deserved a quality murder.

I kicked the captain until I near pitched him into Hell, but his heart still beat, and so I told Edward to bring me the captain's herbs. I stuffed those herbs into Black John's mouth. I even pulled his beard to make room for his last remedy. The captain choked on the herbs, but he was determined to spite me as much as I spited him, and would not die. He spat out the herbs.

I told Bones to fetch me the rum, and Bones rejoined that I had given my first order and that we should mark the occasion with a drink. I took a swig, Edward took a swig, and Bones near drained the bottle. I poured the remainder of the rum into the sea rat's maw. I put my ear to the captain's mouth. "I ain't heard you," I scolded Black John. "What say?" I asked him. "More drink, did you say?" I gave my second order, and Bones brought me another bottle of rum. I poured it into the sea rat and bade him long life, but spite is spite, and the captain spewed out the rum again, this time mixed with blood. Bones, appalled at the sight of the wasted rum, declared it a poor choice of a weapon. I told him that the captain must have a taste for rye, and I gave my third order. I commanded Bones to bring me the bottle of rye, which I poured to the last drop into Black John's open mouth. Black John could swallow no more, but managed to let out a moan, which was the last sound that he made before he drowned in rum and rye and his own damned blood.

There was no one else to murder, so we departed Old Marie's tavern. I left Marie a pair of guineas and a parcel of dead pirates. Bones left Marie seven farthings and the coins that I had spun for Bill. Money never meant much to Bones. He only held rum dear. Edward left Marie a farthing, being some tight with his possessions, like most of them with his breeding.

Edward's coachman met us outside the Flying Horse and took all but me to Cheston at Edward's command. I elected to have me my jaunt. Edward enlightened me on the best place to meet a woman, which he maintained was at All Hallows Barking off Byward Street, as the graves there were temporary but the widows visiting there permanent. And, so he said, in need of comforting.

I instead went directly to visit Cromwell, or rather his head, and that head did look some hopeless all alone on that pike, the last remaining clumps of hair blowing in the Londontown breeze. The skin on the skull was drawn as tight as leather and looked as worn as a pair of beggar's boots, the resemblance to which I can attest with certainty. He had his teeth, however no bill of fare but humiliation had been put before him. And no one paid him much mind, as he had been stuck on that pike for some time. Someone, though, had screwed round his head, and his mouth bore a smirk from the twist. His eyes stared back into Westminster Hall, and so I followed them into the Hall and come upon a grave.

Now this warn't the grave of a man but a grave of another sort entirely.

It was a pit, and inside the pit were other remains. A marble table had been malleted into near oblivion. It had once stood most regally near the south steps of Westminster Hall, where its fragments now rested. The broken trestle and uprights, the once-graceful arch, lay side by side no different than the wracked corpses in the paupers' grave where they buried Tom. No doubt the pieces of this once-magnificent table, a symbol of the monarchy that Cromwell so detested, would be buried soon enough too. Cromwell's crime, his attempt to abolish the monarchy, was still fresh twenty-odd years on, and so this ruined table remained on display as evidence of his crime, just as his head stayed on the pike as the consequence.

If the table no longer whimpered from the weight of the banquets set atop it, it still managed to whisper words to me. Numbers, rather. For there, on the underside of one of the broken pieces of marble, and shaped exactly like a tombstone, were the following numbers as if placed there just for me.

1-1-4-4-5-7-9-12-14-14-14-15-18-18-19-19

I lifted the stone so to see if it might reveal more to me, and as I done so I heard an outcry. I turned and seen the guard coming at me at full gallop with his sword drawn, the tail of his red coat flying behind him. I quickly memorized the numbers, which was some difficult considering that I had no desire to have my head severed from my body and put on a pike even in the best of company. I dropped the stone and reached for my dagger. I had already committed one murder that day and so one more, and inside Westminster Hall, might furnish me an even better command in Old Nick's navy.

I seen another guard, and him running just as fast as the other one, and his sword flashing too. Bad luck, like good luck, comes in threes, and as I did not yet know which manner of luck was to befall me I held up my hands and bade them to stop by shouting, "Long live the King!" They were almost on me by then but faltered, and I met them as kindly as I could, stabbing them both with my dagger. The both of them fell into the pit. It seems that good luck had come my way.

One of the guards fell across a stone of another colour, a red stone, and not marble but common cobblestone and in the shape of a wheel. I had not seen it previously, as it was so small as to fit inside a palm. It was the second cipher wheel, the circumference of which was even smaller than the one in Edward's Bible, and right off I seen that them two wheels worked together. Aye, and that when they were put together they would read so.

Had Edward seen the numbered stone? If so, he had missed the second cipher wheel. The King had tried to murder Edward's family. Cromwell had tried to murder the King. How were the events joined?

Years, my hearty. It took years for me to solve the ciphers, and Edward's association with the head on the pike was but one more such cipher.

I MET MY hearties in Cheston, and we settled there for a few days to be certain that the constables warn't after us. I said nothing to Edward about what I had found but kept the wheel in my jacket pocket just as Edward kept his Bible in his selfsame pocket. I was pleased to tell him that he was quite correct about widows needing comforting, and spun a story about one such woman with flaxen tresses.

We lived high and at our ease in Cheston, sleeping during the day and venturing out at night. Once, Bones asked Edward about the Bible, and Edward told him that he pilfered it at the same time that he stole the watch, as they were in the same pocket of his mark. Bones never raised the matter again, but then he would not be so inclined, as it had naught to do with spirits. The coachman returned, per Edward's instructions, and brought us to a warehouse near the waterside. Edward knew this land like I knew my Bristol.

We saw the ships bound for Newcastle upon Tyne and Sunderland and other ports from our hiding place at the warehouse. When we returned to the Linda Maria the men declared me captain right off, and we come to riches soon after I took the helm, as we captured some of those ships. One of those ships was full of glassware. We traded the glassware for tobacco and sold the tobacco to the Scots. Another of those ships was full of stores that we sold for good profit too, so you may recall.

Men such as we require food and drink to live, but we also need nourishment of a different caliber, and a captain must provide for his men, so I told the crew to fetch Black John's sea chest. They heaved Black John's chest onto the deck, and the men were so eager to see the sea rat's blunt and were shouting so keenly, that they nearly blustered the sails. I split open the chest and his treasure run out of it. Gold, silver, jewels, rings, coins, watches, daggers, necklaces, bracelets, earrings, pistols, swords, sabers, knives, blunderbusses, and more riches than any of us had ever seen, spilled out from that chest. I gave all of them riches to the men. I had what I wanted. The Linda Maria was mine. The second wheel was mine.

I aimed to gather my own treasure. I, confounded creature that I was, did not need anything no more from a dead sea rat. The men swore oaths of allegiance to me until they were hoarse.

Years later, a gale come up that was so powerful that it shook the looking glass off my cabin wall. A parchment that was hidden behind the glass fell to the floor. I saw Black John's scrawl on the parchment as clear as the scars on my own hand. Black John had written the names of every swain that owed him tuppance. My name was on that parchment too. Black John dignified me a liar and a cheat, he did. Aye, and he marked me for death on that parchment too. My Edward fared no better. That was an accomplishment for a lad of his years.

I named Edward my first mate, as although he was young, he was enterprising.

And, what better way to keep him in view?

That is all that there is to tell of my sojourn in Londontown but for one more matter. I kept Bloody Bill's silver plate, the one that he stole in Londontown, and a confounded creature still eats off that plate. So he does.

CHAPTER X.

SOLOMON AND MY HEARTIES

he crimson cipher, "Blood," in Edward's Bible was most perplexing, and Edward maintained that he could make neither stem nor stern of it. He claimed the word to be a marker to lead us off course. Still, I pressed Edward, reminding him that I had warned him not to hold anything back from me. Edward lofted his hands and maintained that he had been forthright with me from the start, and intended to remain so, but that the word baffled him.

"There must be a meaning to the word," I told Edward, as he joined me for a dram in my cabin. "Perhaps part of a map. A heading or a course."

"If we hold these words to be a map," so Edward said, "then 'Blood' must be one leg of the journey, one more cipher to solve." He added that mayhap we would battle them that guarded the treasure, and the word was a warning.

I turned to the last page of the Bible on which the author had written that we should look with favour upon a bold beginning, and as I done so, Edward's parchment fluttered out of it.

Evangeline

"Hold now," I said, as if I had not seen it before. "Where did this marker come from?"

"I have been thinking of the lady," Edward said, and immediately took the scrap and returned it to his Bible. I took the Bible from him and turned to the page that I had seen before, the one that was near blotted out and read the verse.

> And when inquisition was made of the matter, it was found out; therefore they were both hanged on a tree: and it was written in the book of the chronicles before the king.

I feigned to put all my efforts into that verse, turning the Bible round and round and devising systems and schemes for solving it, until I deemed that it was the sheer contrariness of the author that caused him to blot this particular verse even though I knew that Edward had despoiled the page for his own purpose.

"I say that the treasure is in Spain," I told Edward, explaining my interpretation of the verse. "We are after a King's ransom, my hearty." I hoisted Edward by the lapels of his jacket, then dropped him back into his chair. "But this word, 'Blood,' " I told him again. "It must pertain to you and me, as blood follows us everywhere we go with this Bible."

"Blood follows us in any case," Edward answered.

"I maintain that you know more than you are telling me," I said, slapping his knee so to show him that I was jesting. Edward, nevertheless, bit down on his lip as if trying to decide a matter. "Then there are them numbers, '1303,' " I told him. "It is a date. I am near certain of it. But it is not the date of this Bible, as it is too well preserved for a relic. This Bible is not that old, and so the date must have another significance. You might tell your old hearty," so I said to him.

"The musty odor discloses its true age, John," Edward rejoined. "It may be that this book has been cared for all these years and so is rightly preserved, but all the care in the world cannot forestall its deterioration, no more than Black John can cease his decomposition." And with them words he grinned as broadly as Cromwell.

I opened the Bible and turned it so that it caught the light from Edward's lamp. We were in northern seas, and so there was no chance that he might spy the first cipher wheel, but I wondered if I might provoke him whilst I fiddled with the book by candlelight.

Edward would not be provoked. Not yet.

I run my hand over the cover of the book, feeling the smooth grain, and I would swear that Edward's countenance changed to that of jealousy. I handed him back his Bible. "It ain't as if I am stroking your Evangeline," I told him.

Edward coughed into his hand, the gesture of a gentleman, much like that of your Mullet, and I continued. "Blood. Blood, Edward. Blood and treasure. Blood and a king. Blood and a king and treasure. Blood and you, my hearty. Your family's murder. Your family's blood. What might be the link in this chain? I say it is the blood. What say you?"

Edward was cleaning his pistol in his cabin and looked into the barrel, before brushing the wheel-lock with a brush, as if the wind and not I had blown open his door. I inquired if he had heard his father speak of a treasure in Spain.

"It is faulty," he said, still looking into the barrel. "The gun misfires. It is the mechanism." Then he looked at me. "The mechanism, John." I replied that I could care less about his pistol, and he replied that he warn't speaking of his pistol. "The deduction, John. What of the word, 'Blood'?" he asked. "Would it not be just as likely that the author of the ciphers meant for us to take heed of the warning? My family was murdered and perhaps on account of this Bible. There may be another secret in it that we have not yet found. One that we would see if we did not look at this book each and every day. Your theories, some of them, are too elaborate." Edward struck the flint and held it between his fingers. "A treasure. Mayhap even a crown," he said. "Whose crown? The King wears the crown."

It was his turn to look at my reaction. I clapped my hands. "The King's crown would not fit your head," I told him. "Your head is much too large for it. Still, your father's last words, Edward." He lit the wick of his pistol. "And then he pitched you this Bible. And then he was murdered by the King's own men, and so you told me." Edward pulled back the hammer of the pistol and placed his thumb on it. "You were a cutpurse when I found you, and a poor one at that as I caught you, and I will ever think of you as such. So much for your breeding."

He smiled and with his free hand flung open the window to his cabin. He pointed the pistol and called for the men to step aside, whereupon he fired his pistol into the night air. "I have repaired it," he said, waving the smoke aside. "My father never spoke of a crown or a treasure. It may be that our presumptions are wrong, and this is just a simple book, an ordinary Bible."

"I suppose that he never spoke of pirates neither, lad, but here we are as plain as plain can be. Here we are, you and I. And mayhap your father never spoke of gold, but we got it now, don't we? And if he never spoke of treasure, it don't mean that the world ain't filled with it, and that it ain't ours for the taking."

"When you speak so, John, there ain't no other way to look at it," Edward answered, and he avowed that I might, after all, be right as the declamation on the first page did contain them directions to a treasure. He put his pistol in a holster that he had fashioned by sewing up strips of shoe leather and that he fastened to his breeches by another such strap. "But, sure as I ain't Prince Edward Peach, I never heard my father speak of a treasure. I loathe the King, John. He murdered my family and burned all that we had to the ground."

"Excepting your Bible," I told him.

"Excepting that," he replied. "By my father's wits."

"Edward," so I told him, "there is more to this. And the reason your family was murdered is in this Bible. No doubt it is the final secret."

"Do we not see in it what we want to see, John?"

"I am as right as fair weather, Edward. Just as right," I told him, and Edward said that if I said it, then it must be so. I importuned him to think more on the word, "Blood," that mocked us each time that we tried to interpret it, and he said that he would get right to it after flogging one of the men for falling from the mainmast. I congratulated him on his discipline, as it did not do for men to fall from our mainmast. He bowed and left, and it is a wonderment that the answer to one of the riddles come from a man that we had not yet met, from Solomon. And, that we would encounter him under the strangest circumstances in only a trice. If you are anxious to meet up with Solomon again, you have my leave to turn the page, as he appears forthwith.

Aye, but this is some pleasurable.

Even so, you would bear me straight across the Atlantic, but the waters do not accommodate any man. This ship sails its own course by the whim of the breeze. I have always found it best not to fight the sails, but to tack to the wind and let the ship rove where it may go. We abide in port soon enough. It is the same with a man's life. I never trusted those books that Peel gave me, as they always had a plot to them. That was why I took it upon myself to append them. No breezes blowed in them books except those that the authors huffed through them.

A man's life does not follow a particular plot. He is thrown off course by tempests and squalls and whatever else Old Nick can hurl his way. Even your Silver has never tried to fight the sea. It is a matter of respect.

There was no way to expect that Solomon would appear out of a storm, and there was no way to predict that our course would change on account of the tempest. I am unable to amend the past. I can only write it and try to make out the meaning, the same as with the ciphers. The truth can be some obstinate.

Mark this course.

Money is the thing and so it ever was and so it ever will be. You buy bread with it. You buy hearts with it. You buy beauty and intellect with it. Money changes an ill-bred waster into a well-bred gentleman. Money makes a simple man smart. Money turns an ugly man handsome. Sterling gives an Englishman his qualities. And I took that sterling, my dearest. I took it. I gave that Englishman a crooked back and a twisted nib. I took away his breeding. I struck him simple, so I did. And you done the same, but you would still bear me to the hangman. For money. If you are a patriot, then I am a pixie.

Your King promised you a goodly portion of my riches, but he will take them from you. He will take from you what you took from me. So he will. Money is the thing. Even for kings.

You can only hang a man once, my patriot, but I mean to murder you with each word that I write. You call yourself a patriot. You are a thief.

Would you care for an accounting of my riches? You had better take care to make a tally so that your sovereign does not charge you with thievery. Then you will stand before the bench. They will ask you about the treasure of treasures. And then, just like Silver, you will hang.

I will be borne straight to the hangman. But you? They will put you in a pillory. I will write about all my riches, except the one that they want most of all. You can tell your King. Then you can tell the justice in Chancery. Then you can tell the hangman about the treasure.

If I only reach out my hand, I can grab guineas and ducatoons and doubloons. I have armfuls of coins here. I have swords. Gilded, my hearty. I have skins. I have snuffboxes. I have pocket pieces. I have hollands. I have linen. I have spices. I have perfumes. I have silk. I have lace. Good bone lace and no less. I have lockets. I have pistols. I have wedding rings. I have burying rings. I have woolens, and from Ipswich. I have necklaces. I have chains. I have a pewter serving set that we can employ for our last tea together. I have bundles. I have parcels. I have packages. Aye, and I have enough jars of freshwater and drams of rye to last me until the day of doom.

I keep my gold dust, my hearty, in a sheepskin bag next to my pallet. I have one slipper that is filled with ducats and another that is filled with pieces of eight. There are brazils in the pockets of my blue coat. There are rix dollars in my boot. Come into my cabin, my hearty. I would show you my bags of gold, my coins, my jewels, my lockets, and my linens. I would show you my gilded swords and give you a complete accounting.

And the treasure of treasures? Well, we all, rather most of us, prospered in our search for it. I would say that all of the men that sailed with me, save one man, prospered. He took no coins. He ate our bread and none of our meat. Our meat, he said, warn't fit for him. Let us now recall Solomon. I follow the wind.

WE HAD SCUTTLED five stout ships that season whilst Edward and I engaged the meaning of the ciphers, each of them ships bearing more cannons than the Linda Maria. We were superior to them other ships in every way. We were fast, and they were slow. We were sharp in our attack, and they were blunted in their rejoinders. We were resolute in our pursuit whilst they were, each one of them, the Portuguese, the French, the English, and the two Spanish ships, slothful in their retorts.

And so we let the wind take us to the Canaries, where the Guanches are so forthright that it is possible to cheat them of everything they own whilst enjoying the temperate clime all the while.

A squall come up near the Canaries, off the island of La Palma, blowed around the mountaintop and proceeded to assail us. The squall released thunder, rain, and Solomon. I was in the ketch, at the time, with Jimmy Lam and Louis Jay, your old hearties. It must be good to spy them again.

I found, as you may recall, Jimmy and Louis on the same day on the floor of the same alehouse in Nombre de Dios. Jimmy and Louis got in a row over which of them was the better marksman and, after several drams of rum, set out to prove their case to the other. Jimmy had three shots in him, and Louis had two shots in him. I settled the dispute by taking their pistols and giving them sabers.

Bonnet Love, a middling captain that you later caught off Barbados, abandoned them. He was a middling captain, but notable for his enthusiasm for song. He sang, I understand, whilst the noose was put round his neck. I brought Jimmy and Louis on board the ship after Love abandoned them. Love had no use for them after they shot each other. As I say, he was middling.

Now Jimmy was a quarrelsome sort whereas Louis was a clement fellow except when he had the whisky in him. They looked alike. They each had black hair tied in the back. They each had blue eyes. Both men had simple brows and simple minds. They were fair of skin and blistered easy, so they walked about the deck with flour paste on their faces and limbs, and a man might mistake them for rubberkins on Old Nick's crew if he did not know them no better. They each wore a crimson vest, the same colour of the "Blood" in the Bible, and so cut quite a figure, both ghostly and of this world. They tied the bottom bits of their beards with tiny crimson ribbons too. Aye, and as you know, Jimmy and Louis were brothers. I asked them why they took different Christian names and they said that their mother wanted nothing to do with either one of them. They must have been a strict pity to her.

Jimmy, Louis, and I were netting for fish just like the Guanches, which is a fine venture for men such as we, when we are not plundering, marauding, or murdering. We were no more than a furlong from my Linda Maria when our misfortune commenced. I told Louis to row to a cove that was secured from the storm by its cliffs, and after the squall ceased Jimmy climbed a hill to make certain that our ship had not been damaged.

Jimmy pronounced my love in high spirits, and then bade Louis and me to join him at the top of the hill as fleet as we could. He pointed to a beach, where we spied a small boat in another cove. There was a man in the boat and he was slumped forward but still holding on to the oars. We ran down the hill, pulled his boat aground, and dragged the man to shore.

He looked like a minister of some strain. He wore black pants, a long white shirt with tassels, and a straw hat with a wide brim. He sported a thick black beard. That beard, which was ragged and grew in every direction, would have made any other man appear wicked, but gave this man a kindly countenance. The beard suited him and seemed to be as much a part of him as whiskers on a cat. His shirt was torn, but he seemed otherwise unaffected by the storm. He looked fit enough. He was tall, almost as tall as me, and had him broad shoulders. He woke for a moment and shouted to us in a tongue that I had never heard before.

Jimmy was pleased when the man fainted again, and declared that we should not bring him aboard the ship, however I told Jimmy that there was no harm in conveying a minister. I was some pleased to do so, as I figured that he might help with them ciphers in Edward's Bible. Jimmy opined that he was more likely a devil from Nick's fleet sent to trick us. Jimmy and Louis argued about whether the man had ascended or descended to earth. I settled their dispute by saying that if he was a minister, we could feed him to the sharks for good sport, not that I intended to do so, but neither Louis nor Jimmy ever gave up a notion without a struggle. My words mollified Louis. I told Jimmy that if the man was a devil, we could learn some tricks from him before feeding him to the sharks. And that satisfied Jimmy.

The man woke, and Louis put in that we would let him live for a six-pence. The man replied that he had neither sixpence nor the means to get sixpence. But Solomon, for Solomon was the man's name, said that he did not fear death. Then he commenced to sputter in the same strange tongue that he first heralded us.

I drew my sword and told Solomon that I preferred to be damned in my own tongue, and he said that he warn't damning us, and perhaps it was the manner in which he avowed it, but I believed him. Solomon commenced to rock back and forth and mutter some more. Every once in a while he looked at us, but his eyes did not center on us but on some distant point. We tried to ascertain where he was gazing, but could not see anything except the horizon.

Louis pulled a bottle of rum out of his pocket and took a drink. Jimmy grabbed the bottle from Louis and drank more of it. Then they commenced to quarrel about which of them could drink more rum in one sitting. Solomon looked briefly at them when they raised their voices, but it struck me that he did not see or hear them any more than the monkeys chattering in the trees. Jimmy spoke to Solomon, but Solomon did not reply. Solomon's eyes, huge black orbs, ebbed back into their watery pools. A small redbird hopped onto his foot, and the men and I both looked on in astonishment whilst Solomon continued to mutter and rock with the bird on his foot. The bird, eventually, tired of Solomon and hopped away. Suddenly Solomon grabbed the bird. He had seen a snake gliding toward it and grabbed the bird before the snake could devour it.

"Here is a man that deserves to live," I said. "He ain't afraid of snake nor man nor Jimmy Lam nor Louis Jay. We will give him passage. So we will, and whether minister or devil."

Solomon looked up. Them eyes that had looked so dull now looked as cutting as saw blades. He asked if he would be a slave or a free man on my ship. Solomon alleged that he had been a prisoner of the Moors for four years, that they had kept him as a slave and that he had no interest in returning to that profession. He said that he escaped when the squall come up.

I answered him. "Neither slave nor free man. A pirate," I told him. "You have too many years on you to be a cabin boy, so I hereby promote you to starbolin." Solomon tramped a planking that had broke loose from his craft and shook his head when it cracked. "But it won't be easy, and do not believe that you will be rich as soon as we sack the next frigate. Every man has his place, and you must begin nigh the hull. So we all started," I cautioned him. "It takes perseverance, cunning, and devilry to rise on our ship. But, have no fear. We will make you a pirate as surely as a hog has hooves." Solomon declined my offer. I told him that it warn't an offer that could be declined.

The wind freshened, and after our clothes dried we made ready to leave. Just then the body of a boy washed ashore. The sight of the body startled Solomon to the highest degree, and he commenced his incantations again, then suddenly stopped and asked us to help bury the boy. My hearties, who had fought every class of man from England to the Tortugas, dug the dirt and graved the boy upon Solomon's request. They were afraid of him. It may be the only trait that those brothers ever shared, aside from their crimson vests, braided hair, and inspired contrariness.

Solomon heaped stones on the boy's grave and wept so profusely that a puddle of tears formed at his feet. "A slave too," Solomon told us. Solomon cursed the Moors, so he did, and loudly. Jimmy and Louis cowered. "Men need freedom as much as air and water," Solomon said. He turned to me. "As much as a hog needs hooves," he said. I took to Solomon right then, as he had a sound wit. He had thrown my own words back to me, and with good effect, and I laughed and slapped Jimmy and Louis on their knobby backs. They nearly keeled, and I suppose that they would have keeled if Solomon cast his dagger eyes on them instead of on me.

I explained to Solomon about tobacco, tea, rum, and slaves and the profit in them enterprises, and Solomon called it "unholy," and thereupon I told him that was another good reason for engaging in the trade. He aimed those eyes at me again and went on and on about the evil of slavery, and the more that he went on about it, the more I thought about the advantage to it, until I was rightly pleased with myself. I told Solomon so. He spat at my feet. I liked him even better then. He warn't afraid of Long John Silver. He did not seem to be afraid of any man. Aye, and when he threw his shoulders back and told me that his ancestors had been slaves, and went on that he was a Jew and asked me what did I think about that, I gave him my reply.

"I can think of no man that I would rather have on my ship," I told him, though I was some disappointed that he warn't a minister and so able to help me resolve them ciphers. Aye, but later I learned that Solomon knew him most every tongue, having traveled about and even acquired Latin along the way whilst a prisoner of the Moors. "You ain't any breed of Christian, and therefore must be a born blasphemer. Like me. Just like me," so I said. "I am nearly ready to promote you again. I ain't never seen a man so distasteful that a squall gagged on him and spat him out. You have found a true home with us, I say."

"If there is a Hell," Solomon said, "it is on this earth. There are creatures that are worse than devils," he said. "There are men." Edward had said the same to me. I thought that they might find good fellowship in each other on account of their philosophy. Then Solomon bade me to leave him there. I, having never found such a fellow in all of my travels, declined. "One man can do more harm than any devil," he said. Aye, but I enjoyed his wit. I put my sword to his neck and brought him to the ship.

I told Edward to find work for my foundling. Edward said that Solomon was as good with the rigging as any boatswain, but the men would not let Solomon work. Louis rocked back and forth in mockery of Solomon. Jimmy walked aback from Solomon whenever he saw him. Pew flung netting at Solomon's feet to trip him.

Solomon prosecuted the men accordingly. He tore one tar's hat off his head and threw it into the sea for wagging his tongue at him. He stared so fiercely at Louis that Louis finally agreed with Jimmy and become so afraid of Solomon that one day, whilst rocking, Louis nearly fell into the brine. Solomon skipped thrice athwart Jimmy, he did, then laughed at him until Jimmy near went distracted. Solomon heard Pew sliding up behind him and swung a spike at Pew. Pew retreated some, forlornly dragging his netting behind him.

I told Edward to put Solomon in the galley. "He may cook," Edward replied, "but I doubt that the men will eat anything that comes out of his cauldron."

"They will eat everything that comes out of his pot when they get hungry enough," I told Edward. "I mean for him to follow in my own steps. He may, in time, master cookery near as well as me. He might even surpass me and put Jimmy in the pot."

Solomon was a tolerable cook, and Bones declared him so, but Edward was correct, as the men were reluctant to eat anything that Solomon prepared. "Ain't you afraid that he will poison you?" Jimmy importuned Bones. "If he poisons me, I will kill him," Bones replied.

We learned that Solomon knew certain cures, such as for the fluxes, and that he was partial to the leech cures, though not many of the men permitted Solomon to apply the treatment to them. Most preferred sound suffering. There was a rash on one ganger's face, so I recall, that Solomon cured with an aggregation of rice and water. Pew's eyesight grew more afflicted each season that we sailed, and Solomon told Pew that there was no cure for him. "Pew ain't to see no more?" Pew pleaded. "Unlikely,"

Solomon told Pew. Solomon told Bones that he would be dead in seven years from drink. Bones grew sullen, but only for the day, and later, still offended by Solomon's diagnosis, dipped buccan into Solomon's broth. "Improves the taste," Bones said. "Seven years," Solomon replied. Solomon cured another younker of the calentura with a concoction that he made from rum and tobacco. The men almost threw Solomon overboard, so you may recall, when that man died of the ague the next month in Shepard's Bay. He caught it in Barbados, but the men said that Solomon had done him in.

"My father was born in Spain," Solomon told me not long after he joined us. "He left for the Brazils. Then Cape de Verde. He was a trader for a time and returned to Spain in secret." Solomon tapped on his teeth with his fingers. He was given to tapping on his teeth from time to time, but it had no meaning so far as I could discern. He tapped when he was particularly deep in thought. "I was born in Spain too, but not by choice." He stopped his tapping. "A foul land and a foul people." He drummed on his knee with his fingers. He did that from time to time too, and the drumming had no meaning either, at least so far as I could determine. I was glad to hear him condemn the land of his birth, as I would have cut his throat had he said otherwise. "Your country is no better," he replied.

"I would drink to you if I had a flagon in my hand," I said. "I was born an Englishman but I ain't an Englishman unless I have guineas in my hands. Aye, and I am a Brasilero if I am holding brazils. But not a Spaniard. I draw the line at doubloons. I hate the Spaniards. They muddle my seas with their ships. The Dutch muddle my seas too, but the Spaniards are so damned ugly. And they fight too pretty. All flourishes. Like they are throwing kerchiefs over their shoulders." I offered Solomon a demonstration. "That is when I stick them." I removed my sword and thrust it so it just stopped under Solomon's chin. He did not flinch.

"Not all Spaniards fight so," he said. Jimmy was listening to us speak from behind the capstan. Solomon grabbed the sword from my scabbard and, with one swing, sliced Jimmy's hat in deuces. Jimmy near fainted. Solomon tapped my sword on the winch. I was some surprised at Solomon's ability with steel. No other man but Jimmy had seen the display. "An excellent sword," Solomon said, handing it to me. "They said that my father did not pay a debt," Solomon went on. "A lie." Now he was tapping with one hand and drumming with his other hand. "I was sold as a slave on a rover. There was no debt," he said. "I would not take the oath. I would not. To him that died on the cross." Solomon stopped his tapping and drumming. His eyes grew sharp. "I tried to fight. I could not break free. He cut me. I would not take that oath. Look," he said. Solomon opened his shirt and showed me his chest.

Nothing staggers a man that has sailed around the world. I have seen every type of fiend and sailed with many of them. I have seen every type of creature that walks or crawls or flies. But, I never saw anything like what Solomon showed me.

"The crusado," I said with disbelief. That Spanish captain had scored the whole of Solomon's chest with twain marks to form a cross.

"I never took the oath. I never took it," he said.

"Here you will find true brotherhood," I told him. "You are welcome here. Allow the men time. It is fair wind and fair tides here. Mostly, although we have the occasional tempest. There are no classes here. Those that hail from Pie Corner eat alongside those from Southampton. All the same," I told him. "Any man may go his own way as long as it is my way too. We all of us on this ship have a common purpose. Crowns and pounds and ducats and doubloons."

I, and though I do not fancy the admission, was wrong about Solomon. Of course, I was wrong about you too. It strikes me that the sea and Solomon and you and I and damnation are all twined. So we are and so I say. All twined we are.

And now I come to the matter of a hearty and his head.

This hearty of ours was from Plymouth, as I recall, though he may have hailed from Hammersmith. Mayhap the lad was from Hull now that I think about it. When my men revolt and bring you here I will ask you to advise me before I kill you. We had just spied the West Indies on our quest for the treasure, having reckoned the longitude and latitude wrong again by way of counting the kine and the corn, when this tar told Edward that he would be obliged if Edward would grant him free liberty. The fellow asked Edward for fifty guineas, and reminded my first mate that I had promised all my scurvies that they would be paid once we reached the Indies. Edward told him to stand fast and the man stood so, his back straight and shoulders back, as if he was one of your bluecoats. Edward commissioned Pew's tankard and struck the fellow upon the head.

The blow brought the man down, but he warn't bilged and stood. Edward employed the tankard again. The man fell and stood again. Edward bid the men to throw the man overboard, and our hearties surrounded their mate. No man challenged Edward, and the fellow likely would have been cast into the sea for lack of an endorsement, until Solomon spoke.

"He is a man. He is one of you," Solomon protested. He did not tap or drum or rock or mutter. He shouted those words at Edward, he did. Edward was taken aback, as were all the men, but Edward paid Solomon as much mind as one of the gulls that followed the ship, snatched a fowling piece and aimed it at the fellow.

"Stand him against the rail," Edward ordered the men. Solomon strode so he stood directly in front of the man. "Now I will not need to waste another shot," Edward declared. Edward, a man of not many declamations, went on some, saying, "I snuffed Bloody Bill. What is this man compared to that beast?" He did not wait for a reply. "We will save shot today, men. We will kill them both with a single ball. I favour the head. Let us see if they flap their arms and waggle their tongues like a chicken after it meets the butcher's knife. We can wager on it. Then again, they would die slower with a ball through their gullets." Edward cast around for a consensus, but the men could not come to a preference, and so Edward said, "I may aim for the chest." He pointed the fowling piece at their chests and drew it back again. "It would be quite a quick death and likely not as agreeable." He flung his hair back. "There are the legs. However the jumble of limbs would be a chore to mop." He looked at Pew, who looked over the men's limbs to reckon how long it might take him to go about his duty. Solomon spread out his arms to protect the tar, who cowered behind him and begged for mercy, now that his senses had returned. "We shall leave it be a surprise," Edward said. "Our captain enjoys surprises."

And so I did. Solomon struggled mightily, but I pulled him out of the way of Edward's fowling piece. Jimmy and Louis warn't pleased, but I found Solomon particularly diverting, and he did seem to be adept with a sword. Solomon managed to shout, "Let him live!" before I clapped my hand over his mouth. I loosened my grip, as I expected Solomon to defer to the fowling piece, and he screamed, "This is murder!" as if we did not know our own business. Edward glanced at me, displeased.

"Stand this man tall," Edward commanded Pew. "His head is down. I want him to see the powder flash." Pew readily obliged. He lifted his mate's head. "Better," Edward said.

"Take care not to hit Pew," Pew said as he scuttled away. The fellow barely stood. He was ready to unreve at any moment. His head was about to drop again when Edward shot him through it. He did not flap his arms or waggle his tongue.

Pew put his hands in the man's pockets. "Empty," Pew mourned. Another tar hoisted the corpse and threw it into the sea.

Edward struck Solomon with the fowling piece. I grabbed Edward's arm. "Go below," I told him.

Edward flushed. "The men," he declared.

"My men," I told him. "I would have that fowling piece now," I said, and I took it. Edward went below without another word. I should have let Edward keep that fowling piece. Then again, Edward claimed to have killed Bloody Bill. Any court of jurisprudence would have convicted me of that murder. Edward merely abetted me, and happened to have the dagger in his hand when Bill walked into the flinging of it.

Aye, but I should have let Edward blow a hole through Solomon. Edward was my first mate and it did not do for me to show him up in front of the men. Sport is sport, after all. The men had placed wagers and had to settle their accounts by betting on which way the wind would blow, on which part of the ship the gulls would light, when the sun might set, and whether or not Solomon would live through the week. I did not place any wagers.

CHAPTER XI.
SOLOMON'S TRIAL

our lad has rapped on my door and when I did not answer, I heard him chomping on my fare. I believe that he even ate the bones, because I heard him cracking them open and sucking the marrow out of them. He seemed pleased by the poison as, after his last nip, he belched. He padded off in the direction of the kentledge, his footsteps heavier than when he arrived.

We were in the airless Caribbean, and near Magen's Bay, when Edward shot that tar. It is an important point on the compass as so much changed after that day. It was if the weather had broken. The day before we were dancing with the natives on the beach. You even danced. The woman had a flowery dress, and it blowed out as far as Cape Horn, so it did, when you turned her and the breeze caught the both of you. Your hat flew off. Another woman with a platter of fruit and bunches of flowers piled high on her head lifted your hat from the sand without letting a single lime drop. You sat, done with the woman, and had a dram with me.

The weather changed the next day. The wind stopped. The beach was deserted, and all that was left from the night before was a sandal that one of the women had left or forgotten on the beach, and it washed back and forth, into the ocean and onto the beach, until the tide took it away. We repaired to the ship and prepared to make sail. It was then that the tar, drunk from the rum the night before or the scent of the flowers or the sweetness of the fruit, defied Edward. And then Solomon defied Edward too. I took that fowling piece, I did. It was then, when I defied Edward, that I swear the wind departed. The remains of the sandal and the remains of the man, I expect, are in Fair Weather Bay. The remains of that day have not yet washed away.

I drank alone the night that I took away the fowling piece, that airless night. Bones meant to join me for a drink, but quit my company after I brought up the incident. He complained of a sour belly. I wanted a fellow to join me for a drink, a tale, and perhaps a game or two of chance. I ordered Pew, who was skulking about outside my cabin, to fetch Solomon.

I offered Solomon rum, and he refused it. Aye, but that man was stubborn. Then I presented him with a blouse on account that he had rent his own blouse when Edward shot his mate. "It ain't what you might find on High Street," I told Solomon, "but it does have Spanish blood on it." He declined my offer. I told him to choose another blouse. Solomon took a blouse without any blood or history to it. There is no accounting for taste.

"It is night. I am cold," he said. "It is the only reason that I am taking it," so he said. Solomon never did anything natural, and so he had to mutter some words before he tacked that sail to his frame. He crossed his arms. "The only reason," he said. "It is merely that I am cold." He looked about my cabin, and his eyes settled on the pistols and swords and sabers, and then roamed until they settled and stayed on my pantry. "I would bid you a fair night," he said. "The blouse fits," he said. "I was cold." I readied myself for his gratitude. "I am still cold," he said. He did not leave, even though he had bid me a fair night.

"And hungry I would wager," I told him. "Not only cold but hungry. Some edibles then. Cheese. Look at all of the esculents here. Take some. Whatever pleases you." He muttered some words over my wedge of cheese before devouring it. "You must be parched," I told him. "Would you like rum?"

He commenced to drum his fingers on his chin. He did not even give me the courtesy of looking at me when he spoke to me, as if I, who had just given him my blouse and my edibles, was of no more account than that snake that he had caught when I saved him the first time.

"Have we come to an anchor then so soon, you and I?" I asked him. "I would make more of your acquaintance. We are shipmates now." I produced my best and most engaging smile. I opened my hands to show him that I meant no harm.

He turned toward the door. That put me off, it did.

"Are there any words of gratitude in you?" I asked him. "Are there any words that you might afford to thank the man that saved your life? Are there any such words?" I asked him. "There is nothing outside this cabin but dead wind and Pew. I do not have scabies. I do not smell rank so far as I know. I have not served a term in Chancery. Why leave? I have," I boasted, "procured everything that you see here. One way or the other." I was ever proud of my accomplishments and often thought that I should have kept a tally of the ships that I assaulted and the men that I snuffed, so that I could read them on a cold night at sea. But, that would have been a labour of sorts, as there were so many. Mayhap I will derive the same pleasure when I read this history over your bones.

"Thievery," Solomon replièd, tapping his teeth whilst he looked at the stores in my cabin.

"Aye. And murdering," I told him, hoisting my chin so that he could see how proud I was of my achievements. "Such are my talents." He looked at me with those dagger eyes of his again. "I never had a mother or father," I told Solomon. "So I made thievery my father and murder my mother. They give me everything I need. All cheats are my sons. All double-dealers are my daughters. And, we have no creed here. Except blasphemy, my hearty."

"I am not part of your crew," so he told me, and so I answered that modesty suited him no better than me, as I had seen him with a sword. "Parlour tricks," he said. "I can fight. I choose not to fight. Or steal. Or murder," he added. "Yours is the easy way. My way is the hard way. If I save a man, it is as if I have saved the entire world. If I destroy a man, it is as if I have destroyed the entire world. If I save a man, he will have descendants. If I destroy him, he will have no descendants. The blood of your victims cries out. The dead and the unborn."

"Look on it this way," I explained. I shocked him on the shoulder, a friendly gesture, but he was moored too securely to my deck to sway him. "I take from the rich and the poor. I am even-handed. The poor have less to lose and so do not miss whatever I take from them." I took another bottle of rum and two tumblers from out of my cupboard. "The rich. Bless them all. I would be dead before I drew my first crooked breath but for them. They have so much that they do not miss whatever I take from them either," I went on. "The only dishonour is to starve. And I would have starved. I would have been an honest, dead man." I shined the tumblers on my breeches and looked at them in the candlelight. They were clean enough. "One farthing would never suit me," I told Solomon whilst I poured out the spirits. "And what man can say that I will not need more? I might need twenty farthings to bribe the hangman, I might. Mayhap forty farthings. More. Take a dram with me," I told him. "I have an inquiry to make of you." I watched the drink roll back and forth in my tumbler, and it looked for all the world like the waves rolling about us. "It is never enough," I said. Solomon did not take the rum.

"Then," he said, "you will always be poor." He rose to take his leave and as I had not granted it to him, I pushed him back down again. It warn't easy. He was a large enough man and stitched together with strong twine. I was tempted to call him a confounded creature.

"*Audacibus annue coeptis,*" I told him. "Does it have a meaning to you?" I asked, employing Solomon to aid me in resolving the riddles. He nodded. "Would you be so kind?" I asked him.

Edward, just then, promenaded into my cabin. He had taken to promenading ever since I had declared him first mate. I was glad that he had, apparently, forgotten about the incident with the fowling piece and decided to join me. I poured him a tumbler too. "A drink," I said. "To the death of a mate. And his descendants, and therefore a goodly amount. More than he or his issue deserves." Edward and I hoisted our tumblers.

"You as well," Edward ordered Solomon.

"Careful," I warned Solomon. "Mind your answer. You drink with your shipmates. It is our way. By the by," I told him, "Edward will kill you if you don't take that drink with him, and it will not do for either of you to destroy the entire world on account of a tumbler of rum."

Solomon turned to leave. Edward grabbed Solomon by the arm, and Solomon shook Edward off as if Edward was no more than a jib bug. Solomon poured the rum onto Edward's shoes, which upset Edward to the highest degree, as Edward polished the buckles on his shoes most regularly. Solomon had deliberately provoked Edward, but to what end? Aye, but then I knew the answer. Solomon was set on saving the whole world. The fellow glanced at me, and mayhap even smiled, after Edward rushed him. Solomon pushed him all the way back to the door of my cabin. Edward did not expect that, he did not, from Solomon.

"He will not drink," Edward sputtered. "The case is plain, John. Just as it was this morn." Aye, so my Edward did still bear a grudge against me. "It is our way, and so you told him. Allow me that shot now. No, the men deserve better. Swords. Blood, of course. A goodly amount," he said, parroting my earlier words. He told Solomon, "The captain told me once that it don't hurt more than thrice. Once when the sword enters you and once when it is pulled out, and lastly when you fall. I will try to do it in deuces, being a man that likes a challenge. I do believe that Bill was dead before he struck the ground," Edward told me. I was almost pleased to see Edward back in good spirits, even though he still took all the tribute for dicing Bill.

"I will offer you my own sword," I told Solomon. "Assemble the men,"

I told my first mate. I ain't never seen a world saved or destroyed in all of my voyages, and the blue of the Caribbean was as good a place as any for the sight. I suggested to Solomon, after Edward had marched away, that he might live if not for his own sake then out of consideration for me. "I have been attempting to make out that phrase, *Audacibus annue coeptis,* for some time, a long time," I told Solomon. "You might tell me now, in case the sword slips from your hand. What say you?"

"Later," was all that Solomon replied. That and, "I believe you will be amused by the answer."

Do you recall all of the stout men that I commanded in those days? There were lads from Wiltshire. Lads from Liverpool and Septford Reach. Tars from Winterton and Yarmouth and York. Hearties from Litchfield, Brickhill, Hockley, and Westchester. Salts from Dustan, Lancashire, Dover, and Yorkshire. And all of those men, whether they were the sons of charwomen or the sons of gentlewomen, assembled on deck to witness the battle between Solomon and Edward.

I asked if any of the men were of a mind to solicit Solomon's case. No man stepped forward. Edward drew his sword and thrust it poorly. Solomon easily parried it. Then Solomon stepped aback until he stood against the deck rail. The men, who warn't interested in watching a straight and forward hacking, and did not know of Solomon's skill with a sword, escorted Solomon away from the rail. Jimmy warn't among them men.

Pew and providence do not seem likely company but, just then, Pew fell. Pew crawled about the deck perfectly confounded, like the sea crab that he was, until he managed to stand, whereupon he fell into the rigging. The men roared, and Pew yelped. Each wave that lifted the ship cracked Pew's back. The ship capered, and Pew wailed. The men roared louder each time that Pew let out a cry. Whilst the men were so engaged, Solomon climbed the rigging and freed the crab. Then Pew, still heaving for breath, spat at Solomon. Solomon might have considered that the world that he saved on Pew's account might have been better off without him.

Edward pointed his sword at Solomon, and Solomon tapped his sword on the deck.

Edward swung his sword at Solomon and missed. Solomon swung his sword at Edward and caught steel. Jimmy picked up a hatchet, and said, "He is a devil. A devil I tell you."

"Put down your hatchet," I told Jimmy. "Edward is fit to fight man or devil. I taught him to fight myself." Jimmy looked at me askance and gave the hatchet to Bones, who gave it to Pew, who cleaved it into the head of one of my wooden saints.

"Those mutterings," Jimmy said, pulling at his earring. "They put Edward off his steel." Jimmy closed his port eye so better to see Solomon's demise. Jimmy's other eye was swollen from some malady, but he would not let Solomon treat him, as Jimmy preferred a swollen eye to a cure from his devil.

Edward advanced on Solomon, and the sword is sometimes keener than the man, for Edward caught steel. The blow that Edward delivered was hard enough to jag Solomon sidewise. Edward thrust his sword again, but Solomon weaved, and the blow missed its mark. Solomon saw his advantage and struck Edward in the arm. Solomon was no swordsman, or so it seemed to the men, because he could have finished Edward then and there.

It is one matter to cross swords on land and another matter to do so on a rolling sea. The sea, taking Edward's side in the dispute, pitched, and Solomon lost his footing. Bones pulled Solomon to his feet. He set Solomon's shoulders square. "Now bend your knees. Keep your chest stiff," Bones advised Solomon. Then, "No offense to the first mate," he told Edward.

"No offense taken," Edward replied, staring at Solomon with pure malice.

Bones continued Solomon's education, unaware that Solomon needed no direction. "Such is how," Bones told Solomon. "And look at his eyes and not at his feet. Now, fight," Bones told Solomon. Bones was so engrossed in the fight that he had forgotten to pat down his hair, and it rose like the spires in Londontown. Edward made some jibe at Solomon and Solomon answered and Bones warn't pleased. "Hold now," Bones told Solomon, stepping between the men again. "You do not parley with a man when you are preparing to dispatch him," Bones warned Solomon. "It is a common trick. Do not speak. Fight." No doubt Bones was thirsty. "Fight and do not bring any disgrace to this ship," he told Solomon. "Fight now. Fight well. Until Edward kills you, that is." Bones, with those words, concluded his counsel.

Edward and Solomon parried, and it was manifest to all the men, except Jimmy and me, that Edward would soon chop Solomon into haggis. Aye, but then Solomon drew blood. Edward grasped his leg, and as he fell back he delivered a blow to Solomon's leg.

"No slur on either of you," Bones told Edward and Solomon, "but I would one of you kill the other for the sake of my throat. I am parched."

Solomon, bleeding, stood with his legs coiled and sprung with a flourish just like a damned Spaniard. The men grumbled. I suppose that Solomon had been a slave of the Moors for so long that he was bound to have taken up their bad habits.

"Not enough blood," Pew proclaimed, drawing closer to the fight. "Pew can't smell him blood."

"Would you men rather speak on blood or on gold? Answer me that, my hearties," I said in a low voice. They answered me in a shout, as I knew they would.

"Gold! Blood!" Then, "Blood and gold!" they all shouted, whilst waiting for Edward to dispatch Solomon from this scurvy world.

"Gold and blood!" I thundered, now that their pluck was up. "And there is gold and blood!"

"Where?" the men bade me. "Where?"

"There!" I hailed. I pointed nor'east, to Spain, as I had of late concluded that the treasure was in Spain by means of calculating the longitude and latitude over a cup of mash. I intended to take two treasures, the first of them being Don Jorge's treasure and the second being the treasure hidden deep in Edward's Bible. And what use were the two cipher wheels without more ciphers to discover? I had used the wheels on both the riddles and the verses in Edward's black Bible, but to no effect. Solomon knew the meaning of "*Audacibus annue coeptis.*" But what did he mean by stating that I would be amused?

"Not Spain," Bones entreated me. "Not Spain."

Edward and Solomon were fighting on the very edge of the rail, each man barely holding his balance. It was a wonder that they had been able to caper onto it, what with their bloody legs. Solomon had been the first to jump and Edward, after a long breath, followed him. "His blood runs!" Pew shouted, doing a jig as Edward speared Solomon in the shoulder. Pew drew closer to Solomon, always at the ready to grab whatever he might find in a dead man's pocket. "Edward is trifling with him now, Pew says," and so Edward was, offending Solomon with the side of his sword. Edward was promenading again. Solomon looked overboard. "You will not fare any better with the sharks," Edward told him.

"This is just sport for Edward," Bones said, smoothing his hair and looking where he had mislaid his bottle. "It will soon be over." Bones did

not care now if we went to Spain or Barbados or Newcastle, just so long as
he had a bottle with him when we made port.

"I think about gold every night," I told the men, grabbing each of them
by their arms. "I know where it is and how to get it. Now are you with
me?" I asked them. "For if you are not with me, that will be well with me.
I will get me that gold myself, so I will," I told them. I circled back and
stood before each man in turn. "I will not share it then, my hearties. Are
you with your captain?" They did not answer. I shouted at them, "Because
I am bound for gold and bred for blood!"

"Aye!" they bellowed. Only Pew did not answer. "Spain!" the men
shouted. "Gold!"

"They tire," Pew said, and as he said it Edward tottered from the rail.
Solomon leaped from the rail and shoved Edward against it. Edward barely
stood. He looked for all the world like the man that he had set against that
same rail and shot. Then, Solomon lifted Edward's chin. Edward turned
about and near fainted. He lowered his sword. He looked marly, he did,
and ready to take up with the grisly crew.

"A feint," Bones said.

Solomon saw his opportunity, and whilst the ship pitched to the stern,
struck Edward in the head with the handle of his sword. Edward fell.

The men were silent.

Solomon cut Edward's arm and Edward leaved go his sword. At that moment, and without any hesitation, Solomon put his sword to Edward's neck.

"Cut him!" Pew shouted. "Cut him now!" Pew knelt by Edward's side.

"Even a dog deserves to live," Solomon told Edward. "Even you."
Then Solomon threw down his sword.

Jimmy helped Edward to his feet.

Pew jumped to his feet as well. "Cut him!" Pew cried to Edward now.
"You have his sword! Cut him!" Edward stumbled toward the dropped
sword, the sword that I had given Solomon, and took it. Then, from the
strength that comes from the purest hatred, placed my sword against
Solomon's neck. "There is no mercy on this ship," Edward said. "That is
our justice."

I grabbed Edward's arm and he shook me loose.

"You will not kill him," I told Edward. I whispered that Solomon knew
the answer to one of the riddles. Edward looked at me some astonished. "I
only told him the one," I said.

"A man that you spare becomes your enemy," Pew said in his singsong voice, as if he was reciting a nursery rhyme.

"Keep the sword," I told Edward whilst I took his arm again to steady him, as he commenced to reel about the deck.

"But I believe I may have solved it too," Edward said. "The other night. The night that you took my fowling piece. I have not had the chance to tell you." Edward slipped in his own blood, and Jimmy helped him to his feet, and then Edward faltered about the deck again, still holding the sword. He scraped the deck with that sword, he did, as he could not lift it. Solomon looked some peaceful. He might have been an undertaker perusing one of his cadavers. Edward dropped the sword, and Jimmy helped him go below. I told Jimmy to give Edward water and to bind his cuts.

"We cast anchor here," I told the men. "But on the morrow the ship turns toward Spain," I said. And with all the spirit that I could muster, I shouted, "And Spanish gold!" I followed the trail of blood on the deck to the sword and lifted it. I raised that sword high.

The men shouted their assent, so they did, and they brought their shouts to such a pitch that there was no choice but to turn for Spain on the morrow.

I passed Solomon on my way to Edward and gave him proper tribute for his swordplay. Solomon took my arm, and then I saw that he warn't steady at all. It was a wonderment that he did not reel about the deck with Edward. That might have been a jig to remember, even without a fiddler. Aye, but he did not take my arm for assistance. "Parlour tricks," he said, tossing me back my arm almost as readily as he had taken it. "It is no virtue," he told me. He picked up my sword and looked at it. He held it high. It must have taken all of his strength to lift it. Then he dropped it at my feet too. He looked about at the men, drummed his fingers on his chin, and settled his gaze on me before going below. He tottered some, but refused to give way.

"No man on this ship will harm you now," I called after him. My arm was red from where he had grabbed it. I could see the marks of his fingers on it. "At least not whilst you are awake."

CHAPTER XII.
BLACK JOHN'S CURSE

dward warn't in good temper. He would not eat much though he drank a liberal measure of ale. He spoke with Jimmy, but when I asked him to parley with me he said that he was too weak to do so. He was resting, aslant on his elbow on his pallet, when I come to him.

I told Edward, "I would there be some good words between us." Edward had recovered enough of his blood to shift his elbow and rise up from his bed a rung. He coiled one of his curls, but he always had the brawn for that, and set his eyes somewhere amidships, away from me. "I will need you in Spain," I said. "At your best."

My Edward's voice was as thin as the dogvane. I would have supported him with a brace of beckets if he would have let me, so that he could stand upright and parley with me proper. He weared windwards, moving his elbow again, and now looked directly at me. He held that we should proceed to the Tortugas. "It is all a tale," he said, shifting his weight again, capturing another curl. "A sham. My own father must have been taken with it."

"Then the King was taken with it too," I told him. "You solved the riddle?"

"It may be," he said, leaning back on his elbow again. "I recalled the source of the Latin," he said. He righted himself once more and considered me. "It is quite an old verse. I read it when I was in my father's house. I do not know how it did not enter my head until just these past days."

"You never told me that you knew, lad."

"I only just remembered." He arranged his pillow so that he might look on me. "You would have pressed me, John."

"I would have," I admitted, swinging my leg over his chair. "Solomon knows the source of the verse too. He said that I would be amused."

Edward said, "The quote is from a book, a rather famous one. You would not have found it in Peel's tavern. A Roman poet wrote it. Virgil. You must tell me if you are acquainted with him."

"I never had the pleasure of meeting him. I knew another Virgil, but he warn't a Roman nor a poet but a petty thief."

"It is from the *Aeneid*, Virgil's masterwork about the founding of Rome."

"Is our heading Rome then, Edward? Tell me, and I will right the ship."

Edward's chest heaved with laughter. I had not seen him laugh in some time, not since I had batted Pew about the ship with a bowline. "No need, John. The verse was written many centuries past, and is just as I translated it. It means to seek favour as we begin. To 'look with favour upon a bold beginning' and nothing more. Solomon would have nothing to add to Virgil's words. Or my explanation."

"There is more," I told him, rising from the chair and wiping my hands on my stockings. "I have spoken with our new acquaintance. '*Audacibus annue coeptis,*' I said to him, and Solomon laughed most heartily. Just as you laughed now. It was a queer sight to see that man laugh, I must say. He knows it well, so he does."

"But there is no more to it, John. I swear it." Edward fell back into his sheets as if he was falling below the waves.

"A different pair of eyes can sight the same point in the distance and make out different features. The translation is, according to Solomon, just as you said." Edward appeared relieved. "However," so I said, "this fellow, Virgil, wrote about a quest. The hero journeys around the world for the sake of his family. Is that not coincidence? Our hero is a sailing man and in search of his destiny, which is just so you know, a kingdom. Amusing, I would say. I have always held that we are searching for the treasure of a king. Or perhaps a Pharaoh. More likely a king. The King murdered your family. No doubt for the Bible or the secrets it contains." Edward near levitated from his pallet.

"I do not recall much of it."

"Aye, and there is more." Edward was as crimson as the "Blood" in his Bible. "The hero would be a king."

"But, John," Edward declaimed, almost cured now.

"Rest some, lad," I told him. Edward opened his mouth but did not speak. "Aye, Edward. You have spoken too much today. Volumes. You need your rest."

"Solomon might enlighten you on Pharaohs," Edward said.

"I shall ask him. I value your counsel. But another matter before you fall asleep. We are going to Spain, Edward. Not only because the treasure may be there, but because Don Jorge's treasure is there. And, Edward, if we find Virgil in Don Jorge's library, Solomon shall read it to you by your bedside if you are still reclining."

"I am not sure that I would trust Solomon," was all that Edward could muster.

"We need only trust in doubloons for the moment. I see them," I told him. "Spilling out of barrels like wine. Think on it, Edward. A fountain of gold. Dead Spaniards at our feet. Mayhap even the moon rising over the hills. A daring escape under the stars. The Linda Maria listing at first, and then off, the wind filling her sails. I would a crew of Spaniards give chase, so we might blow their ship out of the brine. And someone, another Virgil, would write our tale of daring. And some lad would one day read it by the fireside and be there with us, fighting the damned Spaniards, drawing blood and standing under a fountain of gold."

"It will be our blood that is spilled if we set foot in Spain," Edward replied, falling back on his elbow. "It will be death. I would be at sea when I draw my last breath. Not on land. And most certainly not on Spanish land. There ain't no daring in a dead man. Aye, a daring tale, John. And there will be no one left alive to tell it."

A pallet is but wood and straw and I could have broken Edward's repose with a simple stomp. "You are walty," I told him, reconsidering, and I struck his arm from under him instead. "It is all a tale. Every bit of this curdled world." He managed but a scanty laugh now. "And it is a curdled world, Edward. That is the difference between the landlubbers and us. We see the world for what it is. They sail on milky seas. Seas of cream. We sail on brine. We breathe it in until it scars our lungs and sears our eyes. And what does it matter if we are the only two left alive to tell each other the tale? We still had our adventure. And what if only one of us lives? That man will still bear the tale, even if he speaks it aloud to himself in the night. Even in a Spanish jail before his hanging. No one can ever take it away. It is adventure, lad." Edward shook his head, and when he did, his curls tossed about him as if he was a maiden refusing a man's advances. "It is done. Four men," I told him. "Four men will bring back the gold. There is nothing but blood between those riches and us. Spanish blood, Edward."

Edward sat up in his pallet. The talk of riches must have fortified him. "I think that you would trade us all for silver. And tell us it was in our best interest. You would tell us so even as you threw our bones into the sea. You would tell us that we would have the best berth on Old Nick's crew. John, sometimes I believe that you are Old Nick himself."

"He ain't got my charms," I told Edward. "And I would not trade the lot of you. Not for silver," I told him. "Mayhap for a king's treasure. And good sound murder." Edward enjoyed the boast, as he let loose a sharp laugh. "Aye, murder comes with gold," I told him now that his humour had returned. "Like a carriage comes with horses."

"You took my sword, John," he said, turning weatherboard, sullen again, looking past me. "That Solomon." Edward grimaced, trying to stand. "You took my sword from me."

"That's all bream now. He fights well," I told Edward. "He is handy with a sword. And he knows his Latin. And he is standing on deck. He climbed the trestle trees this morning already. Whilst you were leaning on your elbow." Edward tried to stand again and near fell. He held himself up by sheer will, though it was more likely the hatred that smouldered inside him that gave him his strength. "I am pleased to see that you are recovering. Climbed it with one arm, Solomon did. He favoured the shoulder where you lanced him. That bewildered Jimmy some. I wonder if you can even ascend the fife rails." Edward dressed slowly, no doubt on account of the pain. "I would you let him live, Edward. He is handy with a sword. But, if you do mean to kill him, then go about it and kill him. It otherwise reflects poorly on me, as I taught you your swordsmanship." He listed, and I admonished him to stand upright when he walked on my deck.

Edward struck his hat against his thigh, winced, and followed me topside. The feather in his hat hovered before floating down. He did not totter now. I put my hand on his shoulder and squeezed it. He winced again. "But I would you let the man live," I told him again. "He is so very handy with a sword." I threw in, just before we stepped topside, how the Caribbean was a pleasing indigo that morn.

The men watched Edward, and he gave no sign that he was in pain. He barked orders as if his legs warn't stitched together by cloth and string. Solomon had sewed himself together, as he was skilled in such matters. He strode some stiffly about the deck. The climb to the trestle trees must have been a challenge, but the men said that he did not falter during his climb. He must have been in considerable pain but showed no sign of it. I was rather satisfied with the man.

I had the pleasure to inform Solomon that he would accompany me to Spain, but he warn't grateful at all for the opportunity to slaughter Spaniards. And, he went on, that he was particularly uneasy about Edward joining us on the journey. I assured Solomon that Edward would not cut a whisker off his beard unless I ordered him so, as he was strictly loyal to me. I thought to comfort Solomon by telling him that Bones, who was as good with sword and saber as he was with rum, would accompany us. That, though, warn't much comfort to Solomon. He declared that I should part Bones from his rum when we commenced the crossing. I told him that I would never fraction that pair, as this was to be a stealthy venture, and if I parted those lovers, Bones would wail all the way to Spain.

Solomon, all obstinacy, strode away from me and took his rest nigh the taffrail, at the same spot where Bill used to reside. The men halted. Jimmy looked at Louis. Then the men began their labours again. Pew as usual was pecking about and nearly tripped over Solomon before marching aback, opening and closing his mouth as if he had seen a phantom. Solomon took no notice of any of them. He looked out, not at Bloody Bill's sea, but at a point in the distance that only he could see.

Do you recall the sea at sunset when we left for Spain the following day? The sun blazed on the water, and I sailed my ship plumb down that fiery path. Then the moon shined. A finger of light as white as bleached bones pointed to Spain. I looked about. Bones was snoring. Edward was standing watch, and Jimmy was at the wheel. "Are you following the moon?" I asked Jimmy.

"So you told me," he answered, spinning the wheel as the wind caught our sails.

"Keep to the wheel," I told him. "Aye, it is him that shows us the way. It is his own finger, I say."

"I see no one," Jimmy said. He checked the gaffsail and then the headsail.

"Look keener," I told him.

Jimmy looked at the jurymast and then at the mainsail. He looked all about. He glanced at the mainsheet and the hank. He turned round sighting the loof. He turned his head toward the sternpost, minded the sails again, and looked at the parrel. "I confess that I see no man."

"An old hearty of ours he is, Jimmy. Dead some years now. It is him for certain. The moonlight." Jimmy was about to ask me which hearty pointed the way when I told him. "It is Black John," I said. "Black John and no other is showing us the way."

CHAPTER XIII.

THE CHURCH OF THE PISTOLAS

 asked your Mullet if he had ever seen a castle. I wanted to see if he was still alive after gorging himself on so much of my fare. He told me that there ain't no castles in the colonies. So, you still have your humour, as you sent me a lad from those lands. You must have picked him out of a heap. And no, he ain't never seen a castle, and so I took pity on him and spoke of our jaunt into Spain and the castle that we saw on our way. But then, and before I could tell him more, Mullet was gone, toddling midships.

And, therefore, here is the coast of Spain and just as we seen it. Murcia, it is. And I spy me a castle.

The sea rat would not let go of his ship so easy. It was Black John's hands, and not Jimmy's hands, that grasped the wheel. It was Black John that blowed the air into our sails. Black John was sailing the ship, he was, from the Caribbean seas to the coast of Spain. Black John, no doubt, had spoken to Nick about Don Jorge's riches, and so now this was the devil's business too. Aye, and greedy wretch that he was, Black John wanted those riches, and even though they were no good to him anymore. And, he wanted his revenge too. So it is with wretches such as Black John down in the depths.

Edward, Solomon, Bones, and I slipped into Murcia without anyone spying us. There was a good wind that day, and so, under cover of the clouds, we sailed toward Don Jorge's riches. We lowered our sail when we were nigh the coast and spied the castle atop the hill. That castle was some imposing as it had stood there for ages, stone by stone, with its two turrets. One of the turrets had a hole through it. The clouds and the sky passed through that hole, and it was as if the bleary eye of Spain was watching us as we set foot on land. If I had me a cannon, I would have blown out that eye and put that castle out of its misery. Then again, it might not have been in misery, but contented to watch us on our way to misfortune.

All the kings, queens, princes, princesses, and their knights and court that had lived in that castle were long gone. We ambled past them all with only our wits and Bones's bottle of rum. Ben Gunn might have bid us welcome, as he consorted with dust and demons, but he had not paid me a visitation yet. He only come years later when he was some tired of rowing round the vaporous isles. I would have been pleased to see him in Murcia, dead or alive, as he always told interesting accounts of plagues and retribution. There was a chill in the air and he might have warmed me with a testimonial on damnation.

There ain't no fair breeze that blows in Spain. It is a dusky land, and so the wind blows cold off its coast. The wind changes once on land and turns mild as it huffs through the trees and around the hills. But, not in Murcia. Murcia is mainly desert, and I wondered why anyone would put a castle there. That dust ain't worth fortification. And because it is desert on that coast, the wind does not change and huffs away as cold as ever and chills a body until it shivers. And we did shiver as soon as we stepped on Spanish soil, and so we each took a swig from Bones's bottle. Except Solomon. He strode on against the wind, even though the wind blowed him back toward the sea, trying to expel him once again. I was in Spain and on my way to riches, then, although I had yet to find my way to the treasure of treasures.

Then the desert was gone, and the eye in the turret watched us from the other side of the castle. The sun shined on us, and we stepped into a world of olive groves and grapes and vines with every type of eats on it.

We continued, and the air warmed some, but always with the chill still in it. We did not encounter any Spaniards along our journey. It was a shame, it was, as the blood of dead Spaniards would surely have taken the chill off us.

Bones had his eye on Edward's jacket pocket the entire journey, on account of the bottle of rum was moored there. I ordered Bones to take a swig as soon as we anchored next to an apple orchard. I wanted him peaceable. Bones drank, wiped his lips, and said that he intended to emancipate the spirits interred in Don Jorge's bodega. And, he added, the riches too.

We walked straight into the dawn, and as we walked, we heard the ringing of church bells. That was an insufferable clatter. Men such as us are accustomed to the silence of the sea. I say curse them that live on land and

their bells too. Such as us will rot in Hell soon enough, and the devil will
ring Hell's bells for us day and night. There ain't no need to torment us
with them now. Aye, and all the time we walked those cursed bells rang,
and I would not have been surprised if Black John and Old Nick were taking turns pulling the ropes.

Edward said that he much preferred the sundial on the balustrade on
London Bridge, which don't never chime, but always gives a good reckoning. That sundial, so Edward said, dated from the time of the Romans.
And then he remarked on how most of the numbers on the sundial could
still be read, though they were faded by the years. And, he continued, a
person might mistake that sundial for a mere wheel on account that the
numbers on it were so faded.

Well, sir.

Edward was testing me, so he was, wanting to see if I would mention
the first cipher wheel. Edward must have seen it in the Bible by now. Mayhap he knew it was there all along. Did he truly believe that the sundial on
London Bridge was the second cipher wheel? He must have run all about
Londontown, twisting Cromwell's head, dashing to London Bridge, sporting with the ladies, and arranging for that carriage to Cheston. He was
prolific. Or a liar. Or both.

I aimed to find out soon enough.

We diverted ourselves whilst on our way by speaking on those matters
that the likes of us speak on, recounting the ships that we scuttled and the
men that we murdered, until we come upon a pair of twisted oaks. I recalled Don Jorge enjoining me to keep to the path near the oaks as they
led to the brother's house. Then we come to a clearing, just as he had said
that day on the sinking ship. We crossed the clearing and turned lee.

There was the house and the bodega.

The house stood amidst a field of vineyards, and so finally Bones, and I
would swear that I seen dew in his eyes, had ventured into paradise.

We peered through the windows, and seeing no one about, entered the
house.

This was a grand house, it was, with pewter candlestick holders, fine
linen, crystal chandeliers, tapestries, carved furniture, and the other such
effects. Solomon pulled a dusty book from the oak shelving, blowed into it,
and out come Virgil spouting Latin. He presented the book to Edward,
who cast it across the room. I bade Solomon to see if he could find a book

on sundials, and Edward opened his mouth as if to speak, but instead plunged his sword into Virgil as a proxy for Solomon.

Presently we heard a crash and ran to one of the rooms, where we saw Bones on his back. He had jounced so hard on one of the beds with a bottle of brandy that he broke the bed. Then we heard another sound. Someone else had entered the house.

We drew our daggers and crept close to the walls. I turned and come face-to-face with a dead man.

It was none other than Don Jorge, who drowned the day that the San Cristobal split into deuces.

Bones caught the specter and Edward bound the specter's hands with the tasseled rope that hung from the shutters. The specter maintained, after I told it to vanish, that it warn't dead.

"So you say," I answered. "But you drowned, and so you ain't in any position to debate. You are dead," I told it, "but I am pleased to see that you are not sopped in seawater, as it would be disagreeable to wander the earth as damp as a clam. Still, you are dead, and so there ain't no point in parleying with you anymore."

The specter differed with me, and said, "I am alive, Silver. Silver is your name. I remember. Silver."

The specter insisted that it was alive, and so to settle matters I cut it with my dagger. Red blood ran from him, and I commanded Edward to unbind Don Jorge, as ropes could not hold a fellow that come back from doom so regularly.

Don Jorge rubbed his arms and said that he was rescued not long after we abandoned him. "A Spanish ship," he said with pride. I asked him about the brother, the man that had put him in chains, and Don Jorge said that he had come to an untimely demise. "My face was the last face that he saw," he said. Bones, taking a swallow from the bottle, speculated that the brother had died of fright. Don Jorge heaved up his shoulders and went on to say that his love had died too, and suddenly, after he found her in bed with a shepherd. "An epidemic," Bones said.

I thought it a shame that my Spaniard had all that gold and no relations to share it, and so I told him, whereupon Don Jorge pleaded to keep half the gold. I told him that he could keep half the gold, but that we would be bound out of equanimity to only let him keep half his life. Bones lifted his sword so to slice him median, when Don Jorge said that if we cut him so he would die. I agreed, and advised him that a dead man had no use for gold and therefore we might as well take all of it. That is wit, my hearty.

Solomon told him to take the bargain. Aye, but I was some pleased with Solomon that day.

Bones administered himself with the last of the brandy, and I told him to stay behind and keep watch. And when I told him that he would swim in gold and brandy soon enough, he patted his head and all was satisfactory and at peace within and atop him.

Don Jorge squired Edward, Solomon, and me behind the house to the bodega. There was a solitary candle just inside the entrance, and we walked, under that dim light, down the wooden steps.

Don Jorge lit the candles, and I was able to spy the wine barrels stacked one on top of the other. "The fifth barrel on the crown of the fifth stock," I reminded him. "I would have a drink from that barrel." It took all of us to lift the barrel, and when we set it on the floor I told Edward to take a drink from it. Edward split the barrel with his saber, and a river of doubloons rushed out of it.

Edward commenced to dance a reel, and whilst Solomon and I watched Edward at his hornpipe, my Spaniard stepped aback. Lightly he stepped, so he did. I turned just in time to see him at the top of the stairs. He waved at me just as I had waved at him that day that I left him to drown. Then he shut the door to the bodega sealing Edward, Solomon, and me inside. We were trapped.

Black John was surely pleased to see us jailed in the bodega. So it is with shades. They do not have any other diversions than to snigger at the living.

We threw our shoulders against the door. We broke all the chairs against it. We assailed the door until the light from the candelabra died, and then we sat in silence on the stone floor. The only sounds that I heard were Solomon's low muttering and the muffled beating of Edward's fists against the bodega's wall, until I heard the door scrape open.

The light blinded me, then I saw the farmers. One of them, the one with the red beard, aimed a pistola at my heart. "Do not aim there," I counseled him. "You are not bound to strike anything of importance." He descended the stairs, pistola in hand, and waved his pistola most insistently.

Don Jorge ordered us to drop our weapons, then he marched us to a church and down the marble steps behind the altar. I speak now for all the freebooters in this world. We require us good air, so we do, and the air in that church was most foul. Don Jorge swung open the grate that covered the wall and revealed our prison. We crawled through the opening into the graves, and Don Jorge quickly closed the grate. We put our arms through the grate as he ordered, and he shackled us in irons to it.

There is no need for backed bonds to keep a man in his place, so long as there are irons, I say. There is no need for solicitors or constables or magistrates either, so long as a man is hitched to a grate. Aye, and when one man wants to bring another man to penitence, there is no need for priests or psalms. Only pistolas.

We rotted in that dungeon for days without light or air or food or drink. There is no worse place to put a seaman than in a dirt grave. We shivered there, we did. I have no doubt that we shivered so hard that we rattled the bones of the dead men there.

Your Silver passed the time as agreeable as possible under the circumstances. He thought about his Linda Maria and about Mary too. He thought on Blind Tom and Peel, and once he thought he heard Black John cackling, but it was just a whistle of air through the dead men's bones. And, eventually, your Silver slept soundly in those graves with all them dead men.

We discoursed, at first, about how we would escape. Then we treated on how we would murder the Spaniards. Even Solomon joined in our banter, though he seasoned his words with invocations. I sang every ditty that I had ever heard. And then we were silent. If a heap of creaky bones had called on us, we would have greeted them graciously. Aye, we would have shaken the hands of the skeletons until they crumbled into dust. Those dead men would have been good company to us, but they had grown silent too after all their time in the loam.

Edward was mostly silent. Then all of a sudden he commenced to speak, and I could not tell if he had gone stark or was sorting the ciphers so to pass the hours. He told aught of the Bible ciphers before I could silence him, as I do believe that he deemed himself dead. He even spoke of the cipher wheel, and so now I knew that he had indeed seen it. He spoke of the sundial on London Bridge, and how he had purchased his hat with the blue feather there, as if that was of any consequence. Aye, and he spoke of a treasure of treasures. I counseled Edward to cease, but he persisted in his orations. Solomon, for his part, cited much scripture, and once he started them citations there was no stopping him. And all the while

Edward recited cipher after cipher, repeating over and over how it all began with 1303.

When the farmers finally dragged us out of our graves we were as lame as planks. They walked us to the clearing, then struck us with rakes and hoes, and one of them farmers kicked my leg so hard that he gave me the limp that I sport. Aye, they bloodied us good. We could not stand, so those farmers tossed stones at us for sport. And all the time, the wind that had followed us through the eye of the turret beat us as fervently as those damned Spaniards.

I endeavoured to stand, but fell. That gave the Spaniards good cheer. Nothing cheers a man so much as someone else's misfortune. Solomon hunched over like an old man. He offered Edward his hand, but Edward would not take it, and finally stood on his own warrant.

"Leave the red beard for me," I told Edward. "Take the one on the end. See his rake there. Strike him. Then the next in line. Strike him. Like pegs in a row." Then, "Solomon, do you spy those rocks near the trees?" I asked. "Grab them. And throw them at any Spaniard that strikes your fancy." I pretended to fall, and as I stood I grabbed all the Spanish dust that I could hold, so to blind them during our battle.

And then Bones crawled out from behind one of the oaks. He swung his sword and caught himself a farmer, so Bones did. The farmers fumbled for their pistolas. Landlubbers all. Solomon shambled to the rocks and launched them at our foes. One farmer fired at Solomon, and the pistola flashed, but the ball missed Solomon. The farmers ran for the woods and we hobbled after them, until they stopped to rally, but we advanced on them shielded by the trees. Edward was upon one of the farmers and took his pistola. I snatched the pistola of farmer red beard and shot him through the head. A brace of farmers ran at Solomon, and he struck each of them down with the limb of a tree. Bones drew a bottle and finished off another Spaniard by cracking it on his head. Aye, and Solomon saved Edward's life. Solomon saw the farmer take aim, called to Bones, and Bones cut the farmer down with his dagger.

Don Jorge, the last of them, was still alive and crouched behind a rock. But all men come to their snuffs. Don Jorge fired and missed the lot of us. I grabbed Don Jorge's arm and twisted it until the pistola fell from his hand.

"How do you kill such a fiend?" Edward asked me.

"Without mercy," I answered. "As you might kill the King."

Edward closed his hands around Don Jorge's neck. The colour left my Spaniard's face. He tried to speak, but his tongue waggled back and forth. I put my hand in the Spaniard's pocket and pulled out a key. Don Jorge closed his eyes. Solomon looked away. The Spaniard fell, never to rise again.

I bound my leg with Don Jorge's blouse. "Gold is all I need," I told the men. "It is good for all that ails a man, from goiter to gout. If the dead sentence come down on me, and I was cast for my life, two shillings would raise me up again," I told them.

Edward picked up a branch and made himself a walking stick. The wind was still blowing, and when Edward tried to brush the hair out from his eyes some of his hair come out. He held his blonde hair between his fingers, small dried curls, caked with blood.

Solomon walked slowly, like an anchor dragging the bottom of the ocean. Bones, some pleased with himself, sang all the way back to the bodega.

I turned the key in the lock.

I asked Bones, just before we entered, how he had managed to escape the Spaniards. He replied that he had done what was most natural to him. When Don Jorge and the farmers marched us out of the bodega, he slipped inside it. Bones, thirsty as always, opened a spigot, drank his fill, and fell into a slumber. "I slept in a rum barrel," Bones said, adding that when his time come he wished to be buried inside a barrel of equal attribution. "It was snug there," he said. "I did get me a cramp in my leg, but if I was dead, I do not believe that a cramp would trouble me. I woke the next morning and slipped out after Don Jorge left it again to gather the farmers."

We entered the bodega, lit the candelabra, and Bones, after an obligatory swig, leaped on top of the barrel. Both the barrel and Bones's breeches burst. He sat in the midst of the splinters and gold, triumphant. I am sure that there was never a king in Babylon that looked more proud than Bones.

I told Bones to fetch the Spaniard's steeds and Solomon to fetch the Spaniard's linens. Edward and I apportioned the coins so that they would fit in the satchels that we made from the linens. We slung the satchels over the backs of the steeds, and I damned all Spaniards. My leg afflicted me so much that I threw it over the horn of the saddle and rode so until we returned to the castle and its empty eye. This time I winked at it.

Bones skippered the ketch back to the Linda Maria, and the men raised a cheer as soon as they saw our sail.

No sooner had we boarded the ship, with scurvy Pew piping us aboard, than I saw a tar yoked to the rake. His body was pierced with marlinspikes. "At what man's command?" I asked.

"He insulted you," Bones replied. "Pew told me so before we departed. I did not speak of it, as I knew you had no need to hear such blather. The man said that you warn't as fit a captain as Black John, and that you would never return from Spain. I gave the men the command. In your name." Bones beamed when he said those words as he was so pleased to have done me a turn.

"Pew heard Mister Bones give the command just before you set out," Pew said with a snigger. "And that tar went on," Pew said. "So he did. He said that Edward warn't fit neither, so Pew heard. Now that he is rotted, he don't speak ill no more. He warn't loyal to you like Pew."

Edward struck Bones. "You act only on the command of the captain," Edward told him. "Or on my command."

"Aye, my sir," Bones answered Edward.

Spain sent us one last chill, and it filled our sails. Each man's mouth went slack as he gazed upon them riches, the first of my true treasures. I had spited Black John once more. One by one each man carried his share of the booty below. I told Bones that he could go below, but he patted down his hair and offered to stand watch on deck.

I escaped death at the hands of those Spaniards. So hear me now, my hearty. You will not make an honest man of Silver by hanging him. My memories and misdemeanours are all that I have left now that you took my ship.

Your new hearties never stood high on a quarterdeck. They never looked bow to stern at a score of men. They never saw stars flash athwart the midnight sea. They never felt a sea breeze cross their brow. But you felt it. You stood high on the quarterdeck. You parted the sea with your ship. You commanded men. You saw the stars.

My murder will not save you. Nothing can save you, as I know the answers to all the ciphers.

I stand on the quarterdeck behind the mizzen shrouds and I damn you.

The fever again.

Your Mullet is pounding on my door to tell me that the Atlantic is turbulent this night. He must have him quite an appetite for arsenic.

Look avast you, toward the coaming, then down to the skeg. I will send you to the bottomry.

Where is Old Nick? I would step on his tail. I would tramp on it. Does he not keep up with whispers and hearsay? What sort of a gob is he? Or would he cheat me of my booking? And what jacksnipe is lee of me? Black John himself? I ain't inclined to travel to his dry marl yet. And when I reach his liverless spirit, I will wipe my sword on his cape before I snuff him again.

CHAPTER XIV.

FIT READING

had solved for all the years and all my efforts not one of the ciphers. And, just in case the fever robs me of my wits, I repeat them all below.

We still got us that lovely headpiece.

And them numbers that Edward jabbered on about during our unfortunate incarceration.

1303

We must not forget us the simple declamation.

I have hidden 41 meters from the foundation 6 wooden boxes overlaid in ivory, and all empty, and one remarkable treasure covered in nothing but sackcloth not more than 2 meters deep nor more than 87 meters wide.

The more that I read it the less I believed that the declamation had a whit to do with kine and corn and a Pharaoh that sat on high, as the whole yarn seemed suspect. How could all them ill-favoured kine eat up all them fat-fleshed kine and all them stringy stalks of corn consume all them good stalks of corn? That ain't no world such as I had ever seen.

41:2 And, behold, there came up out of the river seven well favoured kine and fatfleshed; and they fed in a meadow.

41:3 And, behold, seven other kine came up after them out of
the river, ill favoured and leanfleshed; and stood by the other
kine upon the brink of the river.
41:4 And the ill favoured and leanfleshed kine did eat up the
seven well favoured and fat kine. So Pharaoh awoke.
41:5 And he slept and dreamed the second time; and, behold,
seven ears of corn came up upon one stalk, rank and good.
41:6 And, behold, seven thin ears and blasted with the east
wind sprung up after them.
41:7 And the seven thin ears devoured the seven rank and full
ears. And Pharaoh awoke, and, behold, it was a dream.

And I had in my pocket the second cipher wheel that when matched
with the first wheel looked so.

And I found the second wheel on the tombstone, for what else would
you call that jagged piece of marble, smoothed on the underside and engraved with numbers?

1-1-4-4-5-7-9-12-14-14-14-15-18-18-19-19

The ever-present blood.

BLOOD

We may ignore Edward's blot.

And when inquisition was made of the matter, it was found out; therefore they were both hanged on a tree: and it was written in the book of the chronicles before the king.

But leave us not forget his sundial that he chanced on at London Bridge. And always and ultimately Virgil's avowal.

Audacibus annue coeptis

Why is it that each time I write these clues Mullet appears?

I have decided his punishment when I escape. I will have him tied to the rake and feed him until he bursts. I would not be surprised if a flock of partridges flew out of his belly.

———✦———

Y*ou will be pleased that I am quite ill,"* the drudge said.

"*As I told you, boy, you are being poisoned by your captain. You may return later. Rap once if you are alive and twice if you have passed."*

"*How can I rap on your door if I am dead?"*

"*Then it is unlikely that we will be treating with each other again."*

"*It is the fluxes. I have decided to wear an earring."*

"*Against your captain's orders?"*

"*He told me it was better to wear one than to keep pinching my ear. It made him wince, he said."*

"*But a hanging improves his disposition."*

Mullet *laughed hoarsely, and said, "Not any hanging. Your hanging."* Then he said, "*It don't make sense to me."* He waited as if he expected encouragement to continue, but I already knew what he was about to say. "*You did not kill your first mate. He kept that secret from you. The sundial. But you did not kill him."*

"*He was of no use to me dead. Any fool can see such."*

"*Begging your pardon,"* Mullet *went on, "but he did not tell you the origin of the Latin phrase and he, so it seems to me, clearly knew the meaning of* 1303. *And surely even more. One would suppose so given what you wrote."*

"*Aye."*

"*You did not tie him to the rake and flog him or send him to, as you say, darbies."*

"*So that all the men could see? So that they could ask why I was flogging* my first mate? So that he would scream out all that he knew? No, boy. No. He was valuable to me, so you see. Valuable. He had what I wanted, and we each had pieces of the same puzzle. He was of no use to me dead. Dead men, I have found, are not trustable. Not trustable at all. And," I continued, "I did have me words with Edward. You can read it. I was about to write so."

"You might just tell me."

"Boy, you are as unrelenting as stench on a hound."

"Does my captain know what you write?"

"Most all, I would say."

"Then why do you write it for him?"

"It is a testament, boy. A testament. To me and my kind. To our ways. To your captain's duplicity. It is a record. I offer this tale as evidence of his crime. After I retake my ship, I will drop him in the sea chained from his ankles to his neck. You may watch him drown if you ain't yet dead."

"I have no such plans."

"You would know more? I will tell you then. But, silence. For if I hear one word I will cease. One word." The lad took his usual spot at my door, slipping against the frame. "Aye, I spoke to him, my first mate. He said that he had twisted Cromwell's head, so to remove it from the pike, when a constable took chase of him. Edward was partial to Cromwell, was Edward, as Cromwell had acceded to the attempted murder of the King. Edward did not know that he had turned Cromwell so that Cromwell's eyes led me to the pit, the tombstone, and the second cipher wheel. All is not persistence. There is luck in this world too. So a sailing man knows, as the wind may blow foul or fair. Edward did know the origin of the Latin and spoke of it only as Solomon had prompted my interest in it. Them Latin words did hold a secret, and so I discovered later. Edward believed that the sundial was the second cipher, and in his defence he told me about it. He did not keep it from me for long, and wanted to know if I agreed with his conjecture. I did not. How could I as I held the second wheel in my pocket? He was out of his wits when we were in them graves in Spain, and so he went on and on about the ciphers. That is all there is to that."

"You have said nothing about the numbers, 1303," Mullet said.

"I was readying myself when you interrupted me. Now you shall have to wait."

"That is unfair."

"You will learn to mind me."

"Damn you."

I was pleased with the lad's demeanour and so told him that I searched and searched for more clues, so to apply the cipher wheels to them, when all I needed to solve each and every riddle was already on board my ship.

"And damn you, my hearty," so I told the lad. "Now, you have your prospects."

⇒●⇐

We plundered every class of ship from every country. We tore up creation, broke it into bits we did, from Port Royal to the Carolinas, from Savanna Cay to Pimlico Sound, from the Indies to the Caribbean, from the new world to the old world and back again. And as rich as I become, I considered myself poor on account that I did not have me that treasure.

There warn't no depository on the open waters for the spoils that I carried, nor was I of a mind to trust my account to a high-collared clerk that might look over his spectacles and suddenly spy new prospects. No, I was determined to bury my treasure, just like the writer of the riddles. I could not spend all of my treasure, as it would take seven sons and daughters and each of them with seven of their own brood, to spend all that I got, and even then my treasure might outlast that litter. I considered writing my own ciphers, so that someone else might follow them to the ends of the earth. That would be a merriment for a pile of bones if I was given leave to watch the jaunt. Mayhap I already wrote some such ciphers on this parchment. Mayhap. And mayhap I will affirm it so by and by.

We calculated every combination of kine and corn and added and subtracted Pharaohs when we were of a mind to do it, and so come up with different longitudes and latitudes. And we navigated all them places that we charted. We were ever convinced that our latest solution was the right solution, and consequently plotted a course through every puddle of an ocean. We crossed the same seas twice and then thrice, believing that we had overlooked our destination because of a mist or the lack of a moon or the failure to hear the squawk of gulls circling our port of fortune. I told the men that we sailed here and thereabouts on account that I had heard tidings about a ship carrying goods of interest to us.

And then we come upon the clues.

Rather, Pew found them.

Pew never gave up his ways, and he and Bones were tussling about some business when Pew presented a grievance to Edward. Edward decided in Bones's favour and Pew, as if he had some understanding with Edward, protested.

Bones left with one of the few remaining locks of Pew's hair and Pew, so Edward told me, shook Edward's jacket. Out fell the Bible. Pew grabbed it and declared that he would reveal all he knew if Edward did not reverse his ruling and if Bones did not return his hair. "Fair Pew," Pew went on, stroking his head where his hair had resided.

Edward said that Pew knew naught, and Pew replied that he knew the meaning of 1303 well enough, and had from the first time he seen them numbers, and would have told all had I not vowed to kill him if he ever spoke about the Bible. Pew said that Edward's Bible had brought nothing but misery to him, and if it warn't for that Bible that he, and not Edward, would have advanced to first mate. Whereupon, Pew stabbed the Bible with his dagger, and not just stabbed it but scarred it by splitting the inside cover.

I only found out how much Pew knew years later, when Pew told me in order to spare his life for another offence, that being the day that I found a dead man clutching a most interesting clue.

Now it is of consequence that Edward punished Pew by denying him rations for three days and leaving him tied to the rake, but it is of more consequence that Pew had done me a right favour. I come upon Edward just in time, for Pew was running about the ship in search of a place to hide, when two clues fell out from the Bible. They were written in the same hand as the clues on the first page of the book and read so.

AOL JYVDU

And Last Icon

I solved the first clue without delay and kept the answer to myself. I applied the second cipher wheel, turning it until I found the answer.

The translation of "AOL JYVDU" was "THE CROWN," so it was. Aye, but whose crown? And was that the "remarkable treasure"? So it seemed to me. The wheels only revealed that one answer, but it was sufficient. A crown. A crown such as would fit my head. I deserved no less for all my troubles. And here are the wheels once more.

The second clue has already been translated, so we know, to read "On Cat Island." I set the ship on that course once again. I had visited the island many times, as I had solved that cipher sometime ago, but my reckoning of the clue was wrong. I wandered that island looking for a sign or a revelation. I paced it back and forth according to my calculations, each time deriving a new location, and each time come up slack with naught in my hand but soil. The trickster would have his way, and so he did.

I nevertheless recall Cat Island with affection. We must be not far from it now, as I hear the wails of its residents. The island was abundant in fruits, and the animals ate out of our hands as they were so trusting of us. Them that lived on Cat Island did not venture out from their fort of wood and straw to greet us, and kept their livestock and grain inside its confines. They had no need for trade, having all that they desired inside their borders. I don't know how them folks first come to inhabit Cat Island, but they had no place else to go. No place would have them for fear of acquiring the pox. Once in a while they would peek up over their fort and we would see them, their faces the color of pipe ash and bandages hanging from round their skulls.

We stole the lambs from Cat Island at every opportunity and enjoyed them lambs all the way down to their bleats. We took all the fruit that we could carry. Cat Island was a particularly good place to weigh anchor, as so few folks dared venture there on account of the pox. We ate well on Cat Island, and if the screams of the afflicted were some trouble, the temperate gusts there were most pleasing.

I can write with pleasure of Cat Island now, as I am in my hammock, the handle of my dagger between my teeth whilst I wait for you.

We cut our way through bush and bramble for five days this time, looking for signs that might lead us to the treasure. We, again, found no such signs.

I read the clue again.

It did not mean "On Cat Island." It meant, I determined, "No Cat Island." I said nothing to Edward, but he seemed ready to leave anyway on account that he had eaten his fill and found the torments of the tenants distracting.

We had come to our ends and so left that island with naught but the ciphers. We wandered from port to port and land to land, no different than gulls. And that is how we essayed through my middle years, a new heading each day, forever looking for the crown that lay just beyond the next reef and past the next harbour.

Bones spent all of his blunt on drink.

My Edward took to jackets that were flush with silver buttons. He acquired ivory-tipped canes, pocket watches, silk kerchiefs, peaked hats, and all manner of things fit for a grandee. He took particular care of his curls ever since Spain, only hacking his hair twice a year, and even then he had to tipper himself with drink before he could put a blade to his head.

Most of the men, in due course, abided Solomon. One ganger went so far as to declare Solomon the ship's charm, because we never lost a battle after he boarded the ship. Mind you that we never lost a battle before Solomon boarded the ship, but I did not contest the younker's declamation. Jimmy and Louis, those brothers who disagreed on every other matter, concurred on Solomon. They despised him. Louis hated Solomon even after Solomon cured Louis of a rash on Louis's arse in the figuration of Scotland. And Louis warn't partial to Scotland either. Solomon treated the men for all manner of ailments. He fought well too, though he only drew his sword in battle to defend himself. The man had begun to test my patience though, as he asked for liberty wherever we anchored.

And your Silver, he saved his coins. And kept them where he could see them at dusk and dawn until it come time to bury them, as he had little choice in the matter, them coins being so bountiful. He lengthened out his stores of gold and all that glittered whilst he summed them numbers and read that declamation and looked for all manner of answers to the codes, when the answers were so easy and obvious. I can write so now. An answer is always easy and obvious when you have it. Ain't that so, my hearty?

All the blood that we spilled during those years runs together. My history surpasses the devil's own handbook. Then again, a magistrate might go pale if he knew your crimes. He might put out an order to hang you from Bellow's Point. But though you ain't as fit as me to hang in Newgate, do not commence your trembling yet, since if my neck and I come to a mishap, I will greet the devil and wait for you below. I expect to be in flourishing circumstances down there in Hell, for it ain't every day that such as me favours the devil with his society. And, my sir, I will trade my tobacco pipe to the demons and my water jar to the gibbets so that they will torment you at my command. I will wait for you. I will send you to the next level of howling Hell, so I will.

I would murder you with my quill. I would blacken you with this ink. I curse you with plague years, so I do.

I come to love gold for the want of it. I took to thievery for my bread. Your countrymen made me what I am today. They made me in their own image. They starved me. I took their stores. Them good British souls murdered Blind Tom. I murdered them back.

FEVER.

But let us look closer in the glass before the fever takes me yet again. I spy a ship just off Port Royal.

The Marie, so the French merchantman was named.

We hoisted a French flag, then a lantern, and the seamen on the merchantman shortened her sails. We done the same, threw her boatmen our tackles, and become bound and betrothed to those boatmen and them to us upon securing the Marie to our main brace. Our lee side embraced the Marie's weather side, our lanyards crossed, and we were so entwined when the captain of the Marie and I stood amidships. Edward lowered our grapnel. A seaman on the Marie done the same. As soon as we pulled our halyards, the men of the Marie done the same. We threw off our French livery, the captain apprehended his error and barked at his men, but his order come too late. The Marie's halyards and sails were already down. I hailed him. "I take this ship in the name of Long John Silver." At them words, Bones grabbed the gaff and yanked their boatswain into the brine.

There was but one way to escape our grasp and that was to raise the grapnel and cut the lanyards, but I warn't about to wait for the Marie's captain to give that order. Our hawser caught the Marie's prow and them Frenchmen were in darbies.

My men ran through the foreshuttle and jumped from porthole to porthole. We ran amidships over the gangway and began our butchery. We spurred them sailors with our swords and shot them with our pistols. We only lost two men, but the Marie was trimmed with dead men. The captain was the last man standing, and after he spat at Edward, my first mate parted the captain's hair with a hatchet.

It took us no time to uncover the casks that were hidden below the ballast. The Marie and all she held, larboard to starboard, was ours. Them casks were filled with all manner of riches. Silks, woolens, and cambric. Pearls and silver. Gold sheets. Gold powder. Oil, pepper, grain, skins, seeds, sorghum, leather, stockings, lard, perfume. Casks filled with bonnets, buckles, boots, gowns, buttons, thread, sweetmeats, ribbons, claret, feathers, cheese, quills, buccan, needles, a cradle, a fiddle, and a tackle. Aye, and all them riches were ours.

Edward and Jimmy, tight as brails on a sail on account of our good fortune, danced a jig. The men donned the gowns and bonnets and joined them in their skip. One tar plucked at the fiddle and the rest of the men beat on the casks. We hearties drank and sang all that day and into the night at our good fortune. The men conjectured on how they would spend their shares of the riches. Each man made a declaration except Solomon. He sat at the taffrail, as he did from the first day that he took up residence there, and watched us.

"I would get a ship," Edward said. "Fast and with spirit," he said, so my Edward said. "I would treat her as she deserved to be treated. I would dance with her, and no slight to Jimmy, but with more fondness." Jimmy shrugged. "Aye," Edward said. "A fleet ship." He was drunk, so he was. "And we would sway all through the night, murdering and thieving and cheating, jigging faster and faster."

Even though my wooden saints never avowed any change in men nor clime, nor seemed to notice anything of this world, the sails trembled and a line broke free, as if Edward's words had scuffed the keel. Them wooden saints never grinned nor glowered, as all was all, and all was the same to them. But these words marked a difference in Edward. He would not have spoken so without reason and would not have spoken so now, even drunk from rye, if he did not mean to alter our course. Mark the subtlety of his sudden villainy, the challenge to his captain, the assertion that he would have his own ship.

But was it sudden villainy or were his hands on the tiller all along? Had

Edward been directing our course, steering us from shoal to shoal, ever outward and away whilst he resolved the ciphers? Edward finally proclaimed that the kine and the corn had naught to do with the riddles after I had reached the same conclusion, and said so to him. What good chance! Or, had Edward already known so? And if so, why continue the deception for so many years? He needed me, so I say. He could not solve them ciphers by his own merits.

Was this sudden villainy or was Edward loyal to me to the last?

We each had knowledge of the ciphers and each, although we professed otherwise, may have reached different conclusions about their meanings.

And now a matter had changed. He saw opportunity in the Marie. He would have it as his own ship. Greed or deception? Or both? One vice does not preclude the other.

Edward lowered his head for a moment as if thinking on a matter and turned to me. "I would jig with such a ship, and to her honour, as I have been instructed by the master fiddler himself." I bowed. "Aye, a ship with spirit," he said, as his words gusted away on a draft of air.

I decided to allow him his Marie. It was a feint and nothing more so to assure him of my trust.

Aye, and a captain must know the men under his command, and know them well, and so I steered the ship to Port Royal. I called every man to the deck and announced that we would lay in fresh provisions and head for land, and it was a sight to see the men throw their hats and blouses in the air. One man even patted Pew on the back before wiping his hand on the rail.

I called Edward to my cabin and told him that I warn't heading to Port Royal just to take in fresh provisions for the Linda Maria, but to take in provisions for the Marie as well. He asked me why we did not burn the Marie as was our custom. "Why burn a lady?" I asked him.

"Lift up her latch you will see only treenails and trimmings," Edward rejoined.

"An infirmity, Edward," I told him. "The Marie is a lady. What is it to me if she has a round house rather than a hind? It makes no difference," I told him. "She is still a lady. You must remember to treat her so."

"I fail to understand, John," so he said. "What business have I with the Marie?"

Hadn't he asked for the wheel? A cunning lad or a loyal mate? I could not determine.

"There is a matter in your eye, Edward, unless it is dust. It may very well be dust. But I seen it before, some years ago when you looked on Evangeline." The lad stroked his curls. "I was about to say that you must know how to treat a lady. And I am giving you a lady. I am giving you the Marie."

Edward ceased stroking his curls when I spoke them words to him.

"What say, John?"

"Went deaf done you?" I asked him. "You would have your own ship. Your own ship, so you said." I thumped him on his chest. "The best care you will take of her." He did not move. "For I am trusting you with a lady," I told him.

Edward stammered some.

Cunning or loyal? I would choose soon enough. But I had more words for him. A test, if you will.

"And one more matter," so I confided. "I have solved the cipher of the declamation."

Not that I intended to tell the whole truth to Edward. Still, I wondered if Edward might tell me more, something of use while I treated with him.

CHAPTER XV.

CAPTAIN PEACH

I gave Edward the Marie and named her the Evangeline, as a sister to my Linda Maria, but the tars that sailed on that ship soon renamed her the Bloody Evangeline. I created the scourge that had become Edward, just as if I had fashioned him out of wood and string and painted him with pitch. I drew my dirty thumbs across his brow and gave Edward not only a fortune, but also the prospect of the noose and the drop. What more could any blaggard want? I placed my sword in his hand and told him that we would sail topmast to topmast until we found the treasure.

"A privilege," Edward replied, "to sail to the lee of you." And then, "I am your servant." So he told me that day. "Your own servant, John. Ever loyal. Ever true. Ever stanch. Ever thieving. Ever murderous. Ever faithful. Ever conniving. Ever cunning. Ever cruel. Ever steadfast. Ever deceitful. And ever as trustable as you." He took his dagger, cut his palm, then mine, so he done that day. "Blood," so he said. The men cheered, the waves rose up, the sky darkened, and Edward took my hand. Strike me if it ain't true, but just then a tar from the Marie bobbed up on a crest, bid us fair weather, and went under the lather again. He grinned, a laurel of seaweed round his skull.

The fever again, and now with it the shivers and a new malady. Blisters.
"How long has it been? Mullet?"
We are in open water.
This fever must be a cousin to me, as it shows no mercy.
"Is that Tom there?"
My Tom was a square sail his whole life and the wind blowed right through him. Edward and I murdered the sons of Abel. One good turn

deserves another. Cast crumbs on the water and they will come back to you.

———◦◦———

The fever has slacked off. *"How much time have I been away?"*

The Atlantic is cool this time of year. We are in the Atlantic.

The last cipher. Aye, the last one. No, not the last one. "Is that you, Mullet? I must tell you before the fever returns."

———◦◦———

Did you call for me, sir?" Mullet asked.

"I did not."

"I heard a shout."

"The tide, Mullet. The tide. It draws out my fever. It pulls me to shore."

"You must eat."

"Damn you, Mullet. Did you hear me? Damn you."

The lad was silent.

Then, "I heard you, sir," he said, and he tottered away.

———◦◦———

It had always been my supposition, and I shall record it now, that the declamation pertained to the longitude and latitude of the land where the treasure lay.

It is an easy matter to determine latitude. I have me charts that show each parallel, commencing with the equator, which has a latitude of zero degrees. The latitudes girdle the world tighter and tighter until they come to 90 degrees at the poles, where they pinch the world to a point.

The determination of longitudes are another matter, as they run from point to point, north and south, and are all the same length but not of equal distance to each other. Longitudes are rather perverse.

If I were to lose my charts, I could reckon my exact latitude by appraising the height of the sun at midday or the position of the Vesper at night. Any tar can so reckon. I must assess my longitude by estimating the time at a particular site. The world turns upside down and rights itself each day, and so turns 360 degrees. There are 24 hours in each day and so if I rift them 360 degrees by 24 hours I arrive at 15 degrees. Therefore and thereby each hour comes to 15 degrees.

I have ever used Bristol as my primary point from which to reckon, and so one blessed hour away from Bristol is 15 degrees longitude and two such hours is 30 degrees longitude. I warn't never much for keeping charts, as when I am in open water I know the seas well enough to find my way, but the point of the matter is that once I solved the riddle and had me the latitude of the land, I could not establish the longitude of it with any accuracy. I even tried lancing a man that we captured, a good enough fellow until he died from his stabs, every noon and so marked his screams. I thereby knew the exact time in Bristol and marked my charts accordingly, until the man succumbed to science.

And so, even though I had solved the cipher, I could be leagues away from the land as my charts warn't accurate. Still, I now knew my heading, and so I come to my next conclusion. I would tell Edward that we would double our chances of finding the land by traversing the longitudes in two ships. Of course I misdirected him so that he had no chance of finding the land. We would sail together, part, then meet up in Barbados and compare our charts, so I told him over a rum.

"Aye, sir," so he responded, and said naught more. What manner of craftiness was this?

I, of course, never had any intention of keeping our accord. Honesty is an unhealthy attribute and can lead to integrity, and once a pirate has acquired integrity he is as good as dead. His sword loses its cunning and his right arm withers away. And I confess that no matter his answer, I did not expect him to maintain his part of the accord neither.

I expect that Edward knew that I meant to mislead him. Still, he did not mention the deception, and so we crooked arms and shared another goblet of good rum together.

What did Edward know that I did not know?

He was keeping secrets from me. The meaning of "1303." The meaning of "Blood." A blade to his neck might provide the answer, but a blade is a dull instrument when it comes to soliciting a full response, as one is so inclined to use it. It is ever better to persist in artifice. One often learns more from deceit than the hack.

Aye, my answer.

> I have hidden 41 meters from the foundation 6 wooden boxes overlaid in ivory, and all empty, and one remarkable treasure covered in nothing but sackcloth not more than 2 meters deep nor more than 87 meters wide.

The latitude was 41 degrees. It could be no other latitude, as every other latitude took me to a place so distant and inhospitable that it could not be the location. Aye, the latitude was exactly 41 degrees. The trickster wrote that he had hidden the treasure, my crown, 41 degrees from the foundation, and so 41 degrees marked the exact latitude. And where was the foundation? Why nowhere else but Londontown, but mark how I found out.

And here is what I did not tell Edward.

The 6 wooden boxes were all empty according to the trickster, and so I concluded that they should not be counted.

The treasure was buried 2 meters deep and 87 meters wide, but there is no need to dig a hole 87 meters wide for a crown. I put them two numbers, the "2" and the "87," next to each other and the longitude come to no more and no less than 287 degrees. Therefore, so I calculated, the longitude was 287 degrees.

I looked on my chart and placed my compass on 41 degrees by 287 degrees and seen nothing but an ocean of blue on my chart.

Then I seen my error. I should not have measured longitude from Bristol but from Londontown, as the world begins in Londontown.

And then I seen the island, no more than a speck on my chart, mayhap the last place a person might bury a "remarkable" treasure.

But what was the name of the island, as it was not marked on my chart?

Them numbers on the tombstone held the answer. One clue led to another just as one deception led to another. I shall reveal the means of deciphering the clue in time, as there is so much pleasure in maddening you. You know the answer but not how to solve the clue.

You shall wait longer, my hearty.

I believe that I was recounting them malevolent sisters, the Linda Maria and the Bloody Evangeline.

AT FIRST, WE each sailed with half a crew. Jimmy and Louis could not abide each other, but could not bear to part with each other either, and sailed with Edward. Bones sailed with me, and so I raised Bones from first drunkard to first mate. Pew, curse him, brought me ale each twilight until I consented to him staying on my crew. I kept Solomon as he would not have lasted half a watch on the Evangeline, and I still had use for him. Jimmy or Louis would have cut his throat.

We plundered the northern seas, we did, before we turned our keels to the south and the sunnier climes. There was plenty gold for plundering there too, whilst Edward reckoned the location where the treasure might be buried in them six wooden boxes.

I soon learned though that it was a privation to plunder with two ships. Two crews could not board a ship at the same time, as we would scuttle it. Therefore, whilst the men from one ship clambered aboard its prey, the men on board the other ship tarried. We took our murdering turns, so we did, but I lost a good many men in battle as we fought with less of a crew.

It was my initial conjecture that I would only need to lay in half a stock of provisions for half a crew. It warn't so. I had to provide for the men of the Evangeline as well as for my own men, and they all ate like haymakers. I had to fill barrels with biscuits and beer, lay in pounds of cheese and firkins of butter, store granaries of bread, and put aside whole carcasses of beef. Our men sported quality livers, and our larders needed to be filled regularly for the sake of them livers. I would have quartered cattle in the steerage if it warn't already stocked with goods. I would have cured a patch on deck to grow oats if we did not need to tramp the deck.

But a ship ain't a buttery and it ain't a dairy room. She is a ship and needs flints, jackknives, lamps, logbooks, wood, canvas, hemp, cables, and lifts. I even fitted the Evangeline with half my canvas. I sailed with two ships and was twice the poorer for it.

Moreover, the Evangeline was ever in need of timber and copper and iron, as it was ever in need of repair. The Linda Maria was, but for her regular dousing with lye and scouring with brush and wire, as fit and watertight as the day that I first come aboard her. Them saints on her bow never blinked from any grime in their eyes.

"You will sail to the north, and I will sail to the south," I finally told Edward. "You will plunder the top of the world. I will plunder the bottom of it. Mark how I have given you the upper berth," I said. "Then, after two years, we meet in these same waters." Edward removed his hat. I could not help but wonder the amount of blunt that Bones would have paid to have such hair as Edward's that always done Edward's bidding. I suppose that if Edward had been blighted with Bones's hair, Edward might have taken up the drink.

"We are one ship," Edward answered. "We will always be one ship. Ever."

"We split it all, blunt to bills," I told him.

"A drink," Edward said, tossing his hat onto the table with a flourish. "A drink to our good fortune."

And so, my hearty, the Linda Maria and the Evangeline, those malevolent sisters, plundered the open seas. And, the men went forth two by two, though not strictly per the Bible, murdering, as I set the course for our own island of treasure. Aye, that island. Our Treasure Island.

CHAPTER XVI.

THE WHEEL

 woke.

It has been weeks, so Mullet said. He opened the door to my cabin and left me this poisoned food whilst I slept. He looked at me, so he told me, and could not imagine that a man that looked as poorly as I would live.

I have dueled with Mister Fever all these weeks and prevailed. Mister Fever and I stood high on the braces and struck at each other with sabers, and it was a battle such as no other that was ever fought, and if I could defeat that malady, what chance do you have against me?

Solomon, not more than one week after Edward and I parted, bestowed a curse on me. "Seven points nor'west," I told Bones as I set out for the island. Bones turned the wheel so. Thereupon, Solomon told me, "And seven points more damned."

I laughed, so I did. "We are headed for black water now for certain. If I sink, you sink with me," I told him. "You and the other wooden saints on my ship. All go down the same as me." I waited, and he did not disappoint me. He asked me for his liberty, as was his habit, and I denied it, as was my habit. "First you curse me. Seven points more damned, so you said. Then you present a pleading. Denied," I told him, without bothering to return his gaze, as I knew he was staring a breach through me.

I turned from Solomon and treated with Bones. I ordered him to lay to on account of the headwind. Bones's hair blowed aft and up whilst he turned the wheel and then went bunt, as if his mane was finally tired of the effort. The wind gusted, and I told Bones again to lay to.

Now Bones is a man that got his liberty at last and is chased by worse than you or me or any justice in Chancery. Nothing that I might scrawl on this parchment would give a suitable accounting of Billy Bones. This parchment has pallor and so does not bring out the red in Bones's face. This plume does not caper nearly as cleverly as Bones. Bones was a drunkard, but

a sound rover, and maybe one of the best rovers that ever crooked a sword
into a liver. I would need a torrent of quills to relate his rascality. This
parchment is all that is left of our Bones now, and there ain't a blot of him
anywhere else except here.

I am soliciting Bones's case before you. You saw a drunkard, a lout.
But there he is cutting down three men with one swing of his cutlass. Look
at him now. He turns and cuts down three more men.

Soliciting Bones's case is wearisome, but I would finish. I would finish
though the fever is on me again. There ain't a timber of me that ain't
afflicted.

I saw Bones throw a flint glass across the ship, from windlass to transom, and hit Pew square between the eyes.

You see him as a tomfool, just a jack pudding. I see him hale and spirited. Billy Bones was born in a rum barrel, so he was.

And here is Solomon standing before me once more. He has returned
from his watch at the taffrail.

The fever is blistering me from my insides.

One of us will hang and if it is I, it will be a profound disappointment
to the fever.

MULLET SAID THAT we are now in the Azores. He spied him the blue
of Pico Island, and I told him that neither Pico nor the rest of the islands
are blue. The sea plays tricks on sailors, so I told him, and the Azores
have lured many a seaman toward their shores, dashing their ships against
their stubbled coasts. The Azores are to be admired, so I told him, as they
are so sly. Like the trickster.

We may be in the Azores, however I have turned the tiller to the South
Seas. It is there that this tale resumes. Edward, so I believed, was off in the
north while we headed south toward calm waters, and so I was surprised
when I first encountered a storm of some proportion and later encountered
none other than Edward in them same waters. This now is the tale of the
Civility, the storm, the wheel and the changing winds that blowed us to
Treasure Island. It was none other than Solomon, though he did not know
it, who aided me in discovering the true name of our island.

We boarded a ship in the South Seas, an English ship named the Civility, and no name ever suited a ship less. It was a death ship as all her tars
were in the brine, looking rather smart for dead men in their blue jackets

and white pomanders, adrift amongst riches. There were wooden bowls, maps, a fiddle, and a barrel top with nine mens more cut into it. There were chairs, a hand-carved linstock, pepper mills, flagons, and flasks. There was a canister filled with split flint. There was a wooden shot gage. There were lanterns, candles, cutlery, and plates. There were shot, knives, and muskets. There was a sham and a tabor pipe. There were fuel logs, medicine jars, a log reel, sounding leads, and a mallet. There were two brand axes and a bastard culverin. We took all them goods, and then we hoisted two swivel guns by their breeches and brought them on board along with the carriage to the culverin. We did not take the Civility's cannon because we could not free her from her moorings. We even took the timbers off the ship for spare planks.

I entered the captain's cabin and found him relaxed in his chair, his charts spread before him. There was a flagon of ale and a candle on his table, a pair of glasses atop his head, a book on his lap, a nightcap on his head, slippers on his feet, and a woolen gown draped over his shoulders. The captain's face was powdered and he had naught a care in his wigged head on account of the carving knife in his belly. I pried open his fist with the carving knife and two pounds in coppers fell from his hand. I thanked him and bade him a fair night, leaving him two pounds in the hole without any hope of recruit, as it was unlikely that the mutineers that killed him might reimburse him.

The hatch to the steerage was locked, and so Bones blowed the lock off the hatch with his pistol. We found twenty corpses in the straw. "Prisoners," I said, and Bones waggled his finger at the mutineers and rejoined, "No escape now," which were curious words to put to dead men.

We burned the ship and watched her go down until there was naught left on the waters except for our ship and our black souls. The ship's bell rose up in a froth before it fell to the bottom of the sea too. Now them dead men had their bell and could ring it for all their mates in doom.

That eventide I pressed the captain's coppers into Solomon's hands and bade him to see how they shined, telling him that they suited him better than liberty. "A copper begets a shilling and a shilling begets a pound," I told him. "Them are true words. A law of nature, that is. Now rub those coppers between your hands. Rub them and they will shine like shillings. Rub them again, and they will shine like pounds. Rub them even harder, and they will shine like a ransom. Now, tell your captain what you have to say about them coppers." He took them coppers and trudged off to his taffrail, and so I presumed that Solomon had finally seen the error of his ways.

Aye, and then the storm come on us. Rain as sharp as daggers and hail as big as pistol shot fell on us. We shivered so violently that I feared that we would shake the nails in the timbers loose. All hands trimmed the sails and secured the ship, and as strong as I was, I warn't able to hold the wheel by myself and called for Solomon to assist me. I bound his hands and mine to the wheel with rope and rigged our legs to the wheel as well, so that the storm would not bluster us into the deep.

We rode that storm, so we did. We clambered the crest and keeled the bottom of every wave, stabbed by the rain and hammered by the hail. The ropes lashed our legs and arms. The wheel cracked our back. The blasting of the wind turned us as white as them corpses in the water, but we endured it all. When the sky cleared I loosened the ropes, but Solomon said, "It is not done." He drummed on his tooth and aimed a forefinger at a cloud that was now avast the ship. It warn't much of a cloud, and so I told Solomon, who rejoined that we would likely soon be at its mercy.

"Speak to me one of your psalms then," I told him, whereupon he countered that I knew the Bible well enough to speak them myself, reminding me of all that Edward had revealed when we were entombed in the church in Spain. "I would know that Bible's secrets before I expire," I told him. A stout shot of hail fell on the deck just then, no more than two paces from where Solomon and I stood. "Now," I told Solomon. Then the storm commenced its rant again, and I lashed us to the wheel for the second time. The rope cut our hands so deftly that I thought I might lose all my fingers, as it would be like Old Nick to leave a tar with only his thumbs. The wheel turned, and we turned with it like pigs on a spit.

Neither Solomon nor I cried out from the pain. We would not give the other the satisfaction of it, though we were both in agony. We turned with the wheel, shouting to each other. Solomon's eyes blazed. He could have boiled the seas with them eyes. "If you spent all your time, every day of your life reading every letter in Edward's Bible," so he shouted, "you would never understand it." The storm paid no heed to Solomon and continued to beat at us. "Every letter in Edward's Bible," so he bellowed, and at once I knew me the answer. I had solved the cipher on the tombstone.

1-1-4-4-5-7-9-12-14-14-14-15-18-18-19-19

Leave us apply a simple letter code to the ciphers, shall we? The legend reads thus and could be no simpler.

A-1 B-2 C-3 D-4 E-5 F-6 G-7 H-8 I-9 J-10 K-11 L-12 M-13
N-14 O-15 P-16 Q-17 R-18 S-19 T-20 U-21 V-22 W-23 X-24
Y-25 Z-26

Therefore, we may interpret the numbers to read so.

A-A-D-D-E-G-I-L-N-N-N-O-R-R-S-S

It may be that a man needs to be upside down to see the world right, and when Solomon spoke them words about every letter of the Bible, I seen the cipher and the answer.

Mind you I had tried the cipher wheels on this clue but come up with naught but nonsense. And so, while I was heels over head in that storm, I seen all them clues once more, and this one too, and so I heard Solomon's words and applied letters to the numbers but in a diverse order as befitting a man spinning round on a wheel.

I shall reorder the numbers and letters for your benefit.

15-14 7-1-18-4-14-5-18-19 9-19-12-1-14-4

The answer consequently reads as follows.

ON GARDNERS ISLAND

Now, a person might be tempted to rewrite the answer to read "No Gardners Island," for hadn't I misinterpreted the clue to Cat Island? But that would be a false clue, would it not?

Or would it?

All the ciphers lined up as taut as a lanyard.

Or did they?

The men, those of them that were able to stand, unbound us, and as soon as Solomon was freed, he fell upon the deck. I ordered the men to drag Solomon below and I strolled my deck then, sir, and my hearties cheered me.

All the ciphers seemed as simple as Mullet's brow once I had me the answers. I would follow the stars to 41 degrees latitude and 287 longitude, direct to the spot where the treasure lay. On Gardners Island.

The Evangeline was still, to my unawares, in them same waters, and so I hailed her and learned that Edward had lost two men in the storm, one of which was Jimmy, who washed overboard whilst in the rigging. I did not lose a single man.

I wondered if Edward was dogging me. He claimed to have sailed to the north, as agreed, but returned on account of inclement weather. I admonished him on bringing it to me. Aye, but that conversation was not till the following day.

I took a swig of the hot rum that Bones brought me, went below, and slumbered until near the next day. No man could wake me.

Hell would have been a respite from my shivers that night. I must remember to ask the devil's mistress to heap on the coals so that I might canker in comfort. But do not throw lime on me yet, Captain. I still breathe, though my breath ain't much more than sea mist on account of this fever. My tongue still wriggles. It will break off soon enough.

Hear the end of my tale. I light my lantern. I grip the quill.

Aye, and here is your Mullet floundering outside my door, smearing the last pages of this parchment with his greasy fingers. We will see what he makes of his captain soon enough, when I unearth the treasure and then the final bloody secret. We will see then, sir.

CHAPTER XVII.

THE TREASURE

ullet entered my cabin and looked on me whilst I slumbered from the fever. I opened my eyes and he is exactly as I imagined him. He has the look of a broom-boy. There ain't no glint in his eyes. His hair is cut flat. He is as short and round as a plug. He is enough of a dullard to be a peer of the realm.

Later he sprawled outside my cabin, offered me the poisoned food, then ate it to the last limb. I spoke of cannibals whilst he gnawed away, declaring that he would look right sharp with a bone through his nose. He thanked me between bites and advised me that I warn't fit eats for cannibals because of my blisters. I almost took to the lad. The poison suits him, as it has improved his disposition. If Mullet ain't dead by the time I take over the ship, I shall permit him to suck on sweets whilst I gut his captain.

So we are well past the Azores now and in the Dardanelles strait, between the Aegean Sea and the Sea of Marmara," I told him.

"The captain says I have me prospects," he replied.

"Possibly as bait."

"I should not have given you the bearing," Mullet said.

"So you did. So you did. I may have been off beam about your prospects. You may rise to captain one day," I told him.

"Captain," he said, the word barely audible.

"Take heart, lad. It is possible that you may rise to that rank if every other man on board drops from plague." And then, with his usual sigh, Mullet departed.

You have struck a most interesting course, as we are in between worlds, off Asia and the fortifications of Canakalle, and yet away from Europe and the tow of Hellespont. The water runs in both directions here, to each of the great bodies of land. There is the current and the tow, and the Linda Maria is turning about whilst you put us on our final course. The current flows to Europe and the tow streams to Asia, and so here we are betwixt worlds again. I had always skirted Geliboku, taken the blue Aegean and left the Turks to their pipes, but you mean to show me that you are the more daring fellow. We shall us see.

As I wrote, I had incorrectly reckoned the longitudes from Bristol rather than from Londontown, and so I determined the distance between the two and revised my charts. I dipped my nail in lampblack, making blots along the correct longitudinal lines, so if someone should fall upon the charts they would think them blots just carelessness. I set the sails for 41 degrees latitude and 287 degrees longitude, on the edge of the new world, and drafted with the wind at all speed for Treasure Island.

Edward come to a different conclusion about the location of the treasure, and as it was not in my interest to inform him of his error, I allowed him his fancy when we spoke the day after the storm. He was keen that the ciphers led to nowhere else but Britain, although he offered no proof that he would find the treasure there. It was a treasure, so he maintained, that remained in Britain, as the Bible had been kept in Londontown, and that accordingly Londontown was likely both the beginning and end of our wanderings. The other ciphers, he asserted, were false clues meant to distract us. But where in Londontown I asked him, and he replied that he, like me, would have to discover it.

And so I sailed to the south and Edward sailed to the north, as originally agreed, and as if Nick desired to heap glory upon glory, just after I set my course I come upon the Dorchester, a custard pie of a ship, the richest ship that I ever plundered.

The Dorchester was late of the Sandwich Islands, late of the Mediterranean, late of Valparaiso and New Spain and, lastly, late of these same Dardanelles. Her keel drowsed low in the water, as she was clotted with coppers, packed with tea and tobacco, sopped in rum and stuffed with grain. I dipped my spoon into her crust and champed on rials and farthings and pieces of eight.

We blowed a hole through the Dorchester's strake and her foremast fell along with the riggers atop it. We slipped to the Dorchester's larboard, doused our sails, then rammed her and took her wind. We threw our grapnels and lanyards across her bow and bound the Dorchester to us telltale and heart with our hawsers.

Pew, whilst lighting the tinder that burned the Dorchester to slag, said to me, "Edward would be pleased with such a catch. We must tell him when we meet again. We must share our good fortune with him, and all of it. Once, many years past, Pew saw him a Bible. You told Pew to never speak of it, and so Pew never done," he lied. "Pew heard Jimmy speak of it to Edward after it fell from Edward's effects when we parted ways, and Pew seen Edward bade him to silence. But Jimmy spoke of it to another, and them are the two men that died in the storm. Pew is trusty, not like Jimmy, as Pew never said a word to you on that Bible. Pew only makes mention of it now as he wonders if we ain't owed something for them two dead men, as right is right. Pew heard him other matters over the years too and never spoke a word of it, not never."

"As you would not see the next dawn."

"Pew ain't given to the dramatic, but he does like to take in the sunrise."

"We shall keep it so," I told him. I drew a deep breath, and Pew done the same. "For now. So long as you keep that promise."

"Pew is constant," he said, and he scuttled off to watch the Dorchester flame.

We were too portly to sail with dispatch, and I was concerned that we might not arrive at our island before the season changed and the wind raged against us. We flew no flag and avoided all vessels, and the passage took even more time than I had anticipated as we crossed Newfoundland, navigated the Grand Banks, and circumvented Yarmouth, a circuitous route so as to evade all but the chill of the sea.

The men grumbled and fell into a mood as we come on dead winds and sailed into shifting tides. I refused to drop anchor. And then the sea turned.

My Linda Maria whined in a lancing gale in the Bay of Fundy. I poured the men rum and held my dear's wheel until we were out of them waters, and then we sailed plumb for no more and no less than forty days until we reached the coast of Gardners Island, and there we finally dropped anchor.

I scratched "Treasure Island" in the lightest lampblack in the corner of my chart and placed the map behind my glass for safekeeping, in the same place that Black John had placed my death warrant so long ago.

The men wanted to go ashore, and so I let them as there was no harm to it. Mind you that I had found the island but had no notion of where the treasure lay. I stood on deck, the only man not tramping the ground that I had searched for every day since Edward first showed me his black book. The men returned with apples and pears and boars and even a stag, and we feasted, so we did. Even Solomon grinned after making himself a porridge from the roots on the island.

I could not sleep. I walked the deck and waited, but for whom or what I could not say.

Then, and it must have been near midnight, I climbed the rigging. I might have missed the thin finger of moonlight if the clouds had been any thicker, but I followed the light and saw a stand of trees that looked like a bundle of sticks. And then the moonlight was gone, a cloud obscuring the vision, but I had seen it. I had seen that stand of trees that looked exactly like the headpiece.

I was keen to swing all the way from the rigging to the shore and dig up my treasure, and it took all my resolve not to do so, and I drank that night, so I did. Whisky, sir. Whisky, so I drank, until the bottle was empty, and I slept until dawn.

I decided to disembark with only seven men and one sea crab, Pew by name, so to bury my own riches in the woods. Them tars carried sack after sack of my riches to the island, bearing them on their backs like plough horses. I done my share of work too. I tied each sack with a ribbon and numbered each one of my sacks, which come to seventy-three. The coins and jewels and bracelets and such rang out as the men carried them. It was music, so it was, and I might have danced before the men, leading them on, if I was of the mood, and the men warn't so unsightly. The long journey must have, however, taken a grip on the men and, as we come ashore, a lowly tar took it upon himself to protest that all the men deserved to tramp the sand again after so long at sea. They all, so he said, deserved to sleep on the sand. Never mind that I had granted them their leave already and could not allow the ship to be unattended. And, the man appended, all of them that carried my sacks should have them a keg of ale apiece.

Pew, knowing more than he ever let on, told the man that I would make him wealthier than his mother ever fancied when she first spied his foul face, whereupon the man took offense and cuffed Pew. Pew drew his dagger, and the man done likewise. "Hold," Bones told the man. "You might inadvertently split Pew in two. One Pew is foul enough. Two Pews would be a torment."

Pew maintained that one of him was enough to send the man to blazes, and he jabbed but only managed to mangle the air as the man skipped out of range. The tar danced round Pew, and Pew turned this way and that whilst the men taunted Pew, and the fellow called to Pew afresh. Pew thrust, and the fellow skipped. Pew could not pin him, but a hearty with a dagger ain't a hearty to be taken lightly, and so it come to be that the fellow skipped aft and Pew thrust lee, then the fellow skipped lee and Pew thrust aft, then the man skipped lee, and so Pew stabbed, and Pew caught him.

The tar clutched his chest and dropped.

The other men pulled their daggers and advanced on Pew. I ordered them to husk their daggers and when they continued their advance, I commanded Bones to raise his pistol. The men ceased their assault. I pointed to the spot where the men should dig, which, by no chance at all, was the spot amidst the stand of trees where I expected to find the crown. The men went about their duty, and I told Bones and Pew to remain at my side under the pretense that Pew was my prisoner.

The men worked until the sweat ran off them in sheets as the ground was so unforgiving, and whilst they dug Pew begged for leniency and Bones's hair flew up in a fury. I loaded my pistol with powder and ball, and the men cheered, as they believed that the shot was meant for Pew.

Pew believed the same and pleaded with me, pulling at my blouse until he near tore it off, squeaking, "1303. Pew knows him the meaning."

"What clatter is this?" Bones inquired. I told Bones to disregard Pew's words as they were naught but nattering.

Then, "A grave," one of the men called out, pulling a leg from it, then an arm and lastly a hand. I inquired if there was but one grave, and the men called back they had found just one carcass. "Are there any boxes there?" I called to them. "Six boxes, to be exact?" They answered back that aught that was there had already been found, and he warn't in a box but in the loam. They held up the fellow and I seen that he held a parchment of the same pallor as Edward's Bible.

Bones fetched the parchment and I read the words. *Magnus inter opes inops.* So this was my prize, a dead man and another cipher, and no tar on board that could translate the words. Aye, but then I weighed up the matter again. I would oblige Solomon to tell me the meaning of the dead man's cipher.

I ordered the men to plant our riches, the dead conniver, and their mate in the pit, and after I congratulated them on their industriousness, I shot them one by one through their hearts, excepting them that I slayed with my sword.

"The men," Bones said, his hair flying up in the wind.

"They disobeyed an order and advanced after I told them to cease."

"But them were good men," Bones said, his hair slacking at last.

"Not no more," I told him.

Pew buried the men after picking through their pockets. I was inclined to send him to blazes, but he knew the answer to the riddle of "1303." Aye, and I needed both him and Bones to pledge witness to the unfortunate deaths of my hearties by wild beasts on the island.

We returned to the Linda Maria, and as soon as we boarded, Pew said, "Animals. Horrible, horrible. Enormous teeth. Pew saw him lions and tigers. Cats as big as corsairs. Our captain saved Pew. The captain is a quick shot. Quick as quick is. Crows as big as jennies," Pew went on. "Serpents as long as a rattlewatch's shadow. Oxen with horns as sharp as a hedger's axe. Horrible, Pew says."

The men were ready to sail straightaway after Pew's account. And so we did, by way of a southerly breeze to Bristol for supplementary boatswains, Bones drinking his weight in Madeira and Solomon refusing to render me an answer. Solomon bargained for his liberty as recompense and so I locked him in a cabin, and he warn't at all contrite about his punishment and not even after I broke his water jar by way of reply.

All my troubles had come to naught. I had not solved the ciphers, and all I had received for my labours were a dead man and another cipher, though I had found a resting place for my treasure on my Treasure Island.

The Madeira made Bones sickly one night and he near run up the cap, avowing that Ben Gunn had come to claim him. Bones graciously offered old Ben a drink, but Ben refused, as the drink would have run right through him. He swaggered on to tell Bones that he had acquired a nice sum since Bones had marooned him, and that he sailed not for guineas or doubloons, but for souls now. He traded in souls so dark, so Bones told me, that when they come to snuff, there warn't nothing left of them but smoke. Then Ben belayed his rope and told Bones that his captain wanted Bones to join his crew. Bones had aspirations, he did, and asked his berth and lay. I can't fault Bones for the inquiry, but it is one matter to ask about opportunity and another matter to take it, especially when treating with a dead man.

Ben advised Bones that his captain would only take him for a gob and that his lay would be as long as all the evenings in the world. Bones clenched his nightcap when he told me that, so he did.

Ben warn't to be appeased at all and told Bones that there would be no whisky for him on his ship. No rum. Nor ale. Nor even Madeira, but only seawater. He was all principle that night, he was, old Ben Gunn. Bones vowed to make matters right between him and Ben, so that he could have a tot now and then. Lastly, Ben told Bones that he would take him in Bristol. Bones clasped both his hands to his head and tore off his nightcap when I told him that we were only three seas from Bristol.

I asked Bones if there was any Madeira left, as I wanted some words with Ben, and Bones said that he had thrown all of the bottles overboard, except for one stowed under his bunk, a present from Pew. All them bottles, so Bones said, were presents from Pew. I inquired if Ben looked at all like Pew, and Bones remarked that he did notice a fair resemblance during the visitation.

I took the bottle, sniffed it, and knew that Pew had tainted it. I seized Pew by his ear and dragged him to my cabin, then I poured the bottle down Pew's gullet. "Pew has conspired," he moaned. "Pew has conspired grievously." Then he went to sleep directly, and Black John must have sat with Old Nick over a pot of swamp roots to plot Pew's nightmare as Pew screamed all through the night. I should have shaken Pew down to his stern until he confessed his true crime. He had conspired against me, but I did not know the extent of his treachery until later. I had only believed that he had conspired with himself to torment Bones.

I importuned Pew to tell me what he saw that night, and first it was Kwik and Smith, rotted through and through. Pew maintained that they abetted Ben's conspiracy. "Pew will never trust a cadaver again," Pew said, denying that he had tormented Bones. "Then Ben Gunn appeared before Pew, just as he done to Bones, and looked on himself in Pew's glass. He was as thin as gravy and accused you of abandoning him, and so Pew set him to rights and told him that he was naught but dregs. Ben carried a bible with him as always, though Pew don't know of what use it would be to Ben in the nether kingdom. Lest it got them ciphers in it," Pew added, whereupon he clasped his hands over his mouth.

I accused Pew of tainting the Madeira, and when he denied it I told him that I would provide him with a tainted brew each night. Pew dropped to his knees, spat on my boots, and rubbed them with his sleeve until he seen his reflection in them. "Pretty Pew," so he said. "It would not do for Pew to die in the captain's cabin over such a matter." I grabbed his neck, and his tongue wriggled out whilst he tried to speak.

"Tell me all," I bade him.

Pew twittered like a parakeet. "Ben's breath was intolerably foul, and he warn't to be peaceable, and so Pew ordered him away. Aye, but then he startled me. He skulked back a few steps and said that Edward had pushed Louis off the bowsprit and into the sea. Pew asked how Jimmy fared now that he was dead, and Pew was most displeased to hear that Jimmy was tied to the brails of a fourmaster and did naught but watch his brother walk the sea bed in vain."

"And what did Ben say about my island?" I asked Pew.

"Aught but what we already know," Pew replied. "Ben preferred his own island, the one where you marooned him, though it don't got near as much gold as ours. Pew distinctly recalls Edward telling Jimmy of a land of gold and Jimmy saying so to Louis, and Louis, out of spite, telling a swain. And now all of them dead according to Ben, and Ben would know. Aye, Edward's Bible fell, and Jimmy seen it, and before we parted them two had their talk. Jimmy and Louis were preacher boys, but Pew never spoke a word of it to you as Pew don't tell tales. They knew Latin, all the good verses too," Pew confided. Then, "Ben seen all and told all. Pew only knows what he sees and hears for his own self."

"Them numbers," I ordered Pew. "Tell me their meaning."

Pew hesitated, looking all about, as if a younker might be under my bunk, before telling me, "1303 is a date. A date that such as us should revere. Pew says that he might even recount more if the captain spares his life." I put the point of my dagger to Pew's neck. "Pew says that 1303 is the date of the greatest thievery of all time. Pew says that there was a time when Pew was considered to have prospects for a career in Chancery. No one ever minds Pew, fair Pew," he said, stroking his cheek. "No one inquires as to his health or relations or parentage, but they tell poor Pew to do this business and that business. It might interest the captain to know that Pew's father was a magistrate, and he told Pew many tales whilst flogging poor Pew. One such tale was about a crown." Pew looked up at me. "A crown," he repeated. I sheathed my dagger. "Pew's father was run over by a coach and four. Pew happened upon him that same night. By chance, as they never proved otherwise and even though I had my father's gold watch in my pocket."

"You killed your own father, Pew?"

"Not Pew. Never Pew. Pew says it was the shay that run over him as it was such a dark night. And rainy too. Squall weather. And Pew never seen him until the hooves trampled him into the cobblestones."

"Repeatedly no doubt."

"The horse reared some," Pew replied. "I rode directly to the shipyard as Black John was ready to sail. The ship left that very evening. Black John was to be charged for some crime, so my father told me, by way of coincidence. The evidence disappeared that same night."

"Timely, Pew."

"My father always spoke to his Pew kindly when he warn't flogging him. He taught his son all about justice. That was how I learned the meaning of 1303."

"There ain't no shay here, Pew. Just you and me and my dagger. Tell me."

"It is always this business or that business with Pew," he carped again. "But Pew is loyal. He never spoke on Edward's Bible to no one. Nor on the date. But Pew will tell the captain as the captain has made a particular inquiry. Is the captain ready for Pew's reply?" he asked. I was inclined to cut him till there was naught left of him to put in a cupboard. "You see, 1303 is the date that the Crown Jewels were set in the Tower of London, taken there after they were stolen that same year from Westminster Abbey. Pew can feel his father's whip. Burglary, burglary, he used to tell Pew. There is no reward in it. Only loss to all concerned."

"We know us better. And you know best of all, Pew. So tell me more."

"All the treasure was recovered. Almost all the treasure, so Pew recalls the account. The Crown Jewels were placed in the Tower where they are guarded by six black ravens. Aye, and guards too."

"Almost all the treasure, Pew?"

"So Pew's father told him. Does the captain not feel the sting of the lash? Pew is ever in pain. And there is more. More to the tale. Much more. The Crown Jewels were stolen again. Melted down by Cromwell. Pew knows him all about it. The captain must know him too. The warder clubbed to death. All such trouble. Such trouble. Pew can still hear his father warning him that he would chain him to a bedpost. The hooves on the cobblestones. The whistle of the whip. Can you not hear it too? Blood is the answer. The answer to all and everything. I hear it coursing. Aye, the blood," Pew said before I cut off his ear.

"Now you need no longer be troubled by what you hear," so I told him.

Pew fell to the ground as the ship pitched, one hand on his head where his ear had resided and the other hand grabbing for his ear, which rolled about my cabin. He tried to screw it back to his skull but warn't successful, and so I offered him some words of encouragement. "I imagine that your eyesight will improve now as well." Pew reeled about my cabin and left it in a dead run, and thereafter always wore a red bonnet around his head.

Pew had said, "Blood," and "Blood" so the trickster had written in Edward's black book. I recalled the name of one Thomas Blood who had stolen the Crown Jewels in 1671, which would have pleased Cromwell if he warn't on a pike. Edward's Cromwell. "Blood" was not a clue but a name.

And I had left Edward to ramble round the world. I had even given him his ship. Where was Edward now and what had he discovered? He was in search of the treasure and if he found it I would not have it unless I found him and took it from him. It was my treasure. It was my crown and belonged atop my head.

And I had given him his ship, his very own ship to search for my treasure.

And that warn't all to the matter of Bones and Pew and Ben neither. Ben paid regular visits to Bones from then on. Bones commenced to talk to Ben at night, and insisted that I could see Ben too, but I never saw Ben, but only Pew in his red bonnet, and no matter how many times Bones pointed out Ben on the transom.

CHAPTER XVIII.

A TAVERN IN BRISTOL

———◆———

Mullet is moaning. I tried to cheer him with a song about the severed head of an alderman who got axed by his wife, but Mullet moaned all the more.

"Your captain cannot very well drop you into the Atlantic, as he is respectable now. Respectable men do not drop cabin boys into the Atlantic. Apparently, they poison them."

"I never seen a man in a red bonnet. But what about the dead man's cipher and what happened in Bristol?" Mullet inquired.

"As coincidence would have it, that is what I intend to write next. Your captain must have told you all about Thomas Blood, or you would have bade me to tell you. And he told you about the Hawkins boy too. And Bones. And what become of Pew. Nevertheless, I will write about it all in time. Even about Mister Blood."

"I know all about Blood."

"You know naught. Straight naught."

———◆———

Where was I to go? All my travels had led to a dead man and another piece of parchment. Yet another cipher.

And where was Edward? What ciphers had he solved?

What was the meaning of the dead man's cipher?

Solomon insisted that he be given his liberty, attempting to trade it for the translation of the verse clutched in the dead man's hand. Each time that I threatened to kill him he laughed, and so I locked him in his cabin until he was disposed to be of aid to me.

I decided to repair in the town that I knew me best. I returned to Bristol.

I tramped to a certain tavern nigh the seaside. Aye, the Three Goats.

I smelled the smoke from the coals, banged on the door, and called for Peel. No answer. I struck at the door with my walking stick. An old lady opened the door but a splinter and asked me my business. All that I could see of her was the shades around her eyes where she had rubbed them, smudging her paint. I gripped the brass knob.

"My pardon, miss," I told her, whilst she scowled on account of the late hour of my call. "Now where would you be keeping Peel?" I asked, slipping on a smile that was all innocence. "I need a night's berth," I told her. "And breakfast. Eggs and ale," I said. "My name is Silver. John Silver."

"John Silver you say. Is it John Silver?" she asked me. "I recall that my dear departed spoke of you." She opened the door a frap wider. I could have blown her and the door down with a yawn. "Eggs and ale?" Her nose was long and bony and come to a point. She toddled her fingers around the door one by one and grasped it as best she could. She looked me over bollocks to bulkhead.

"Dear and departed? Not Dick Peel?" I asked. She licked her upper lip and told me that Peel had passed on five years ago. The hinges of the door scraped as she leaned against it, and the fire in the hearth guttered, then flamed. She removed her fingers from around the door. "And how shall I address you, madam?" I asked, but I knew her name well enough. I recalled her. Aye, I recalled her, and all I could think of at the moment was poor Peel and his book of accounts. He must have devoted passages and passages to her in his ledger. He must have bit off the tip of his plume when she finally consented to wed him. She likely fed him that plume with his morning biscuits, and mayhap that was how my patron come to his end, at the nub of his plume.

"Judith," she answered me. Her voice had the timbre of rusted gallows. "Silver, you say," she creaked. "You are not someone else asking for eggs and ale?" She closed the door a crack, and I could no longer see the light from the fire.

"Judith, I would enter this tavern," I told her. "You may remember me. I brought you your meals from time to time. I was a boy then, and now I am a captain." She near chawed off her upper lip. "We were thick, Dick Peel and I. Captain Silver, so they call me these days." The shadow of the fire disappeared. "I was named by none other than Black John in this very tavern. I will sleep in the room overlooking the seaside," I told her. "My old quarters. You were a lovely," I lied, but she did not reply. "You may tell your customers that Long John Silver slept here," I told her. "It will be good for business."

"I will tell them that Judith shut you out this night." Thereupon, she slammed the door. "Away," she declared. I could hardly hear her through the door, thick as it was to keep Peel and his profits locked inside.

"I would we be more like relations. Your mister and I were on the best of terms, Madam," I protested.

I only fancied one night's berth. I had spent my entire term at the Three Goats working out how I would depart it, and now I wanted naught but to sleep in my old quarters again. Peel would have been knocked for six by my exploits, and likely would have dropped tuppence for a new ledger to write them down. But Peel was gone, and Judith warn't interested in acquiring me as a relation, not even for the night, and there warn't no one left in Bristol to tell about my deceit and double-dealing, unless the pinching constable was still wheezing about town.

I heard her scamper up Peel's stairs. "No doubt Peel hired a coachman, madam, as soon as he was undone. To speed him away from you," I bellowed, whilst I hammered on her door. If she replied, I did not hear her. I imagine that she was under her covers with a carving knife.

It was a shame I say that so fine an establishment burned down to cinders, and so soon after I left that crone under her covers. I had only recently taken up the pipe and must have been some careless with my tinder.

I traversed the dusky lanes of Bristol, and having been taught to see by a blind man, did not need lamplight to find my way. I pulled away the bricks in one lane, reached inside the wall, and pulled out a blanket. It was Tom's blanket, it was. The wool was mostly gone. Mites are as greedy as men, I say. I threw the blanket over my shoulders, left the lane, and tottered over the stones until I spied a dim light.

The Black Dog was near the mouth of the great western dock, and was filled with tarts and tars, with my men telling tales of our travels under the skull and bones. Thin Jim, the proprietor who warn't thin no more, was drunk. He bade me to sit at his best table and tell him my pleasure. I called for ale, and a woman approached me. Pew trooped a grenadier around a hearty that lay dead drunk on the floor, preparing to reach into his pocket. My lass flicked a crumb from the table at Pew. "I never catch all the names," she went on, putting her hands around my waist. "You are all Bills and Mikes and Jacks. And, there ain't no difference between any of you in the dark. I never catch all the names, especially the ones that ain't evident. Such as the name of the drunkard's mate, the one that I could see clear through. He said that it would please him if I poured his mate a drink, but there warn't no one there." I looked about the tavern. Bones was gone. I pushed her off me. The woman called after me, "He asked me to skip with his mate, and I would have for the right coin, even though I could not see a hair of him. Now I recall his mate's name. Ben, it was," she cackled, nearly tripping over a hearty felled on the pine.

Pew was pulling on his bonnet so to protect his other ear, and warbled that Bones had left with his sea chest. Then Pew darted under a table and went on that Bones had confided in him, though Pew warn't able to hear him particularly well. Bones took a map, so Pew said. "What map would that be?" I asked Pew, and he replied that it was a map smeared by lampblack. Ben told Bones, according to Pew, to take it as amends for his crimes. I lifted Pew by his neck and held him so whilst he flailed about. I flung him atop a table and he skittered off it with a firm clutch of his bonnet.

My men searched the River Avon and called into the Avon Gorge for their mate. They searched from Giant's Cave to the Severn Estuary for Bones, from the Cotswold to the Mendips and from the Black Mountains to the Forest of Dean. But mostly they searched the taverns, picking through sotted seaman, until they finally found him in a tavern by name of the Admiral Clifton.

I sent Pew to the Admiral Clifton in hopes that Bones might skewer him and so save me the bother, but Bones only put a dagger to his throat and told Pew that he had quit the sea trade. "The lady of the tavern spat on Pew," Pew complained. "A foul woman," Pew said. "She goes by the name of Hawkins. Julie Hawkins. A son but no husband. And a lodger," Pew trilled. "Name of Trelawney. Squire Trelawney, so Pew believes he heard them address him." Pew held his hand to where his ear had been. "A squire. Old." I pulled at my collar and Pew tugged at his. "Pew would venture that Bones told them, at least the boy," he whispered. "Told them about our"—and Pew turned his head sideways and sang—"island."

I told Pew to return to the Admiral Clifton and press a pound note into Julie Hawkins's palm, so we might speak with our dear mate. Pew peered inside, entered, and quickly scuttled out.

"The birds have flown!" he piped. We searched Bones's room. All that remained of my hearty was his sea chest. Shiling, Whitman, Pew, and I stood watch until daybreak, when the boy and his mother returned, and then Shiling and Whitman sprinted up the stairs. I heard a shot and Shiling tumbled down the stairs. He tore at his chest until his eyes widened, and his arms fell limp to his sides. Then Whitman backed down the stairs followed by Julie Hawkins, who was pointing a pistol at him. It was Bones's pistol. The boy stood behind his mother, and they looked right defiant too, they did.

Mother Hawkins's head was dainty, but rested on shoulders as large as mattocks. Her legs were muttons. Her hair was thin and long and hung about her, seemingly some despondent. Her neck was as thin as a spar, but her hands were near as large as my own mitts. No part of her matched any other part, and even one of her nostrils flared out whilst the other one hid behind it.

The boy had tawny-coloured hair and deep brown eyes. He looked able for a lad of his years, and I put his term at twelve. He had broad shoulders that suited him better than they done his mother.

"We come calling," I said with a smile. "For one Billy Bones." I gave mother and son a smile, all cordiality, and I continued. "We heard that he took up residence with you. Temporarily," I added.

"You are Silver," the boy said instantly. "He said that you would come for him. He spoke of you too," the boy said, pointing at Pew.

"Pew and Bones were shipmates," Pew replied, bobbing his head up and down.

"Pew. He said Pew, Mother." Jim clenched his fists. I took to that lad right off, I did.

"No need for a pistol," I told Julie Hawkins as melodiously as I could manage. "I come to visit with my shipmate. It seems that our Mister Shiling frightened you. That is our Mister Shiling on the floor." Jim advised his mother to aim the pistol square between my eyes. Jim had him prospects, he did.

"The captain said that you would call for him," Jim said, patting his hair just like Bones. "He said that you would murder him."

"Aye, a captain. Captain Billy Bones. That is right," I said. "Right as dry powder. He would be a captain now," I told the lad. "Murder him, did he say? Murder our own shipmate? That is a rich tale, that is," I said. "One of his best. A question." I leaned forward. "Was he drinking some?" I asked. "Rum perchance? I knew him to tell a tale or two with spirits in him. But murder our own shipmate? Never. We come to warn him of danger."

"Grave danger," Pew chanted.

"Danger, Mother Hawkins," I told her. "There are men after him, and so we dashed in here. There ain't no time to tarry. Billy Bones owes a debt, and his creditors, crafty sorts all, are at his heels. We come to pay that debt. Where is our shipmate?" I asked.

"Dead," Mother Hawkins replied. "He was fond of the rum and finally drank his fill. Drank himself to death," she put in. "Dead, sir. Rotting dead." I told her that I had twenty guineas to pay his creditors and offered to settle his bill with her, as I would rather she have the coin than his creditors. "Jim, what say?" she asked. Jim suggested that she shoot me. Aye, but I took to that lad.

"Jim is it?" I asked, holding out my hand. "A fine name for a fine lad," I told him, retrieving my hand after he refused to take it. "I would see our Billy Bones, Jim. One last time, so to pay last respects. Where is my old shipmate?"

"Doctor Livesey's," Julie Hawkins interceded.

"But his sea chest is for me," Jim said. "He promised it to me. He swore an oath and spat."

"That is no more than right then," I said. "If he made a pledge and spat, then that chest is yours. And right you are to tell me, Jim."

Julie Hawkins lowered Bones's pistol.

I was charm itself, I was. Pew was silent for once and Whitman took to fluttering his eyes at Julie Hawkins. There is no telling with some gobs. They take to all classes of ships.

I inquired if I might see Bones's sea chest one last time before a brief respite at Doctor Livesey's, being as I was sentimental from my flagstaff to my forefoot. Julie Hawkins told us to walk in front of her. "I walk slowly," I apologized. "The stairs are a chore for a man with sea legs and a limp. And how do you fare, Mister Pew? No need to reply," I said. "Mark you, Jim, that he does not see well with that bonnet on his head. It is to cover his topmast. No hair there, Jim. Not a hospitable clime above his neck. The bonnet falls over his good eye on account that there is nothing to hold it. Best take care lest he tumble. There is one soul at the bottom of the stairs already."

Pew grabbed Jim's arm. "A strong boy. Help poor Pew. Would you, lad?"

Jim batted Pew away.

"No harm," I said. "Mister Whitman here, who has been silent, will go first. He does not speak much," I said. "But when he does, every declaration is true. It might as well be," I appended. "He don't have him much of a tongue left." Whitman produced what remained of his tongue and grinned. "I will follow Mister Pew to make certain that he does not pitch down the stairs."

We proceeded to Bones's chamber.

"I am true to my word," I told Jim. "His chest is yours, Master Hawkins. All yours. You were fond of our shipmate, and he was likely fond of you if you brought him rum. He told you tales. Am I correct, Jim?" Then, "Did he ever speak of a shipmate, one Ben Gunn?" I asked.

"Not so I recall," Jim answered. "He spoke about him," Jim said, pointing at Pew. "He said that he was unsightly but did not do him justice, as to call him hideous would be praise." Pew pulled down on his bonnet. "The key, Mother," Jim said, and she pulled it from her apron and gave it to him. "Raise your pistol, Mother." He was already giving orders, good lad.

"We will see what all sea dogs come to now. Give Mister Whitman the key to your chest, Jim," I told Jim. Whitman turned the key in the lock and lifted the lid. "Look here," I said. "A spyglass. A fine one too. Look through that glass, Jim. What do you see? A ship? Men heaving to and fro, swinging from the ropes?"

"He saw them without the glass, Mother," Jim said.

"Sea eyes, Jim." I looked inside the chest and proclaimed, "Nothing else, Jim. A lesson to us all. He sailed around the world and ended in a box. Come you, men. We are away." We walked down the stairs with Bones's pistol at our backs. "But your payment, madam." I dug into my purse. "I count twenty guineas," I said, and proffered the money to Jim, who placed it on the table. Whitman bowed to the mother. "Aye, but he is partial to you, Julie Hawkins," so I said. "Still, we depart. Give me your hand, Jim. I would wish you the best of luck." And as I said them words I grabbed his wrist and told Julie Hawkins to lower her pistol. "Pew, is your sight so poor that you can't see them guineas? I leave you one Shiling instead," I told Mother Hawkins. "And now you will take us to the doctor," I told her, but I spoke too soon.

Just then a man entered the room, a man that was unassuming in every feature but one. He was holding a pistol. "Squire Trelawney, shoot them all," Jim proposed.

Trelawney ordered us to stand fast, and old as he was he still spoke with the air of a blue coat. You would have taken to Trelawney. He told me to release Jim, and so I done, just as Whitman grabbed Hawkins's pistol. I advised Trelawney to lay down his arms as Whitman would not miss him, but Trelawney countered that he would not miss us.

"Pew must live," Pew pleaded. "Fair Pew," Pew sputtered, stroking his face. "No punishment does Pew merit. Firstly Black John, then the captain and Edward, Pew served. Pew only served others," he sniveled before attempting to dash out the window. The squire fired at Pew, and Pew curled up on the floor of the tavern, a dead sea crab, red bonnet and all. Whitman fired at the squire and struck him. I grabbed Jim. Mother Hawkins screamed. And all was near square, but I still wanted my map.

CHAPTER XIX.

DOCTOR LIVESEY

Mullet has ceased his moaning.

"*You have expired, Mullet. Do not deny it.*"

"*The weather has calmed but for the summer rain, sir. We will be in port within a fortnight. Captain said. We have had naught but fine weather on this crossing.*"

"*All inclement, lad. All inclement.*"

Mullet bade me to go on about the map, and so I done, but not before he told me that he did not believe me. I assured him that my tales warn't just turnips and trumps, and nearly told him the exact spot on the island where I finally found the treasure. Well, sir, now I know the game and the play, and so here is my hand.

Whitman stole two steeds and hoisted Julie Hawkins onto his mottled gray, grasping her apron strings along with the reins whilst I rode the black with Jim. Men in toppers and ladies in adornments rolled and strolled through the streets, past idlers, but mostly past litter after litter of children, as if them unfortunates warn't no more than mist. They paid no mind to the strays nor anyone else for that matter, and whether them sorts were breathing or stiff as planking. Smollet saw this world right when he spied you on the Rose Atoll. This is a turvy world, and we all hang by our heels.

WE ARRIVED AT Livesey's house. A man so pale and lean that he could have been a cousin to the skeleton on our island opened the door.

"You mean to see your shipmate," the doctor said in a voice that boomed too loud for his beam. "No need for pistols," he told Whitman. Whitman held his aim. Livesey looked at me, and said, "You would be Silver. The limp." Again, I wondered what else Bones might have told these landlubbers. Livesey importuned us to put away the pistol. "I am mostly hollow," the doctor said. "Fair warning. There is some meat on me. Not much though, so a shot might pass right through me." He peered into my eyes. "I know Latin, my fellow," he said. "*Magnus inter opes inops.*" I told Whitman to withdraw the pistol.

Livesey took us to a chamber behind the parlor. There, on an oaken table, was Bones. "Perished no more than a few hours ago," Livesey said. "A poor man in the middle of treasure. I speak not about your mate," Livesey said, "except to inform you that those were his last words. That is the translation. A poor man in the middle of treasure. Fine last words too. I would not have thought that a man such as him would know Latin."

"He did not," I told Livesey. "He seen them words in a dead man's hands."

There was no hair left on Bones's head, except for a single lock, as the doctor had shaved it off him. I expected Bones to rouse from his slumbers and pat the lock back down. Livesey took a scalpel and clipped the last lock. Bones did not protest. Livesey, hobgoblin that he was, had been preparing to hack Bones open when we arrived.

"The rum done him in," the doctor said. He picked up a bottle of laudanum, shook it, then put it back on his shelf. "Saw him at the Admiral Clifton." He took another bottle and placed it close to his nose. "Salts," he said. "No." He put the bottle back. "Took my own sup there. I like the corn pudding." He reached for a bottle and opened it. He smelled it and rocked back on his heels. "Lime," he said. He looked about and wiped his cadaverous hands on a pale duster.

"On what else did my mate speak?" I asked.

Livesey ignored me. "Julie Hawkins here is a master of the corn pudding," Livesey rasped. "I told him that the rum was killing him. His eyes. Yellow. Yellow skin too. The liver." Livesey chuckled. I suppose that Bones amused Livesey because the dead are comforted by their own kind. "Threw a bottle at me once," Livesey said. "Do you recall, Jim? Threw it straight at me. Missed. Hollow. Nothing here. Hit the wall. Remember that, Jim?"

"I had to mop the floor," Jim stated, never taking his gaze off me.

"Peel's tavern only cinders now," Livesey rasped away. "Said it was you, she did. The widow, Judith. Almost died in the fire. Long John Silver," he said, waving his lancet. "Back in Bristol, she said. Long John himself."

"A shame she survived," I replied.

"Treated Black John for scurvy once. Gave him goldenseal. Other curatives."

"What do them words mean, a poor man in the middle of treasure?"

"Naught but what they mean," Livesey answered. "Your shipmate spoke of you," the doctor went on. "Long John Silver is coming for me he said. And Pew with him. Silver is lame he said. Pew is blind in one eye and deaf in one ear he said, with neither a left eye nor a right ear. Your eyes are fine," the doctor told Whitman, crooking forward for a better look. "You got both your ears."

I told the doctor that Pew was dead. Livesey did not seem surprised, so mayhap those cadavers had already had their tea. If so, and was I on better terms with Livesey, I would have told him to knob his pocket to verify that his watch was still there.

Jim told Livesey that we shot Trelawney. The doctor aimed his bony finger at me, shook his head, then his bottle of lime. He might have liked Trelawney but no doubt planned to slice him open too. He checked the bottle and seemed pleased. He had enough lime for everyone.

I bade Livesey to tell me if Bones spoke of one Ben Gunn. Livesey dropped his lancet. I made ready to pick it up, but Jim jumped betwixt us, and I could not help but find the lad ever more impressive.

I was certain that Bones had told them about the treasure and considered it likely that he had given them the map. Bones could explicate to no end when he was in his cups.

"I depart your premises," I told Livesey, "and thank you for your hospitality." I turned. "But I am taking the boy. You may keep Billy Bones. Look inside him, Livesey. You will find nothing in him but the dark."

"No! Not my Jim! Not my only Jim!" Julie Hawkins shrieked.

"I am trading you Bones for the boy. I need a cabin boy. This lad suits me." Jim's mother pulled at her mane and pleaded with me, and so I assured her that there was no need to fret. "I plan to make a man of young Jim here," I told her. "I will take him to sea, I will. We are in need of a cabin boy, and this lad is some enterprising." I commanded Whitman to direct his pistol at the good doctor. Whitman done so, shifting his feet back and forth. He must have had some Scot in him on account that he changed his loyalty from foot to foot, as if he was changing allegiance from crown to country and back again.

Livesey offered to trade his life for Jim's life. I refused, as Livesey's bones were barely stitched together. I told Julie Hawkins to step aside lest my hearty shoot Livesey, but she did not budge, and so I told her that after Whitman shot Livesey he would shoot her.

Jim, enterprising lad, broke free of his mother.

"They will not harm you," he told his mother. "Or you," he told the doctor. "Not on my account." Julie Hawkins come at me as quick as a cat and, just like a cat, scratched my face. I pushed her away.

I ordered Whitman to shoot her.

"Stand up for the lad. His mother. Keep your own counsel," Livesey told Whitman. Whitman faltered. "Good," Livesey said. "Now shoot Silver. Shoot him. Shoot him," the doctor implored Whitman. Livesey nearly rasped himself hoarse. I wonder how many buckets of lime Livesey used in his time. He was practically foaming at the prospect of dipping his finger inside me.

Whitman shambled back some and handed me the pistol. He had taken to Julie Hawkins, all right. A gob should not spend too much time away from port. It prejudices his reasoning. I took a last look at Whitman. He had been ever accommodating before he turned contrary. I shot Whitman flush. Julie Hawkins screamed, so she did, and collapsed on the floor.

Jim told me that he would come with me if I spared his mother and Livesey. After Julie Hawkins righted herself, Jim avowed that he would one day shoot me with the selfsame pistol that I held in my hand. Julie Hawkins thereupon collapsed into Livesey's arms, and they both of them tumbled to the ground. Livesey managed to spout, "One more matter. The treasure, Long John Silver. Your Bones spoke of an island. We know no more except that there is a man on your ship who knows all. Release the lad now, for pity sake," Livesey said. "We have told you all we know."

Solomon. Solomon knew.

"Silver does not trade for words," I replied. "It ain't no bargain."

"Scoundrel," so Livesey said, and I wholeheartedly agreed with him. I backed out of the laboratory advising Livesey and Hawkins to mind their tongues until we were free, and I most gently closed the door.

I gave a fellow a guinea to row us to the reeds and towed Jim into the skiff after cuffing him so to stay still. "Do you feel that breeze?" I asked him. He did not reply. "Watch how I trim the sail," I said. Jim looked away. "Do not think about your mother. You will not see her for some time."

"Damn you," he said.

"Spirit, that is," I told my charge, and showed the lad how to work the rudder. "I will teach you to curse better than that too," I told him. "There she is," I said. "That lady is the Linda Maria. You will sleep well at sea. All lads do."

A gob of no account piped us aboard. Most of our new gobs warn't much better than stover, on account that the better men had already been recruited for the season. Smollet was a gob of little consequence, however he swaggered some proficiently, and so I named him my first mate.

"It is my sincere pleasure to provide a cabin boy for you black hearts," I told my men. "His name is Jim Hawkins. Mind your manners now. He is a fierce lad. Bones is dead, my hearties, and Whitman is done in too. Pew snuffed as well." Just then, and before I could continue, a wave slapped at the ship and coursed over my wooden saints. "Make sail," I ordered the men. "Bristol will soon be after us. Give the order, Mister Smollet. Take the lad below and put him with Solomon."

"They will hang you," Jim told me.

"They surely will," I answered. "They surely will if they catch me, young Jim Hawkins. But until then we have us a treasure to find."

CHAPTER XX.

A SECRET

I asked Mullet if he would like to know the last secret. He nearly choked. You are magnanimous, as you are poisoning him with a pageant of a meal. He ate a joint sopped in mustard sauce and an onion pie. He groaned when he ate the derby cheese topped with cream. He managed to grunt, "Stilton," before he collapsed, whimpering, "Aye. The treasure." You should not throw this lad into the brine but bury him in a porridge pot.

Mullet, if you are reading this, remember to steer clear of the porridge pot.

The lightning will now flicker. The rain will streak my deck like black tea from Nick's own bowl and thunder will split the hull. The storm is finally upon us.

Leave us recall Solomon, the map, Jim Hawkins, our island, and my treasure. A crown indeed, sir.

One tar, by way of greeting, clouted Jim on the head. Jim grabbed the ganger's hand and bowed back his wrist until the man's knees buckled. There was nowhere for the man to go but upwards, and nowhere for Jim to go but downwards, and so before either of them could reach their destination, my hearties grabbed Jim and bore him to Solomon.

Solomon huddled in a corner of the cabin, his head on his chest. Smollet brought the lantern close to Solomon. Solomon held his hand over his face so that he remained in shadow, and Smollet treaded aback. "The captain locked him in this cabin on account of his oaths," he told Jim. "Contemptible curses. The man called me a pusty boil. Do not look at him," Smollet cautioned. "His eyes, boy. His eyes. Daggers." Smollet was the middlemost of men, except when you murdered him. And then he made an excellent corpse on account that you puddened him to the plansheers, so when the wind blowed aft to lee, he bade a farewell to the world.

Solomon turned his head and spoke one word. "Liberty."

Thereupon, I sent Smollet away.

"Bones is dead," I told him. "He took a certain map. Pew gave it to him. I no longer need the map, but others may find it of use."

"Next you will ask me about the cipher. You do not understand the meaning," Solomon said.

I locked Jim in the cabin with Solomon for the night as I had devised a plan, and like all my plans, it was a good one. "Tell me the meaning in the morn," I told Solomon, and bade him and the boy a peaceful night.

"You are a poor man in the middle of riches," Solomon told me as soon as I unhinged the lock the next day.

"I already know the answer, but what is the meaning of it?"

Jim was shaking from the chill, and so I tossed my jacket his way.

"You have a world of riches and what do you do with it?" Solomon importuned, tapping his teeth. "You bury it in the sand and have nothing. That is one inference. And what if you never acquired your riches?" He did not wait for me to answer, but said, "You would still not see the wonder of the world, and would be a poor man in the midst of riches." I countered and told him that the dead man must have meant more by the cipher as he held on to it all the way into eternity. "He may have failed in his quest, just as you have failed," Solomon said. Aye, but his words stung me. I rejoined that I had not failed.

"The crown," Solomon said, tapping his teeth most vigorously.

"Aye, that," I said. "My crown," at which Solomon laughed most heartily.

"Edward was most diverting during our respite in Murcia," Solomon said, laughing once more. "And almost all who knew of Edward's Bible and the ciphers in it are dead, and with no crown on their heads. Jimmy, Louis, that tar that Louis told, Bones, Pew. You are a reckoning man. I have heard you say it. That leaves you, Edward, and me." He tried to stand, but his legs were weak from his confinement. "And Jim here. And the rest of Bristol. And, by now, most of Londontown." And then, damn him, he laughed again.

"But we will reach it first, so we will," I told him. Thereupon, I presented Solomon with my challenge. I informed Solomon that the boy would choose one of us as his guardian. I would grant Solomon his liberty if Jim preferred him by the time we reached the island, but would keep Solomon confined until the last day of doom if Jim preferred me. Solomon could end the challenge at any time by so stating the true meaning of the dead man's cipher. Solomon protested that the contest was inequitable to the lad and that he had already told me all. "We commence now," I replied.

I made certain that Jim ate a hearty breakfast of salted cod and brown bread. I showed Jim the cleat, how to belay a rope to the cleat with a pin, and subsequently described the backstay and how it supports the mast and leads down abaft. I let him know that he would be clambering the mast soon enough, sharp lad that he was.

I do enjoy good sport, so I do.

I instructed the boy during the day, and Solomon offered him accounts at eventide of how he might better himself and so the world. What were his soppy accounts compared to my salted cod and brown bread? Nevertheless, I sent a man to skulk outside Solomon's cabin and deliver me a report. Jim asked Solomon, so the man said, if I was going to murder them, and Solomon said that I might if it pleased me. True enough. Jim asked how Solomon might help him, and after Solomon pondered some he told Jim to never lose hope. He did lay in that my ship had traveled the world, but never sailed to anywhere but misery and back. Then Solomon told Jim that he had hidden something from everyone on board the ship. And here was a treachery, sir, almost worthy of me. Solomon produced a drawing. It was a drawing scratched from lampblack, just like my map, and it was of a crown of gold. Solomon had known all and had never spoken a word of it to me.

But how would he have known without the Bible or the ciphers or the wheels in his hands?

Bones. Bones must have told him what Solomon could not infer from Edward's discourse in the depths of that grave in Murcia. And how did Bones know? Pew surely told him before he poisoned him with the drink.

Pew's conspiracy, his grievous conspiracy. With Edward.

I spoke to Jim about Londontown as he aspired to see it one day. I kneaded my stories with ample supplies of butter, meats, and sweets. I spoke of adventure as well. I told of battles in the China Seas, Java, Beaufort, Madagascar, Barbary, Bonaire, Cartagena, New Granada, Eleuthera, Antiqua, Basse-Terre, Isabella, La Vega, Port-de-Paix, New Providence Island, Nevis, and Tortuga. I declaimed on frigates, reefs, alehouses, jigs, and even the crook of Old Nick's nose, so I did, and young Jim listened.

Jim, in turn and in time, told of his life in Bristol. It warn't much like my life, as he had a mother and, for a time, a father. He had a roof over his head and a bed. Jim never spoke of Bones, the treasure, or the island.

He did tell my hearties after they gave him rum that Solomon snored. Aye, and, that Solomon taught him a song.

Now here is the song that Solomon taught Jim, so Jim told them, and so they told me.

> *A cry is heard*
> *Weeping bitter weeping*
> *Rachel weeping*
> *Rachel weeping*
> *Rachel weeping for her sons*

One tar, the fellow that you evened out with the balls from the shot locker when you took my ship, told me that Jim's eyes damped when he heard the ditty. I told the mister that it was sea spray and naught more, and he told me that there was more to the song, and so I told him to sing it to me and not to leave any of the misery out of it.

> *Her tears fall on the ground*
> *Always falling always*
> *Rachel always*
> *Rachel always*
> *Weeping for her sons*

Another tar said that Jim asked Solomon about this Rachel, but Solomon did not answer him, and so the tar offered that Rachel must be Solomon's mother. I told my hearties, whilst I pondered the matter on the foredeck, that we would teach the boy a song as well.

The wind was moderate the following night, and so we anchored and prepared a feast from stores we acquired in Algiers. I set Jim on the fore boom so that he could dangle his legs whilst watching us at our cookery. Smollet lugged French hens from the hold and we boiled them in a double-hulled pepper pot, the fleur-de-lys covering them out of diffidence. We roasted a pig that had followed us from market, and as the pig was insistent on being roasted, we accommodated him, salting him for good luck. We brewed a broth of fish, poured rum in the cauldron, topped it with whale oil, and lit the brew. The cauldron bubbled, black smoke billowed from it, and the oil brimmed over and into the scuppers.

One fellow took up his fiddle and stomped his feet on deck until the bowsprit had no choice but to prance to his tune. All hands hunched over the brew and plunged their mugs into it. I took Jim off the boom and the men fully rigged him in calico and silk and, at my command, topped him off with a most becoming crown woven from green plantains. That poxed Solomon.

"Would you like to hear a song?" I asked Jim. "A good seafaring song? That ain't got no puddle of tears in it? We don't know any songs but lively ones, and they all go with roasted pig, boiled hens, fish stew, and a fiddle." I had the men allot Jim a draught. "Down your drink," so I told him, and so he did. "Open your ears, boy. Here is an authentic and faithful account of the fate of another crew not so lucky as we. A cheery song it is too." Thereupon, the fiddler struck the tune and I sang.

Oh I saw one night a terrible sight
Whilst the wind was piping free
A lad sat on the binnacle pat
Whilst his head hanged from the crosstrees

I near fell about before the fiddler struck the next verse.

Oh I saw one night a terrible sight
Whilst a gale was blowing hard
The thunder roared and the old gob snored
Whilst a bolt blowed up the yard

I commanded all my hearties to join me in the song.

Oh I saw one night a terrible sight
Whilst Nick brought the ship north a lee
The cock-bell hung from a serpent's fang
Whilst the serpent drank up the sea

Oh I saw one night a terrible sight
Whilst the water churned to steam
The cabin boy spat his fish bones abaft
Whilst the fish spat the boy back aflee

I was doubled over with cheer, I was, and so I bade Smollet to sing the last verse.

> *Oh I saw one night a terrible sight*
> *Whilst the first mate bade for more pay*
> *The captain laughed until he swallowed the gaff*
> *Whilst the first mate called out, "Give way!"*

I sleep the righteous sleep of the corrupt, so bless me, I say, but that night, I woke. The pig warn't as accommodating as I presumed, even though I was cordiality itself when I bit into him. I summoned Jim.

I spoke on roving and the open sea and how no one on board a ship ever drops from the vapours. I enlightened him that only landlubbers cultivate such ills, as we stick to simple scurvy. I recounted battles among the outlanders and other suitable subjects for a growing lad, and then I fell asleep. When I woke Jim was standing over me with a dagger. I considered lashing the lad, but spirit is spirit, and so I told him to save his strength for the morrow.

I ordered Smollet to work Jim hard that next day, and so Smollet put Jim in the rigging, ordering him to climb it all day. The men carried Jim out of the reefing line at dusk. His face was as red as an alderman's nose and his eyelids were shuttered tight. Solomon doused Jim with whale oil and covered the boy's face with tobacco leaves soaked in the balm.

Solomon and I were playing for the highest stakes. This was better than any game of bones, a game of turn and turn about, and I intended to prevail.

"Are you able to keep a secret, Jim?" I asked him. "I expect that you are able and I expect that you have some secrets. Ain't that so, Jim? But here is one, Jim. Do not tell the men. I am more milliner than monster. That is on account that I am ever mindful of my profit. Ever, lad. The world is just profit and need, I say. Now you tell me a secret, Jim. Give the captain a word," I told him.

And so Jim gave me that word. "Liberty," he said, and I expect that I turned as raw red as his own face then. And Jim warn't done. "Turn this ship about," Jim said, as if he and not I was captain. Now ain't a day in the rigging with naught a care and only the timber and the sea below liberty? It is, and so you know, sir. There ain't no greater liberty than that, but Solomon had put words into the boy's mouth.

"So I will, Jim," I told him. "I will grant you your liberty. I will turn this ship about. I will bring you back to Bristol," I told him. He threw back his shoulders. "You will return rich, Jim. A true rover. Strike me down with lightning and try me in a court of thunder and doom if it ain't so, Jim. But, Jim, I ain't catching a northerly back to Bristol just at the present." Jim slumped some, so he did, but drew himself back up like a true Bristol lad. "We are headed for fortune, Jim. The island, Jim. What did Billy Bones tell of the island?" Jim spat. "A rejoinder like a barrister," I told him. "Mayhap you will defend me one day from them that would end my nature prematurely."

"They will send a ship after me. They will chase you all the way to your island, and you will hang." And now I had the lad.

"That may well be, Jim. But where will they send that ship, as Bones never gave you my map? So how will they find it?" Jim replied that he had heard Bones speak of it. I complimented him on his reply, a well-considered falsehood. "I tell you on the curls of your dear mother's head, Jim, that you will see a treasure. Such as only a Bristol boy dares to dream. A crown of gold according to Solomon." I detected a gleam in his eyes. "But what do you care about a crown when you have a rendering of it?" I asked him. "I heard that Solomon drew it for you. That was right generous of Solomon, that was. He offered you parchment, and I only offered you gold. He done you a turn, he done." I sent the boy to Smollet the next day, and Smollet put him back in the rigging and kept him there the remainder of the day.

I treated with Solomon just before the moon rose, importuning him to strike me with his best secret or his best curse. I reminded him that I could lance him at any time but I was a sporting sort, and so would rather he tell me all he knew without me bleeding him of it. I added that Jim would take to the mast sooner or later and tell me all, then Solomon would lose the bout. He chose neither a secret nor a curse, but rather a deception.

"Your Mary," Solomon said. "Your Mary preferred Edward," so he said, drumming his fingers on his chin.

"No. Not Edward. It was Evangeline that took to Edward. Not Mary," I told him.

"Edward told me. Your Edward," Solomon said. His eyes were daggers again. "Liberty," he said. Aye, the man knew how to perturb me. He enjoyed the sport, I say.

I took his hands and turned them over. "But look here," I told him, pressing my forefinger into his palm. "Is that a secret there? Do I spy me a secret?" I dropped his hands. "I will prevail," I told him.

SOLOMON LIED. WHAT do you say, my silent sir? Do not palter. Jabber on with all haste as the fever is coming on me again.

You may come closer. I see you in the shadows. Come closer. This fever is pulling me to the fathoms, and I must cut your throat before the tide pulls me under the waves.

Now back again.

Near port, Mullet says. How does he still live? Aye, the treasure. He cannot fall until I tell him the spot. I remember.

THIS FEVER IS no match for me.

Take a swallow with me, my hearty, whilst I tell you the best part of this tale. Draw on your pipe and drain your drink. Take another. My tale is near as sweet as my brew. Drink up, my hearty.

Aye, Mullet. Aye, the tale. We will be in Londontown presently, and one of us dead by the noose. Well, sir.

There ain't no better way to train a lad than by hard work, and Jim stood watch until he dropped. One salt taught Jim to mend a sail and another salt drilled Jim in the jig. A fellow from Heysham instructed Jim on how to slip through a porthole like an eel. A Welshman parleyed deeply on deception and an Irishman orated profoundly on daggers. Mind you that it warn't all good times for Jim. He carried the breakers fore to aft, twisted the handspike until he went indigo, and performed every labour that Smollet could devise to turn the boy into a tar. Jim soon enough, and by his own choice, slept on deck with the rest of the men whilst Solomon crabbed below. The boy was mine.

Days passed and, when we spied Treasure Island, Smollet hailed me so to take the skiff to the strand, but I decided to wait until daybreak, so to taunt Solomon before going ashore. I needed no lantern to see him as the light of the moon, my moon, caught his eyes. He had lost, and I had won. I told Solomon that he would remain my captive till the end of his days. He would be my witness and given liberty only to watch my every iniquity, and then he would be jailed again. I must say, and so I told him, that the sea would be greener and the sky higher with him attending all my evils. Moreover, I told him that Jim was now a proper rover, with as much heart as my wooden saints. And why shouldn't it be so, as hadn't I shaped him just as the ship maker had wrought them penitents? Solomon looked at me some forlorn, then he spoke what I had already determined.

"Bones told me all," he said. "He come to me for a cure. A cure from Ben Gunn, but it warn't Ben Gunn scratching his back but Pew. Pew pouring that bottle down Bones's throat and telling Bones all about the treasure. So you would kill Bones and promote Pew."

"I would never make a sea crab my first mate."

"Or, perhaps he told Bones just for the mischief of it. Pew knew all, and your Edward told Pew to mind you every moment. To watch you. To follow you and tell Edward all. And Edward would share the treasure with Pew, as Edward had almost solved it when he had been in Londontown. And perhaps Pew was waiting for Edward to return. And if you killed Bones in the meantime, or Bones killed you, that would be—" And here Solomon struggled for the right words. "A feather, so to speak, in Edward's hat."

"I have no more need to solicit you."

"Then there is the matter of 'Blood,' " Solomon said.

"Aye, the seas are filled with it."

Solomon so forlorn only a moment ago now fell about. "Blood," so he said. "Blood told and tells."

"Aye, Thomas Blood. I am near on speaking terms with him, though he is dead. He wrote the ciphers," I told him. "It is his Bible that Edward no doubt purloined, the clever lad."

"You indeed do not understand at all," Solomon said. "Liberty," so he said.

"Some folks want their fortune buttered," I answered, and with them words I left him to dream of my crown.

I slept soundly. Too soundly, my hearty.

I woke to Smollet battering my door.

"They fled!" Smollet cried. "Both of them! Solomon and the boy!" Smollet went on. "And with the lee boat!" Smollet cried.

"After them!" I shouted. "After Jim! After Solomon! Every other man! Lower the boats, men!" If I had told them to set the course, they would have rowed all the way to the China Seas, flogging the waves with their oars.

My hearties ran all about the island, they did, but I marched plumb to the dead man's grave, Smollet and a parcel of other men trailing me. We strode past the brambles and hedges, and Smollet, so low to the ground, cut his legs on the thorns. He bled, and that is good, I say. A man should bleed for profit.

We reached the clearing, and I spied Solomon's drawing of the crown pinned to the mound with a twig. I swore to bury Solomon on the very spot and told the men to dig.

I pledge to you that the dead man and my lifeless hearties sighed after Smollet heaved them out of their hole, pleased to be relieved of their duty. That crew had pits for eyes and tufts of hair on their skulls. I recognized one seaman by his shock of hair and almost bade him to sing, as he was a smooth warbler in his day, until a worm crawled out of his eye. The clothes of the men were rotted through, and their bones were off beam, and I wonder if some of them were yet alive when we buried them as they were contorted so.

I ordered my men to stand aside when they tapped my chest, and they jumped out of the breach right quick. I hoisted the lid and looked inside. All my riches were there.

And here is where you and I come to our discord. What was Solomon to you?

Leave us raise a tumbler to them that never sailed and ambled lightly on this earth, whose treading made no sound. Leave us toss off a tumbler to men that no one will recall.

You turned on me, you did.

I am sporting these drinks and so will say whatever I please.

If you come across me on a duty day, and I look parched from my hanging, tender me a drink. I might not take that drink on account that it was you that sent me swinging, but the gesture would please me. We were shipmates.

And now we are close to settling all debts.

One of our fellows found us and announced that he had captured Solomon and Jim. He doffed his hat and wiped his brow, saying that Solomon went on about a crown buried on the island, and that it was the King's own crown and this man said he would like to sport it. I shot the fellow in the chest. By the tide, that was more good fortune. I had discovered another mutineer.

CHAPTER XXI.
LAST DEBTS

————

Mullet looked in on me last night whilst the fever was on me. I turned and he scampered out and latched my door again.

"You look rather fit for a poisoned lad," I told him.

"You have done me an injustice," Mullet grumbled. "You are fiddling me from seeing a hanging as you appear to be near expiring from the fever."

I recommend stuffing Mullet with horsehair and setting him in your quarters, as he would make a fine footstool. Aye, but I may have misjudged the lad, as he may be the most sturdy of fellows, having survived your poison. And now he will hear of your deceit.

"I told you I ain't inclined to die," so I told him. "But, you may have you your hanging."

"Very well indeed, sir," he replied.

————

The men bickered over which of them should have the pleasure of dashing the two mutineers and by what means. One proposed hanging, and another recommended marlinspikes. One advised pistols, and another advocated swords. The men each made their cases for the appropriate means of murder.

These are the men that you snuffed. I would resurrect Bloody Bill and Bones, and even Pew, and mind you even Black John, to form an argosy against you. I would raise those sea dogs just to swig to your demise. Aye, but there are some feats that no man can manage, not even Silver.

The men formed a circle round Solomon and Jim, and I bade Solomon to mind what moved men. It warn't prayers nor pleas nor petitions but swords that moved them, so I told him, and Solomon looked straight through me and said that we warn't men but mongrels. I patted his pockets whilst my men held him, and told my hearties that he had nothing to offer us for his life. And then I told Solomon that I would let him go free for a farthing, but he was intent on maintaining his stubbornness to the end.

"My liberty," he replied.

I would let Solomon live for a ha'penny, so I said, and toddled around him as if I was considering his circumstances. He importuned me to spare Jim, and I told him that I might if he or the boy had anything of worth. I drummed my teeth just as Solomon done, then I reminded him that he had a drawing of a crown. I promised to set him and Jim free if he pulled the crown from his drawing, and then I marched them to the clearing. I handed Solomon the parchment and now he had nothing to pay for his life but words, the words that I most wanted to hear, the words that had taken up most of my life, the secret revealed, the location of the crown and its significance. Only them words would turn his debt to good account.

Jim broke free just then, and dodged Smollet for a time until the lad faltered in the woods and was recaptured. Jim was ever impressive, and I almost reconsidered his case, especially when he cited me as a butcher upon his return. There ain't naught wrong with a dram of disrespect. The world is built on it. If all men went about respecting each other there would be no betterment. Everything we have is at the expense of others. Do not tell me differently, my hearty. Your King is paying you for my neck, ain't he? You are sailing under his orders, so we have all heard in port, and he pays you at my expense. I would tell him over tea, tainted tea mind you, that you do not sail for him and that his reward is naught compared to the riches you will receive if you find my treasure. And them riches, sir, come at his expense.

Solomon was determined to confound me to the very end, he was, and even on this, his sizen day. He told me that he would give me what I most wanted, whereupon Jim shouted that I should be struck dead where I stood, and that put Jim in even better figure. It is a crime that Jim never acquired a career as a rover. I blame you for that felony. I warned Solomon not to trifle with me and informed him that there were all manners of murdering a man, and that I did not particularly care to mangle him. I told him that I could fix it so that there warn't enough of him left to pour into a flint glass. I pressed on and told him that any palter would lay hard upon his case.

I pulled my cutlass from my scabbard, and Solomon turned his back to me. He wanted a swift death, but I would not grant it to him, and told him that my cutlass was too good for him.

I ordered my men to make a rope out of the vines on the island, one that would be a credit to the Bailey, and to bind Solomon and Jim to the same tree.

One ganger said that Solomon was spreading curses on them, and another ganger agreed, and Jim put them to rights and told them that Solomon warn't cursing but praying. I told the men that I would trim every one of them if they did not go about their duty directly.

Now there ain't no more of them men on this ship. Mayhap, as the magpies are screeching ever louder, there will be no more Silver neither on this ship soon. But a hundred years on, my hearty, none of us will be rambling regardless. Think about that. No more Silver. Mayhap there will be no more hearties then too, and the seas will go slack and all men will be sober. What a dreary plot this world would be then.

I stabbed Solomon's drawing with my dagger, held it to Jim's neck, and ordered Solomon to tell me all he knew of the crown. And so Solomon spoke at last.

"History," so he said. "Your history. It does not lie."

"It would not dare," so I told him.

"This," and he freed one of his arms from the rotted vines and pointed at the drawing, "is your history. It is a matter of liberty," he said, tearing at the vines. Aye, but he was intent on galling me to the end. "Do you not recognize it? Do you not know what it represents?"

"Your life," so I told him, some proud of my counter.

"It is the crown of the King of England, your own King, but he does not wear it on his head. It was taken from him."

"And buried here by the thief of all thieves," I declared. "By Thomas Blood or one of his fellows. So I already know. But the man should have taken the King's head with the crown, as one is no good without the other."

"That is not so," Solomon said. "The King's crown is buried on this island and his head is buried in Londontown. It is the crown of Charles II, your Georgey's antecedent, taken from your King by Oliver Cromwell. And you will tell me that you know that too."

"I do, and I read it in Peel's own history book when just a lad, and left it just as it was written without no appendage as it was so amusing. Cromwell took the crown from right off his head."

"And allegedly the crown was melted down with all the other regalia. The orbs, rings, spurs, swords, scepters. Priceless, that crown. Not just bejeweled with diamonds, sapphires, rubies, and emeralds but with mystery and majesty," Solomon said, forgetting for a moment to pull at the vines that bound him.

I fixed my eyes on his drawing. "Four crosses on all sides of it and one more at the top. Two arches of gold crossing, like longitude and latitude."

"This is what you have been looking for, the stolen crown, never melted down but taken and brought here," Solomon said.

"The dead man's deed."

"Perhaps, but I doubt so. The dead man was a pauper in the middle of riches. The crown is here. It is here. And it should have been melted as were the others by Cromwell."

"We warn't on speaking terms when last we met. Otherwise, I would have taken the bother off him."

"Do you know why he took the Crown Jewels? To prove there is no divine right among kings or sovereigns of the sea, such as you fancy yourself. Liberty. It is a matter of liberty. We are all peers, and there is no mystery among us but what we make."

"I would solve this mystery. Where is the crown?"

"Blood has it. You would manifest him a thief."

"Aye, Thomas Blood."

"Not at all, Silver. Not at all. Not Thomas Blood but Edward Blood."

"I never had the pleasure of meeting him. Or gutting him for that matter."

"You have eaten with him. Shared mugs of ale with him. Even perused his family Bible. The Bible of the Bloods. Passed on from generation to generation, but defiled recently by Cromwell's most loyal servant, a regimental officer."

"Aye, Thomas Blood, and so I said. I know me the history. He was tried and set free by the King, and even after the murder of the old warder who kept the Crown Jewels. I seen Edward's blood and it is the same colour as yours and mine."

"Have you ever seen another colour? Now Silver, why would the King set that man free?" Solomon asked. "Even I do not know the answer to that question, but I imagine that Edward knows. And then there is this man, the man that buried your prize on this island according to Thomas Blood's precise instructions. I do not know his name. Perhaps a faithful friend, but murdered just the same and just as you murdered your own men and at the very same spot."

"You have not yet acquitted yourself," so I told him.

I drew my dagger across Solomon's throat until a trickle of blood run from it. "Aye, all the same colour. You know more and you will tell me more."

My men, who had heard all, shouted for me to spare him until he disclosed the location of the crown. Jim likewise shouted oaths at me, but to cut them both free, for Solomon had done as I bade him.

"I can only presume," Solomon told me.

"Presume correctly," I advised him.

"That the answer is in Edward's Bible. Something that you missed. And for that, Silver, you need your Edward. Blood will tell."

I told Smollet to have the men fetch two lanyards from the ship, as I wished to bind Solomon and Jim tighter whilst I determined their fate. I had no more need for Solomon, as he had told me all he knew for the sake of the lad. No sooner did Smollet send the men than they returned.

"Sails! Sails!" they shouted. "Cannon fire!" one of them put in. "And the flag!" another man shouted. "A Bristol ship!"

"Doctor Livesey," Jim said, quite calmly, as if he had expected Livesey to cross the threshold just then for tea. "You against an English ship," Jim said. "Fitted with a crew. They will blow you away," Jim so stated. "You, your ship, all of you. And take your own treasure," the lad said. "Bones's map of this island," he said proudly. "And the crown if they can find it. I gave them Bones's map. They will take you before the day is done," Jim declared.

"Every man to the beach," I ordered the men. "To battle. And you," I told Jim. "You will see how I scuttle a Bristol ship."

"But there are two ships, Captain," one tar said. "One a Bristol ship. But the other ship, Captain, she is the Bloody Evangeline."

"Edward's ship! This will be a battle. And here I am on dust and mud. To the beach, men! Bind our mutineers well. More vines. Bind them now, damn you!"

My hands are jouncing. I can barely hold this plume.

The fever. It is on me once more.

I fight you both, though you each yank at me so to pull me apart, like them two in the headpiece of the Bible.

—❦—

I will not answer you.

I ain't screaming. I ain't raving. Leave me be, I say.

I will finish my tale.
Take heed again, boy.

And one more matter, now that I look on it. *Don't that bundle of sticks look just like a crown?*

I will not take your food. You will not poison me. I will not take it. I would rather die of the fever.

Aye, the tale.

We ran to the beach, the better to see the dismemberment of the Lucky Hands.

The weather is of paramount importance in any affray at sea. A captain must change strategy and tactics, with much depending on whether there is a steady wind or a sudden gust, if the waves are swirling or still. The position of the sun is of paramount importance. That day the wind was frivolous, flurrying only now and again, and the sea was calm. The Bloody Evangeline and the Lucky Hands traded positions, the Evangeline advancing on the Lucky Hands until, like a reluctant suitor, the Evangeline fell aback.

The Evangeline then, seemingly rashly, turned to, thereby risking a broadside from the Lucky Hands.

The Lucky Hands fired and missed, and the Evangeline, having tested the gunnery of the Lucky Hands, found it wanting. It may be that the conscripts of the Lucky Hands were brave, but leave us consider the facts. The Lucky Hands set out right quick after I departed Bristol, and so its men, for all their bravery, were not only untested in battle but also unfamiliar with their ship. Edward's men were experienced and knew every plank and knothole of the Evangeline. Moreover, they were the best of men, the middling ones having succumbed to swords and sabers in prior battles.

Edward returned fire, even though he knew that he had no chance of striking the Lucky Hands, and was thereby able to observe how her men responded. They ran about the deck awaiting orders. One man misfired from the mizzenmast, his shot drowning in the deep.

Then the wind blowed, and Edward sailed the Evangeline over the swell and, having perceived that the men of the Lucky Hands could not fire accurately in tranquil water, and knowing that they would fare no better whilst the gun platforms reeled, approached the Lucky Hands and fired. The Evangeline missed the Lucky Hands, fate saving that Bristol ship for the moment, the swell rolling the Lucky Hands away from Edward's gunnery.

Then quiet again. And no man on land made a sound neither whilst we watched this battle.

Edward learned even more about the Lucky Hands as she rolled rather heavily over the swell. He now determined that she was weighted more than the Evangeline, and that the Evangeline could maneuver swifter than her adversary.

Edward drew the Lucky Hands closer to shore, where the wind, as if often does when nigh land, turned contrary. A wind always favours the fleeter ship, and therefore this was an excellent ploy by Edward, allowing the Lucky Hands to believe that the Evangeline was beset by the same ill wind that blustered the Lucky Hands' sails.

Edward shortened his sail and slowed his course. The Lucky Hands followed suit, seizing the opportunity to converge on the Evangeline from the rear with the sun behind her. The Evangeline listed leeward and even nearer to shore, but still in enough depth to turn and attack.

And so she did.

Edward engaged the Lucky Hands, quickly lengthening the Evangeline's sails and consequently catching all the wind. She tacked, and the Evangeline was now behind her. The Lucky Hands fought for the turn, but too hard. Her sails blinded her batteries, and she was sightless when she shot at the Evangeline.

The Evangeline raked the Lucky Hands, pride of Bristol, with a broadside through her stern once, then again, and the pride of Bristol listed, the men falling from her gundeck into the brine. Edward stood on the foredeck and waved his hat, a crimson hat, and as he done so, the Evangeline fired its cannons repeatedly until the Lucky Hands was no more than yard and hull. The Lucky Hands went down spouting froth and foam and the last gasps of Bristol seamen. Her spine cracked, her bow broke, and her mast come down. Her barrels bobbed until my men lanced them, making a game of mumble peg out of all that murder. And then she went down final, the windstaff the last to submit to its fortune.

The Bloody Evangeline hoisted the red flag. No quarter.

Them men of the Lucky Hands that were still alive abandoned her, and Edward fired his cannons once more. Some of the Lucky Hands' boats were away, and then my men entered the fray, recklessly firing on the Lucky Hands' crew. A crew needs a captain. I would have ordered my men to stand fast had I been aboard the Linda Maria, as the honour of the disposition belonged to the Evangeline, as she had brought the ship down.

One of the boats from the Lucky Hands overset and the men in it drowned. They were some skilled at that, burbling and gurgling and flaying at the waves. The other boats that were away rafted to shore, my hearties cutting down every man that bounded to shore, so you recall. Livesey survived the attacks, and I seen him look about as if he was lost, until one of my tars gored him through his heart. That distressed me, as I would have much preferred to hang Livesey alongside Solomon, and a merriment that would have been, as I would have settled all debts on one tree.

The men from the Evangeline and the Linda Maria rowed to shore.

I bade my men silence as to all Solomon had told me.

Edward stood in his boat. He sported blue britches and that crimson hat. Aye, and he had a feather in his hat and a brocade jacket. I grabbed him by his shoulders. "Is this my Edward?" I asked. "Edward Peach. And looking like a grandee." Edward's curls ran down to the middle of his back, where they were bound with a black ribbon. He wore a beard, or at least attempted one, as only a few tufts sprouted from his chin. But for that beard, you could have put a frock on Edward, handed him a basket, and walked him down High Street. Every man would have doffed his top to him.

"Just so," he said abruptly. "And here is Silver. I would speak to you on a matter," he said.

No doubt there was more murder to come, but I had the drop on the dandy. He did not know that I had discovered his true name and why the King had burned his house to cinders. There would be ample time for me to tell him when my blade was in him. Murdering always comes first. A person should murder each day before biscuits, as it improves the disposition. Aye, and a murder after supper benefits the digestion.

"Your men broke those barrels," he said. "We chased that ship," he said.

"And you caught her." I slapped Edward on his back. "You must acquaint me with the men. I would commend them."

"But the barrels," he said. I told Edward that them barrels warn't filled with naught but breech water now, and, as we had agreed to split everything all even, we would share us that brine. I told him that the Lucky Hands had followed me from Bristol, and Edward gave an account of how he had come to find me by chasing the Lucky Hands until he reached the island. I, in turn, told him how Bones had given his hindmost oaths in a bar in Bristol, where he had spoken of the treasure.

"Is this the island?" Edward inquired.

"If it is, I have found naught but dead men on it."

Edward looked some pleased.

The Linda Maria and the Evangeline sailed round each other, as neither Edward nor I had given the order to drop anchor and lash the lines, but it was no matter as most of our men had already rowed to shore. There would be time to bind our ships together again, place the gangplank between them and then celebrate our good fortune in blood.

Aye, but it was hot that day on the island, and whilst Edward fanned himself with his hat, he told me that his men were greedy sorts. I commended him on his choice of men. Then I told him that I had kept a secret from him. I pulled the feather out of his hat and cast it on the sand. One of his men, Adam Flaning, so his mother called him, handed it to him and Edward flicked it away. I decided to have a spot of fun with my old mate.

"Now this secret. It ain't a thing for your pocket," I told him. "By the by, you cannot take it with you, but it has good worth, Edward. Tell me if it ain't so when you look at it. What would you bid for it sight unseen? And half of it will not do. Half of it would not be of any value. A riddle."

"We know our riddles, Silver." He smoothed out his jacket. "Good worth. But I cannot put it in my pocket," he mused. "Too large no doubt." He slapped his hat against his thigh and smiled but did not answer me.

"What would you bid on the open market?" I asked him. "In Londontown," I went on. Whilst he considered his answer I threw his hat into the water. "Make a declamation," I told him. Edward watched his hat float into the shoals.

I told him that I would let him off easy, mate that he was, and bade Edward to take my arm so to help me on account of my hobble. After he done so I clamped my own hand on his arm. Our men gathered behind us. "Walk on, fellow scoundrel," I told him.

Edward's humour lightened. "I expect that you can still bite through a crown," he said.

We come to the clearing.

"There is your treasure," I told Edward, pointing at Solomon. Solomon and Jim struggled mightily to free themselves, but to no advantage.

"This? This is my bounty?" he asked. "What would I want of him?" he bade me, kicking a clump of dirt at Solomon.

"You may hang him of course," I told Edward, then I pinched him on his arm, and whispered, "He may know a secret or two about your Bible."

Solomon, as soon as he saw Edward, did not solicit his own case but implored him to ferry Jim back to Bristol. Solomon reminded Edward that he had spared his life once, whereupon Edward replied that the sun was in his eyes that day and, as he recalled, the ship had pitched.

"I will not share a farthing with you, Silver," Edward said, Flaning sidling beside him. "You have brought nothing to the table but a curse tied to a tree and a cabin boy. I have paid enough to you over the years. Evangeline cost me nothing, and so I named the ship after her. I paid your Mary for her accommodations." I did not fathom his words, and so I told him. He smiled again. "She come cheap, Silver. Less than most tarts. I am captain of the Bloody Evangeline, and this is a bloody business," he said.

"My Mary asked me to live in the Carolinas with her. She had property," so I said.

"I have never known a person to lie," he replied. Then he laughed and threw off my hat. I had never seen him laugh so before. "Almost all of the men had her," he said. "Even Pew. Not Bones though. Too drunk or too loyal. She was particularly pleasing, Silver. I grant you that."

"Aye. A bloody business. Enough," I told him. "Mind your words, Edward." I was ready to pull my saber.

Flaning spoke. "Take care how you speak to Captain Peach," the man said.

"Aye, a bloody business it is, Edward. What is the right name for a man such as you? Captain ain't good enough. Not Captain Peach. It ain't got no bells to it, such as they ring in Londontown when they hang a man." I drew my dagger and cut both our hands before Flaning could move, and clasped Edward's hand in mine. "Sealed in blood. Blood, Edward. Blood."

Smollet trudged to my side.

"Meet Adam Flaning," Edward told Smollet. "First mate and good with mattocks," Edward asserted.

"Keen with them," Flaning said.

"Tell him to toddle away," I told Edward, and so Edward done, and I ordered Smollet to step back too. I bade Edward to show me his Bible. He slipped it out of his jacket pocket. "I would have half your Bible," I told him. "Per our agreement. No more and no less. Half. Split into deuces. We shall cleave it and hear it moan its last secret."

"I could kill you now," Edward said, and I should remark for posterity, so much as it may exist without me, that he warn't smiling nor laughing no more.

"You may kill me, or try, but I will tell all before I go down, and your men will turn. Even your man, Flaning, so good with mattocks. I expect that he is as good with mattocks on your head as he is on mine. Trust your old mate," so I told him. "I have solved the last cipher. And it is you, Edward Blood. Grant me that. And the right to see the crown."

"My grandfather was loyal to the King."

"It is a blight on his soul, but we shall forgive him."

"He spoke of the crown with his last breath and was heard by his nurse. He hid the crown on this island and murdered the man that buried it. And that man is a pauper in the middle of riches, strictly dead, and so that crown won't never do him no good."

"He held a scrap of parchment telling me so. Telling me that the treasure was not buried here, and that I was a pauper too, as I had not yet found the treasure."

"And more, Silver. It warn't the King's men that come after me, but the Prime Minister's men. It was them that murdered my family and drove me to the streets with nothing left to remember them but this Bible."

"Blood runs in your family," I told him, hacking him on his back like old times.

"Them men were on us before the same dawn. My father gave me the Bible and left it to me to solve the ciphers, though I always knew the prize."

I must set down my oars for the moment, as I have been rowing so relentlessly. This blasted fever. I barely have time to finish this tale, my history to date, and skate it under the door to your lad.

Speak to me, my hearty, and ask me how I fare. I will tell you that my hand is as curled as the canvas. I have a proper claw now. My heart is afflicted, as heavy as a barrel. My timbers are stiff, as I have stooped over these words since you locked me in here. But still, what other man is my match? Not you, sir. Not you nor any tar. Not a gob of the King's navy. Not a cutpurse that calls himself a captain. Not a man born to wealth. Not any such man such as you.

I will finish this tale. I will finish it out of spite.

There was another matter on which I wished to treat with Edward. I bade him to also confess that he lied about Mary, but he replied that he had told the truth. Edward put a spar in my back with his claim against Mary, and that spar pierced my back.

THE FEVER.

You are holding the spar, I say. Now you turn it. Mary, you said. A lie.

Is that Ben Gunn there?

It is Ben. Is that Ben?

I told Ben to stand fast. I ain't ready to tack on to this crew.

Spite, my hearty. Spite. And here is Billy Bones beckoning me to join him in a draft. And here is Bloody Bill, but he ain't speaking. Spite too, my hearty. It is stronger than fever. All spite.

LEAVE ME LIVE, Sir Fever. Leave me live long enough to slay the man that put me here. He lies. Sleep, you say? Sleep? Aye, so I shall. You will not come for me yet. Not until I finish this tale. I must finish this tale.

And then I will cut the man down. He is afraid of me still, he is. I will cut him down everlasting.

So I shall sleep, but a pledge on board a ship is a pledge. He is a dead man.

What do you say, fever? Sleep? And so I shall.

Do not forget to wake me.

MY HEAD IS thick this morn. Is this the morn?

The captain is a coward. He could have killed me whilst I slept. I hailed him. He did not reply.

Mullet again. One day more till port, he says.

The air is thick with gulls. I smell the char. Chimneys.

There is a lad in the corner. Look. A man has covered him with his cape to cool him. A great black cape.

I have a dagger at my side. Here is my hand, and here is my dagger, sir. Come for me.

The captain wants you to take food," Mullet said, "so they can stand you up when they put the noose around you." I told Mullet that I was too weak from the fever to eat. "It ain't the fever," Mullet said.

"It wracks me. It shakes and shivers me. It ain't the fever? Then what is it, boy?"

"Hunger," he answered.

"I have all the food that a man could want here, boy."

"All spoiled," Mullet told me. "Rotten," he said. "But you would take no other. It gave you this hunger."

"Aye, a good tale too. So your captain must have told you." I tacked to the wind. "If you free me, I will tell you the exact site on the island, Treasure Island. All my riches, boy."

"Aye," he said, then he said no more, for he took his leave. Did he mean to free me, or to inform you that I offered the dunce a crown?

It was spite, it was. Spite. I presented Solomon to Edward, but Edward warn't grateful at all.

"You may put the rope about Solomon's neck," I told Edward. "A hanging will suit you. Your words will be the last words that he hears. Make it good sport. Tell him that you will set him free on Threadneedle Street. Marry him off to a countess. A murder does wonders for a man. Then dash him. Mind you to listen closely to his last words. I would know what a man such as Solomon says at his end."

Edward walked to where Solomon and Jim were bound and put his sword to Solomon's chest. The men gathered round Edward so better to witness the murder.

"Are you afraid?" Edward asked Solomon.

"I am," Solomon answered.

"Take notice," I told Edward. "He will beg you for his life. His last words."

"Spare the boy," Solomon said.

I bade Solomon for a final curse. "Look at me," I said. "Look at the man you hate most in this world. A final curse if you please. Your summation."

Solomon did not address me. He looked at Edward, and only at Edward, and said one word. "Liberty," he said. Then Solomon raised his eyes, and Edward lofted his sword.

Jim pleaded with Edward to spare Solomon. "He saved your life! He saved your life!" Jim kept on.

"There ain't no one in arrears here," I threw in. "Kill him," I bade Edward, so as to finish the only other man that might guess the location of the crown.

Edward looked about as if he was lost, and that is how I recall Edward looking the first day that he come aboard the Linda Maria. Edward squared his sword, then he lowered it, then he squared it again whilst young Jim screamed.

Edward lashed at the ropes that bound Solomon. He swung his sword again and freed Jim from his rigging too.

"Confound you," Edward told Solomon. "This is on account of Silver and not no other matter." Then Edward told me, "They go with me. I take them in trade for the barrels," so he spoke and loud enough for all to hear. "And you owe me more than this. Remember that. Now make way," Edward ordered his men.

"Curse you then. Take them. Take them both," I told him. "I will not forget this either."

"Do not. Now tell your men to stand away," Edward said, as if he was giving me orders. But, I done so, my hearty, as your man, Flaning, was pointing a pistol at my head.

But then you drew me aside and spoke into my ear, telling me that I would see the crown. You told your men to stand back and we walked into the trees and you opened that Bible and tore it in half, just as I had bade you to do in jest. There was a swell in the binding and around that swell a parchment. "I never solved the riddle of the island," you told me. "You led me here. I would not have found it otherwise. Try as I might, I never solved the longitude nor latitude. Nor could I discover the name of the island. All credit to you."

"Well, there is a difference between us. You must admit such."

You flounced up and about as you were so restless. I was anxious too, mind you, but held my temper better. You jigged, so you done. You slapped your chest like the cannibals that chased us on Skeleton Island some years past, before they took their eats of one of our hearties. Your body quivered whilst you turned about, and I would not have been surprised if you had screwed yourself into the very ground where we stood from all that turning.

You pulled at the parchment and took it from your Bible and a gem was wrapped in it, a ruby no less, and it caught both the sun and the moon as the sun was setting and the moon was rising. And on the parchment was a map, and I swear that it is true but we were standing not more than ten paces from the treasure.

"And 1303 was the date that the Crown Jewels were first stolen," so you told me. "But they were returned. So what use is the date? I could not answer it, but then in Londontown I seen the answer. It was on a grave too, but a different grave. That of Anne Hyde, the wife of King James II. She was buried in 1671, the date that the Crown Jewels were stolen again. The date of her death was March 31. I come upon her grave whilst in the Abbey and there it was, March 31, the third month and the thirty-first day, the same numbers as 1303 with a bit of a switch of the order of the digits on account of the perversity of the riddler, as if he was writing them numbers from the other side of the grave. And, so you may ask, what led me to her grave? The sundial on London Bridge. The same sundial that appears in the Bible, and both round as a subaltern's arse," Edward said.

"The first cipher wheel," so I said.

"It is a sundial, Silver. A particular sundial. The sundial on London Bridge, which points at three o'clock, sir, to only one place."

"You are going to tell me that it points to Westminster Hall."

"Just so. And if you follow the light, it leads to Anne Hyde's grave. It was I that turned Cromwell's head and led you to Westminster Hall. I put the second cipher wheel in the pit. I had the wheel fashioned. I knew that you would find it, enterprising as you are. The same numbers that you found on the wheel were scratched, by the by, on Lady Anne's grave. A most enjoyable desecration. I presumed that you did not mind the clue. I know that I did not mind that you solved it for me. How did you solve it, Silver?"

"You might ask Anne Hyde, but I doubt that she would answer you. A simple matter of transfiguring the numbers into letters. Quite simple, really. But you need answer a question for me, Edward. How did you know to find the map in the black book?"

"Who held the Bible all these years? None but I. You merely copied the ciphers, but I held the Bible. I never let it out of my custody. Except, of course, when I wanted you to find it."

"Hardly true."

"I paid Pew well to watch you."

"I did not need to pay him to do my bidding."

"And so he never done it. He only done my bidding. I took him into confidence, just enough mind you to keep him from telling you. But Pew is of no matter now. You inquired about how I knew of the map. I knew when my father put the Bible in my hand and told me not to take the parchment out from it until I found the island. The map is of no use without the island and the island is of no use without the map. Them were his last words. Shall we look for the crown now? It has been a long journey."

"One more matter. What does Solomon know? You spared his life."

"No more than me. And now, no more than you. Consider it not an act of kindness that I spared him, but of malice. Well, Silver. Are you ready?"

And there was the tree waiting for us after all these years, grizzled by wind and weather, with a black gash across one of its limbs from when it was struck by lightning. But this tree would not be torn asunder. We walked the ten paces to it, Edward turning his head this way and that to make certain that no one else was about.

And there was another gash on the tree, and this one made not by lightning but by a man, by the trickster himself, as I recognized the script. He had carved the trunk with the following words of encouragement:

Audacibus annue coeptis

And so we done as he bade us and looked with favour upon our bold beginning, and each placed our hands into the hollow of the tree, just below them words, and pulled out a man's blouse, now faded but likely once as red as the setting sun. And then we drew off that drapery and there was the crown.

The gems that gilded it caught the last of the light, and those gems shined like a rainbow on our hands, as we both grasped the crown. Aye, and that gold shined so that it near blinded us.

We held the crown by the double arches that crossed each other at the crest, one hand each on the arches, and turned it round so that the four jeweled crosses turned too, and we must have turned the crown round and round at least a score more times, but not enough turns for all the seasons that we pursued it. You tugged and I tugged at it, but as I was the stronger one, I took it and placed it on my head. You were obliged to try to tear that crown off my head, and so I was obliged to hold you back with a wave of my dagger. I held you at bay and refused to relinquish the crown until I had counted every stone, and there were no more nor less than 444 stones on that crown, and in every colour that the devil had devised when he crafted this world.

It was only then that I took your dagger and handed you the crown. You ran your hand over the four fleur-de-lys and the cross mounted atop of the crown, and as you cradled it so to put it on your head, I put them daggers to your neck.

The crown fits only one man, and so it warn't fitting nor proper that you should wear it, and anyway, I and not you had found it. I might have let you hold a scepter if we had found one, and if you would not have skivered me with it. I would that we had found two swords with the crown, and that we would have made great slashes whilst climbing the branches to the peak, hacking away at each other until we stripped that tree of all its fruits and leaves. We could have battled whilst the tree bowed with each of our strikes. Mind you that I would have given you the blunter sword.

"It is mine," so you said. "My family kept the secret all these years, kept it in my Bible. It belongs to me."

"This is a fine crown," so I said, taking it from you. "And nobody but John Silver holds it now. It is more than a fortune. It is more than a country. More than a land and its people."

"Is this patriotism? Loyalty to your King at last after all these years from Long John Silver?" so you asked me.

"Not at all, Edward," I answered, turning the crown so that it caught the light once more, the gold and jewels sparkling and flashing. "Another lesson for you, Edward. You are apt to speak when you should be still and apt to be silent when you should utter. I had not concluded my declaration."

"My pardon then," he said, eyeing the crown. "A last lesson from the captain."

"I was about to say, prepared to say that after all these years, and as I look on this crown, that it is more than just a fortune or the symbol of a nation. I imagine it on the head of your King, and as such and in that capacity, it is a hat for a sotted old man."

I draped the crown in the cloth again and placed it back in the hollow of the tree.

"It is mine, Edward. Not yours. It was never yours. Your family was the custodian of the crown, and only that, keeping it until a man worthy of it should wear it. I am that man, and that is my crown."

"Aye, Silver. A hat for a sotted old man," you said, whereupon I cut you athwart your cheek with your own dagger.

"I have spoiled your looks, Edward, but now you will recall me whenever you look upon yourself in your glass. I leave you with your life. Unless you mean to take the crown, in which case I will kill you. There is no need for you to live."

"Or you for that matter. Do not forget my men."

And so we made us another bargain and agreed to leave the crown where we had found it, where it had been safe from both lightning and the likes of us for all these years, and to return to our ships. We agreed to circle the island one last time and that if either ship returned to the island, the other had a free hand to fire on the other, which would have been a pleasing conclusion to our rivalry. Whereupon we returned to our ships, keeping each other in our sights until nightfall when we anchored, and I returned to the island in the yawl and took the crown.

I took that crown, so I did, and my treasure too. All seventy-three sacks, carried by seven men, just as before. They carried them sacks aboard my ship and carried them off again when I hid my treasure and reburied the crown. And then I murdered them men and left the corpses for you. You may have them stout fellows, if you ever find them, and with my best wishes. And, sir, you may take them in trade.

Only I know where them riches are now. I would tell you to harken to every tale of murder over these past fourteen years since we parted. If you do, you will find bones scattered on every shore of every land. And I confer them bones on you too, for let it not be said that John Silver warn't generous to an old mate on occasion.

You should have taken the treasure that day. You had more men than me, and better men, but you feared me. You knew that I would have hacked off every one of your precious curls before any man drew his sword or threw his dagger. That, sir, is your weakness. You value life more than spirit. And that, sir, is my strength. I value spirit more than life, and that is why I have always and ever bested you.

I presume that you returned for the crown right quick, despite our bargain, after I had already taken it. I regret that I could not have looked upon your face when you discovered it gone.

And so what better way to make amends with a dear mate than to sail under the King's flag and capture him, to keep him locked in his cabin under threat of execution until he tells you where he has hidden the crown and the rest of his treasure? All of it is mine. All of it.

So many years now. So many years. How long you have searched for me? How long you have searched for my treasure?

And that is how we parted ways, you and I. That is how we parted ways, ever since and evermore, until now.

CHAPTER XXII.

MY HEARTY

I am afflicted by the fever.

What a bony hand I have now that I look on it. My hand is as thin as a spirit.

Edward, I will not tell you where I hid my treasure.

You set Solomon and Jim free. You released them in Bristol no less. The boy is most likely an apprentice to a tea merchant by now. But young Jim should be a rover. The lad should have a price on his head just as you once did.

This world is some dusky and some ruinous.

You should have quartered Solomon. You must have let him live to spite me. Men need spite to live as much as they need food and water. We both grew fat on it.

I ain't ready to die.

I sailed around this world fourteen times in fourteen years since I last spoke with you, blaggard, but I have not lived enough. I ain't done. I would do more. More, I say to you. More, I say.

You caught a dead man, Edward, and there ain't any sport to that, there ain't.

I am parched. These are waterless days.

You marplot. Blaggard.

What sport is there in hanging John Silver?

The years since we last met were full of profit and plunder. I have gold, blaggard. More gold.

This is my deck that you walk. This is my ship.

You set Solomon and Jim free, not for King or country but for spite and naught but spite.

I will gull you, I will. I will die from this fever before your King can hang me.

Think on that whilst you walk my deck.

Parched.

We were mates. Hearties.

The fever.

My Linda Maria may founder yet. She does not care for your clammy hands. The Linda Maria is true to her Silver, ever true.

I am drowning in this fever, boy.

I only have rum and blockade. You took my water.

My treasure.

I would swallow my riches, but you would carve me open for them. Lay me open and blunt would come spilling out of me, so it would.

Look at this fellow with red hair in my glass. He has a saber with an ivory handle.

Mate?

Mate or foe?

Speak.

He is standing shoulder to shoulder with me.

I am speaking to you.

That is Smollet's sword that he dropped when Flaning cut him. My men fell like misfortune.

I killed five of your men. One man wore a ducat on a chain around his neck. You strode the boom. Calling out the orders to murder my men.

All dead now.

"Spare the captain," you said. "Tell me where the treasure is, Silver. Tell me."

"I damn you!" I returned.

"I am taking you to England then," you said. "Where they will hang you, Silver."

"It ain't much likely," I replied, whilst your first mate pinned my arms behind me.

"It is more than likely, Silver. I will stand in the yard when they hang you," you said. That was a hot day too. Or mayhap it was the fever already on me. No, it was a hot day. You opened your jacket. You loosened your blouse.

"And you? They will hang you too," I said, and those are true words, my sir. They do not know the extent of your treachery. A cutpurse, so you ever were.

"They will stick a ribbon on me. A ribbon, Silver," you replied. Another smile. Damn you.

"They will hang you," I told you. See if it does not come to pass. I am right. I have always been right. I am right in all matters. You said that you would stand in the yard and watch me whilst I swing. "Make certain to take your hat off," I called to you.

"Your Solomon is free," you told me then. "I gave him his liberty, Silver," you said. "The lad too. All free. All free men." You took your hat and placed it on my head. "Not quite a proper crown."

"Blaggard," I told you, fighting to free myself of Flaning. He was the younger man, but I still managed to free my leg before we scuffled to the deck. "You are no more than a blaggard," I hissed.

"Aye, a bit more," you replied. "A bit more, Silver. I am free. I am free too. Of you."

"I will cut you down. I will cut you down," I said, whilst I kicked at Flaning.

"And rich. I am rich, Silver," you said.

"Never free of me. Never free," I said, almost breaking away.

"Take him below," you ordered Flaning.

"I will fight you!" I called. "Sword to sword. Sword to sword, I say."

You turned your back to me.

"Secure him in his cabin," you told Flaning.

"I will give you a gold piece," I told Flaning. Mark my sharpness even then. "I carry one such in my purse." Then, "There is a blade on the deck," I told him. "Look there," I told him. "You will be captain of the Evangeline in less than a tick if you let me go."

"You ain't so great, John Silver," he said. "Long John Silver."

"A captain, Flaning," I told him.

"He wants me to free him, Captain." Flaning laughed.

There are all manners of crimes in this world, boy.

My sea will never forgive you. Not ever. She will scuttle you one day. So I say.

You marched my men before you and took a saw blade to them that would not swear full blood to you and your England. I will give them men good berths on any ship that I command in the nether. Abide me on the underside, my hearty. Take care though. Nick waits by the braces for both of us.

I would like to see you when my sea blows you over. I would like to see that. But, the fever.

Still, I will cheat your King of a hanging.

I have my treasure, and you will never know where I buried it. And so you will never be free of Silver. You will search for it high and low and never find it.

They will speak my name a hundred years hence, I say. Long John Silver. But they will not remember you.

Long John Silver.

I spy the chimney smoke. Londontown, it is. There is no mistaking it. Your men are pulling the ropes. A good day for a hanging, a fresh wind, but I will not accommodate you.

Long John Silver threw a shadow across the sea.

Here is Blind Tom's black cape. Now it is midnight in the back alleys, those Bristol alleys. Look at my shadow. Here is Black John's cane. And here is that cursed church in Spain. We are in Don Jorge's cellar. Here is my shadow. Here are Bones's drunken slumbers. Here are the men that I murdered. Look here. Look at the grieving widows.

Now try to find my treasure once more. Look here, the crown and the jewels. Here, man. Do you not spy them? Look closer. Here. The greatest treasure. Aye, you son of the sea, here in these tales, here in my history, here in these curled and blackened pages. Look closer I bid you, as I have the treasure, not you.

Look closer, so I told you. Here. Between these pages. More ciphers. But they are meant only for them that can solve them. Will it be you? I think not, my sir. You will be otherwise occupied on a platform between two crossbeams, and then there is that hood that renders it some fiddly to read. Think of me, won't you, when the horses draw out the gallows.

I have always been a sporting sort. And so, my hearty, the last contest. The treasure is still buried, but it is deep inside this testament.

Aye, your eyes are most likely gaping now, just as when the hangman will wring his rope around your neck. No doubt you consider this to be a deception, and so let me enlighten you.

Did you truly believe that I would leave my riches for you? Did you presume that I would allow such as you to have my treasure, and after I discovered it? Would you suppose me so guileless after all these years? I took it all.

The crown that you found in my cabin is false. I would never sail with it no matter how much it pleased me to look in my glass with it topping my head. I hid it along with my other riches.

If you march through Piccadilly with that crown on your head, you may garner a few shillings for your trouble. A jig may bring you a few farthings more. You, sir, have a counterfeit treasure.

Them gems on your crown are no more than glass. Pew could have stuck one of them in his dead eye. The manufactory is from the Savoy House in the Strand, in the Londontown that you know so well. We stood there once many years ago whilst you picked my pocket, and there, not two throws of a dagger away, is the flint glass shop where I had them gems made to my specifications. Aye, flint glass. Naught more.

You may well pass the shop on the way to your hanging, but mind you not to bother to look in on the shopkeeper, as he come to a sudden demise.

Aye, and that crown is gold, but not such as you or I covet, but a base mixture of lead and, as I recall, copper and a bit of gold dust, but not enough to bite into and have a proper meal.

I have buried the crown and the treasure elsewhere. Where? Look, so I told you. Look. The answer lies in this, my own black Bible, my history. The ciphers are all here. All you need do is reckon them. Of course, if I do not find myself in Newgate Square tomorrow, I might assist you.

—◦—

I smell Londontown, lad."

"We are nearly there."

"Still keen to see a hanging?"

"Ever so. But you may die of the fever if it pleases you."

"Nothing pleases me, lad. Except for a murder here and there. That, and treasure, and so it pleases me to tell more about the treasure. Them clues that fell from the Bible after Pew sliced the inside of the Bible were false."

"You found the crown."

"But why would one clue be true and the other one false? I will write them clues for you again."

AOL JYVDU
And Last Icon

"I had rendered the first clue to mean 'The Crown' and the second clue to refer to Cat Island. Neither clue was correct. There was no treasure on

Cat Island. Nor a crown. The answer of 'The Crown' was a misdirection, the same as when Edward wrote 'Evangeline' in the Bible, so to lead me astray. The same as with the kine and corn. All palters designed to blow me off course and direct me to the one cipher that your captain could not resolve. Be certain to tell your father."

"My father, sir?"

"Just listen, lad. We searched for different treasure. I for the crown and your captain, shall we call him, for all of the Crown Jewels. The crown is but one part of the regalia, as the regalia consists of crowns, rings, scepters, robes, spurs, bracelets, and even spoons. And I have found them all. They are with my other riches, buried, hidden away until someone worthy can find them. The King's crown was on my Treasure Island, and I have replaced it with another, as I have written, but I found the rest of the Crown Jewels. They were never melted by Cromwell."

"But they were."

"Stolen by Thomas Blood, to be sure. Thomas Blood killed the warder. Put a sack over his head and clubbed him to death. Or stabbed him to death. I don't right recall. The King's men caught him and jailed him. Blood would not answer any questions during the trial, allowing that he would only answer to the King. So they brought Thomas Blood before the King, and the King pardoned him. And the King done even more for the rascal. He restored Blood's land grants in the bargain."

"You are saying that the King had a hand in the thievery?"

"He is royalty after all. He spared Blood so that Blood would do him a service. That service being exactly what I done myself. Blood made a false set of the regalia for the King and hid the real ones away. He buried one crown on Gardners Island, our Treasure Island, and the rest elsewhere. For safe-keeping. Even them royals need blunt now and again. What better way to pay for navies? Your captain knew this, and his father knew it too, them all being Bloods, the secret passed on until one King could abide it no more and wanted it back. Them kings are greedy sorts. And the Bloods gave it all back but for one crown, so to bargain with the King, and were killed for it."

"What proof is there?"

"The Bible itself. Edward was given the Bible with the ciphers, the purpose being to expose the King and his kind."

"But the captain sails under the King's flag."

"The better to guile him, boy. The better to make him pay for what he done. But Edward could not find the crown. I had it. And so he come for me."

"Where is the crown?"

"With the rest of the Crown Jewels. You must search for them."

"But they were returned. So you said. So I heard you say."

"I have them as I took them, lad."

"They are in the Tower of London."

"They are not. Of course I had me an accomplice. One of the guardsmen, a strapping fellow, enterprising too. Quick as quick can be. Aye, but he hates kings and queens and all them that tortured his mother, as if she knew anything at all about the matter. He come upon his mother in their tavern, a dowel through her head. Poor Jim."

"You wrote that they were set free, him and Solomon."

"And they were and then they parted ways."

"You wrote that Jim was likely an apprentice to a tea merchant."

"Not just likely but accurate. He made his way to Bristol, found his mother, and waited for me. Boys are loyal to their mothers. Ain't that so, lad? To the world he is an apprentice to a tea merchant, but to me he is brass knobs all the way. Mind you that I bested Solomon, so I did, and that is some satisfying too. Jim stole the Crown Jewels. We set it up, him and me. He gained employment in the guards after I gave him the name of Hyde. There were those that said he bore a striking likeness to the Hydes of Londontown, all trustworthy gentlemen and gentlewomen. One of them Hydes was a queen so we know. I got me the inspiration for the name from your father's account of the grave of Lady Anne."

"I do not believe any of this."

"No matter to me, lad, though it is the truth. Just as I had a counterfeit of the crown constructed for your captain, I done the same with the other regalia. For a price. I paid dear, but as I have always said, there is dear and there is dear. And one by one, Jim took each piece and replaced it with the counterfeit."

"You are balmy from the fever."

"You may choose to believe so."

"I will tell my father."

"An admittance. Good for the soul so I hear. As is a hanging. You are likely to see one upon your return. Your father's hanging. Does anyone else know that you are his son?"

"None."

"Good lad. Good lad. Mind you what I told you. The clues are all in my testament. Take it. Hide it. Do not search for Jim. You will not find him. He goes by another name now. Not Hawkins nor Hyde. And may I say good fortune to you?"

⸺◆⸺

I have buried that treasure and a dozen more treasures, and a dozen more after them, as all them treasures warn't never enough for Long John Silver, and so I buried a dozen more too, more than any Pharaoh that drowned in the sea.

But do inquire of Mullet, and even though that ain't his true name, I prefer to recall him as such. You threw your bones, and I guessed your play. You would never poison him, not this lad. Aye, we are both of us sporting sorts. Whom else would you trust but him?

He has your gait.

And he ain't a dunce at all. I suppose him some clever, as it takes cunning to act so ignorant. I wrote it all down for him. Not for you. He is, all in all, a handsome lad and not as I described him. He is a deception through and through, just like his mother. I could not provoke him no matter how much I tried. The lad has will, so he does. I attribute that to the mother too. He has him that lilt in his voice, and that is like his mother too, for Mary spoke so.

And I would recognize them eyes in a hailstorm. The same eyes as her. The same eyes.

Now, just so you know, the boy told me his history too and only on account that he said I was a dead man. His mother must have spoken of me kindly, and that is why he unlocked my door and looked in on me from time to time. And that is why I never put my dagger to his throat.

He told me the truth just this past day as we were so near port, but I already knew it, and I told him so, and your son told me that I was the greatest captain that ever sailed these seas. Me, sir. Not you. And so I told him of my deception, my counterfeiting of the crown, and I wonder how you will deal with your lad now. He knows that your treasure is false and mine is true, and just as your father passed the book of ciphers on to you, I passed my testament on to your son. My history will not end with me.

You never cared for Evangeline. It was Mary that you wanted, my

Mary. You would have all that I had and so you went back there to take her, and a boy opened the door.

Your boy said that Mary cried when you took him from her, just as Jim Hawkins's mother cried when I took that boy away.

Look at this parchment. Look at me in this dim cabin. My shadow falls crosswise. This is my hand. The lantern catches it and marks the new heading. Treasure. The compass always and ever points to treasure, my treasure.

Ask Mary's son for the heading. I wonder if he will assist you. I think not, as he can have it all for his own self one day if he solves the ciphers in my book.

I would be a lad again.

I listed on the rail my first night on the Linda Maria. I was a boy. The daystar was setting. I saw my destiny spread out across the water that sunset, a golden hand filled with riches. Tom told me that those who go to sea never come back. Aye, but he was right.

I am burning.

My hand cannot hold the quill. This hand never thwarted me before.

EDWARD, IT SUITS me to tell you again that I taught you the sea. I taught you the compass, the stars, the pistol, and the sword. I gave you this world, my own world. I gave you your ship. I gave you your glory, no other than me. If it warn't for me, you would have hanged already, cutpurse that you are.

Mayhap you would have rather been a hay trusser or a spade digger.

This fever be damned.

I am a rich man, Edward. I died a rich man.

How can these vapours that I cannot see be stronger than me? How can this fever be stronger than Silver?

I WILL SEE you between Bristol and Hell soon enough. The devil is building a torchlight parade for me. He will build one for you too, soon enough.

Why should my candles burn after I ain't here to see them?

I dropped my dagger.

The fever is taking me.

I saw the Indies. I sailed all around this world.

Silver.

I sailed all around this world.

I am not telling you where I buried my treasure.

⎯⎯►◄⎯⎯

T*he prodigal has returned for one more throw of the bones.*

The lad has confessed. Good lad. Stout lad. He has kept the parchment for himself. He has not shown his father a word of it.

"*And what will you tell your father, boy?*"

"*That you told me the treasure is on Skeleton Island. That there is a fort there. A man by the name of Israel Hands that may be your Solomon. That he guards the treasure. Or not, as you were some unclear on the matter whilst you slipped in and out of the fever.*"

"*Is the parchment in a safe place then?*"

"*I have hidden it behind a mirror. Bound it in twine.*"

"*Not my mirror?*"

"*The same.*"

"*He will find it.*"

"*He will not, sir. He trusts me.*"

"*Lad, you are formidable.*"

"*Just so, sir.*"

"*Send him in a shore boat to Skeleton Island and leave him only the oars.*"

"*I shall instead send him to a port near Spain, concealed by the rocks and baffled by the winds. We mended our mainsail there.*"

"*Your father could be dreadful careless at times.*"

"*Aye, sir. And he will never be found there, though he may spend his days there pleasantly enough. It is a lush land but stony land, a land of Mexican Indians and other peoples of good humour. A Negress of uncommon beauty found him most favourable.*"

"*It ain't proper at all, lad. Him being betrothed to your mother, although not strictly, but still in a manner.*"

"*And I shall leave him not a guinea so to forestall any wanderings. I shall take the helm. I am ready, or shall be ready by then. The men will harken to me. I will tell them of treasure. I have drawn a map.*"

"*I would see it.*"

"*A matter, sir. I would you know that my mother spoke of you often. Even when my father finally found her. She ran out clutching her apron, looking all* to make *Silver* accurate—in my fashion—by describing life in England, the deprivation on board a pirate ship, life in the seaside ports of call, and the intrigues of the time. I did create a monster in Silver. I maligned Jim Hawkins's mother. Trelawney and Livesey did not fare much better. Billy Bones has quite a bit of life in him, more of a part than in *Treasure Island*. Ben Gunn is determined to haunt both books. Israel Hands appears by reference only at the end of the book. Mister Arrow has a walk-on role. Smollet is reconstituted. New characters, notably, Mary, Evangeline, Black John, Peel, Mullet, Solomon, and Edward shape the plot. I would like to believe that I gave young Jim a good, albeit tainted, future. As for Mullet, in many ways a stand-in for Stevenson's Jim Hawkins, I presume that he may be destined for a marly and bleak future even if he finds the treasure. Revenge, like spite, is an ill wind. That would be up to you, the reader. It is out of my control now.

Although . . .

There is the matter of another treasure described by Silver. He might be speaking the truth. Or not. As I am on good terms with the author, I can note without equivocation that if the author did hide a treasure, he would have done so deep within the pages of his book. He is not as skilled as Silver at deciphering kine and corn and other codes, and so he would have to use another ruse, find another way to bind the reader and his tale together.